PROMISES TO KEEP

CHAR CHAFFIN

To Kella –

*Love the Book
you're
With!*

Char Chaffin

*Thank
you!*

SOUL MATE PUBLISHING

New York

PROMISES TO KEEP
Copyright©2011
CHAR CHAFFIN

Cover Design by Rae Monet, Inc.

Published in the United States of America by

Soul Mate Publishing

P.O. Box 24

Macedon, New York, 14502

ISBN: 978-1-61935-100-4

eBook ISBN: 978-1-61935-33-5

www.SoulMatePublishing.com

The publisher does not have any control over and does not assume any responsibility for author or third-party Web sites or their content.

For Don, Sue Ann, and John;
their unswerving support and confidence,
that someday I'd publish this book, kept me going.
I succeeded because you believed in me.
I love you all.

And for Faith,
who already holds my heart in her tiny hands.

Family is everything, and mine is the best

Acknowledgements

My thanks to the Posse: Theresa, Donna, Robin, Carol. They are my sounding board and often my sanity, the kind of friends that last a lifetime. And a special thanks to my publisher, Debby Gilbert, for offering me that all important, first chance.

PART ONE

Friendship

Chapter 1

Shenandoah Valley
June

Annie Turner fell in love with Travis Quincy on a hot summer day, over a tangled fishing line and a bucket of night crawlers.

From the moment he walked up to her in the sunlight and smiled at her, nothing else seemed to matter. Her frustration, as she struggled with the twine attached to the end of her homemade bamboo pole, wasn't important. Anger over wet knots that resisted all her tugging, irritation because her brother Mark hoarded his new rod instead of allowing her to borrow it . . . All magically gone, the very second Annie looked up into blue eyes as warm as the sky above, and lost her heart.

"Need some help?" He squatted down next to her on the ground.

She nodded, a flush heating her cheeks. *Stop staring at him, Annie.* She couldn't get any oxygen into her lungs. *Breathe, Annie . . .*

After what seemed like an eternity of gawking at him, she cleared her dry throat. "I—my line got tangled, over in the reeds. I don't think I can fix it. There's not enough weight on the twine." Her pulse sped up when he leaned in for a better view of her mangled pole. There were glints of blue in his thick black hair and his eyelashes were longer than hers.

He's so cute. She barely kept from sighing in his face.

He carried a small oblong box, which he set on the ground as he reached for her pole and examined the knotty lumps of twine. "Did you make this? I've never seen a homemade fishing rod before."

"It's not a very good pole," she admitted. "I've made better ones, really." For a few more seconds, she stared at him. "You live in that big, pretty house on the hill." As soon as the words left her mouth, she wished she could have snatched them back because they sounded so dumb.

"Yeah. That's where I live." He shrugged. "It's just a house." He cocked his head as he looked at her. "What's your name?"

She tried hard not to blush. "Annie Turner. And you're Travis Quincy. I see your daddy in town once in a while." More dumb words. She wanted to kick herself.

But Travis nodded and replied, "Yeah. He's got an office on Market Street." He gave up on the mangled pole, and tossed it down. "It's too messed up to fix. You got any more twine? Maybe you could make another one."

"I only took one piece. I didn't think it would tangle like that." If she'd been alone, she'd have stomped on the broken pole and tossed it into the pond. Now she'd have to give up trying to fish, and go back to the house. She'd been cooped up all week in the kitchen, helping her mama put up jam and chutney. Finally able to escape, Annie had run all the way to Bogg Pond, clutching her battered old beach bucket that she'd crammed with worms and wet leaves. She couldn't wait to get her hook into the fattest night crawler, and catch her first bullhead of the morning.

She'd wasted too much time goofing with the knotted twine. And as soon as she returned to the house, Mama would grab her and drag her back into the hot kitchen to work. She'd miss out on a prime day of fishing . . . not to mention a chance to talk to the cutest boy in town.

Resigned, she got to her feet. "Thanks for trying to fix it. I'd better get on home."

"You can still fish if you want. Use my fishing rod." He reached for his oblong box and flipped back the lid. Inside, a rod, reel, and some sinkers and hooks nestled in molded foam. He pulled out the sections and screwed them together, then threaded the line and attached the reel. He held it out to her and she reached for it, but changed her mind and pulled her hand away.

"I can't. What if I break it? I break stuff all the time. My sister says I'm a klutz. I've never seen a rod like this, anyway. It looks like it cost a lot of money." Annie's fingers itched to give it a try.

He shrugged again. "I guess. I got it for Christmas last year, and this is the first time I've had it out of the box."

With the toe of his sneaker, he rattled her dinged-up beach bucket. "Tell you what. I forgot to bring worms, and you need a rod. Why don't we share? We'll take turns. Maybe we could have a contest, too. See who gets the most fish. Winner takes all the fish, all the leftover worms, and the fishing rod."

"That wouldn't be right. You said it was a gift from somebody. Anyhow, I break things, I already told you."

"Who says you're going to win, huh?" He gave her a challenging look as he dug in the bucket for a worm. "Maybe I'll win it all. I'm a very good fisherman." He hooked the worm and stood, holding the baited rod out to her. "Besides, I have other rods I fish with. So even if you do win, I don't mind giving this one away."

Annie rose as well and flashed him one more uncertain look, before her own competitive nature kicked in. She took the rod from him.

"I'm a better fisherman than you are." She stuck out her free hand to shake on the deal, and he grasped her fingers firmly.

She swung her arm back to cast out, already anticipating a pile of bullheads so heavy, she'd need a wheelbarrow to carry them all home.

"I guess you're a pretty good fisherman after all," Travis commented, a few hours later. He poked at the string of fish Annie finished tying to a clump of marsh grasses. Eleven fat bullheads flopped around in the shallow water. "I only caught three."

"Some of yours are longer than mine." She stood and brushed dirt off her knees. "But I did tell you I was better." She smirked up at him in the afternoon sun, and he elbowed her in the ribs. Her grin widened. In one short afternoon, they'd become friends.

She didn't want to go home yet. This was the most fun she'd had all summer, away from her snotty sister, her dumb brothers, and all the work she got stuck with during canning season. She didn't really mind helping out; sometimes it could be fun. But hanging out with Travis Quincy was a whole lot better.

She held out his fishing rod, but he waved it off. "You won fair and square. Keep it."

"I can't." When he looked puzzled, she tried to explain. "My folks wouldn't let me . . . it's a fancy rod, right? They wouldn't let me keep something so expensive." She didn't want to make him mad, but taking that rod would probably hurt her parents' feelings. They couldn't afford to buy her anything half as nice.

"Well, if you're sure," he replied.

She nodded, relieved that he seemed to understand. He took the rod and started to break it down so he could store it back in its box. "You can borrow it anytime you want, okay?"

His generosity surprised her. "Okay." She waited until he stood, then shyly offered, "You can have some of my bulls, Travis. If you want them, that is." The smile that spread over his face was worth losing a few of her catch. Thrilled she could give something back to him even if it was only some fish, she busied herself with using the remainder of her twine to string the biggest fish they'd caught. She'd keep the small ones for herself.

As they trudged down the narrow path leading toward Boggy Creek Lane, he said, "If you don't have to go home yet, you could come over to my house for a while. Maybe have some lemonade. I'm thirsty, aren't you?"

She glanced at him, startled at the flush riding high on his cheek. He sure looked hot and thirsty. Come to think of it, so was she. But, go to a boy's house? Annie hesitated, unsure. Silence stretched between them, broken only by the hum of cicadas and an occasional cricket.

Be brave, Annie. It's only lemonade. Still, she stuttered when she agreed.

As they got closer to his house up on Thompkin Hill, nerves churned in her stomach. His folks might kick her out for smelling like worms and fish. By comparison, Travis looked as if he'd lounged by some expensive pool all day. She envied him his spotless tee shirt and pressed jeans. Dirt was probably afraid to jump on his clothes. She sighed in resignation. Dirt always seemed to come looking for her.

A wide, white porch wrapped around the front of the house. Beyond double doors, the hallway they stepped into had a crystal chandelier that hung from what looked like the tallest ceiling in the world. Tables covered with vases of real flowers and silver-framed photos sat in the corners. She swore she saw her own reflection in the floor. She didn't know where to look first.

As she paused in the massive hallway, sweaty with nerves, a low, cultured voice floated down a curved staircase.

"Travis? Is that you? Where have you been? You were due home an hour ago."

The voice grew clearer and Annie saw a tall, thin woman descend the staircase, one hand trailing along the polished banister. She couldn't help but stare. This was someone's mother? She looked like a model or a movie star!

Thick, black hair, drawn back into a smooth bun, crowned her head. She wore a sleeveless dress, formal enough for somebody's wedding, and dainty pumps in the same shade of pale blue. As she moved closer, Annie saw her eyes were identical to Travis's, but there the similarity ended, for there didn't seem to be a drop of warmth in them.

"Travis, you smell of the pond. Your sneakers have dirt on them. And who is this. . .child. . .you've brought home?" The woman's voice spiked sharply.

Travis wiped his feet on the thick runner in front of the door, before he caught Annie's hand and pulled her forward. "We've been fishing. Annie, this is my mother, Ruth Quincy." As he spoke, Travis inched her closer to his mother and her silky perfection. Annie saw her shrink back to avoid their grimy hands.

She stammered out a breathless, "Pleased to meet you, ma'am." Her voice echoed around the elegant hallway.

"Indeed." With one word, Travis's mother dismissed her and frowned at her son. "You are late for your riding lesson. Desmond can't wait forever. He has other students to see to." She eyed the string of bullheads he carried. "I suggest you dispose of those horrid fish and prepare for your lesson."

"I can't dump our fish. They're some really large bulls. I'm going to give them to Martha, and—"

"You will *not* bring those foul things into my kitchen. Martha has more important tasks than dealing with slimy fish caught in a nasty pond. She's already preparing dinner. Councilman Cabot and his family are dining with us tonight.

I repeat, throw them out and attend to your lesson."

Annie cringed to hear the way this woman spoke to her son. Her mama would never talk to her and her brothers and sister like that, even when someone broke a glass or one of her brothers walked through the house in muddy shoes.

She knew Mama would pull her into a hug or tickle one of her ribs when she came home with her load of tasty bullheads. Even when Mama made her help out in the kitchen, she found ways for everybody to have fun. This tall lady with the silky dress and the perfect hair probably didn't know what the word "fun" meant.

Just before Mrs. Quincy turned away, Annie said, "It was nice meeting you, ma'am," which she either didn't hear or chose to ignore. Her back as straight as a steel pole, Travis's mother walked toward the staircase. She paused when a side door opened and Mr. Quincy walked out, his pipe in hand and a folded newspaper tucked under his arm.

He reminded Annie of her daddy, tall and lean with twinkling eyes and gray speckled through his dark brown hair. He wore slacks and a dress shirt with the sleeves rolled up. When he spotted her, he winked, then turned to kiss his wife's cheek. She smiled, but her eyes narrowed as she looked pointedly at his wrinkled shirtsleeves.

Mr. Quincy murmured, "Don't fuss, Ruthie. It's Saturday, remember?" To Travis he added, "Now, what's that I see, Trav? Bullheads! My favorite fish in the entire world. I bet if you ask Martha nicely, she'll cook them up for us later, what do you think?" He sent another wink toward Annie.

His wife glared at him. "Don't encourage your son in his uncivilized behavior. Martha is *not* cooking a mass of vile fish. Travis, do as I say and throw them out."

"Now, Ruth. Bullheads are to be savored, not tossed out with the garbage. I'm sure Martha won't mind cooking them. And if for some reason she can't, well then, Trav and I will man the kitchen and the fry pan. Won't we, son?"

Travis nodded eagerly at his father's suggestion. Ruth Quincy didn't seem to find the idea worthwhile, though. To her husband she accused, "You let the boy run wild in the summer, and I won't have it. Spending a valuable Saturday flipping about in a dirty pond isn't part of his weekend schedule. Desmond has now waited thirty minutes, and Travis has yet to clean up and present himself for his riding lesson."

She might have said more, but when Mr. Quincy laid his hand on her bare arm and squeezed gently, she stopped talking. The tight look on her face was probably due to lots of anger.

"Ruth, this is Thompkin, not Newport News," he admonished. "It's summertime and of course a boy wants to hare off and have some fun, especially when he has a cute little friend like . . . I'm sorry, we weren't properly introduced. I'm Ronald Quincy, Travis's father." He held out his big hand to Annie.

She grasped his fingers. "I'm Annie Turner. I really like your house." Her admiring words just popped out, but Mr. Quincy chuckled.

He whistled at the number of fish Travis still held. "Fishing must have been good today. I used to go all the time when I was your age, Annie. Sometimes I'd catch the biggest, wiliest old bullheads. And the ones that got away? Why, they were huge!" With both hands he measured the longest bullhead anyone could imagine, and made Annie giggle over his silliness.

She smiled at him happily. "Can I go fishing with you someday?" Ruth Quincy gasped in horror. Annie winced at her own boldness, but Travis and his father laughed, sounding almost identical.

It was obvious to her Travis had inherited his father's easygoing personality. Mr. Quincy beamed. "Well, of course.

Nice to meet you, young lady. You come back anytime. Travis, take those fish into the kitchen and clean them for Martha, there's a good boy. And don't worry about Desmond and your lesson. I'll call down to the stables and send him home."

When Travis's mother growled under her breath, his father continued, "Ruth, before I dress for dinner, I need your advice on a very urgent matter." He took her arm and led her away.

Travis let out a relieved sigh. "I hope Mother didn't upset you. She can be sort of strict. And Dad likes everyone. He's really friendly. Let's go get some lemonade now, and then we can gut and clean the fish before I give them to Martha. She's our cook," he explained.

Annie's nerves, having melted away during Mr. Quincy's reassuring presence, flooded back with a vengeance at the word "cook." God, it was like another world here. A huge, fancy house, a fancy mother, and now a cook. Riding lessons, too. Annie trailed along after Travis as he headed toward the kitchen.

How on earth they could ever be friends when their lives were so very different?

Chapter 2

Shuffling her feet, Annie walked down Spring Street. For some reason, today she paid attention to the shabby neighborhood where she'd lived all her life. Railroad tracks ran behind their house and rattled with freight trains every day. Smelly Crum Creek churned through the narrow ravine alongside the old tracks. Crabgrass grew through the cracks and gaps in the sidewalks on both sides of the street. Their house needed paint, and three broken boards out on the back porch should have been repaired years ago. Her brother, Danny, fell through them last summer right after his fifteenth birthday. He busted up his left leg, which sent his twin, Frankie, running off in a panic for help. The rest of the kids got stuck with Danny's chores while he lay in bed and complained about everything.

Mark, the oldest, chose to enlist in the Air Force right after graduation. Bobby, fourteen, lived just to irritate everyone. Annie's twelve-year-old sister, Susan, liked to boss her around and lord it over her because of their two-year age difference.

Susan, blond and pretty, already had tiny breasts growing underneath her tee shirts. When Annie drifted into the bedroom she shared with Susan, she caught her sister staring at her own body in the mirror and hesitantly touching herself in awe.

Annie gaped at her. Whirling around, Susan pointed at her bare chest and exclaimed, "Look, aren't they simply fabulous?"

"I don't see anything. You're dreaming, Suze." Annie

wrinkled her nose in disgust.

"Don't call me *Suze*! You know I hate it. And I do so have them. You're just jealous 'cause you know it'll be *ages* until you get anything on that flat, bony chest of yours." Susan ducked the pillow Annie lobbed at her, snatched up her shirt, and ran for the door, yelling, "Mama, Annie hit me!"

Annie sank down on the edge of her bed and stared at her own reflection. She didn't want to be mean to her sister, but lately she'd been wishing for more. She wanted to look like Susan, with her curling blond hair and big blue eyes. Instead, she got stuck with boring brown eyes and hair as straight as a stick.

She'd soon be eleven whole years old, but she still looked like a little kid. Annie held up her hands. She wanted to take piano lessons, but her hands were small and so narrow. Well, it wasn't as if her parents could afford such a luxury. With a sigh, she tore her eyes away from the mirror.

She prowled around the room she shared with Susan, poked at the faded curtains at the window, scuffed her toe on the threadbare carpet. Being poor was no fun at all. Her daddy worked hard, long hours for what money he earned at the Interbake factory, fifty miles away outside of Harrisonburg. Every night he'd come home, worn out, and fall asleep in front of the television in the living room.

It took Mama most of the summer to can all the vegetables they grew, spending her time in the kitchen with the old pressure cooker. Sometimes she burned her fingers when the rusty gauge acted up. Mama worked hard, too.

Impatient with herself, Annie forced her thoughts away from where they'd wandered. She wasn't ashamed of her large family, not one bit. They did all right. So what if she had to wear Susan's hand-me-downs? At least her sister took decent care of her clothes.

Annie knew why everything bothered her today, the

way she looked, her house, and her life: it was Travis Quincy.

Not only were they the richest family in Augusta County, they'd also founded Thompkin. Everyone knew the history, of how Duncan Quincy made a fortune in the silver mines during the Colorado Territory Rush, then came back to the Shenandoah Valley and built himself a town. He'd named it after his bride, Lilah Thompkin.

It seemed a long way from her old house on Spring Street to the Quincy mansion on Thompkin Hill. And Travis came from that local royalty.

Get a grip, Annie. She made a face in the mirror as she walked past it.

Travis had talked to her, laughed with her. Invited her to his house, treated her like a friend. Her mouth curved into a smile when she realized she had something her dopey sister didn't have. With a lighter heart, Annie headed downstairs.

That evening, while Mary Turner supervised kitchen cleanup, Annie asked, "Mama, do you know Ruth Quincy?"

"Well, not really. I know of her, though we've never actually met." Mary glanced at Annie, who carefully stacked plates in the cupboard. Curious, she queried, "Why do you ask?"

"I kind of met her, today. Well, first I met Travis." While Susan squealed in disbelief, Annie rushed on, "And we were fishing together and then afterwards he asked me to come to his house for lemonade and I met Mrs. Quincy. Their house is like a *mansion*, Mama."

The dishes abandoned, Annie spread out her arms in as large a circle she could make. "They had a light hanging in their hall *this* big. And the hall is lots bigger than our living room *and* kitchen together."

"You're lying," Susan hissed. "You didn't go over there.

Why would Travis Quincy want to fish with you, anyway? He's so gorgeous, and you're a flat, *skinny* thing." She flung her dishcloth into the sink as she faced Annie. Only Mary's quiet admonishment kept her from saying more, and she subsided into a fuming silence.

Mary watched Annie's cheeks bloom red from Susan's angry words. "Annie, tell the truth. Were you at the Quincy house today? Did you really meet Travis?" It wasn't that Mary didn't want to believe her daughter, but it seemed far-fetched a boy like Travis would pay any attention to a ten-year-old girl from the wrong side of town. Oh, the Quincys weren't any better than her family, she knew this. But they *were* rich and, because of that, probably unapproachable. In all her years living in Thompkin, she'd rarely seen Ruth Quincy in town.

Annie rubbed away her tears. "I'm not lying, honest. I was at the pond trying to fish, and my line was all knotted up. Travis was there, too, and he tried to help me, but we couldn't get the knots out. He forgot to bring worms so I shared mine with him, and he let me use his pole. We caught lots of fish." Suddenly crestfallen, she added, "Only I left mine at the pond. I bet they're all dead now."

She brightened again as she finished her story. "Then we went to his house and I helped him clean his fish, and their cook Martha gave me lemonade and a brownie, and I got to meet Mr. Quincy, too. He's a lot nicer than his wife," she confided.

Susan grumbled, "I can't believe you got inside their house. I've wanted to see it forever. What's Travis like? Is his voice as dreamy as his face? Did you tell him about me?" She fired rapid questions at Annie, who only blinked at her, while Mary hid a smile behind her hand.

Annie stammered, "He's cute and all. You know he is, Suze. You've seen him around town. And why would I tell him about you? That's so dumb."

"*Don't call me Suze.* And it is *not* dumb!" Susan screeched. "I bet you didn't meet Travis Quincy at all. Why would he want to hang out with a bratty kid like you? You're such a liar—"

"Susan, *enough.* Apologize to your sister right now."

As Susan mumbled a resentful apology, Mary scolded, "I don't know what gets into you sometimes. You know better than to say such hurtful things. I think you should finish up in here, and Annie can get started on her bath. And I want you in bed early tonight." Mary pulled Annie toward the stairs when Susan protested about how life was so unfair. Mary rolled her eyes as she herded Annie upstairs.

In the bathtub, while Annie scrubbed herself, Mary brushed the tumbled hair back from her daughter's forehead. More and more, she resembled her daddy, and Henry Turner was the love of Mary's life. It thrilled her to see his wonderful features on Annie's delicate face. Mary also knew Susan, as the older sister, enjoyed feeling superior.

Unfolding a towel, Mary wrapped it around Annie and patted her thin shoulders dry. "Honey, you know not to let Susan make you feel bad about yourself. Don't you?" She cupped her hand under Annie's chin, raised the wounded brown eyes to hers.

"It wasn't that, Mama. I don't really care about the mean stuff she says. I hate it when she doesn't believe me. I wouldn't lie." Annie sniffed while Mary handed her a tissue.

She took her daughter's hand in hers, squeezing the small fingers. "I believe you, and so does your sister. I'll bet that's why she's mad. She wishes it had happened to her. Although I honestly can't see Susan up to her ankles in pond muck, wrapping a worm on a fishing hook." They both laughed at the idea of girly-girl Susan trying to bait a hook. She wouldn't be caught dead fishing at any pond.

"So, tell me about this Travis. Is he a nice boy? I've met his father a few times, over the years. He's a good man."

"Did you go to school with him, Mama? Did you know Mrs. Quincy in school, too?"

"Goodness, Mrs. Quincy is younger than I am. I'm probably closer to her husband's age. But no, I didn't go to school with him. He went away to the academy. Travis probably goes there too, I'd imagine."

"Then in another couple of months, he'll be gone. That's just *unfair*."

Sympathetic, Mary nodded. "Yes, I know, honey. It's kind of unfair. But look at it this way. If you and Travis are meant to be friends, then you will be, whether he's here in town or away at school. If he goes to the academy like his daddy did, then I bet he comes home on the weekends sometimes, and for the holidays. And you have two whole months more to go fishing and have fun, before he'd have to leave. Right?" She gave her daughter's shoulder a comforting rub.

"I guess. If his mama lets him. She sure didn't like me. She called me 'this...child...'" Annie mimicked a lady's highbrow tone perfectly, and Mary was torn between chuckling at the imitation, and outrage at Ruth Quincy's attitude. "I don't think she likes kids much."

"Well, maybe she's never had an opportunity to be around any children other than Travis. I suppose we could ask her to tea on a day when the boys are all home, fighting over the television, and tromping through the house with their muddy shoes. That might give her a taste of what extra kids are all about."

When Annie giggled, Mary hugged her, reveling in the sweet warmth of her child in her arms. How could anyone not love her Annie? It was inconceivable.

"Come on, Munchkin." She smiled when Annie groaned at the old pet name. "Off to bed. We have to can sweet relish first thing after church. I'll need you and Susan both to help me. And no fighting in the kitchen tomorrow, okay?"

"I'll try. But if Susan calls me skinny and flat one more time, I'm punching her out."

In the room the girls shared, Annie tugged off her towel and wriggled into a nightgown, crawled into bed, and snuggled with her pillow. Mary kissed her forehead and whispered a soft 'good night.'

As she moved toward the door, Annie mumbled, "Mama? Do you think I'm pretty?"

A tender smile bloomed across Mary's face. "I think you're very pretty, honey. Inside where it counts as well as outside where everyone, especially your friends, can't help but see it." She blew Annie a kiss and slipped out into the hallway.

Chapter 3

A light breeze rustled the thin marsh grasses that shielded one end of Bogg Pond. Travis sat on the largest flat rock, chin in hand, his tee shirt damp and stuck to his back. *If I had some danged scissors, I'd hack up my jeans and turn them into shorts.*

Anything to cool himself down.

He glanced over at Annie, poised at the very edge of the pond, her knees slightly bent as she grasped the rod in one hand and played out line with the other. She looked as sweaty as he felt, but it didn't seem to bother her. Heck, nothing really bothered Annie when she was on the hunt for bullheads, not the heat, the mosquitoes, or the thick, steamy air. He had to admire a kid like that.

"Aren't you hot?" he called over, ignoring the Number One Fishing Commandment: *Thou Shalt Not Get Loud Around the Fish.*

"Shh." He could just hear her over the chirping crickets. "I've hooked one and he's gonna fight me."

Wildly envious because his line was empty, he snorted, "Bulls don't fight. It's not like you're fishing for trout."

"This one'll fight." Her soft voice got smug.

Travis jumped down from the rock. He had to see this for himself. Annie always seemed to get the largest bulls. He'd like to have some of whatever magic she used to catch them. He strode to her side and peered over her shoulder, just as she jerked her arm. The hook caught firmly in the fish's mouth, and they both gasped at its large splash.

"Holy heck! Where did he come from?" Travis's jaw dropped as he sized up the fat bullhead Annie now struggled to pull in. He brought his arms around her, caught the rod with one hand, and helped her pull the line with the other. Together they yanked, tugged, and finally landed a bull he swore was as big as a catfish.

Annie dragged a grimy hand over her forehead and left behind a smear of worm slime. She gaped down at the flopping monster. "I've never seen a bull that big. Maybe it's really a cat."

Travis stepped away from her and knelt down to get a better look. The head might be broad enough for a cat, but it still looked more like a bull, and the coloring was right. "I think it's a plain old bull." He prodded it with a finger, and the bull whipped and pulled at the line Annie still held. "Maybe this is one of those wily bulls Dad always brags about." He grinned up at Annie, who chuckled.

"We should take it back to your house and show him. He'll flip when he sees what we've got." She knelt beside Travis, and between the two of them, they unhooked the large fish from the line. Travis got hold of it with both hands and dumped it into the cooler he'd brought. Four other fish lay, submerged and listless, in the large, water-filled cooler. The new bull eclipsed them all.

He stood, wiping his hands on the seat of his jeans. "I bet he *would* flip. But he's not home. He's in Newport this week." He waited until she jumped to her feet, then moved to the flat rock and climbed onto it. Annie followed and clambered up behind him, grabbing onto the back of his shirt for balance.

In silence, they watched the ripple of marsh grass as the breeze strengthened. Travis didn't feel like talking, and Annie wasn't one to push it. He liked that about her. He glanced sideways as she pulled her knees to her chest and rested her chin, her attention caught by a low-flying heron.

Since they'd started fishing together, they hung out at the pond almost every day he could wrangle out of whatever dumb plans his mother insisted on making for him. Even when the fish wouldn't bite and all they did was sit on the bank and swat flies, he had fun with Annie despite the three-year gap in their ages. His dad liked her. Too bad his mother didn't.

Thoughts of his mother put a frown on his face. Annie noticed it, and elbowed him in the ribs. "What's wrong with you? Mad 'cause I got the biggest bull?"

He elbowed her in return, careful not to push too hard and knock her off the rock. "No, I'm not. Well, maybe a little." He snickered when she stuck her tongue out at him. "I was just thinking about junk I have to do when I get home. Stuff I was supposed to do all day. I kind of took off without even starting on it."

"What kind of stuff?" Annie shifted on the rock to face him, her eyes lit with interest. For some reason she found his life fascinating and loved to hear him talk about it. He couldn't imagine why.

"It's nothing." He passed it off with a wave of his hand.

"Oh, come on. Tell me all about your junk. Maybe I can help."

He stared at her in consideration, and shrugged. "Okay. Can you play golf? Take over my fencing lesson? Read the next ten chapters of *The Quincy Legacy History*, for me?"

"Huh?"

He cracked a grin at the confusion on her face. "All the junk I have to do. My mother loads it on me every summer, like she can't stand to see me have any actual fun. Golf lessons and riding lessons and stupid fencing lessons. Dusty old books full of deadly boring facts about my Quincy ancestors." His grin faded as suddenly as it appeared. "It's like she doesn't want me to be happy. This summer is worse than all the rest of them, because she's started going off about politics."

"Oh, Travis. I'm sorry your mama drives you nuts." Annie rubbed her hand over his shoulder.

She sat quietly beside him. Travis knew she sometimes wondered if he had that great a life. She probably compared his relationship with his mother to the way Mary Turner treated Annie and the rest of the kids. In that respect, his life came up way short.

Annie prodded, "What does your daddy think? He's so nice, Travis. He seems a lot more . . . um . . . ." She seemed to struggle for a word that wouldn't show his mother in a bad light. Finally, she said, "He seems really easygoing. Kind."

Travis lifted his hands, dropped them again. "Ah, Dad's great. He never pushes, he just lets me do what I want in the summer." He sighed. "As long as I get good grades in school and I'm willing to try for Yale, Dad's okay with me goofing off."

"You're going to Yale? Wow. I want to go to college, too, any college. If I could go, I'd never ask for another thing in my life."

"Well, I'm going to try getting into Yale. Dad went there. He wanted to get in by himself instead of using Legacy funding, so he went for a full scholarship and got it. That's the way I'm going to do it, too. Like my dad," Travis vowed. He blushed as he met Annie's admiring gaze and jumped from the rock, his hand outstretched for hers. "Come on, let's take off. If I'm going to get that scholarship on my own, I guess I'd better start earning it. I've still got ten moldy chapters of Quincy stuff to read."

She slid down and landed lightly on her feet next to him, looking up into his face. "You can do it. I know you can. You can do anything you want to, Travis."

He ducked his head in embarrassed acknowledgement, and a smile lifted the corner of his mouth as he walked over to the cooler and hefted it by its thick handle. She scooped up their rods in one hand, grasped her bucket in the other and matched his stride.

As they walked along Boggy Creek Lane, he mumbled, "Thanks, Annie."

Ruth Quincy creamed the makeup from her face as she reviewed the evening's festivities. The dinner party with the Cabots, a weekly summer tradition, had proved to be quite successful. Councilman Jeffrey Cabot and his wife, Janice, enjoyed the same level of social status as the Quincys. Ruth smiled as she thought of their daughter, Catherine. Such a darling girl, sweet-tempered and biddable.

Born a mere three months after Travis, both families greeted Catherine's arrival with such joy. Within a year, Ruth and Janice began to plan a wedding between their beloved children. It just seemed fated.

A brief frown marred her smooth brow, as she recalled the many ways her son squirmed out of his social duties toward Catherine. They might be far too young at thirteen to think of an engagement, but it was important they maintain an eye toward the future. It was time to reel Travis in and impress upon him his responsibilities.

"What are you thinking about that's putting a frown on your pretty forehead, Ruthie, my love?" Ronald's voice sounded right at her ear. Startled, she jumped and pressed a hand to her heart. She glared in the mirror at her husband, who had silently entered their suite, and now stood behind her chair with an unrepentant smile on his face.

"Honestly, Ronald, must you sneak about the room?" She took a few deep breaths as she reached for her hairbrush.

Ronald removed the brush from her hand and began working it through her hair himself. The familiar, rhythmic movement soothed her as he commented, "And where else would I sneak, hmm?" He ran his fingers over her hair. "You didn't answer me. What were you concentrating on so fiercely?"

"Nothing dire, I assure you. Just thinking about how lovely Catherine is, how much she's grown up in the past few months." She paused as she met her husband's eyes in the mirror and noted the firm set of his lips and the narrowed eyes. "What? I can't think about the dear child?"

"Don't. Just—don't."

She pretended not to know what he was referring to. "Don't what? Don't say she's a lovely child? Well, she is."

He sighed as he laid the brush on her vanity and grasped her shoulders, turning her around until she faced him. With stern inflection he said, "You know what I mean. Don't start your matchmaking. They're only thirteen, for heaven's sake. You've been campaigning for a wedding ever since Catherine was born, and you know it."

Ruth shrugged, dislodging the gentle grip on her shoulders. "What if I have? Travis has to make a good marriage. He has to have an heir. He's the only direct-line Quincy. Yes, I know," she snapped, anticipating his next remark with sudden temper, "it was my choice not to have any more children. My choice to put the burden of future Quincy generations on his shoulders alone. You know how I feel about herds of children running about, Ronald. I had enough of dealing with children when I wasn't much more than a child, myself," she reminded him.

"Yes, I know. How young you were, with all the responsibility of caring for your baby sisters. I know, Ruthie. And I've never given you any grief about not wanting another child, although of course I'd have enjoyed giving Travis a younger brother or sister. Perhaps it's why he enjoys the Turner girl's company—"

"I don't care what he enjoys. I don't want that girl anywhere near Travis." She turned from the mirror and her eyes locked onto his as she faced him. "For God's sake, she's a *Turner.* I cannot and will not bear her bad influence on our son."

"Ruthie, she's just a little girl. Her parents are decent people. I knew Henry Turner when we were both boys, and he's hardworking and honest. Mary Turner is gentle and kind. I met her a few times, right after Henry moved the family from Roanoke. None of their children, to my knowledge, have ever been in any kind of trouble. They don't have much, but they're good parents and worthwhile citizens of Thompkin."

"No Turner has ever been worthwhile. I don't care how young they are or how removed you consider them from that vile old man who fathered Henry Turner. I will never forget." Her eyes stung with unshed tears. "I will never forgive." Her fingers caught his shirt in a tight grip as she gulped in a ragged breath. "I want that girl to stay away from Travis. I want you to promise me. If I can't do anything about them living in our town, then I can certainly do something about any of them coming around our son."

Saddened, Ronald stared at his wife. He ached for her, for the girl she'd been and for what had happened in her life to cause such bitterness and hatred. Lord knew, he understood. But there came a time when forgiveness had to occur. Otherwise she'd never move on.

He leaned in and gave her a gentle kiss, enclosed her in his arms and held her as he struggled to find the right words. Finally he realized the best way to handle it was the simplest. With regret, he pulled away until he could look into his wife's eyes. "No, Ruth. I'm sorry, but I can't. It isn't right we do this to Travis, to Annie Turner."

She stiffened in protest, and he smoothed his hands over

her loose hair, cupped her cheeks tenderly, slipping them over her shoulders. He entreated, "Let it be, honey. That little girl can't hurt you. Nothing can hurt you any longer except for the memories you're unwilling to release. Can't you see? You're a different person now, a stronger person. A bigger person, too."

But he knew his Ruth was also stubborn. He felt her withdraw, until there was a foot of space between them and the frozen blue of her eyes kept him at bay. She stood tall, her spine steel-rod straight, and when she spoke, her voice was calm and remote, icy.

"Very well. I can see you've made a choice, and put a Turner before my happiness and well-being. I won't speak of it again. You want your son to consort with scum, then so be it. I'll look the other way." Her soft lips tightened. "But I will remember, from this day forward, that once I asked a simple request of you, and you refused me."

With those words, Ruth turned and walked toward the bedroom door, opened it, and stepped through. The door swung shut behind her as tense silence filled the room.

Weary, yet resigned, Ronald crossed to the bed. For certain, he'd sleep in it alone, and not only tonight.

In the old mother-in-law quarters, Ruth looked out the window into the moonlit night. It was warm in the room, but her chill went to the bone. She rubbed her hands over her arms in an effort to regenerate body heat. She refused to walk back to the master wing and retrieve one of her warmer robes from her dressing room. She'd rather freeze all night than encounter her husband while she felt such fury and hurt.

Part of her knew he was right. It happened years ago, and all of the key players—her mother, Willa, and stepfather, Greeley, among them—could no longer hurt her.

The misery of her younger years she could easily heap at her mother's door, since Willa had used her as slave labor. Ruth grew up neglected, beleaguered, and loaded down with more responsibility than any young child should ever have to face.

But that didn't mean her own son should shirk *his* responsibility, she reminded herself. It was vital to the continuance of the Quincy Legacy for Travis to marry well and produce superlative children.

Hadn't she and Ronald given—and would continue to give—their son every opportunity?

Advantages Ruth had never enjoyed. With reluctance, her mind drifted over nuances of her past.

She'd once stood, a stranger outside this very house, and pounded on the door, desperate and afraid. Her hands curled into fists now, as she pushed the memory away. She straightened her shoulders and stiffened her spine. She'd stopped being that person years ago.

And she'd found her safe haven. As the wife of Ronald Quincy she'd gained a warm and caring family, a husband and son who loved her. When Ronald's mother was alive, she'd treated her like a daughter, and Ruth had loved Amelia Quincy dearly. She'd mourned her mother-in-law's death. From the first moment Ruth entered Quincy Hall that miserable, rainy night so long ago, Amelia became "Mama" to her.

She enjoyed such security here at Quincy Hall. Still, there remained a residual kernel of the young, frightened girl with the rain-drenched hair and clothes, who'd banged hard enough on the door of Quincy Hall to carry cuts and bruises on her hands for days. She hated knowing her fears remained, causing strife and frustration between her and her family.

Of course she wished she could get over it. Only the memory could truly hurt her.

Restless and agitated, she circled the room. She didn't want to spend the summer angry with the two most important men in her life. Neither did she want to become a doormat for them to trample on her feelings and aspirations.

Perhaps a touch of reverse psychology held the key. Surely Travis's fascination with the Turner girl would wear thin by the end of the summer. After all, hc'd be back at Newport Academy, and the girl would continue on at the local elementary school with all of her common little friends. By the time he came home for the holidays, this budding acquaintance—Ruth refused to label it anything else— between them would be long gone.

She nodded decisively, relieved. Travis would revert to his usual thoughtful and obedient self, once summer was over and he was back at the academy.

Chapter 4

Determined to hoard as much summer fun as he could, Travis slipped out of his room right after breakfast, eased down the back stairs, and let himself out the kitchen door. He'd left the moldy old Quincy book open on his bed. He'd propped the dumb sword—okay, *rapier*, according to his fencing instructor—in the corner of his room. On a sunny, hot day, prancing around holding a goofy sword wasn't his idea of fun. Not when a bucket of worms and fishing with Annie awaited him. Anxious to escape, Travis reached the end of the driveway and took off at a sprint toward town, and the turnoff for Bogg Pond.

As he walked down Boggy Creek Lane, Travis thought about the past month and a half, how hanging out with Annie had changed his outlook on all kinds of things. With her family, he didn't have to be a big deal, no one special. Just a guy named Trav, another local kid with pond water on the legs of his blue jeans and traces of summertime sweat on the back of his neck.

He liked it, a lot.

Even better was Annie herself, who had fast become his very best friend. He could tell her anything, and she'd really listen to him. About the only thing he hadn't told Annie was the way his mother tried to choose not only his friends, but his future wife, too. Jeez, he wasn't stupid.

Travis hitched the two fishing rods over his shoulder, his sneakers stirring up dust as he walked faster. As usual, thinking about his mother's agenda irritated the crap out of him. He knew what she was up to, with her frequent invitations to Catherine Cabot and her parents. Somehow Mother had gotten it into her head—the same way she'd gotten golf lessons and riding lessons and dumb fencing lessons, for God's sake, into her head—that someday he'd marry Catherine.

That wasn't going to happen. Talk about boring, she gave new meaning to the word. Several times over the summer, his mother more or less demanded he accompany Catherine on some sort of outing, and each time he'd found ways to avoid it. His freedom meant too much to him to waste it on a pale, silent kid like Catherine.

As he rounded the far edge of Bogg Pond, he saw Annie in her old, faded jeans and muddy sneakers, her green tee shirt already damp with sweat. A big smile wreathed her face when she spotted him, and she started running. The bait bucket she carried swung in her hand and her thick braid bounced on her shoulder. Without conscious thought, Travis picked up his pace. Beneath the hot summer sun, they sprinted toward each other.

They met in the high grass along center Bogg Pond, both breathing fast in the humidity. Travis looked at her as if he'd never seen her before, this girl-buddy of his, three years younger than him, but in many ways so much smarter, so much more alive. Rich in all the things he didn't have. Things he never knew he missed until he'd discovered them through her eyes, her life.

She dropped her bucket on the grass and the load of night crawlers and leaves threatened to spill out. He loosened his grip on the two fishing rods he carried, and they slipped to the ground. He couldn't stop staring at her.

She really was . . . cute. Big brown eyes, pretty hair, a smile that didn't quit. Half tomboy, adventurous, nothing grossed her out or made her squeal in disgust, not even the slimiest worm or the ugliest fish. She wasn't afraid of snakes or spiders, liked frogs, read tons of books, just like he did.

They shot hoops together, and she could beat him at one-on-one if she put her mind to it. She told him some of the dopiest jokes he'd ever heard.

His very best friend, Annie. Someday she'd grow up into the kind of girl who'd be perfect for him to love, to share a life with. It hit him with sudden certainty.

Holy smokes.

Less than a foot away from her, he gazed right into her wide eyes. One of his hands reached for hers. Grimy from worms and leaves, clammy with dampness, it fit into his palm like it belonged there.

He said the first thing that popped into his head.

"I'm going to marry you someday. When we're out of school and I'm home for good. When we're old enough that nobody can tell us what to do. I don't ever want anyone else. Just you." His defiant and passionate words might not make sense coming from a kid his age and aimed toward a girl who was still in grade school, but it seemed the right thing to say to her.

"I think that's a great idea." She sounded dazed. "I don't want any other boy, either. It was always you. The first time I saw you, it was you."

Maybe she was too young to make a promise like that. But he knew she meant it.

He swallowed, hard. Emotion tightened his throat and made it difficult to speak. He cautioned, "We can't tell anybody. They'd say we're too young to talk about it or think about it. I don't want to make your folks mad, Annie. And my mother would probably freak out. So, our secret. Okay?"

She nodded, solemn. "Our secret. Until you think it's safe to tell."

As they faced each other in the hot sunlight, an odd calm settled over him. Yet with that calm came the need to seal their bargain with more than words. As if she read his mind, Annie tugged on his hand, raised herself up on her toes. She brushed his cheek with her mouth. The shy, butterfly-light touch made him smile.

He scooped up the rods and bucket with his free hand. Toward the shallow edge of the pond, they settled on their favorite spot of flat rocks, digging into the worms for the choicest bait. The humid summer breeze enveloped them and the sound of crickets and cicadas broke the silence.

It promised to be a great day.

Chapter 5

August

Annie tossed restlessly, punched her damp pillow into a mangled lump, finally gave up and threw it on the floor. In the bed across the room, Susan slept like the dead, as usual.

The sobs Annie muffled left her with a headache. She flopped back on the tangled sheets and blinked away a fresh bout of tears.

Travis's mama had sent him off to that academy, weeks before school was supposed to start. Annie knew it she'd done it on purpose, because she hated the friendship between them. If she only knew how they really felt about each other, his mama would pitch such a fit.

Earlier that day, Annie waited at the flat rocks for him, hot and cranky in the humidity. He'd torn through the waist-high alfalfa that grew in the pasture near the pond shore. She frowned in bewilderment. Travis never ran unless he had to.

"I can't stay. I'm not supposed to be here at all." Out of breath, he pushed damp hair off his forehead. For once, at least since she'd known him, she saw dirt smeared on his clothes.

She pointed at him. "You're wearing a real shirt. How come? Did you run out of tee shirts?"

He shook his head and sank down next to her on the rock. His eyes snapped with temper. "Mother is making me leave for the academy today. I wasn't supposed to go for another few weeks. She packed my stuff and told me last night. Damn it!" He pounded his fist on his knee and jumped up to pace around the rock cluster.

She followed him, sudden tears in her eyes. He turned and looked down at her as he caught her hand and twined their fingers together. "I think it's because Dad saw us the other day and must have said something to Mother. My folks never saw me hold hands with a girl before." He glanced down at their joined hands and she gasped, remembering the other day. His daddy had driven by and waved to them as he made the turn for Thompkin Hill.

Miserable, she whispered, "My fault. I should have paid attention. We never walk close to the hill together—"

"It's *not* your fault. We didn't do anything wrong."

"But, our secret—"

"It was stupid to try and keep it. I was stupid for making you promise." Still holding her hand, he leaned against the rock. "Look, my mother knows we hang out together a lot. I guess she thought once I was away from school I'd forget all about you. Probably figured you'd forget all about me, too."

Annie's rebuttal was out of her mouth almost before he could finish the sentence. "I'd *never* forget you. How could I?" She flung herself against Travis. "You're the *best* friend I've ever had." His arms closed around her as she whispered, "You *belong* to me." Her eyes raised to his, emotion splintered her voice. "You're going to m-marry me."

For long seconds they held each other, while the hot August sun beat down on them.

Finally, she stirred. "Your daddy won't make you go." She mouthed the decisive words against his shirt.

"No, Annie. My dad's not here. He went to Roanoke, some kind of business meeting." He drew her away, to peer into her face. "He won't be home for another two days. My dad's driver is taking me to Newport in a couple of hours. Mother's orders."

His mama did this behind his daddy's back. It upset

Annie so much that she started to cry, and pressed her wet eyes to Travis's shoulder. He stroked his hand over her hair.

There wasn't anything left to say. They trudged down the lane, this time only as far as the turnoff for the older side of town, and Spring Street. No reason to add to his mother's already unreasonable attitude, no need to give her any more excuse to split them up.

In the few minutes before they parted ways, both clung to the hope they'd stay friends and spend more time together, come the holidays, until they got older and could choose for themselves.

While those promises echoed between them, Travis walked away while Annie watched him go. She waited until he was out of sight before she turned toward home, her eyes blurred with more tears.

Now, hours later, she replayed the entire morning. Waking up, so eager to have another day with him, to her last glimpse before he rounded the bend on Boggy Creek Lane. She dragged her pillow from the floor and pressed it to her wet cheek as she turned on her side.

She sighed and closed her eyes. Christmas vacation couldn't get here soon enough.

PART TWO

Romance

Chapter 6

Five Years Later
December

Susan Turner flopped on her bed and scowled at Annie, dashing around the room half in and half out of yet another outfit. "For crying out loud, it's not even a real date. How many more times are you gonna change your clothes?"

Frazzled, Annie snapped, "Don't bother me, okay? Don't even talk to me, not unless you want to help and tell me if this looks better than the blue dress." She spun around to face the mirror, dissatisfied with her reflection. The dark pink skirt and pullover was pretty but made her look like a child. The last thing she wanted to look like was a *child*, for heaven's sake. She flung a pleading glance over her shoulder at her older sister. Susan had a hundred times more fashion sense than she'd ever have.

With an exaggerated sigh, Susan rolled off the bed. Her critical once-over assessed and then dismissed the pink outfit. "You look cute, but too young. The blue dress is better." She chewed her bottom lip thoughtfully for a second, then offered, "I guess I wouldn't mind if you borrowed something of mine."

Annie turned to stare at her sister. In all the years they'd shared clothes, not once had Susan ever offered to let her borrow something new. She'd get Susan's hand-me-downs and that was about it. But now Annie worked at the Coffee Hut two hours each afternoon and all day on Saturday. She had some money of her own, half of which her parents made her put away in a savings account. But she'd been able to buy herself a few things, and found the joy of owning something nobody else had ever worn heady beyond belief.

For one glorious moment Annie basked in the unfamiliar glow of her sister's affection. Then her eyes narrowed in suspicion. "What do you want, Suze? You have to want something. You need money, right? You want me to do your chores on Sunday so you can sneak out with Matt again. You want—"

"Oh, cripes. I don't want anything. And *don't* call me *Suze*. I thought I'd be nice for a change and do you a favor." Susan aimed an accusing stare at Annie. "You're seeing Travis tonight, aren't you?"

"Just for a little while. They're having that big holiday party up at Quincy Hall this evening, so he can't stay for long. I want to look good for him, though." Annie tugged at the hem of the pullover and wondered if an upswept hairstyle would lend her some maturity.

"He always comes home the week before Christmas." Susan's voice held just enough wistful envy to please Annie, who immediately felt rotten for gloating. Her sister used to have a thing for Travis, and he tolerated her only because of Annie.

It was mean of her to needle Susan in light of such unexpected generosity, and Annie relented. "I promise I won't call you Suze any longer. You're really going to loan me something? Whatever I want?"

"Anything but my black velvet pants and top. And you can't borrow stuff if it doesn't fit you in the chest 'cause it'll look silly on you," Susan added.

Annie didn't take offense at the deliberate provocation, for how could she when it was the truth? She turned sideways and viewed herself in the mirror, resigned as always to the sight of her small breasts and boyish hips. The superior smirk on Susan's face didn't help to bolster her confidence, either. Well, they'd been at each other's throats for most of their lives. She shrugged and swung back to the mirror.

Susan rested a hand on Annie's shoulder. With their reflections almost cheek to cheek, her sister idly commented, "I have some blush that would look fabulous on you. And this new lip gloss. You should try it. Tastes like peaches. You know that new outfit I bought, the pleated wool skirt and matching sweater? I haven't worn it yet. I bet it would really look good with your hair and skin. You want to try it on?"

Annie blinked at her. "How short is the skirt? I can't wear a short skirt." All of her Sunday churchgoing skirts and dresses brushed her calves.

Susan stuck her head in their closet in search of the outfit. "I don't see why you can't." The tightly packed clothing muffled her voice.

It took some rummaging, but Susan finally unearthed the outfit and handed it to Annie, whose eyes grew covetous as she held the skirt against her. The hemline flirted a good four inches above her knee. "Mama will throw a fit if I wear a skirt this short." She stroked the soft wool and ran a finger along one of the pleats before she laid it on the bed next to the dark green sweater. It was the prettiest outfit she'd ever seen.

"You'd be surprised what Mama might say. Maybe she'd say it's about time you started dressing like you're sixteen instead of six." Susan unzipped Annie's demure pink skirt. Down her legs it slid, leaving her wearing the knit pullover and a pair of white panties with tiny roses scattered all over them.

With a strangled cough, Susan pointed to the panties. "You've still got those stupid things? I gave them to you three years ago! I can't believe they're not faded and all stretched out." She poked a finger at Annie's ticklish hipbone and made her flinch. "I can't believe Mama hasn't tossed them out."

"She did. I fished them out of the trash," Annie muttered, ignoring Susan's sudden whoop. "They're comfortable, all right? I like them." She frowned at her sister. "Stop laughing."

Susan gave a final chuckle as she yanked the pink top over Annie's head. Her eyes goggled and she huffed theatrically at what she found beneath. "Not *another* undershirt. Annie, you have to start wearing your bras. I know you've got some. What are you, a baby? Your clothes won't fit right unless you play up what you have. Granted, it's not very much, but at least you're not totally flat-chested."

She tugged at the undershirt and had it off before Annie could squawk in embarrassment. It landed on the floor. "I swear I'm going to burn all your dopey underwear, just wait and see." Susan raided Annie's dresser and tossed her the first bra she found. Annie caught it in mid-air and stared at it for a few seconds before putting it on.

She turned sideways and looked at herself. Her sister was right. The bra did help to shape the slight curve of her breasts, and made them look like more. A smile caught at the corner of Annie's mouth as she picked up the skirt and stepped into it. Maybe this time she'd look closer to sixteen than six.

Five minutes later, she viewed her reflection with wonder. Amazing what a decent bra, flattering clothes, and some makeup could do. She must have mumbled it aloud, for Susan nodded.

"*This* is the way you want Travis to see you. You'll knock him clean over. In fact," she leaned in and gave Annie an awkward hug, "you can have the outfit. It would never look this good on me. Consider it an early Christmas gift."

It took Annie a full ten seconds to overcome her shock at her sister's sudden generosity, before she turned and wrapped both arms around Susan in a tight, emotional squeeze. "I'll do your chores on Sunday. You can sneak out early for Matt. I'll—oh, thanks, Suze. You made me look so nice."

"Nice? I made you look *hot*, Annie Turner. And don't you forget it." For once, Susan didn't bother to give Annie grief for calling her *Suze*. She wiggled out of Annie's arms, stepped over to her nightstand, and pulled open a drawer. "You need to accessorize," she declared.

Annie watched while Susan tossed a dark leather clutch purse onto the nearest bed, and searched in her jewelry box until she found a silver chain bracelet and matching earrings. She handed them to Annie. "Put these on. Don't lose them."

"We're only going for a drive, not to some fancy restaurant," Annie pointed out. "I don't need all this stuff. Not that I don't appreciate the offer," she hastened to add.

"Doesn't matter. You want to look polished and put together, don't you?" Susan thrust the purse at her. "Use this. I know you hate purses, but you should bring some lipstick with you tonight. And the front door key, too, in case you get back really late. And take some money. Do you need any?"

Baffled, Annie cupped the bracelet and earrings in her hand. What was going on? Her sister never lent out money or jewelry. Maybe she was coming down with some horrible illness.

"Well? Put them *on*." Susan barked at her impatiently as she waved the purse in her face.

Annie fastened the dainty bracelet and hooked the earrings in her lobes while she eyed her sister as if she'd lost her mind. At Susan's urging, she slipped a tube of lipstick into the purse, added her house key and a few dollars from her piggybank.

She turned toward Susan and held out both arms. "Am I polished enough?"

With a grin, her sister pushed Annie toward the door. "Travis won't know what hit him."

Chapter 7

Ruth stood in the doorway, scanning everything one final time. The dining room table gleamed with her mother-in-law's wedding service. Fine bone china, a soft cream with delicate silver leaves and tiny flowers edging the scalloped rim, created a lovely place setting. Each Waterford goblet and wineglass sparkled and the ornate silverware lay on dark red damask napkins. Three floral arrangements of poinsettia, winter white roses and holiday greenery set in low silver bowls graced the long table, flanked by candelabras fitted with slender red candles. It made for a magnificent display.

The room glowed with elegance and quiet dignity. Mama Amelia would have been so pleased to see her possessions holding a place of honor at the holiday table. For Ruth, it was a gesture of love to the memory of the woman who had been more than a mother-in-law to her. Nothing but Mama's heirloom china would do for such a special occasion.

Ruth smoothed the skirt of her deep green cocktail dress. The silk Chanel creation fit the mood she sought to emulate, elegant, yet festive, with its subtle beading and soft, draping neckline. Wearing the diamond earrings Ronald had presented her on their tenth anniversary gave her additional confidence and poise.

Yet she brushed at sudden tears that threatened to fall and ruin her carefully applied makeup. At the holidays, she missed her Mama Amelia so much. Sometimes the ache stayed with her for days, even after all these years. Mama Amelia always knew what to do in any given social situation. Her gentle guidance had changed Ruth from a wild-haired, frightened child of fifteen into a lady who wore designer clothes with ease. One who knew how to keep a fine house, set a lovely table, entertain influential friends, make an important man a devoted wife who was an asset rather than a liability.

Sparing a final sigh, she glanced at the diamond-encrusted Piaget on her wrist, and gasped at the time. Their guests would arrive in less than two hours. Ruth hurried upstairs.

She looked toward Travis's rooms and stopped, her hand raised to the door to knock and hurry him along. And she almost cursed aloud in frustration as she recalled why her nerves stretched to the breaking point: her errant son.

Earlier, he'd rushed into the master suite and caught his father in a hug, pressed a kiss on her cheek. Then Travis breezily declared, "I put my luggage in my room, and now I'm headed over to Annie's for a while. I'll be back in time for the dinner." He cut through her heart as he walked out the door, turning his back on his responsibilities with no more than a cheerful smile.

Two hours later, Ruth still trembled with an all-consuming urge to grab her son by the neck and shake him until he promised to behave. Until he promised to stand next to Catherine Cabot and pledge himself to her as befitted a Quincy.

Deep, calming breaths. Ruth gulped them in as she uncurled her stiff fingers. Ladies didn't clench their hands into fists. Forcing herself to relax, she descended the stairs, calculating the amount of time she could spare until her guests arrived.

It was time to have a talk with her husband.

Parked on Hickory Knob, warm and snug in the front seat of his silver BMW, Travis cradled Annie in his arms, the radio muted in the background and snow melting as it hit the windshield. Neither noticed the snow, or cared what songs were playing. They were too busy holding on to one another, trying to stuff four long months of longing and loneliness into one perfect moment of reunion.

He'd wanted to go straight to her house instead of dropping by Quincy Hall, but he knew it would infuriate his mother if he didn't come home first. Even so, the brief time he spent with his parents chafed at his patience, and he knew he'd have to listen to his mother's angry tirade later on when he got back to the Hall. He wasn't looking forward to it.

But he made it to Annie's in record time, trying to be mindful of the slick streets, so anxious to see her that he came close to landing in the ditch twice. Annie waited on her porch, wrapped in a long coat, her hair hidden under a bright red knit hat. She'd come flying down the steps toward the car as he killed the engine and jumped out. He'd ended up with an armful of excited, teary-eyed girl before he could close his door.

He lifted her off her feet and swung her around in a wild circle, his mouth fused to hers. They kissed madly in the wet snowfall, only coming up for air when Travis realized how soaked they'd become. He'd bundled her into the car and by mutual agreement they'd headed for Hickory Knob for some much-needed alone time.

Their reunion in the cramped front seat of his Beemer passed all too quickly. Her hat lay on the floor near her feet, and Travis wound his fingers in her thick hair, holding her close for yet another kiss. He couldn't get enough of kissing her. Nothing had ever felt so right.

"When do you have to be back?" Annie rested her head on his shoulder.

He nuzzled her ear and felt her shiver. "Mother's

already mad at me because I wasn't home for more than a few minutes, so I guess I should head back now. I don't want to. God, Annie." He sat up straighter and gazed at her in the dim glow of the dashboard. "These dinners are the pits. Mother always invites all these people she thinks are so important, and they sit in the dining room and talk politics. Dad mostly tolerates them. He never did like politics. And he tires so easily these days. I worry about him all the time." His father had suffered a debilitating stroke two years ago, and had been confined to a wheelchair ever since.

Annie frowned and commented, "I thought he was doing better. Mama saw Martha at the bank a few months ago, and she told Mama your daddy's doing fine." Her words trailed off as Travis shook his head.

"No, I think it's getting worse. Dad used to go into the office a couple times a week, but it's harder now for him to get around with that wheelchair. Dan Marley—he's Dad's assistant—comes to the house almost every day." Helplessness overcame him, as always, when he talked about his father's failing health. He looked at Annie and saw concern for him and for his father on her face. She grasped his hand as he whispered miserably, "I think Mother and Dad still fight a lot over me. Over my future."

"Oh, Travis. I'm so sorry." For a few minutes they sat in silence, Travis lost in his own thoughts while Annie held his hand.

Determined to lighten the mood, he shook off the gloomy thoughts, and smiled at her. "Anyway, the party is mostly filled with people my parents' age. It's beyond boring. It's all I can do to sit there." He pretended to sulk to make her giggle, gratified when she did.

"You're so cute when you pout." She grinned at him and nuzzled a kiss to his neck. "Maybe you can sneak out right after dessert. They don't make you do anything, do they? Like play the piano or dance, or something?"

Horrified, he gasped, "*No.* Don't even think it. I don't want to give them any ideas. It's bad enough already. My mother will probably insist I take Catherine for a walk, which is pure agony. It never seems to matter to Mother how cold it is, either. She still makes me do it."

"Catherine? Is that somebody's dog?"

Immediately, an image of Catherine Cabot tied to the end of a leash flashed in his mind. He choked on his own sudden laughter. "Jesus. No! Catherine is a girl, not a dog."

"Oh? What kind of girl? A little girl? An older girl?"

He heard the insecurity in her voice and quickly reassured her. "She's the daughter of some friends of my mother's. Her mother and mine have some half-baked idea we should get together, but Catherine knows I love you."

"You've never mentioned her before."

He raised Annie's face until their eyes met, and saw a trace of doubt in hers. "Catherine's not important, sweetheart. She's never been worth mentioning at all." With relief, he watched as her eyes cleared, and she nodded.

"Okay. But tell me about her now."

"Catherine's all right, I guess." Travis leaned back in his seat as he spoke. Annie snuggled closer, her eyes never leaving his. "When we were younger, her family came over a lot. She'd just sit there and stare off into space. I swear, she's the only kid I know with less personality than any of the fish we used to pull out of Bogg Pond." He enjoyed her startled snigger and pressed a kiss to her temple, rested his lips against the silky curve of her cheek. "I'd rather be with you, at your house, with your family." He eased away so he could look in her eyes. "The last time I saw Catherine, I made sure she understood who holds my heart."

"Me." It was half question, half statement. But he could feel Annie sigh as she fully relaxed against him, and he drew in a thankful breath.

"Yes. You." He kissed her mouth lingeringly.

"Too bad I can't be at your dinner. I'd keep you from being bored." Annie snuggled even closer.

"You could come, you know. To the dinner. My dad would be happy to have you there." Travis's voice was casual, but his heart pounded as he thought about it, about walking into Quincy Hall with Annie's hand firmly in his. And he tried to picture the way his parents would handle it, how his father would greet her with a smile and maybe even a hug. How his mother might stand there at Dad's side and either freeze up or do a slow, mean burn.

The more he thought of it, the more he convinced himself of its rightness. He was nineteen years old and in college, for Christ's sake. He could invite anyone he liked into his home and to these silly dinner parties. His mother had shut Annie out for years. Christmas could be the best time for her to finally understand what Annie meant to him.

With a frown, Annie shook her head. "Travis, I don't think so. It's not such a good idea. Your mother—"

"My mother has been rude to you for over five years. It's never made sense to me, other than she's just a snob." He took hold of her shoulders in a gentle grip. "I love you. I want to marry you. Sooner or later my mother has to accept it. I'm so tired of her obsession with what she thinks is the kind of life I should be leading. It's *my* life. My decisions." He moved closer and kissed her again, held her close.

In the idling car, poignant holiday music gave way to the local news. Snowflakes swirled past the windows. Travis pressed his forehead to Annie's. "I'm old enough to choose the kind of life I want and the one I want to spend it with. I choose you." His lips brushed hers. "I chose you a long time ago."

"Travis, I—I'm not really dressed for a fancy party."

Travis thought she looked like an angel. "You're so pretty, Annie. It doesn't matter what you wear, you'd look beautiful." He cupped her face in his hands. "Even when you had leaves in your hair and worm slime on your nose, you were the prettiest girl I've ever seen." She pushed indignantly at his shoulder and he let her, then caught her close and hugged her, hard.

Against her ear he vowed, "You're perfect, so say yes. Come to the party with me."

Her eyes filmed with tears, Annie nodded. She refastened her seatbelt when he put the car into gear and sat back in her seat, holding on to his free hand as they drove the few miles over to Quincy Hall.

"I can't stay very late."

"I know. You can call your parents when we get to my house. Tell them I'll have you home by eleven. Okay?"

Annie took a deep breath and held it. "Okay."

Travis gave her fingers a hard squeeze. A new chapter of their lives was about to begin. He didn't know how ready they were. But it would be all right, as long as they never let go of each other.

As they turned into Quincy Hall's long driveway, he told himself they'd have a great time, that for the first time ever, the holiday party would mean something special to him because Annie was at his side.

He pushed away the mocking voice of fear, determined to shake off a sense of foreboding.

Ronald, dressed in his best suit, stated, "No, Ruth. I will *not*. You should know better than to even ask it of me." He faced his wife with the same assurance he'd always possessed. In his wheelchair he should have appeared weaker, but he had never been, and would never be, a weak man.

Ruth regarded him as if stunned, her blue eyes icing over. Travis's eyes, Ronald thought with sadness. The two most important people in his life shared the same coloring, the same eyes. But Travis's were warm and guileless. Had Ruth's eyes always worn such an edge? Had he fooled himself all these years, made her into someone he wanted her to be, only because he loved her so much?

He wheeled himself closer. "Ruthie, listen to me. Our son is nineteen years old, a college man. All too soon he'll begin a life of his own, and as an adult, he's more than entitled to it. I'd like to think he'll include us in that life, wouldn't you?" He gestured toward her, a plea for her understanding. "He's drawing away from you, my love. Can't you see? You're pushing him away with your unyielding stance. Please, Ruthie. Please think about what you're doing."

Her eyes never faltered. Cold and angry, they refused to thaw. They bore into him as she retorted, "I *have* thought. For over five years I've thought of little else. And I've felt pain at having to admit to myself, time and again, how you put your son's foolish impulses before me. Travis is still a child. He knows nothing, *nothing* of the world outside our door." She paused to take a breath, pressing a fist to her chest. "Understand me, once and for all. I will never acknowledge a relationship between our son and that girl. I will never welcome her into this house. If Travis persists in pursuing this insanity, I will find a way to stop it. You have my assurance, trust me."

Her words cut Ronald to the quick and he closed his eyes briefly, dropping his outstretched hand into his lap. It hurt to admit he'd never sway her. The prejudice she felt against the Turner family ran too deep.

And Ruth's anguish, at what had been done to her when she was even younger than Annie, still had the power to control her, warp her. Distort her. He couldn't let it go on. He should have dealt with it, gotten her the help she needed, years ago.

As he tamped down his own anguish, he said the words

she'd no doubt never forgive him for. "All right, Ruth. If that's your final decision, so be it. But you understand *me*." He sat ruler straight in his chair. Though it sent shooting pain along his spine, he refused to let the knifelike twinges get the better of him. "I may be in a wheelchair, but as long as I have all of my faculties, I'm telling you Travis will be allowed to see whomever he wants to see. His friends are welcome in this house."

He noted the fury on her face and stressed, "If you cannot behave toward those friends in a civilized manner, then I will ask you to move to another part of the Hall when our son is entertaining them here. I will not have your blind bigotry ruin our child's happiness and his future."

Her mouth dropped open in shock. "Are you *threatening* me?"

"If you see my decision as a threat, then yes."

He would have said more, but the anguished voice of his son broke in. "*Stop*! God, both of you just stop it!"

The color drained out of Ronald's face at the sight of Travis framed in the drawing room door with tears in his eyes. Snow still clung to his coat, and huddled close to him, visibly distressed, was Annie Turner.

Oh, Lord. How much had his son heard?

Ruth released a hiss of fury and moved toward the door. Hastily Ronald maneuvered his wheelchair between her and the couple who stood like statues in the open doorway, clinging to each other's hands as if lost.

Ruth growled, "Move out of my way, Ronald."

"No. I don't think that's a good idea." He held firm between his wife and son. "I believe you have guests to attend, Ruth. I just heard the sound of a car motor, which tells me our friends are starting to arrive. Jenny will get the door, but you should be in place in the dining room, ready to receive them. I think you should go there. Now," he stressed, when she didn't respond. For several seconds, their eyes—

and wills—clashed. Finally Ruth turned on her heel and walked out the side door. He watched her go with a heavy ache in his heart. But the face he showed to Travis was as calm and loving as always. The smile he sent Annie's way was gentle.

Before he could say anything, Travis pulled Annie farther into the room and shut the wide doors behind them. Still in his coat and boots, he moved to Ronald's side and dropped to his knees next to the wheelchair. Tears slipped down Annie's cheeks as Ronald hugged his boy, trying to ease the hurt he saw in those expressive blue eyes.

When Ronald held out his free hand, Annie stepped closer to the wheelchair and sat on the thick carpet with her head on his knee, clutching his fingers.

Travis moved out of Ronald's embrace and sat back on his heels. When he looked at his son, Ronald saw such love, as well as weariness and sadness, in his young face.

"Dad—"

Ronald shook his head, cautioning, "Not now, Trav. I know you have questions. Lord knows I don't have all of the answers. But shortly we'll have a lot of company, and any discussion will have to wait until later."

He smiled at Annie, curled next to his chair with her cheek still pressed to his knee. "It's good to see you, Annie. You've grown up on me." When she raised a blushing face to him, he casually brushed a wayward tear from her cheek and teased, "If I were twenty-five years or so younger, I'd give my rascal son a run for his money."

The teasing had its desired effect. Annie giggled and squeezed his hand. "I'm glad to see you, too. I'm so sorry, we should have told you. . . I should have stayed home."

"Shh. You have nothing to be sorry for." He reached into his pocket for a handkerchief and pressed it into her hand. "Dry your pretty eyes, my dear, and I'll see you both at dinner." He patted her cheek fondly.

"Dad, I don't know if it's a good idea for us to stay to dinner—"

Annie protested, "Oh no, Travis, you have to stay. I should go—"

"You are *both* staying. Period." Ronald allowed no further argument. "It's Christmas and a time for celebration. You two are going to eat turkey with me until you explode. Annie, do your parents know you're here?" She shook her head. "Then why don't you give them a call and let them know you've been invited for dinner? Travis, take off those boots, they're still wet. And where are your manners? Help Annie off with her coat."

"Yes, sir." Two voices spoke at once. As Ronald noted the tender regard they had for each other, he sent up a silent prayer that someday he'd see Annie walk down the aisle of a church right here in Thompkin, and marry his tall, handsome boy.

In the meantime they had a dinner to attend, and he had some hard decisions to make.

Chapter 8

Festive holiday music played softly in the background, while the laughter and chatter of Quincy Hall's dinner guests rang above the clink of crystal and silverware. Another successful party was well underway, and Ruth sat at one end of the table, smiling, gracious, lovelier than ever.

Seated across from Travis near the head of the table, Annie toyed with a piece of roast turkey. Her nerves prevented her from eating much, and she hadn't said more than a few words since dinner began. How easy to smile, though, when she saw for herself the way Travis and his daddy enjoyed each other's company. If only Travis's mama would join in, too. In her opinion, Mrs. Quincy missed out on a lot.

She glanced around, awed by the magnificent, intimidating room. Worried about acting dumb, Annie tried to concentrate on her table manners, but only managed to move the food around on her plate, knowing she wouldn't be able to swallow much.

She didn't belong here. She shouldn't have let Travis talk her into it. Everything about her seemed less than it should be. Her appearance, her level of social graces . . . her ability to hold her own next to Travis and his elegant family.

Then she caught the smile Travis sent her across the table. She saw his daddy wink at them both as he forked up a bite of chestnut dressing. Suddenly it was easier to breathe. Annie rescued a carrot slice she'd buried under her turkey, and nibbled on it as she returned Mr. Quincy's wink.

The noise level of animated, cheery dinner conversation grew, along with Ruth's anger and frustration. She hadn't eaten more than a taste of anything. The blame for her inability to enjoy her own party rested on the slender bit of trash seated near Ronald, smiling at her besotted son.

It was all Ruth could do to remain calm. It wasn't fair. She would *not* tolerate it. Right in the middle of the fourth course, she began to push back her chair. She had no set plan, but right now her decision to rid her dinner table of a Turner overrode her sensibility.

Then she noticed how desperately Catherine Cabot, seated a few chairs away from her, stared at Travis. When Catherine turned back to her dinner, she looked up and for a second or two her distress was plain to see. Realizing Ruth watched her, the poor girl's cheeks flamed and she hurriedly ducked her head.

The thought that Catherine might be humiliated if Ruth incurred any sort of scene kept her from embarrassing the dear child. Ruth relaxed in her seat, confident no one nearby noticed she'd almost committed an inexcusable action at her own dinner table. Now wasn't the time. She took a deep breath and nodded to Jenny when she whispered the dessert course was ready. As the maids cleared the entrée plates, Ruth chatted with several of her dinner companions seated on both sides of the table, and silently plotted the confrontation which would ensue when all her guests were gone and the family was alone.

She deliberately caught Catherine's attention and smiled at her, causing her face to brighten. Such a darling girl. She'd make a wonderful daughter-in-law.

When Jenny set the raspberry and Bavarian cream mousse in front of her, Ruth decided she had an appetite after all.

After the party, with Annie close by his side, Travis faced his father in the study. "Dad, it's gone on long enough. Maybe we were both kids when Mother's attitude started, but we're not kids any longer." The look on his face reflected his determination.

Ronald stalled gently. "Son, your mother needs to be responsible for any explanations you demand. But I also think she's not ready to answer those questions." He glanced over at Annie, observed the shadows under her eyes that hadn't been there when she'd first arrived with Travis. The poor girl was exhausted.

"Why don't you take Annie home? We can talk later. I know I promised you an explanation right after the party, but right now I'm tired and in need of my rest. We'll get this straightened out, Trav. You have my word." The smile he kept pasted to his face faded as soon as they turned and walked from the study.

He wanted nothing more than to clear the air with his wife. When he wheeled himself in the direction of the dining room and peered through the open doorway, the only occupant of the room seemed to be their day maid, Jenny, shrugging into her coat.

"Jenny, where's Mrs. Quincy?"

Startled, she faced him, a hand over her heart. "Lord, Mr. Ronald, you gave me a turn. I thought you'd gone upstairs with Mrs. Quincy." Jenny took a deep breath before buttoning up her coat. "She's in the master suite, sir. I'm all finished. I sent Alice home, and I think Martha went up to her room. I'll be back early tomorrow morning to help serve the holiday luncheon."

Ronald nodded to her absently. He'd forgotten about Ruth's annual luncheon for the ladies of Thompkin with whom she socialized. It made clearing the air tonight all the more important.

"Thank you, Jenny. And thanks for the extra help

tonight. You didn't have to stay, not after the full day I know you put in."

"I was happy to do it, Mr. Ronald. See you tomorrow." Jenny turned and bustled toward the back door. Ronald wanted to tell her to just use the front entrance and be done with it, but he knew she wouldn't. Ruth trained the staff well, and not even Martha would have dared to use the front door, at least not when Ruth was around. It was just another small spot of frustration for him.

When he was a kid, Martha would sail out the front door with familiar confidence. He recalled several times when his mother and Martha went Christmas shopping together. Employer and employee they might have been, but they'd also been friends. Another difference between Amelia Quincy and his Ruthie. His mother treated the staff like family and consequently, they'd all been loyal to her. But to Ruth they were servants, nothing more. He loved her more than his own life, but he wasn't blind or obtuse, either.

He wheeled over to the elevator, which he'd had installed when he finally accepted he'd be bound to a wheelchair for the rest of his life. As the doors swished closed, Ronald rested his head against the padded chair cushion and wished he didn't feel so exhausted. Most of the time he handled the repercussions of his stroke fairly well, considering he was confined to this damned chair. But stress always complicated things, and today had certainly held its share of negative emotion.

He'd never been able to make Ruth understand that the circumstances of a person's arrival into the world had no bearing on their overall worth. Her past was proof that anyone could rise above the circumstances of their birth. How such an important lesson had escaped Ruth's instruction, he didn't know.

How was he going to smooth this mess over?

The silence in Travis's Beemer was broken only by the occasional swish of the windshield wipers. Annie sat with one hand tucked in her pocket and the other pressed against Travis's knee. Through her woolen glove she could feel the heat of his skin and the way his leg muscles tensed and relaxed as he shifted and accelerated. They both needed the contact.

"Are you okay?" At his concerned inquiry, she turned to him, and her heart melted as she saw the way he gazed at her. At a stop light in the middle of Thompkin Square, his hand cupped her cheek. When she nodded, he smiled and the pad of his thumb brushed against her lips, before he turned his attention back to the road. To her, the caress felt like a kiss.

Before they approached the turnoff for Spring Street, she grabbed his arm. "Can we just park somewhere for a while? I don't want to go home yet."

Slowing the car, he pulled to the side of the road and shifted into neutral, then glanced at the illuminated clock on the dash. "Annie, it's almost eleven. I promised your mother I'd have you back by then. I don't want to get you in trouble with your folks."

"They won't be mad. They trust me, and they trust you, enough to know if I'm late there'd be a good reason. Please, Travis. Just for a little while."

Her tense shoulders sagged in relief when he nodded. "Okay. Maybe your daddy won't pound on me too hard for keeping you out past eleven."

Without another word, he turned the car around and headed for Boggy Creek Lane. Luckily for them, the wide lane wasn't too muddy with melted snow. He parked the car and killed the headlights, but left the engine idling. In silence, they unfastened their seat belts and reached for the comfort of each other's arms. She wanted Travis to kiss her so badly, but once he did, chances were they'd both be unable to stop.

And they needed to talk out what happened that evening.

Travis pulled back to look into her eyes and whispered, "I'm so sorry my mother acted that way. So sorry she hurt you."

"I just want to know why. Don't you? Don't you want to know why she hates me, Travis? She's always hated me, right from the first. I used to think she'd hate any girl who liked you, but it's only me, isn't it? She likes that other girl, that Catherine, doesn't she?"

"Yes. I don't like to admit it, but you're right. And I want to know why, too." His palm soothed over her hair as he mused, "For some reason Dad thinks she needs to be the one who tells us. Whatever it is, I think it goes way deeper than just being snooty because I want to be with you and not Catherine Cabot."

"It's because our family is poor. Your mother thinks I'm not good enough for you." Defeat, angry pride, maybe both, colored her voice. She heard it for herself.

"It doesn't matter what she thinks. It never did. And I'm not a minor any longer. Maybe I can't legally drink yet, but I can vote, and I can marry the girl I love." Travis cupped her face between his hands and kissed her, deep and long. Her fingers grasped his wrists as she returned the ardent kiss.

As their lips parted, he huskily assured, "She can't make me give you up. She can't stop us from getting married, not now, and not ever."

When Travis kissed her, Annie believed him. When he held her in his arms and the wild beat of his heart pounded against hers, she felt safe, protected, focused.

She told herself she was silly to feel such panic and dread, crazy to think Ruth Quincy could ruin their future. Travis was legally an adult. Her folks would welcome him with open arms.

While snow fell all around them and coated the windshield, Annie reveled in Travis's embrace. They'd plan their future together, regardless of his mother's bad opinion of her and her family.

Finally he eased away and rested his cheek against hers. "I love you so much. I wish we could stay together all night. I don't want to let you go, but I have to take you home. I don't want your folks to worry."

She nodded and slid back into her seat.

When they reached Annie's house, he insisted on going in with her to explain their lateness to her folks. They tiptoed up the steps and through the front door. Except for a lamp glowing in the living room, the downstairs was dark and empty.

In the kitchen, her mother had left the light on over the stove and there was a note propped against the saltshaker on the table. Annie picked it up and read, "'Went to bed. Pie in the fridge if you're hungry. Hope you had fun, love, Mama.' They didn't wait up. I wonder why? They won't even know I'm late, Travis."

He slung an arm around her shoulders. "They trust us. Hey, don't look so sad," he admonished as she raised confused eyes to his. "This is a good thing. They don't think you're a baby any longer, and your mom left pie. Life is good. Let's eat."

She laughed at his eagerness as he opened the fridge. Shoulder to shoulder at the table, they dug into the crumbly blueberry pie and ate right out of the pastry plate. When she looked up and grinned at him through a mouthful of berries, Travis grinned back.

Life *was* good.

Chapter 9

Humming softly, Martha stepped into the dark kitchen, only to stifle a shriek of surprise at the sight of Travis seated in the shadows at the table, hunched over a mug of coffee. "Travis Quincy, you about scared ten years off me, and I guarantee I can't afford to lose even one!" She felt for the switch on the wall and flooded the kitchen with light. "What are you doing up so early?"

"Morning, Martha. I'm loading up on caffeine. I'm going to need it." He knuckled the sleep from his eyes. "I've been up since four, thinking about everything. I'm not letting another day go by without finding out why Mother hates Annie so much."

Martha stifled a sigh as she moved to his side and brushed a hand through his tousled hair. "Honey, you sure you want to do this? What would it solve other than to get your mama so angry?" She pulled out the chair closest to him, then sat down and laid her palm on his arm. Beneath the faded Newport Academy sweatshirt he wore, his muscles were tense.

She chose her words with care. "Travis, your mama isn't going to change her mind, just because you make her admit the reasons for not liking your gal. You know that. Your mama is who she is. She loves you and she wants the best life has to offer you. If she thinks that best isn't your sweet Annie—"

"But she doesn't even *know* Annie. She doesn't know her family. They're great people, Martha. They love *me*, not because my last name is Quincy. And Annie doesn't care, she never did. I've loved her since I was thirteen. We're meant to be together. It's all that matters."

"Oh, honey, I've got eyes to see! I remember the first time she came here, what a cute little thing she was." Martha smiled in remembrance. "She's grown into a lovely young woman. I know she loves you for all the right reasons." Her smile faded into lines of concern. "But love isn't always enough, Trav. You're enough of an adult to understand what I'm talking about."

Travis threw up his hands in a gesture of frustration. "So what are you saying? You think I should just let it be, let Mother continue to hate the girl I love and never understand why? You think that makes a better foundation for our future? Because we've got a future together. With or without Mother's blessing, Annie and I are going to get married someday."

"No. You will *not*, Travis. Believe me when I say this, you will not marry that girl." The voice came from the doorway of the kitchen and had a hard edge to its usually cultured overtones. Startled, Martha and Travis both swung around.

Ruth stood there, poised and polished in severely tailored, dark gold wool slacks and an ivory cashmere sweater. In her eyes Martha saw no warmth, only an implacable determination.

"Travis, you and I are going to have the discussion we should have had last night." Ruth's tone held ice. "I expected you home at a decent hour, and you chose instead to squander your time with that girl."

She turned to Martha. "You will please leave the kitchen. Travis and I need our privacy."

"Not in my kitchen you don't, missy." Martha ignored her hoity tone. "You want to fight with your boy, take it into another room. I've got a luncheon to cook. *Your* luncheon, in fact. So you just scat, and Trav, you go with her."

Travis pushed his chair back and stood, waiting, but Ruth refused to budge. "I'll thank you to remember you are an employee of Quincy Hall. You will never speak to me again in such a manner. Is that understood?"

Slowly, Martha got to her feet. "I will speak to you in any manner I like, when I think you're acting like a snooty brat. Which, right now, you are." Her voice was quiet, but not at all subservient. "I've lived here a heck of a lot longer than you, Ruth. If you don't like the way I act, then you'd best take it up with Ronnie."

"Don't call him by that common name!" Ruth's temper visibly flared.

"He was Ronnie to me, long before he was a husband to you," Martha retorted. "Now if you will excuse me, I have food to cook."

Ruth couldn't get enough air in through her tightened throat to speak a word. Her hands clenched and unclenched as she stood in front of Martha, who in one quick minute reduced her to a fifteen-year-old girl again. All of her breeding, along with most of her learned refinement, seemed to slide down the drain as she stood in the kitchen of her own home feeling like an outsider.

"Mother. You wanted to talk to me. Let's talk." The low command made her spin around. Travis stood near the doorway with a hand extended to her. Numb, she allowed him to take her arm and pull her from the kitchen, across the foyer, and into the study. He shut the door behind them and guided her over to the plush love seat near the bay windows. She sank onto the overstuffed cushion.

First her cook, and now, her son. Like strangers, both of them. Treating her horribly, as if she were of no consequence. When had their opinion of her disintegrated so much? Ruth folded her hands together in her lap to still their trembles.

She made herself really look at her son. When had he gotten so tall? Ruth suddenly found herself in the uncomfortable position of having to rethink the way she needed to relate to her own flesh and blood.

He was still so young, despite his outward maturity. He'd barely begun to tap into his formidable potential. Somehow, before it was too late, she had to reach him, get him to understand what he was tossing aside if he continued to pursue this madness of a "future" with a Turner. She had to make him see.

Perhaps a bit of reverse psychology . . . She spread her hands in appeal. "I am sorry, Travis. It's difficult for me to look at you and not see the baby boy I rocked to sleep. You have grown into a splendid young man, right before my eyes, and I have refused to notice."

He frowned at her. "Mother, if you've refused to see I've grown up, then it's your own problem. I stopped being a child two years ago, when I started prep school. And whether or not you can accept it, I'm old enough to marry without your permission." He leaned back in his seat and crossed his arms.

She almost smiled at that defiant and naïve statement and pose. It seemed she might have more of an upper hand, after all. But she had to play it with care, for Travis was highly intuitive. Just like his father.

"Travis, I never tried to keep you a child. But it's my job as a parent to guide you in the right direction. You are a Quincy. By birthright you are the only heir, a title which carries great responsibility." She paused and considered her next words. If she could appeal to her son as one adult to another, which he seemed to crave, she might actually get somewhere with him.

She took his silence as a good sign. "I expected your teenage years to be trying for both of us. Your small rebellions, the way you wanted individuality. I'm not so far removed from my own adolescence that I don't recall how important that individuality is. But you are not a teenager any longer. You are on the threshold of embracing your Quincy duties."

"I'm also on the threshold of becoming engaged to Annie Turner. Whether you like it or not, she's a part of my future. I'm marrying her as soon as she turns eighteen. If I wanted to marry her tomorrow, I have a feeling her folks would agree to it. They like me."

The touch of smugness she heard snapped her deliberate calm. Exasperated, she retorted, "Of *course* they like you. For God's sake, Travis, you are going to be worth millions of dollars! I'm sure they'd like nothing better than to get their grubby hands on you. The fact that you currently moon over their daughter probably thrills them to death. Are you blind or stupid—or both?"

Travis's jaw tightened. "You know nothing of their family, Mother. You never once tried to understand why I feel the way I do about Annie. You never once tried to get to know her. Hell, you've never even said a civil word to her. All you've said, over and over again, is how trashy the family is. How inferior they are. I guess money talks with you and everything else walks, huh?"

He surged to his feet. "I'm not going to listen to any more. You hang onto your bigotry. You hold your hatred close and see if it's a good substitute for the respect you think I owe you. Someday Annie and I will start a family together. You'll have grandchildren, but they'll never know you."

He strode to the door and flung it open just as Ruth scrambled off the sofa and shouted after him. "Don't you walk away from me, Travis! We are *not* finished discussing. We have *not* resolved this situation."

Travis turned from the open study door, his face like

stone, his eyes glittering chips of ice. "This 'situation' as you refer to it, is a person with a name. It's Annie Turner. Get used to hearing it around Quincy Hall, because I'm going over to her house right now and getting down on one knee. I'll be engaged to her so fast it'll make your head spin. That's a promise, not a threat." He strode toward the coat closet.

As he shrugged into his jacket, Ruth came up behind him, caught his arm and whirled him around to face her.

She'd never in her life felt such fury. With stiffened fingers she clamped onto his arms and shouted, "She comes from filth, Travis. Do you hear me? *Filth*!"

"You tell me why you think that way!" Travis pried her hands from his arms and crushed her wrists in his grip. She winced in pain and tried to pull free, but he held fast.

His voice dropped to a soft menace. "You tell me. Or else I swear I'm walking out of this house and never returning. You can take the Quincy legacy and the will and all those goddamn history books and burn them. You can keep the millions, too. And I'll gladly explain to you just where you can shove the whole 'Quincy Heir' crap." His eyes burned into hers. "I have had all I can take, Mother. You tell me why you hate the Turners, or you'll never see me again."

She pulled against him and wrenched her wrists from his grasp. Massaging her sore skin, she grated, "If it will stop you from making the biggest mistake of your entire life, I'll gladly put myself through the pain of telling you. But first, you get your father down here. I have a feeling you won't believe me. Your father will verify everything I say. Go on." She nodded toward the staircase. "Go and get him. By now, I imagine he's awake."

"I'm already here, Ruthie." She jerked at the sound of Ronald's calm voice. In the open elevator, he paused, fully dressed, his face pale and tense.

As Ronald manipulated his chair into the foyer, Travis

rushed to him and fell to his knees, catching one of his hands in a gentle grip. "Did we wake you? I'm so sorry, you need your rest—"

"Son, it's all right." Ronald patted Travis's cheek, and met Ruth's eyes as she stood in the foyer, her hands clenched into tense fists. He gave her a faint smile. "Why don't we go back into the study?" His gaze held a wealth of love and patience.

Looking into the faces of her husband and son, Ruth felt the fury and bitterness drain from her as quickly as it had built. How could she ever think she could hide it? Pretend it didn't exist and had never happened?

If she'd been better able to master her emotions, perhaps the friendship between Travis and the Turner girl would never have gone any further than a few summer fishing sessions. By her own inept attempts to control, she'd helped it blossom into something far stronger than she could fight against with conventional means of discipline.

She'd failed to consider the powerful allure of forbidden fruit, and now she had to face the consequences of her failure.

Ruth took a deep breath and held it, then released it. She felt the familiar fear and tamped it down. Years ago, when Travis first walked through the front door holding the brat's hand, she'd somehow known this day would come, though she had done her best to deny it. Out of the corner of her eye, she spotted Martha in the short hallway between the foyer and kitchen, her hands twisted in a dishtowel, her eyes wide with concern and worry.

Well, there would be no more secrets in Quincy Hall, would there? Martha already knew some of it. After all, she'd been in the house that unforgettable night.

Ruth smoothed a hand over her hair to assure it hadn't fallen from its elegant twist. She touched the square-cut diamond on her left finger, as if to further reassure herself, and cleared her dry throat.

"Franklin Turner . . ." Her voice faltered alarmingly and she fought the urge to run for the wide, curving staircase and lock herself in her suite of rooms. She rubbed a shaky hand over her mouth and tried again, this time in a firmer, stronger tone.

"Franklin Turner, Annie Turner's grandfather, kidnapped me and raped me, repeatedly, when I was fifteen years old." Her eyes stung with tears, and they slid down her cheeks as she rasped, "That's the legacy your precious girlfriend brings you, Travis."

Chapter 10

Ruth leaned her head against the settee cushion in the study, and reached for inner calm. If she kept her story clinical and detached, it might be easier to get through the awful narrative.

"I was raised in a poor family. 'White trash,' most people called us. My mother and stepfather were illiterate, backwoods, abusive and neglectful. Willa, my mother, had little common sense when it came to her children, but Greeley Mason, my stepfather, had none whatsoever." She was silent for a second or two, remembering more than one occasion when her parents would come home from a night of heavy drinking, their loud voices awakening her and her half-sisters, Lindy and Lulu.

Her older brother, Junior, had already run away from home by the time her sisters were out of diapers, and it fell to Ruth to care for them, for her mother would just as soon have kicked them out of the way as look at them.

"My home life was the stuff of nightmares, Travis. Greeley was a brawler, a gambler, and he spent most of the money Willa brought home from whatever waitress job she had at the time. Before I reached fifteen, she'd been fired numerous times. She came to work drunk, and she stole from the tip jar. She flirted with all the male customers, and then cheered when Greeley picked fights with them for daring to talk to his wife. More often than not, during the fistfight he'd pick their wallets, too."

"Where did you live?" Travis's words were a hoarse croak, as if he couldn't wrap his mind around the kind of life she described.

"I was born in Harlan, Kentucky, and my biological father died in the Harlan mines. Willa brought Junior and me to West Virginia, where she met Greeley. We lived there until I was about twelve, then we were evicted from our rental and had to leave. For non-payment, trashing the place, fighting. We weren't by any means ideal tenants." She moved her shoulders in a resigned shrug, finding a familiar numbness stealing over her as she recounted a past that felt as if it had happened to some other young girl, years ago. "Greeley brought us to Thompkin. His older brother, Nate, lived here in a small trailer, and we all moved in with him. I slept on the sofa with my sisters, and Willa and Greeley took the other bedroom. The walls were paper-thin, and we heard a lot of fighting." She saw the distress on her son's face when she added, "As well as the sounds of . . . other things."

Ruth was unaware that she still cried, until she brushed at her eyes and her fingers came away wet. She coughed, but her voice thickened as she held her emotions at bay. "One night, Willa was at the bar getting drunk as usual, and Nate had gone by train to visit a lady friend who lived in Alabama. My sisters were asleep, and I was in the kitchen doing my homework."

Bitterness coated her throat as she dredged up the painful memories. "I'd met evil already, in the form of my stepfather, but even I had no idea just how deep his foulness penetrated, how low he could sink."

With a sound of distress, Travis shifted from his seat to come to her side, but she raised a hand, effectively holding him off. She would get through this on her own, damn it.

"The night that forever changed my life started with rain and quickly escalated to a thunderstorm, wet and windy. I sat at the kitchen table trying to stay awake long enough to complete a geography essay, but I found my attention drifting. Perhaps I'd even dozed a bit.

"When the kitchen door flew open, my first thought was that the wind had done it. Sometimes the old door didn't close properly. I barely had a chance to acknowledge Greeley's presence before he moved to the table and yanked me up, out of my seat."

Her book crashed to the floor and the pen flew out of her hand as Greeley dragged her toward the open back door. She stammered, "I didn't do anything! What's the matter? What's going on?"

"Shut up, yew lil' bitch. We're goin' fer a ride." His voice was a mean growl, and the hand he'd clamped around her arm hurt. He pulled her down the porch steps and shoved her into the front seat of Nate's beat-up Chevy sedan, climbed in after her, and revved the engine. He peeled out of the driveway so fast, she could hear gravel spit. She cowered on the seat, chilled to the bone in her thin tee shirt and shorts, bewildered, afraid.

They drove in the wind and the heavy rain, weaving all over the road. Even from where she sat, Ruth could smell the whiskey on Greeley's breath. God only knew how long he'd been drinking that day.

"Well? Ain't yew wonderin' where I'm takin' yew?" He glared at her as he took a sharp right turn. The car almost flipped over. Hanging on to the seat, she swallowed tears of panic and fright, knowing if Greeley saw them, he'd just get meaner.

She managed a shaky, "Y-yes, sir."

In the greenish light from the dashboard, his smile was awful to see. "I'm takin' yew t' yer new daddy." His grin widened when he saw the shock and confusion on her face. "Name o' Franklin Turner. An' yew better be good t' him, else I'll be hearin' about it."

"I don't—where's my mama? I want my mama!" Now Ruth sobbed, far past fright or anything she'd ever felt in her life that had scared her. Tears poured from her eyes, and her entire body shook, hard. When Greeley reached over and backhanded her, the blow knocked her against the side window. She curled her body into a tight ball of misery and anguish, while he told her exactly what her "new daddy" expected of her.

"He'd been gambling again." Ruth pressed against her eyes to ease the ache behind them. She hoped Ronald could see what it cost her to speak of her past this way in front of their son, who listened, pale and stricken. "While I cowered in my seat, Greeley told me how he'd bet all the money in his pockets, had gone from having a large pot of cash to just a few dollars to call the last hand. He'd bragged of holding three of a kind, all queens, and how he'd just known for sure his hand couldn't lose. Well, he was beat by a better hand, and the man who held those winning cards was named Franklin Turner."

"Annie's grandfather." Travis's voice shook.

"Yes. Her grandfather. Apparently as well as being a child molester, he was also a gambler and a drunkard. I couldn't say how old he was back then. Perhaps in his mid-forties." Ruth clenched her hands into tight fists, her only outward sign of distress. "Greeley didn't have anything on his person worth giving to Turner, who demanded his money and threatened to beat Greeley to a pulp unless he paid up.

"And then he remembered he had a fifteen-year-old stepdaughter at home. Greeley told that vile man all about me. How young I was, how pretty. How innocent."

Ruth had to stop and take calming breaths, had to force out the rest, before she went mad from having to dredge up the horrible memories. She would finish it, though. She would get it out, and then would never speak of it again.

"I suppose I don't have to tell you how eagerly Franklin Turner snapped up what Greeley offered."

She should have wrenched the door open and dove out, risking injury, rather than stay in the rattletrap station wagon curled into a tight ball of terror. Should have risked running down the highway in the rain, in hopes that another car would come by and rescue her.

But there weren't any other cars on the road. She prayed they'd get pulled over by the police, who would then see Greeley's condition, figure out she was being kidnapped and arrest him for all kinds of crimes. Of course as luck would have it, there was never a cop around when one was most needed.

She rocked on the seat, her arms wrapped around herself, and her entire body trembled violently. She'd been pawned off the same way a drunk would pawn his last possession just to buy a bottle. As if she were less than nothing. Less than human.

Oh, God.

Rain pounded on the roof of the car as it jerked to a stop in a parking lot, deserted but for one lone car. And she knew there was a monster in that car, waiting for her.

Fresh panic and terror surged through her as Greeley got out and strode around to the passenger door, tugging it open. He caught hold of her arm and hauled her across the seat, the ripped cushion underneath scratching her bare leg. She landed on the wet gravel on her hands and knees, whimpering.

Greeley forced her to her feet and pushed her, pulled her toward the car. As they got closer, the driver's door opened.

Ruth got her first look at Franklin Turner.

"He was tall and heavy, the most frightening thing I'd ever seen. When he looked me over, I could see the eagerness in his eyes, and it was all I could do remain sane from the fear. Greeley had to hold me upright or else I would have fainted.

"He cursed at Greeley for leaving marks on my arms, but he was just as cruel when he grabbed hold of my hair and pulled my face into the light from the street lamp. He must have liked what he saw, and I am sure he saw a lot, as much as my wet clothes probably revealed. He dragged me toward his car and Greeley followed, assuring him I was a virgin as promised. Then he offered Franklin Turner my baby sisters, too. He told that monster Lindy and Lulu would be 'ready' for him in just a few years. And they both laughed as they shook on it."

"Oh, my God. God." Travis looked sick, and Ruth could find it in her shattered heart to pity him at that very moment, for she knew she'd stripped some of his innocence from him.

But there was still more to tell.

"I don't know how long he drove, or where he was driving to. I sat in the front seat, blind to anything except the hard grip he had in my hair and the way his breathing sped up every time he looked over at me. When he suddenly stopped the car, I knew there was nothing or no one to save me."

He opened the door and yanked her out by her hair. Ruth screamed, trying to fight him. It was like a gnat trying to fight a giant. He pulled her beneath him in the back seat.

She couldn't break his hold.

He panted into her ear, things he wanted to do to her, things he expected her to do to him, awful things—while rough hands tugged at her clothes and rougher fingers pinched and probed. The pain of what those fingers did to her recoiling body forced another scream from her raw throat, and she tried to strike out with one hand. He easily pinned it down. He dug painfully into her tender skin to hold her still as he covered her lips with his and thrust his tongue inside her mouth.

She couldn't breathe, couldn't move. And she knew if he did this, if he raped her, she'd somehow find a way to kill herself rather than live with the shame of it.

Yet it was human nature to fight when cornered. Ruth tried to incapacitate him the only way she knew how. She kicked out with her bare feet, trying to catch him in the groin. She had seen her mother do that to Greeley when he'd gotten drunk and mean and rough, and it had just about killed him. Please God, let it work, this time.

But his big hands blocked her move, and he knocked her leg to the side as if it were nothing more than a pesky fly. He even chuckled as if amused by her attempts to protect herself.

Franklin Turner was strong. He maneuvered between Ruth's legs, pulled her arms above her head so hard, they felt wrenched from their sockets. And Ruth had no way to protect her body any further against him, because he'd gotten his pants open.

Before she could take a breath to scream again, he clapped a palm over her mouth to hold in the sounds she made as he raped her.

"I must have blacked out, for when I came to, the car was moving again. I could hear him, just whistling along to the radio as if he hadn't a care in the world, while I lay bleeding on the back seat. I remember throwing up, but I doubt he heard me over the radio's ear-splitting volume.

"I'd lost track of how many times he'd hurt me. I knew he'd do it over and over, if I didn't get away. He'd lock me up somewhere and use me until there was nothing left of me. I'd never had a date, never been kissed before. And now I was broken, ruined, dirty. If I'd had access to a knife right then, I'd have slit my throat."

Travis made a sound deep in his own throat that sounded as wounded as she felt, and Ruth gritted her teeth against the need for his sympathy. *Almost finished.* She pressed hard at her aching forehead.

"I had to get away. I fought back the terror and made myself think. The rain was still coming down. I could hear the wind against the windows. If I flung open the back door and tried to jump from a moving car, I'd hurt myself, and it would be easy for him to stop and go back for me. I'd end up with broken bones, maybe worse, and the monster would still have me."

If he touched her again, she'd go mad. She'd rather die than go through it, day after day, feeling him pushing into her. Destroying her.

She kept an eye on the back of his head while she fumbled for her torn clothes and dressed. Maybe she'd find something on the floor of the back seat she could use to knock him out. There'd be a chance the car might flip over, or worse, hurtle over an embankment. It was still better than doing nothing and sitting here waiting for him to stop the car again and climb into the back with her.

She kept her movements as subtle as possible and prayed he wouldn't notice. Luck was with her, because he must have thought she was still unconscious. He never looked over his shoulder or checked the rearview mirror.

Rooting around on the floor, she could have cried aloud with relief when her fingers tapped over what felt like a metal case. Sliding forward, she peered over the seat and saw a tool kit. There might be a hammer in there. Maybe a wrench and a screwdriver. All potential weapons.

As stealthy as she could, she eased open the latch, which gave without a sound. Her fingers searched for the largest tool. Her hand closed over a hammer.

Now, she had a weapon. She wasn't defenseless and helpless any longer.

Across the room, Ronald watched her with tears in his eyes. They brimmed over, slid down his ashen cheeks. Ruth glanced at him once, and the sight of his emotion bolstered her. She murmured, "I held that hammer in my hand for what seemed like eternity, though it couldn't have been more than a minute or two. I was so frightened, thinking I could kill this man for what he'd done to me. Then I told myself I'd never have the courage. He'd stop the car and have me in his hands again. I'd never get away from him.

"Finally, I decided it was now or never. I had to take him by surprise. If I waited until he stopped, then he'd see what I held in my hand and he'd surely use it to kill me. So I moved behind the driver's seat and waited until the car swung around a curve. And I hit him in the back of the head, as hard as I could."

Travis exclaimed, "Jesus! What happened?"

Ruth smiled grimly. "He slumped against the steering wheel and we spun out on the wet road. I clung to the seat as the car flipped over and ended up on its side in the ditch. It was a miracle there had been a guardrail to keep it from going over the embankment, because when I finally crawled out from the back seat, I could see how close we'd come to one of those hilly areas where there's usually a gully. The car could have crashed at the bottom of it." She dragged her chilled hands over her damp face.

Exhaustion gave her shoulders an uncharacteristic slump, and she was thankful there wasn't much left to tell. "The point is, I got away. I can't tell you how many miles I ran. Maybe two. Probably more. In that rain and wind, nothing looked familiar, none of the landmarks. I was numb with cold, in pain, bleeding, and still petrified out of my mind. My feet hurt from running barefoot on the road."

Sheer inner strength alone had enabled her to push through her narrative without falling apart. The necessity of somehow drilling into her son's brain the imminent disaster of pursuing a future with the Turner girl . . . it was worth what she'd suffered to relive the horror.

Before her son or husband could jump in and say anything, Ruth finished it. "After what seemed like forever, I saw lights. A lot of them. I had reached the bottom of Thompkin Hill, though at the time of course I had no idea. I trudged up that long driveway, thinking it was another road, and then, as if I somehow knew salvation and safety was just ahead, I began to run again. By the time I'd reached the porch and was pounding on the door, my hysteria had returned with a vengeance. When your father opened the door, I fell into the foyer, and into his arms."

She allowed herself one glance at Ronald as she spoke. There would be sympathy for her in his eyes, and she hated herself for seeking it. She wasn't a broken, traumatized child any longer, and yet her confession reduced her to what she'd struggled for so many years to overcome.

He must have seen the price she paid for rehashing the entire ordeal, for Ronald wheeled to her side and reached for her hand. He stroked his thumb over her skin.

Without asking her, he chose to tell the rest. "Your mother was soaked to the skin, bruised and bloody, unable to speak of what had happened to her. I brought her upstairs, and Martha and your grandmother attended to her. She slept for almost twenty-four hours, and when she awoke, she was screaming from a nightmare, the first of many she'd have over the next year or so.

"We tried to get her to tell us what had happened to her, but it was almost two days before she could speak coherently. We tried to convince her to allow the family physician to examine her, but she cried so piteously that we let it go, afraid to terrify her any further. It was week or more before she said Franklin Turner's name." Ronald carried her hand to his lips as he spoke and kissed it gently, bringing fresh tears to her reddened eyes.

She watched the emotion, the shock and outrage, flit across her son's expressive face, and knew what he was thinking. He'd try to rationalize, make excuses, based on what he thought was love for the Turner girl. Romantic, sensitive despite his level of intelligence, he remained a teenaged boy in the throes of first infatuation. She emitted a quiet sigh, and waited for his reaction.

With a jerk, Travis rose to his feet and paced the confines of the study, clearly in turmoil. "No wonder you've never wanted to leave the house." He turned and faced her. "All this time you've been afraid, haven't you? I used to think you just had some kind of agoraphobia."

She nodded, embarrassment heating her cheeks. "By now, I'm sure I do. I'm certainly not proud of my weaknesses, but as your father said, I had horrible nightmares and found myself unable to leave the safety of Quincy Hall." She shrugged. "In time, it didn't seem to matter any longer. I stayed within these walls and cultivated a network of acquaintances who were content to visit me." She offered a faint smile. "The rich and powerful are often regarded as eccentric, too. No one has ever questioned why I cloister myself."

Travis shook his head. "I'm trying to sort through all of this. Turner is a common enough name even in small towns. How can you be so sure this Franklin Turner belonged to Annie's family?"

Her lips parted to respond, but Ronald cut in. "Travis, I knew Henry Turner when we were both boys. Although I only saw Franklin Turner perhaps once in my life, I remember Henry speaking of his father. I remember when Franklin left his family destitute and his wife broken. He'd been a gambler all of his life. I sat on the bleachers at the ball field listening to Henry rant about his father. I think we were maybe thirteen or fourteen at the time. Franklin Turner took all of the money from the family's savings account and skipped town one day. He didn't leave them a single dime."

Travis looked back and forth between them. Ruth could see the struggle on his face and her heart ached for him. Finally he protested, "I can't believe it. I *know* these people. They're hardworking, honest and good. Maybe Mr. Turner's father left them and never came back, but it had to be a different Turner who did this to Mother. A monster like that couldn't be related to Annie and her folks." There was conviction in Travis's voice, but beneath the conviction was the plea of a little boy who didn't want to believe bad things existed in the world.

Ronald confirmed, "It's the same family, son. Genetics sometimes don't mean squat when it comes to family characteristics. Franklin Turner was a horrible human being and yet his son is kind and decent. You've heard for yourself the kind of woman your maternal grandmother was. It doesn't always follow, does it?"

While Travis pondered his father's words, his mother cleared her throat and brought his attention back to her. Tears still glittered in her eyes, but her expression held determination. He wanted to go to her and hold her, comfort her for all she'd endured while just a child herself. He wanted to cheer on her behalf, for the way she'd overcome the misfortune of her family, her heritage.

But her next words froze him in place. "Travis, this has been one of the most difficult days of my life, telling you what happened to me. I'd always prayed I wouldn't have to, but you needed to be told. Knowing the full story, I'm confident you won't be inclined to follow through with your rash and impulsive plans. As far as I'm concerned, we can let the matter drop, and get on with our lives." She held out her hands to Travis, expecting him to rush to her side.

Shock immobilized him. Did she think he'd snuggle into her embrace and tell her he'd never see Annie again, all on the strength of what had happened to her at the hands of a man who was two generations apart from Annie?

She didn't get it. Maybe he didn't, either.

He chose his next words with care. "Did you go to the police? What about your mother and stepfather? Were they arrested for what they did to you? After all, they were trying to sell their own child, right?"

In spite of her calm front, Travis knew he'd offended her. However, her reply showed no hint of temper. "No, the police were never told. That was my fault. I had such a hard time speaking of it, as your father said. By the time I was able to mention names, he was no longer a threat to me. Willa, Greeley and my half-sisters had left town and I never saw them again. I never saw Nate Mason again, either. In that disgusting old man's case, I suppose he received his just desserts for what he did. He died that same night."

"What? You killed him?" Travis gasped, shocked.

Her lips curved briefly. "I will never know for sure if

that hammer to his head did it, or not. To this day I couldn't tell you how hard I swung it. Hard enough to knock him out, that's all I can be sure of. When the police found Franklin Turner's car in the ditch the next morning, he was dead inside it. An autopsy revealed he'd also suffered a massive heart attack. It was impossible for the pathologist to tell for sure if death had been caused by the blow to his head or from his heart attack, or possibly both."

"Ruth, you know it wasn't your fault—" His father broke in.

"No, I don't." She waved a hand in denial. "I will never know. I can only tell you I'm glad he's dead, and if it was indeed my hand that killed him, then I'm proud of the courage it took for me to swing that hammer. For what he'd done to me, I doubt I'd have been labeled a murderer."

Travis flinched at the ugly word. No one in his right mind would slap that label on someone who'd been through such a nightmare.

He still needed answers, though. "Did the police ever question you or Dad? Did you ever find out where your parents went?"

"I always assumed they went back to West Virginia. I ceased to care about them the night my stepfather tore me from my chair in that kitchen and thrust me into a nightmare. As for the police talking to me," she paused, closed her eyes for a second, "they never knew of my ordeal. Your father never reported anything. Not that I'd been taken by Greeley Mason. Or given to Franklin Turner. I couldn't have borne anyone else knowing what happened to me, Travis."

"But your family, they must have been known in town. Thompkin isn't that big. Your sisters, suddenly missing from school, wouldn't that have raised suspicion?" He was persistent in his quest to understand everything.

Once again, his dad answered for her. "It's surprising, but no. Folks like Willa and Greeley Mason, living on the edge of town in the lower rent areas, often slip through the cracks. The school system was resigned to those children skipping school. Many of the people in the trailer park were transients who would pick up and go at a moment's notice. I assumed Willa and Greeley did the same thing. Believe me, I checked."

His father sought to reassure both of them. "Trav, your mother wanted it to be over. I had a hard time letting it go, once she told me everything. But for her sake, I did just that."

"And your sisters?"

Her eyes narrowed. "Half-sisters. They have Greeley Mason for a father. That dooms them, in my opinion."

"And what about you, Mother? You were born poor, came from people who would sell their own kids to pay off a debt. Yet you found a way to rise above the circumstances of your old life, didn't you? With a loving husband, a nurturing mother-in-law, you got past the bad and heaped on the good. It's something to be proud of, wouldn't you say?" Travis watched for his mother's reaction.

"Yes. I am proud of what your father and I have accomplished. You are our greatest achievement." She shifted on the sofa, confusion on her face. "Why else would I be so concerned for your well-being, your future?"

At the soft sound of distress his father made, Travis knew he understood where the questions were leading. He plowed ahead with determination. "Well then, Mother, wouldn't you say Henry Turner has risen above his father's rotten deeds, too? He has a good job. He has a loving wife and six well-behaved children. Two are working steady jobs and saving money for college. Their oldest son has been accepted into the officer training school the Air Force provides. People like and respect Henry Turner. Wouldn't you say he, the same as you, found a way to move beyond the legacy of neglectful, abusive parents?"

It didn't sink in at first. The meaning behind Travis's

observation seemed initially lost to her. She started to speak, paused, frowned. Then, one of her hands gripped the sofa armrest, hard. She bit off an expletive better suited to Willa Mason than the wife of Ronald Quincy, sprang to her feet, and stood, quivering.

"How dare you." She bore down on Travis. "How *dare* you compare my life with *any* of those trashy Turners. You know nothing. You understand *nothing*. What I suffered, what I endured at the hands of that monstrous old man. To think my own flesh and blood would turn on me this way. To think you'd choose to believe the worst of me and the better of them!"

He knew her hurt ran deep. Yet, sometimes the only way to heal a wound was to cauterize it. Travis sighed in defeat. He sent his father a helpless shrug, and lifted his coat from the arm of his chair. Slowly, he pulled it on and zipped it up as he crossed to the side door.

With a deep, fortifying breath, Travis faced his mother. "I don't believe the worst of you, Mother. I couldn't. But I *do* believe better of Annie and her family. I can understand why you would do all you could to bury what happened to you."

His eyes burned with emotion as he gazed at his mother's ravaged face. "It breaks my heart to know you had to go through something so terrible. But it changes nothing for me, except to be thankful Henry Turner grew up normal, became a good husband and father. Someday soon, the Turners will be my in-laws. If you can't accept it, then there's nothing more to be said." Tears slid down his cheeks as he whispered sadly, "I love you, Mother. Maybe one of these days we'll be able to come to terms with all of this." Turning away, he stepped into the foyer.

He was almost to the front door when his mother's shout hit the dead silence between them. "If you walk out that door, Travis, you leave without the support of the Quincy family and its legacy. Do you understand? You'll be cut off, penniless. You'll have nothing. Do you hear me? *Nothing*!"

Travis walked through the front door and closed it behind him.

Chapter 11

Watery daylight shone between the trees as Travis drove toward the older section of town. The snowfall from the night before still coated the bare limbs and remained on rooftops, making a pretty holiday picture. He hardly noticed.

Less than a quarter mile from Annie's house, Travis pulled to the side of the road and let the motor idle while he scraped his hands over his face and wondered what the hell he was going to say to her family. He'd bet money they knew nothing of Franklin Turner's fondness for young, virginal girls.

The Turners used to live in Roanoke. He remembered Annie telling him how her parents moved back to Thompkin after Mark's birth. They'd have never returned to town with a scandal hanging over their heads if they'd known about it.

Jesus, what a mess.

He'd looked forward to a day of Christmas shopping in Charlottesville with Annie. Maybe a movie later on before heading back to town. Now, all he could think about was the fury on his mother's face when she figured out her story hadn't affected him the way she hoped. No doubt she thought he'd recoil in horror, drop all contact with Annie, and then immediately call Catherine Cabot for a date. As usual, his mother had underestimated the importance of Annie in his life and in his future.

Not any longer. She knew exactly how much he and Annie wanted each other.

His mother was more than capable of making trouble for the Turners. He knew his dad could control some of it, but his mother had a lot of influential friends in town. A few phone calls, some words in a half dozen willing ears, and the town's attitude toward Henry Turner and his family could quickly change from "well-liked and respected" to "undesirable and unsavory."

Thompkin was a nice place, but it was also a typical small town. Gossip fed the grapevine, and everyone knew each other. Older people in town thought his relationship with Annie was "sweet." As if it were a summer breeze passing through, to blow away like so many dried-up leaves come autumn.

Would Annie's folks put pressure on her to stop seeing him, if his mother started any kind of trouble? The Turners cared about him, and they approved of him for their daughter. If they hadn't, they would have put the kibosh on the friendship a long time ago. But they'd yank her out of his grasp if association with him and his family caused her pain.

His mother was capable of anything. No matter what, someone would get hurt.

Confused about everything except his need for Annie, Travis tried to set aside his worry as he shifted back into gear and headed toward her house.

While she waited for Travis, Annie peeled apples for pie, a mindless task handled easily with low thought process. Nearby, her mother rolled out flaky pie dough. Mama always made sure everyone got their favorite dessert, each Christmas. Apple pie, chocolate brownies, peach cobbler, pumpkin pie . . . Christmas was a bonanza of deliciousness because her mama thought to please her family. Even the blueberry pie she and Travis enjoyed last night had been made just for him.

Annie's heart melted as she watched Mama's capable

hands lay the dough in pie pans. How lucky she was to have such a caring mother.

"Mama? Mama, I love you." The words burst from her throat as Annie tossed down her paring knife, launched herself out of her chair and straight into her mama's arms.

Her mama moved the pie pans aside and hugged Annie tightly. "I love you too, honey. Are you ready to tell me what's making you so sad? Did something happen at the Quincy's dinner last night?" she prodded.

"Travis's mother is a bitch! Oh, I'm sorry, I shouldn't have said that, but it's true." Annie condemned the woman, asked forgiveness and reaffirmed her original assessment all in one fast hiccupping breath. She pressed her damp cheek into her mama's neck. "The way she treated Travis and his daddy last night was awful." She looked up with blurry eyes. "She was mean to them. I don't care for myself, I know she hates me. I know it's because she thinks she's better than anyone else. But she hurt Travis. I can't stand to see him hurt, Mama."

"I know, honey. Travis is a good boy. What else happened last night?"

"She was really mad I was there. She got Mr. Quincy all upset. He was nice and acted calm, as usual, but I could tell he was upset. He was so sweet to me. Why can't she be nice, too? What makes one parent so mean and the other so nice, and they can stay married to each other? I don't understand it."

"Neither do I. But honey, she's his mother. Right or wrong, the way she deals with her son is her business. And she does love him."

Annie wrapped her arms around her mother's neck and clung. "I'm so lucky, Mama. I wish Travis could be as lucky as me."

"Oh, honey. Nothing you could ever say to me could be sweeter. Thank you."

For several seconds they cuddled together as Annie struggled to get her emotions under control.

Finally, her mother stepped back. "My pie crust is drying out, young lady. You pick up that knife and keep slicing. And I hope you and Travis enjoyed the pie you gobbled up last night. Not a crumb left for your poor father to put in his lunch this morning. Just who did you think you were fooling, covering the empty plate with foil?" Her voice held just the right amount of teasing admonishment to shake Annie out of the sniffles.

Annie managed a smile as she picked up the abandoned apple. "It was good pie, Mama. Thank you." She blinked away fresh tears when she felt her mother's hand brush over her hair.

Ten minutes later Travis knocked on the door, and Annie's heart burst as it always did when she saw him standing in their small foyer. He opened his arms and she flew into them, uncaring if her mama or anyone else saw. He swung her off her feet and she released a breathless giggle.

"Put me down! You're all wet." A light snow mixed with rain had kicked up in the time it took for him to park the car and walk to the door.

He rubbed his cold nose against her neck and made her squeal. "Just a little snow. You'll have to tough your way through it." He pulled back and grinned at her, but she saw tension around his eyes. "Are you ready to go?"

"You sure you still want to? You look kind of tired." She traced the edge of his eyelid with a finger. "We don't have to do this today, Travis."

"And miss out on watching you buy out the mall with all that Coffee Hut money you've been hoarding? No way. I'm fine, sweetheart. Get your coat and let's take off." He squeezed her once more before letting her go, and Annie turned to lift her coat from the hall chair.

As she slid her arms into the sleeves, her mama came

in from the kitchen, wiping her hands on a dishtowel. "Mind those slick roads, Travis. And don't forget dinner tomorrow night, all right? Mark got home yesterday, and he says he wants to talk to you." She laughed when Travis's face went white.

"Uh-oh. My big, bad Air Force brother wants to 'talk' with my boyfriend," Annie chuckled. "Maybe we should shop for a weapon while we're in Charlottesville."

"Annie, don't tease him." Her mama ruffled Travis's hair and tugged on the lock that always seemed to curl over one eye. "I doubt Travis will need to arm himself." Her hand cupped his face before she stepped back toward the kitchen. "Not too late, you two. No speeding and fancy driving, you hear?"

Travis was still pale from the mention of Mark. Her oldest brother loved to intimidate the younger kids, and Travis had gotten his share over the years. She heard him swallow with an audible gulp as he answered her mama. "Yes, ma'am. I mean, no, ma'am." He grabbed Annie's hand and pulled her out the door. She didn't stop giggling until he shoved her into the front seat of his car.

Standing in the middle of the study, her arms wrapped protectively across her chest, Ruth's bitterness showed on her pinched, angry face.

"You have *no* right to dictate to me when it comes to raising our son. No right to tell me what I can't take away from him if he fails to do as he's told and refuses to obey. He's a child, Ronald. You have let him control his own life for far too long. You rewarded him when he should have been punished. You gave him the lofty idea he can choose his own path, even though that path will be destructive to this family. So don't," Ruth's breath hitched in her throat, "don't stand there and tell me I have no right to take away what our son sees fit to destroy."

Ronald fought the urge to yank his hair out in frustration. "Ruth, listen to yourself. Our son is not some spawn of Satan, trying to rip apart the Quincy name and annihilate the entire town while he's at it. And he's *not* a child. Open up your eyes and see. See what kind of man our boy will become. I'm proud of everything he's accomplished so early in his life, proud of where he's going."

Lord, he was tired. It was almost an effort to sit upright, but he forced his spine to stiffen, and gripped the arms of his wheelchair. He had to make her see reason. Before she tried to do something she'd forever regret.

Finally, he said, "Ruth, there isn't a thing you can do to oust our son from the family will. It's set up much the same as it was when I was a boy, except Travis's name replaced mine in the wording as my sole heir. You know this. I explained it, years ago."

"What if I told the Board of Trustees you weren't in full possession of your faculties, Ronald?" Her voice lowered, turned sly. She looked at him with glittering eyes. "You said yourself Travis is old enough to choose his own future and mate. What if the board got wind of the scandal surrounding the girl our son has chosen? You think they'd wax sentimental over the course of true love, versus the kind of damage a merger with the Turner family would instigate?"

He could only regard her with crushing disappointment. "You'd reveal your past after years of secrecy, all you went through, just to spite the Turner family and make the board doubt my ability to run the legacy?"

It had come to this. To bend their son to her will, she'd rip her privacy wide open to the opinions and gossip of a typical small town and its small town mentality, ruin the name of a good family, break her son's heart. All in an attempt to control not only Travis's life, but Annie's, too.

And, in an indirect way, Catherine Cabot's as well, for she'd never stopped trying to force a match between Trav and Catherine.

It was too much. It had to stop.

His chest ached, heart sore from the confrontation and the fury of what had been spoken in this room, this morning. He needed to rest. But first he had to nip it in the bud, once and for all. Then he could rest.

Weariness dragged at him as he struggled to maintain his authority. "Ruth, there's nothing you can do to hurt the Turner family. Let it go, for God's sake. It's over. If you want it in terms of black and white, then fine. You have lost the war, my love. Stop this insanity, *now*. Or you'll lose your son's respect and affection, too." With nothing left to say, Ronald wheeled through the side door of the study.

Numbed, Ruth sank onto a side chair. He wasn't going to change his mind. He wasn't going to stop their son from this path of madness. She buried her face in her hands as she recalled some of Travis's final words.

"Someday soon the Turners will be my in-laws."

She couldn't bear it. The thought of her son's blood mingled with the trashy Turners caused her own blood to freeze in her veins like ice.

Mingled. A child.

Merciful heavens, what if there was a child? Ruth dropped her hands from her face as fresh horror assailed her. Of course, there'd be a child. What else did trash do, but impregnate each other and beget *more* trash?

As soon as she thought it she chastised herself for lumping her own son in with the kind of lowlifes who only wanted to fornicate and thus make babies the world could surely do without. Travis wasn't *anything* like those Turners.

Even at his most defiant, after he infuriated her past the point of reason, he wasn't anything like them. Deep in her heart, she had faith in her son and in his sensibilities. He was merely under some kind of spell. It was that horrid girl's fault, all of it.

She didn't know what sort of influence the Turner family had over her son, but she would find out. And then she'd obliterate it.

Obliterate them.

The urge to hibernate appealed to Ronald as he wheeled into his suite. Maybe he could pretend the morning's heartaches had never happened. But life went on inside Quincy Hall, regardless of the family dynamics. He supposed it would have to.

He pressed chilled fingers to his temples to ease the pain of another tension headache. He'd been getting them more often. His nurse, Phoebe, clucked over him daily. She'd take his blood pressure and order him to relax more often. His doctors, too, told him to let go of any stress, or risk a second stroke. He'd tried, Lord only knew. He released a great deal of the daily responsibilities to his board of trustees and to his assistant, Dan Marley, who held the position open until Travis graduated from Yale.

Weary and sad, Ronald maneuvered his chair to the French doors that led onto his private terrace and looked out at the glitter of sun-dappled snow on the sculptured landscaping. How long had it been since he'd sat in the sun and enjoyed its warmth on his face? And how many years had it been since Ruth sat next to him on one of the pretty marble benches, holding his hand?

After today's painful revelations, another relaxing interlude with his wife might never again happen.

He should have gotten professional counseling for Ruth and helped her to find whatever closure possible. Instead, he'd allowed her to bury her head and her emotions under a blanket of false security, and he turned a blind eye to her increasing phobias. Now he needed to fix it as much as he could. He needed to do right by his son.

Even if it meant hurting the woman he loved so much.

Phoebe Sherman paused in the kitchen doorway and viewed the late-morning bustle with a smile on her freckled face. The aromas coming from the huge stove and oven were heavenly. She needed to get upstairs and see to Mr. Ronald, but she couldn't resist a fast visit to the kitchen, especially when it smelled this wonderful.

Martha chattered with Jenny and Bette, the other day maid, as she deftly frosted a layered cake. The long butcher-block table was already covered with crystal dishes heaped with delicious food. Glazed fruit tarts and an elaborate tower of cold shrimp took up space next to bowls of dipping sauces, several pies, and trays of cheeses. A wide silver tray of thinly sliced meats almost edged out a fancy display of delicate iced petits fours. There would be champagne punch and an assortment of crisp and fruity wines from the Quincy's extensive wine cellar.

Phoebe sighed in delight. She and the rest of the household staff would have their own fun luncheon in the kitchen later on, for Martha always prepared more than enough food each year.

She smiled at everyone and announced, "I'm going up to check on Mr. Ronald. Save me some of that cake, Martha, if you know what's good for you." Phoebe made a face at Martha and was happy to see her co-worker grin at her. They needed a bit of levity today, when Mrs. Quincy and her lady friends would just about run Martha and the maids off their feet, catering to their every whim.

Martha shooed Phoebe out the door, flapping her apron. "Go on with you. I'll put together an especially delicious plate for Ronnie's lunch. And don't worry, no roast beef. I'll make sure he has several slices of turkey, and some shrimp, too."

"You're a saint, Martha. I've always said so." With a wink, Phoebe ran from the kitchen before Martha could snap her apron again. The great hall was empty and quiet, the drawing room door tightly shut. Either Mrs. Quincy was in there, or in the study. Phoebe shrugged and headed up the stairs. Maybe she'd cajole Mr. Ronald into a short nap before his lunch. She stepped through the door of his suite with a lingering smile on her face.

That smile faded into white-faced horror when she looked toward the windows.

Chapter 12

In the passenger seat, Annie sat with her hands folded together, staring down at them. Other than some details about her oldest brother's recent engagement to Sissy Walker, the girl he'd dated through high school, she'd been quiet almost all the way into Charlottesville. Travis didn't mind. It wasn't as if he didn't have a lot to think about, either.

He wanted a long, fun-filled day with Annie. The two of them, hand in hand as they strolled along the crowded streets like any other couple in love. Maybe a cup of coffee in a cute little cafe somewhere along Main Street and some holiday shopping, a late lunch, some more shopping. Maybe a stolen kiss, here and there throughout the afternoon. A leisurely drive home with another sweet kiss under the porch light.

Just some more normal time with his girl was all he wanted.

He reached for her and drew her close. She uttered a broken sigh as her arms curled around his neck. He breathed her in, his mouth against her temple, and brushed a caress over her cheek until he could reach her lips. He loved the way they parted for him, so responsive. When he pulled away, her face glowed, and he felt a thousand percent better.

She whispered to him as she pressed her cheek to his. "Are you okay now? Because we can stay here as long as you need to, Travis. We can go back if you'd rather do that, too."

"And miss shopping with you? I don't think so." He mugged a goofy face at her and got her to giggle. The sound warmed his heart.

He played with a lock of her hair. "Let's get something to eat first. What are you hungry for? Anything you want." Travis knew exactly what she'd choose.

And sure enough, she answered, "Big Mac. And lots of fries. Maybe an apple pie?"

With a laugh, he gathered her closer, a final, tight hug, then let her go. As he helped her from the car, he commented, "I don't think a little squirt like you can eat that much food." He caught her hand as they walked down the busy sidewalk.

She swung their joined hands between them. "No? Then why stop at McDonald's?"

"I knew you'd nag me if I didn't."

She huffed at him as he tugged her up the sidewalk, past the familiar golden arches. "I never nag."

"Uh-huh." Travis pushed her inside and up to the first line they came to. She stood in front of him, a slender slip of a girl with a huge smile on her face and boundless love in her heart, so real, so palpable, he swore he could taste it as he wrapped his arms around her and rested his chin on her shoulder.

Mine. She's mine. I'll never let her go. I'll never lose her. Not for anyone or anything.

Three days from Christmas and with years and years of loving each other stretching ahead, it was easy to believe.

Ruth stood in the foyer and wrung her hands as she watched the emergency team take Ronald out the front door on a stretcher. An oxygen mask covered most of his face and what was visible around the mask appeared gray and drawn. She took three steps toward the open double front door, and froze.

Martha, behind her with Ruth's coat in her hands, pushed at her none too gently. "Ruth, we have to go." When she didn't budge, Martha pushed again and grabbed one of Ruth's arms, trying to force it into the coat. "I said, let's *go*. Now. Your husband needs you."

Ruth yanked her arm away and wrapped both of them around her body as one of the emergency team members strode partway up the steps. He called, "Ma'am, we need to get on the road. Are you coming or not?"

She didn't answer, and the team member shook his head in exasperation and ran back down the steps. He shouted over his shoulder to Martha. "We're taking him to Rockingham Memorial." He jumped in the back of the ambulance, and they raced down the long driveway.

Martha cursed aloud, something she seldom allowed herself to do. She whirled from the open doorway and grabbed both of Ruth's arms, then shook her. "You listen to me, missy. That's your husband in the back of that ambulance. He needs you to be his wife right now, not some scared girly who can't step out of her own damned house. Phoebe is pulling the car around, and you're going to get into it with me, and we're all driving to the hospital. *Now*."

"No, I can't. You know I can't. The ladies will be here any minute. We have a luncheon to serve." Ruth trembled in Martha's grip. The distant stare of someone in deep shock might have been in her eyes, but her voice was eerily calm.

"Oh for God's—I don't have time for this. Jenny!" The young day maid came running as Martha hustled Ruth toward the doors. "Call everyone on the luncheon guest list and tell them it's canceled. Do *not* tell them why, you understand?" In tears, Jenny nodded as Martha pushed and pulled Ruth down the porch steps. Ruth fought her every step of the way.

Wild-eyed now, she resisted, trying to dig in her heels. "*No*. I never leave the house. Ronald promised me I'd *never* have to leave the house. Let *go* of me!"

Relentless, Martha dragged her by both hands, yanking her up when she tripped on the slick concrete steps. The car waited at the bottom of the stairs, the rear door open with Phoebe nearby, ready to trap Ruth inside and slam the door before she could leap out. Martha muscled her onto the seat. She jumped into the front after Phoebe locked Ruth in the back and dashed around to the driver's side. They roared down the driveway before Martha got her door latched.

Martha turned a grim face to the younger woman as she maneuvered the slippery road. "Phoebe, she's losing it. What on earth are we going to do?"

Phoebe blinked away a sudden flood of tears. "We'll take care of her. We'll take care of them both."

They sped toward Harrisonburg as Ruth sobbed in the back seat, demanding to be taken home.

She didn't once mention her husband.

Annie peeked inside the brightly patterned bag for at least the twentieth time and sighed once more at the soft, pale yellow sweater nestled atop red tissue paper. Out of the corner of his eye, Travis saw her moon over the gift and had to stifle a grin at her excitement. It was only a sweater, but Annie reacted to it as if he'd given her a bag of pure gold. And there lay the difference between her and other girls he'd met over the years, both in Thompkin and at the exclusive all-girl boarding school adjacent to the Academy.

Annie didn't know his impulsive gift was expensive cashmere. It was fluffy, soft and in her favorite color, and he'd thought to give it to her. That was enough to thrill her, and she'd jumped into his arms and kissed him.

Annie blushed when she looked up and caught Travis grinning at her. "You think I'm silly." She wrinkled her nose at him as she fingered her new sweater, and leaned toward him to kiss him yet again. "I love it, Travis. I can't wait to try it on." He started to remind her she could try it on any time she chose, and she shook her head. "No way. You know how clumsy I am. I'd either rip it or spill something on it before I could even get it home."

"Then I should go back and buy you the green one, too." He started to rise from his chair, and she grabbed his arm in both hands.

"No! Travis, you can't buy me another sweater. You've given me way too much already." She pulled him back into his seat. "You don't have to buy me things."

"But I like buying you things. And you want to know why?" Travis cupped her face in his hands and brought her close. She nodded, her beautiful eyes locked on his. "I like it because you've never asked for anything in return. You give and give of yourself, and never think anyone is going to give you a thing back, and then when I do, you're always so surprised. The day I fell in love with you was the day you gave me half your fish and all of your worms." He watched her eyes fill up with tears.

She uttered a tremulous sigh. "Travis . . . oh, I want to marry you. I'd give anything if we didn't have to wait." In the middle of a food court in the mall, they leaned into each other and kissed, the gesture a pledge between them. At a nearby table, a few boys Travis's age whooped and whistled as their girlfriends shushed them.

Ignoring the hooting, Travis held her closer. "I don't want to wait, either. I love you so much." He pulled away, to look into her eyes. "Will you wear my ring, Annie? Right now, today, will you let me put a ring on your finger and wear it, even in front of your folks and mine?"

Her bottom lip quivered as she nodded. "My folks love you, Travis. They'll be happy."

"Even Suze? You think she'll be okay with this?" It was a feeble joke at best, but they both needed some humor before they drowned in the overload of emotion passing between them.

Annie rested her head on his shoulder and wiped the tears from her cheek. "Susan will want to kill me, but she'll hug us both. She gave me the outfit I wore to your party. It was hers, but she said I could have it. And she said—um—never mind." Annie pressed her lips together.

"What? Did she upset you? I'll wring her neck if she upset you."

She was quick to reassure. "No, honestly, she wasn't mean at all. She just said you wouldn't know what hit you, when you saw me in my new clothes." Her blush was adorable. "She even asked if I needed any money."

"Are you sure it was Susan? Maybe it was an alien or a clone."

She pinched him. "Don't make fun of my sister."

When he took her hand and pulled her from her seat, she protested, "Now where are we going?"

He guided her into the first jewelry store he saw. "I'm getting you a ring. And then I'm going to ask you to marry me." When he looked at her, Annie's eyes had gone huge with emotion.

"Now? Right now? Before you say anything to your folks? Travis—"

"Right now, Annie." He nudged her toward a display case loaded with diamonds and precious gems.

"But—"

Travis clapped a playful palm over her mouth, shushing her, and grinned at the young salesclerk behind the glittering display case. "Hi. We just got engaged. Do you have anything that matches her eyes?"

The salesclerk returned his grin. "I have some deep smoky topaz. It's not quite as dark as her eyes, but I think you'll like it. A plain setting, or with baguettes?"

While Annie gulped, he settled her into a leather chair placed in front of the display case, and replied as if he'd been buying jewels all of his life. "A solitaire, preferably emerald-cut. Gold setting, diamond baguettes. Nothing too big," he picked up her left hand and kissed the back of it, "since she has very delicate fingers."

"I have something I think you'd like." With a smile just for Annie, the salesclerk headed toward the rear of the store and disappeared behind a door. Annie sat there wide-eyed as Travis pressed her hand to his cheek.

"Travis, you can't afford this. You need your money for school."

"Yes, I can. What I can't afford is to let another day go by without the world knowing you belong to me, Annie Turner." When her eyes filled yet again, he groaned, "Not another tear! You'll make me think I'm torturing you instead of getting engaged."

Before she could respond, the salesclerk was back with a small tray lined in white velvet. She chose a seat across from Annie and placed the tray in front of her. Rings lay against the velvet, some plain and others fancy. Glints of pure light shot through many of the faceted gems, and every one was breathtaking.

She tore her gaze from them with a beseeching look at Travis. "I can't choose. I don't know—"

"I'll help you." His face suddenly sober, he selected a ring from the center of the tray. Deep and pure, the stone was not too small, but not so large that it would overpower her hand. Emerald-cut, as he'd requested, and in a simple, yet elegant, gold setting, framed on two sides with tiny, perfect diamonds. He took her left hand, slid the ring on her finger. It fit as if it had been waiting for her.

He lifted her hand until the ring was close to her eyes. The stone was just a few shades lighter. Against her skin, it glowed and pulsed, warm and pretty, just like its new owner. With his other hand he cupped her chin, brought her lips to his, and kissed her. For long seconds, he kissed his Annie. Slowly, he released her and gazed into her starry eyes.

"Marry me, Annie."

Her lips trembled, then parted. She cleared her throat. Spoke through a dawning smile.

"Yes."

Chapter 13

"What have we got?" Bernard Grayson, the cardiologist on duty at Rockingham Memorial, rushed into Emergency, the ER nurse running to keep up with him.

"Stroke. Patient's second. Male, approximately forty-six. EMTs brought him in from Thompkin. His family's with him. Three women."

"Three women who might go hysterical on me. The day just gets better and better," he muttered as he entered the cubicle. The patient's vitals were choppy at best, with an elevated BP and pulse, irregular heartbeat, and gray-tinged skin. The right side of his face appeared palsied. Bernard picked up the chart.

Ronald Quincy, of Thompkin. He frowned at the vaguely familiar name. Two women stood beside the bed, and a third sat in a chair placed beyond the privacy drape, rocking back and forth with her head in her hands.

Bernard addressed the woman closest to the patient. "Are you Mrs. Quincy?"

She raised red-rimmed eyes. "What? No. I'm Martha Knowles, Mr. Quincy's cook. This is his private nurse, Phoebe Sherman." She indicated the woman standing next to her, her eyes also swollen. "Mr. Quincy suffered a stroke two years ago, and Phoebe has been with us ever since."

He nodded to the distraught woman. "I'll need to talk with you later. Is Mrs. Quincy here?" He pointed to the emergency contact sheet attached to the chart, adding, "Ruth Quincy?" Martha released the patient's hand and walked to the chair behind the privacy curtain, bent down and whispered to the woman hunched there. Bernard turned just as the woman shook her head vigorously. Martha murmured to her and took her arm, trying to ease her to her feet, and the woman again shook her head and tried to pull away.

He glanced at Phoebe. "What's going on here? Is that Mrs. Quincy?"

She nodded toward Ruth. "That's her, Doctor. Ruth suffers from a form of agoraphobia. She's only been away from her home a handful of times in over fifteen years. The last few years it's been impossible for her to step outside at all. We had a heck of a time getting her here." She lowered her voice and added, "We're trying to reach her son, Travis."

Sighing, Bernard laid the chart down, stepped over to the chair and squatted down until he was level with the wife, who had once more buried her face in her hands. "Mrs. Quincy, I'm Doctor Grayson. I need you to calm down and focus on the questions I'm about to ask you."

"Can you give her something to relax her?" Martha asked.

"No." Bernard placed a hand on Ruth's arm, taking note of the way she shuddered and recoiled. "Mrs. Quincy? Listen to me. Your husband has suffered another stroke. It's caused paralysis along his right side, which I understand mirrors the damage his first stroke inflicted. Yes?" He glanced up at Phoebe, who nodded. "All right, then." He brought his attention back to Ruth. "I need to know what your husband was doing prior to his stroke."

"I don't want to be here. You can't make me stay here." Ruth wrenched her arm from his grip and struggled to her feet. Martha and Bernard both took hold of her and pushed her back into the chair. Ruth burst into tears and slumped sideways.

Bernard signaled the ER nurse, who came over and took the sobbing Ruth off his hands. "Put her in the waiting room for now. Have Grace stay with her." He indicated one of the older ER volunteers. "I'll make sure to talk to her before we move her husband to ICU." Grace stepped to Ruth's other side, caught her arm, and spoke to her in a low, soothing voice.

Bernard returned his attention to Martha. "Well now, what about the son?"

Martha moved toward the bed and stroked the hair back from Ronald Quincy's damp forehead. "He doesn't have a cell phone. He went Christmas shopping in Charlottesville with his girlfriend. I spoke to her mama and told her what happened. She'll tell Travis as soon as they show up there."

"Unusual to see a young man without a cell phone."

"Yes," Martha agreed. "But his mother didn't want him distracted at school."

Bernard glanced at the monitors, noting the slightly improved vitals. He picked up the chart again. "Why don't you head into the waiting room and sit with the wife? I'll schedule Mr. Quincy for some tests. For now, his vitals are holding. Not much we can do until he regains consciousness."

The early-evening light was pearly and soft when they left the busy mall. Annie held Travis's hand and as far as he was concerned, all was right with the world. He didn't have to look at her to know she was smiling. He laid their joined hands on his thigh and felt a thrill when she seemed content to leave hers there.

The ring on her finger glinted up at him. It was exactly right, too. He cleared his throat as he eased out onto the highway. "It's been a while since lunch. Are you hungry again? Do you want to stop and get something to eat?"

"No, I'm not hungry. Are you?" The look she gave him was half-shadowed, almost mysterious.

A sudden attack of nerves made him catch his breath.

"Not really. It's still early. Do you want to go see a movie?"

"I—" She paused, then rushed on, "I just want to be with you. I want to sit next to you somewhere alone. Just us, Travis." He heard the plea in her voice. "I don't want to go home yet. You'll have to go back to your house, and your mother will still be angry. Can't we stay out a little longer? Can't we just go somewhere and be together? Alone?"

He broke out in a sweat at the immediate picture her words conjured up. Did he want to be alone with her? More than anything. But he also knew his own limitations. He couldn't be with her and not want to hold her. Couldn't hold her and not want to kiss her.

Couldn't kiss her without wanting to touch her, all over.

She was only sixteen, and he wanted her so much, but he wasn't sure how ready they were. At nineteen, he was inexperienced by his own choice. Most of his Academy buddies dated steadily and had sex with their girlfriends. Busy with his studies, Travis crammed as many classes as he could into his days so he'd graduate early, his single-minded goal to get it done as soon as possible. Coming home to Annie was all that mattered.

In a few weeks, he'd pack up his car and head to Yale for spring semester. His schedule would be insane, with no time to himself. The next time he'd come home to see Annie would be early summer, if all went as planned. He knew there was no way her folks would let her travel to Yale on some weekend to be with him.

But they'd just gotten engaged. An engaged couple had the right to take some time for themselves, didn't they? He needed it, and so did Annie. With that decision already firmed up in his mind, he turned at the next intersection he came to.

She raised her head and glanced around as he maneuvered off the highway and onto a side street. "Travis?"

He slowed down and entered a parking lot. A lit sign on

the side of the lot said, "Shenandoah Inn." She blinked at it for several seconds, turning to him with uncertain eyes.

Travis cut the engine and unbuckled his safety belt, twisting in his seat to her. "I think we should get a room. I want to be with you, Annie." His voice threaded out to a hoarse whisper. "I want to make love to you. We're engaged. We're getting married as soon as we can. But right now, I need you, so much. Please don't say no."

Her hand was cold in his and her fingers trembled, but she came into his arms when he urged her closer. Pressed to his heart, her mouth met his in an ardent kiss. And it was so new yet so familiar, so right, like coming home after a long, hard, impossible day. Their families were far from there and they were alone in the encroaching twilight. It was their own private existence, where they ruled and made the decisions.

Tomorrow would come and with it, too many troubles to count. But for a few hours tonight, they were newly pledged, and the world was theirs for the taking.

"Annie? Please."

She kissed him on both cheeks, and again on his mouth. "Yes, I want to. I want you to show me. I want to learn from you."

He choked out a shaky laugh, his forehead touching hers. "Annie, I—I don't know how, either. I've never done—I've kissed only you. You know that."

"I know. We'll learn together, Travis."

"Then wait here." One more kiss, and he was out of the car and walking into the inn's office. He returned shortly with a key attached to a large plastic disc with the room number stamped on it. He opened her door and helped her step out. Annie clung to his arm while he locked the Beemer, and he gave her what he hoped was a reassuring smile as they walked to the row of rooms on the first floor of the inn. His hand shook when he inserted the key.

The room was chilly, so they turned on the heater

under the single window. Curious, Annie poked around. "I've never been in a motel room before." A bed and two nightstands took up one side of the room; a table and three chairs crowded the other. Everything looked plain, but clean. Travis couldn't claim to have been in many motel rooms, either, but this one had everything they'd need.

He dropped his coat on the table and sat on the edge of the bed. He should use the bathroom, but he didn't want Annie to hear him do it for fear it would embarrass her. He should brush his teeth. How could he kiss her unless he had clean teeth? He should take a shower. Annie deserved a fresh-smelling lover, right?

And why the hell was he nervous, anyway? This was Annie. He adored her. It should be the easiest thing in the world, coming together this way, loving each other like this.

Shouldn't it?

For endless minutes they sat there, their eyes meeting and then glancing away. Tension stretched between them like a tightrope.

Travis found some of his nervousness easing off as he watched her. She was so beautiful in the dim light of the room. The glow from the lamp cast gold over her hair. Her eyes seemed apprehensive. He could understand the fright, because this was a huge step for them. He'd always assumed when the time came for them to make love, everything would fall into place, and they'd know what to do.

Stupid. This wasn't the movies. This was real life.

His Academy buddies often ragged on him for not going out with them during the week, after classes, and getting drunk or chasing girls. To be honest, several times he'd been tempted. It was lonely in the dorms. What held him back was the thought of Annie, waiting for him.

He'd lie in bed and picture her sweet face and her bright smile. He'd strive to recall the silky texture of her hair and how good her arms felt around him. He'd compare her to some of the girls he saw around Newport, and they'd all come up lacking. Nobody seemed to fit him the way Annie did. They were meant to be together, simple as that.

And just as simply, the rest of his nerves eased. His worries about clean teeth and perspiration also disappeared. Travis smiled at the girl he loved, and watched her smile back at him.

She rose and unbuttoned her coat, draping it over one of the chairs, then took a few steps and reached for him. Their fingers clasped as she sank down on the bed and nestled close. Travis brushed a hand through her hair, and Annie sighed, her head on his shoulder.

He palmed her cheek and raised her face to his, searching for reassurance. "Are you—all right—with this, Annie? We don't have to do anything if you don't want to."

She nodded. "I'm okay with it. Honestly."

She kicked off her boots, slid over on the bed and stretched out, her eyes locked on his. She grasped the edge of her sweater to remove it, but he stopped her.

"I want to." His low words made her blush. She nodded again and relaxed.

He knelt on the bed next to her, and his hands trembled as he pushed her sweater up and slipped it over her head. Underneath, she wore a pale pink bra that was as innocent and demure as Annie. She shivered when he traced the edge of it with his finger.

"Cold?" He didn't even recognize his own voice, raspy and thick.

She shook her head.

"Good."

He reached for the button of her faded jeans, paused, then took a deep breath and unfastened them, pulling them off and down her legs. She was so tenderly-formed; shapely thighs, pretty calves, dainty ankles. She wore panties with tiny hearts all over them. Her skin still had a trace of the tan she'd acquired over the summer.

She overwhelmed him. He didn't know where to touch, first. He forgot about taking off his clothes. Travis could do nothing but stare down at Annie in amazement at how lovely she was. He feathered his fingertips over her stomach and felt it flutter. Nerves, anticipation, he had no idea which, but it excited him. He couldn't stop looking at her.

When she tugged at his own sweater, his gaze snapped back to hers. She swallowed, hard. "I want to see. Travis, can I—?" The words seemed to stick in her throat.

"Oh, God, sorry." He fought the urge to fidget and tried to remain still while she undressed him. Somehow she got everything unbuttoned, and soon he wore only his briefs. The heat rose in his cheeks and felt almost as warm as the pretty blush he saw on Annie's soft skin. For a few seconds they remained side by side, their hands clasped, hardly daring to breathe.

With hesitant touches and shy caresses they came together on the cool sheets. He trailed kisses over her, and each one tasted like heaven. He touched her, marveling at the differences between a woman and a man, how skin could take on such a sheen of silk when it stretched over slender bones.

"Annie—" He wasn't sure what he wanted to ask. Permission to continue, assurance she wasn't scared? It didn't matter because she seemed to understand without further words. She stroked her fingers over him and made him shudder. This time when he kissed her, she clutched his hair with both hands and held him tightly. A moan slipped from her lips, and he swallowed the breathy sound.

He wanted to inhale her, absorb her right through his skin. And he was glad he'd waited for her, glad he'd never given his innocence to another girl. Annie was the only one who could appreciate it. They'd waited for each other. What could be more perfect?

Her muscles quivered as he brushed his lips along her navel, and her legs moved restlessly when he nibbled on the tender curve of her breast. When he pressed against her, instinct took over. Their bodies blended together as easily as their love, sweet and true.

He'd never belong to anyone else.

She turned her face into his neck; her fingers gripped his shoulders. Her breath came in short, hot bursts. He found her mouth with his and kissed her deeply as their bodies moved, clung, shuddered. How could something this amazing be anything but right?

He looked into her face and saw the same wonder he could feel. He slipped his hands beneath her hips and pulled her closer. Closer. And just like that, the final link—the one stretched between their souls—forged and held. Permanent.

In the quiet, warm room, he made love to Annie with the eagerness and endurance of youth. The shadows at the window deepened into evening as they lost themselves in each other.

Chapter 14

Ruth sat wedged between Martha and Phoebe in the waiting room outside ICU. Martha tried to get her to drink a cup of coffee, but she'd knocked it away. She didn't want any damned coffee. She wanted to go home.

This wasn't supposed to happen again. After the first stroke, Dr. Perkins, their family physician, told her Ronald would be fine. That all she had to do was alter his diet and add daily rehabilitation. Well, she'd done all he'd prescribed, hadn't she?

She had Martha prepare special meals. She'd hired Phoebe—much as she hated to have another domestic in the house—to assume live-in status and to assure he received that daily rehabilitation the quack doctor had ordered. She'd even contracted to have a goddamn elevator installed. And for what? So Ronald could still be in danger of having another stroke? Forcing her to leave the security of her own home and sit in a hospital, in a stuffy room that smelled of stale coffee, smelly feet, and worse? Expecting more doctors to come forward and tell her that Ronald was now a vegetable. That's what happened when someone suffered another stroke, they became little more than a rutabaga.

It was intolerable. She needed to go home.

"I have to go." No one seemed to hear her, so she felt compelled to repeat herself. "I need to go home. I have to leave now. *I want to go, now.*" With each repetition, her voice grew in volume and resolve, from a whisper to a shriek.

Martha slapped a hand on her shoulder and trapped her in the chair with one strong hand. On the other side, Phoebe gripped Ruth's arm.

"Are you insane? Take your hands *off* me. *Don't touch me.*" Ruth twisted in their grasp.

"Sit still, Ruth." Martha's tone bordered on the insubordinate. Incensed, Ruth struggled with Martha and pulled against Phoebe's hands.

With a muttered curse, Martha leaned into Ruth and pressed an arm across her body. "Shut the hell up. I've had it with you. Show some spine. And while you're looking for that spine, show some love and dedication to your husband. We're waiting right here until Travis comes. Your son, remember him? You need to be strong for him."

Ruth glared at Martha. "My son is a traitor. My husband is dying, and where is his son? Out somewhere, God only knows where, consorting with filth—"

Martha pinned her down. "Ronnie isn't dying. Get that thought right out of your head, Ruth. He'll be fine. We'll take him home where we'll all care for him. Including you. If I hear you speak one word about him dying when we get in there to see him, I will personally pop you one, right between your eyes. I mean it. You watch your mouth when we go see Ronnie."

"He won't even be aware that we're in there, I tell you. He's a vegetable, he's—"

Martha's open hand smacked across her cheek, snapping her head back. Ruth gasped in shock. Phoebe froze in her seat, gaping at both of them.

A light rain misted the air, but the temperature wasn't cold enough to form ice on the roads. Two more miles and they'd be at Annie's house. Travis drove slowly, reluctant for the evening to end.

The hours they'd spent together at the Shenandoah Inn

hadn't been enough. They'd used all of their time in a fever, making love as if they'd never get another chance.

He wanted more time with Annie but couldn't anger her parents by traipsing in late, looking as if they'd been doing exactly what they *had* been doing. Her folks liked him, but her father also had a gun.

"I don't want to leave you." Annie's soft voice roused him from his own bleak thoughts, and he turned to smile at her as they stopped for a red light.

"I don't want to leave you, either. But I have to get you home, before your parents worry." He signaled left and took the last street toward her neighborhood.

"Will you come in for a minute, Travis? Will you walk in and speak to my parents?" She didn't have to say anything more. He knew what she meant. Talk to her folks, show them the ring, and ask for their blessing. The necessity of it made him nervous as hell. He knew when they looked at their daughter, they saw a girl barely old enough to have a serious boyfriend, much less a fiancé. It could go either way, and added to the mix was the knowledge they'd sealed their engagement with far more than a kiss.

Could her mother tell what they'd been doing, look into Annie's eyes and sense it? Some people claimed they could see lost innocence in the eyes. Not for a second did he regret the hours they'd spent in each other's arms. But he didn't want to cause her mother any added worries, either.

"Travis?"

He shook off the panic and smiled at her. "I'll come in. I'll ask your parents, Annie. We'll do it the right way."

They pulled up in front of the house, and he helped Annie out of the car. Hand in hand they walked toward the house. Before they could even step inside, Mary met them at the door, her face etched with worry. "I'm so glad you finally made it back. Travis, your father is in the hospital in Harrisonburg. He had a stroke. You need to get there, right now. Mr. Turner and I will take you, but we have to go, immediately."

All the color drained from Travis's face as he tried to process what she'd said. "My dad? Another stroke? But how? When?"

Henry came up behind his wife. "Late this morning, son. After you and Annie left for Charlottesville. We have to go, Travis. I'll drive. I don't want you going by yourself. Come on, now."

His mind blank with shock, Travis moved toward the driveway as Mary locked the front door behind them and Annie started to cry.

In the Turner's old station wagon, Travis sat in the back with Annie close to his side, while Henry headed for the freeway. Guilt piled itself on, until Travis's shoulders slumped with despair. *I shouldn't have left the house. I should have stayed right by Dad's side.*

What the hell had he been thinking? He knew his mother, knew the kind of awful things she could say when angered.

A warm hand engulfed the fist he clenched on the edge of the front passenger seat, and Travis blinked through blurred eyes at Mary as she turned in her seat. She soothed her palm over his tight knuckles. "Honey, there wasn't a thing you could have done. A stroke hits hard and fast. You could have been sitting right next to him, and he'd have still had it. You understand me? Don't you take this on, Travis. Don't."

"I could have been there when he had it. I could have been by his side." Travis spoke low, but the adults in the front seat heard him.

"Travis, honey, that kind of thinking weakens you, and right now you need to be strong. Your mama especially will need you to help her—"

Instant fury boiled through him. "Help her? She did it

to him. I know it. They were fighting last night." He turned an agonized face to Annie. "And this morning, too. It was bad. My mother caused this."

"Oh, Travis, no. Please don't say that." Annie slid her arm around him.

Mary tightened her grip on his hand, until his tense fingers relaxed. "Travis, listen to me. Your mama and daddy might have been arguing, but that's not what caused this. Married folks argue all the time, and it doesn't cause anything but maybe some hard feelings. Mr. Turner and I have our spats, and we get over it. Your folks will, too. There isn't any blame, here."

"Yes, there is. I shouldn't have left him alone with her. So the blame's mine, for doing that. She shouldn't have said the things she did. You don't know—you can't imagine—" He couldn't finish for the anguish that clogged his throat. He dropped his head on Annie's shoulder and sobbed as she held him.

Twenty minutes later, Travis rushed out of the ICU elevator ahead of Annie and her parents, and straight into Martha's arms. In her embrace he started to tremble, suddenly a child again, trying to accept the bitter knowledge his father wasn't Superman, after all.

"How is he? He'll be all right, won't he?" Travis's voice was deep but hoarse. A young man held her, but a boy's fright was behind the words he spoke.

Martha rubbed his back to soothe him. "He's stable now. It was touch and go for a little while. Phoebe got the oxygen to him fast, so that's a good thing." She cradled his face in her palms, her thumbs brushing over his wet cheeks. "Now, you take a moment and calm yourself before you go in there, Travis. You stand here and take a few deep breaths, and you go in without tears. Your daddy might not be awake, but I believe he's aware, and you don't need to be crying all over him. Okay?" She released him.

Travis nodded and hurried toward the private ICU room. Martha fished a handkerchief from her pocket and blew her nose. She'd cried more than her share today. When Annie and her family walked toward her, she wiped away fresh tears.

"How's he doing?" Henry kept his arms around his family as he greeted Martha.

"He hasn't regained consciousness yet, and that's not always a bad sign. His vitals are better, that's a real relief. Thing is," Martha glanced at the open door of Ronald's room and spoke quietly, "we don't know how long he was upstairs after he had the stroke. We don't know for certain how long he might have been deprived of oxygen."

"He's not going to die," Annie burst out. "God wouldn't let him die. It would kill Travis to lose his daddy."

Her father hugged her close. "Honey, the doctors here are very good. They'll do everything they can to help Travis's daddy. Now, I want you to go sit down with your mama, okay?" Henry passed Annie to Mary, who led her into the waiting room.

He turned to Martha with a more serious expression. "How's he really doing? I figure you didn't want to get into it with either of the kids."

She heaved a worried sigh. "It doesn't look good, Henry. This stroke caused more damage than the first one he suffered two years ago. His right side was affected this time. He'll probably be bedridden for the rest of his life. The cardiologist assigned to Ronnie is positive some brain damage occurred due to restriction of oxygen."

She dabbed at her sore nose. "Ruth has been a handful, I can tell you. She fought us every step of the way when we drove here. Phoebe and I had to babysit her like a two-year-old."

"Can she take over for Ronald temporarily, concerning the businesses?"

Martha's shoulders lifted in a weary shrug. "As far as I know, Ruth never concerned herself with the legacy and its holdings. She only left the Hall maybe six or seven times, total, after she and Ronnie were married, and for the last few years, she's never walked beyond the front door for any reason."

"I had no idea her agoraphobia had gotten so bad." Henry shook his head. "If there's anything we can do, you have only to ask." The sincerity in his voice was almost Martha's undoing, and she battled her own emotion. It was vital to remain as strong as she could, for Travis. God knew the boy would need some added strength, and it was a sure bet he wouldn't get it from his mother.

Ruth hurried along the ICU corridor. She couldn't have taken one more minute in that airless room, listening to yet another doctor drone on about nursing homes and hospice care. She'd needed to escape. The ladies' room had been the only place she could think to go where she might be alone for a few minutes.

Out of the corner of her eye, Ruth noted Phoebe walking toward her, and she sped up. She didn't want to talk to anyone. She strode past another, larger waiting room where the low ebb of voices briefly caught her attention. One of the voices sounded like Martha's. And why on earth should she care, anyhow? Martha had been horrid to her.

As for her errant son, she'd decided to forgive him for the appalling way he'd behaved earlier. He was still such a child, despite his adult appearance. She'd take him in hand as soon as he arrived at the hospital.

Ruth felt much calmer as she walked toward the private ICU rooms. She knew what she had to do, for herself and for Ronald. First and foremost on her agenda was to swallow her own bubbling hysteria, which would serve no purpose but to make her seem weak and ineffectual. She was now the head of the Quincy Legacy. It was time she acted the part.

Stepping into Ronald's room, she saw Travis standing by the bed, holding his father's hand. Fury threatened to choke her as she remembered the misery her son had caused her, but she tamped it down. Now wasn't the time or place.

"Travis." She watched her son's shoulders tense before he turned to face her. Tears stood in his eyes, ready to overflow. His face was pale, his clothing rumpled. Ruth clasped her hands together at her waist and waited for him to acknowledge her.

Aside from a brief nod in her direction, Travis ignored her. He angled away from her and leaned over the bed, still clasping Ronald's hand. "Dad, can you hear me?"

"Travis, I wish to know where you've been. You should have arrived here hours ago. Your father needed you." Ruth wasn't above using guilt when it served her purpose.

"Dad, it's Travis. I'm here. Can you squeeze my hand?" All of Travis's attention was on his father, and Ruth felt the fury gather, dispelling her newfound calm. She fisted her hands together until her nails bit into her palms.

Despite her efforts at self-control, her shrill voice rang in the room. "Travis, he can't hear you, he's a vegetable! He's dying. Your father is leaving us."

His head jerked back and he sent her a hateful glance. "*Shut up*. Just shut your mouth." He took a few steps toward her and growled, "I know this is your fault. You were yelling at Dad when I left the house. He wasn't supposed to have any stress. No tension. Why couldn't you have just left him alone?"

Refusing to let him see how his words cut her, Ruth

glanced at Ronald, who lay still as a stone in the bed surrounded by machines, their tubes snaking all over him. Her gaze swung back to Travis, so tall and handsome, a perfect balance of her and Ronald.

The boy received everything in the world as his due: privileges, advantages. Obviously such bounty had spoiled him. Though he might not accept it, Travis needed her. She had to believe it was never too late to reestablish necessary boundaries, instill discipline.

A few steps brought her closer to her son's side, but his forbidding expression kept her from touching him, as she strove to assert authority and reason. "Travis, listen to me. It's true your father and I argued after you left this morning. But the stroke could have happened at any time." She gestured with both hands, stretched them out in entreaty. "We must work together to help your father. He'll need constant care once he comes home. You must put away your childish thoughts now, and begin the maturing process I know you are more than capable of."

Travis didn't respond. Instead, he pulled a chair close to the bed and sat in it, all of his attention on Ronald. After a few minutes, she sighed and walked toward the open door. A restorative cup of tea might be in order. She'd have a nurse fetch her one.

Unfortunately, there wasn't anyone at the nurses' station. Frustrated, she went searching, prepared to chastise the first nurse she saw for deserting her post when she was needed—

And she ran right into Annie Turner, standing in the middle of the wide corridor next to the nurses' station.

Incensed, Ruth spat, "*You*. How dare you come here?" She marched forward as Annie retreated a few steps, then escaped to the waiting room. Ruth followed, determined to remove her forcibly from the area if necessary, and came face to face with Henry Turner. Behind him stood a woman, her arms wrapped protectively around the girl.

Ruth paled, but held her ground, and when she spoke, her voice remained satisfyingly firm and steady. "Kindly take your daughter from here, Mr. Turner. There is no place for her at my son's side." This was her turf now. She had the upper hand here. It made no difference that she controlled a hospital waiting room and not Quincy Hall.

His wife spoke up. "We came to offer our help, Mrs. Quincy. If you or Travis need anything, then you have only to ask."

Ruth gave her the most cursory of glances and once again addressed Henry Turner. "Your family's presence here is disruptive. Please don't force me to call for Security, Mr. Turner, for I can assure you—"

"Mother." One firm word came from Travis as he stood in the doorway of his father's room. In that single word she heard a strength so akin to Ronald's. When he walked to Annie and took her in his arms, it was all Ruth could do not to reach out and strangle her for her usurping presence. *It should be Catherine, here with Travis and offering comfort.*

Ruth's entire body stiffened when Travis bent and kissed the girl on her mouth, and then reached out and hugged the Turner woman. Hugged her, as if she were of importance! Ruth clenched her teeth, determined to bear the outrage without screaming in frustration. They'd leave soon, these accursed Turners, and then she'd deal with her son. Ruth held onto that thought.

Travis returned the tray and left the cafeteria. The hamburger he'd forced himself to eat sat like a lump in his stomach. He'd choked down less than half of it. But the food had given him an excuse to get away from his mother. He'd needed the reprieve more than the meal.

He wished she'd go back to Quincy Hall. He dreaded having to spend any more time with her. Disheartened and depressed, Travis returned to his father's room. All he wanted was to be alone with his dad, talk to him some more and hope he'd either wake up or respond with a squeeze of his hand.

His mother rose from her seat by the bed when he walked in, but Travis ignored her and crossed to the other side of the bed. When she sat and looked over at her husband, the man she supposedly loved above all others, Travis couldn't see any emotion on her face. No marriage was perfect, but he'd always figured they at least loved each other. Now, he wondered just how much love his mother was capable of feeling, for anyone.

She turned toward him and quietly stated, "He's going to require a great deal of care. Nurses around the clock. I'll have to hire at least two more to relieve Phoebe. The doctor recommends a nursing home, but of course that's out of the question. A Quincy cannot live away from Quincy Hall. It's unacceptable."

When he didn't respond, she sighed and made a show of straightening the blanket over his dad's legs. "I intend to assume responsibility of the legacy holdings as soon as I obtain Power of Attorney. Until you are of an age and educational level to step into your rightful place as heir apparent, key board members will assist me." She fussed with one of the pillows, the image of a loving wife, but her eyes were chilly when she looked up from her ministrations. "You will return to Yale as soon as possible, begin spring semester, and remain through the summer."

It was a direct order, and Travis bristled in silent protest as she added, "I expect you to complete as many extra classes as possible. The sooner you complete them, the sooner you will graduate. You will then take your place at my side, with the board relinquishing all Quincy holdings and duties as deemed appropriate to your balance of maturity and readiness."

Travis's consternation, as she outlined his immediate future so coldly and emotionlessly, spun into blind fury. Under her thumb through college as well as after graduation when his life should, by all rights, finally be his own? He didn't think so. And in the tension-thick room, unspoken between them, was the ever present specter of Catherine Cabot. His mother didn't have to say her name. Travis sensed her there, unwelcome. Unwanted by him, but as always pushed to the forefront.

He couldn't, wouldn't live like this.

He faced her with stronger resolve. "No, Mother. I won't go back early or take classes through the summer. And I won't be put under your thumb. Dad wouldn't want it that way." He released his father's hand and stepped back from the bed, standing tall. "I'll stay on my present schedule. I'm sure the board will do a fine job with the family holdings—"

"You will *not* disobey me, Travis." Soft and frigid, the words stabbed at him. "Trust me when I say this. You don't want to show me your rebellious nature right now. You will do exactly as I say, when I say it. Or so help me, I will make you regret every instance of disrespect you have ever shown me." Her eyes narrowed on him with relentless intent. "Starting with your precious Annie."

Chapter 15

May

Annie tossed the potato peeler and half-cleaned potato aside when the phone started ringing. She ran to the hall table and snatched up the receiver. "Hello?"

"Annie?"

Her knees wobbled as she heard Travis's anxious voice. Annie sank onto the rickety old cane-backed chair next to the hall table and clutched the phone.

"Annie? Is that you?"

She cleared her throat and took a fortifying breath. "It's me."

A long pause. Neither of them said anything. She couldn't hold back the sudden tears sliding down her face. Never, never in the last, almost six years, had either of them been at a loss for words with each other. Never had they been unsure of what to say. It broke her heart.

"God. You're crying, aren't you? I'm so sorry, Annie. Please talk to me. Please say something."

Her throat ached. "Where have you b-been? That's all I w-want to k-know."

"I just got home. I'm up at the Hall. Can I come over? I need to see you, Annie."

"I didn't mean—I . . ." She gulped in another sob. "Why did you stop calling me? It's been two months! I've been so worried."

"That's what I need to talk to you about. And I want to

see you. Please let me come over."

For several long seconds she sat there with the phone clutched tight in her hand. She wanted to see him so she could tell him off for ignoring her. She wanted to grab hold of him and never let go. Confusion and hurt warred with need, until she felt sick to her stomach.

Her folks would be gone all day and most of the evening, helping Danny and Frankie set up their new apartment in Charlottesville. Bobby and Susan wouldn't be back for hours. That gave her and Travis time to talk, and—

Stop it. She hadn't heard a thing from him in almost two months. Before there could be anything else between them, she needed explanations.

"Annie?"

She pulled her attention back to Travis, who sounded even more anxious. "I'm so mad at you." Her voice cracked. "I'm so angry, Travis."

She heard him utter a broken sigh. "I know you are. I don't blame you, but I can explain—"

"You can come over now." She didn't want to hear anything else from him until she could look him in the eyes. She dropped the old-fashioned phone back into its cradle and dashed away fresh tears.

It was the first time they'd parted company over the phone, without saying, "I love you." Something bad was happening to their love.

And Annie knew it had started in January, right after Mr. Quincy came home from the hospital.

That last night together, before Travis left for Yale, they'd gone for a drive. With no real destination in mind, they spent some time cruising the streets, and ended up parked on Hickory Knob just to watch the snow come down.

They cuddled close and spoke in hushed tones, almost as if they were afraid they'd be overheard.

"I can't come back until May, but I'll call you at least once a week. Martha told me she'd keep you posted on my dad. So you'll hear from her once in a while, too." Travis pulled her as close as their coats would allow, and nuzzled Annie's ear as he spoke.

"I wish I could go see him. When does he get to come home?"

"Another week. Mother has to make the final arrangements for the extra shift of nurses. Dad needs someone with him around the clock, and it's a sure bet Mother won't spend much time with him." His voice held enough bitterness for her to notice, but she wisely hadn't commented. So much animosity lay between Travis and his mama, and Annie didn't know how to help other than just being there for him.

They still had the optimism of youth and such a strong basis of love, however, all tipping the balance toward them and their future. They kissed and touched, then kissed and touched some more, until with a groan of need, Travis pulled Annie onto his lap, both of them cramped and bent in the compact BMW.

He undressed her with eager fingers, enough to reach her skin, and likewise, she unzipped and unbuttoned his clothes, until bare, shivery flesh could meet and meld together. They moved against each other, held on with such urgency, and Annie had cried out in his arms as she experienced for the first time the kind of pleasure that made intimacy so magical.

Words, as usual, weren't necessary between them. With their bodies they said everything vital, everything important.

He drove her home, parked on her street and kissed her over and over. When he finally let go, Annie floated through her front door secure in the knowledge that her life with Travis was just beginning, and nobody could ever take it from her. She fell asleep that night with her hand curled around the ring on her finger as wonderful dreams filled her head.

It was pointless to dwell on that night. She'd only get upset, and right now she needed to think with a clear head. Hurrying through her chores, Annie carted the pot of stew over to the stove and turned the gas on low. She'd probably forgotten half the correct spices, but in her present state of mind, it was a wonder she could recall her own name.

He'll be here soon. She sank down on the nearest chair and pressed a hand to her heart. It pounded hard and fast beneath her fingers. Everything felt wrong, upside-down. She pushed the heavy hair out of her face and reached for whatever composure she could find within herself. No more tears, and no excuses. She'd be firm with him. Grown-up. And she'd get the answers she needed to explain his behavior.

After Travis left for Yale, Annie's daily nuisances of high school and chores, her sister's relentless teasing, and her brothers' typical idiocy, her loneliness—all of it was bearable because she got to talk with him each Friday night. She lived for those phone calls.

Then, the last weekend of March, they just stopped.

At first, she thought his Friday classes must be overwhelming him and he couldn't get away long enough to call her. He'd surely call as soon as he could on Saturday. Then Saturday passed with no word from him. Annie fretted and worried, until Susan told her to knock it off or she'd kick her morose butt down the stairs and out into the yard. Even Mama was short with her. Annie figured she overreacted, so she forced herself to calm down and to be patient.

Two weeks into April, she still hadn't heard from him. Uneasy about bothering him when he was so busy with classes, she'd finally tried calling his cell phone, but he never answered. She'd left messages at his frat house. He didn't return them. By late April, Annie was angry and confused. There wasn't anyone she could speak to over at Quincy Hall, and she felt uncomfortable asking Martha about Travis. Besides, she knew Martha's hands were full helping with Mr. Quincy, who stayed in bed most of the time after that second stroke did so much damage.

Annie's balance was out of whack. She and Travis never had even a slight disagreement in all the years they'd known each other. Sometimes it seemed as if they shared one mind. This sudden, unexplained break unnerved her. Nobody knew all of her hopes and dreams the way Travis did. For over five years she'd counted on having such loving support in her daily life. She'd planned a future with him: marriage, children, celebrating their love forever. Now, there was nothing, not even a letter.

By early May, she more or less resigned herself to not hearing from Travis. When his birthday came without any contact from him, she just gave up, her heart in pieces. For some reason, he'd withheld himself from her.

For a full week she cried, ignoring her family's attempts to get her mind off Travis and his desertion of her. Only the fear that she'd fail her final exams if she didn't get a grip on herself kept her from falling into depression. She mopped up her tears, dove back into her classes, and worked hard to recover what she'd lost from weeks of apathy. She still missed him horribly, but told herself it was his loss.

Some days, she even convinced herself.

As she walked into the living room to wait, Annie swore she wouldn't cry like a baby. When Travis arrived, she'd act like a woman, with grace and dignity.

Then she heard his car as it squealed to a quick stop in front of the house. With a deep breath, Annie moved to the door, placed her hand on the knob, and wrenched it open before he could knock.

His eyes seemed to glow as he stared at her. One look at him and Annie forgot her anger, her resolve to be calm and mature. The door hadn't fully closed behind him before she jumped into his arms and clung as he covered her mouth in a desperate kiss. More forceful than he'd ever kissed her before. More passionate.

They kissed with fervor as Travis pushed her up against the door. He leaned into her, held her so tightly that she couldn't breathe. His hands rushed over her, stroked beneath her tee shirt. She hadn't bothered with a bra when she'd dressed that morning and now, as she felt Travis's hands cup her, she was fiercely glad of the omission. Annie arched into his caress.

Suddenly he picked her up. She wrapped her legs around his waist as he stumbled up the stairs, carrying her to the room she still shared with Susan. They fell onto her bed and the old mattress sagged beneath their combined weight.

This isn't right. She yanked at the buttons of his jeans, tugged at his shirt. *Don't be stupid, Annie.* She could hear the sob in her throat and gasped for air as she wriggled out of her shorts, loosened by his fingers. *This is a mistake.* Yet she didn't back away.

Her hair was in her eyes. She shook it out of the way and lifted her arms for him to pull her shirt over her head. His mouth skimmed her bare skin, and, shivering, Annie clenched her fingers around his neck and held him fast.

Her panties hung off one thigh, and his briefs were down around his knees. She still wore a sneaker. She didn't care. She couldn't stop. Couldn't think of anything except the need to crawl inside his skin and never come out.

When he pressed against her, she opened her body to

him and clung. He fused his mouth to hers and she kept her eyes open, unwilling to let him out of her sight as he made love to her. Yet even as she clutched him, so tight a sliver of paper couldn't have passed between their driving bodies, her mind wouldn't ignore the inner voice asking why he'd cut her from his life.

She cried brokenly against his neck when she tightened, climaxed. Travis buried his face in her tangled hair as he reached for his own release.

The room was silent, but for the sound of their labored breaths, her soft sobs, and the words he murmured in an attempt to soothe her.

"Why haven't you called me, Travis? Was it just your classes keeping you busy? Or is it something else?"

She sat up in the mussed bed, her hands locked around her knees. Now that they'd satisfied their first urgent rush, she was determined to get the truth from him.

With a sigh, he leaned into the pillows stacked against the narrow headboard. She heard hesitation in his voice. "Classes *have* been tough. And it's been hard to find enough time in the evenings to even eat dinner, much less make phone calls. But that isn't an excuse, Annie. I let you down, and I'm sorry for it."

She started to speak but he held up a hand to stop her. "Just listen, okay? Mother has pressured me almost nonstop since I got to Yale. She wouldn't let up on the idea that I should schedule my classes semester to semester with no break in between. She expected me to stay at school and work my ass off. She didn't seem to care how burned out I'd be if I took classes spring semester through the summer months and then ripped right into fall semester. I wanted to go against her, but—well, I had to do as she ordered."

Distressed, she reached for his hand and soothed her fingers over his palm. He gripped her fingers. "The dorm phones were always jammed, especially on the weekends. After Mother agreed to let me have a cell phone for emergencies, it was a lot easier calling you on Fridays. I heard from Martha once in a while, but she'd never get into much detail about how Dad was doing." He dragged his free hand through hair that already stood on end. "So I kept slogging through more homework than I'd ever seen in my life, and worried a lot about Dad." He brought her hand to his mouth for a kiss. "Talking to you once a week was my salvation, Annie."

His words might be sweet to hear, but she couldn't accept them at face value. "If that's true, then why did you stop calling me?"

"Mother cut me off in April." At her gasp, he nodded. "It's true. I picked up my cell phone to call you, and got a message it was no longer in service. I couldn't understand it because I knew the monthly statement was paid. I found out Mother canceled everything. She'd seen the billings and realized I talked to you every week for hours." His hand tensed on hers. Sarcasm sharpened his tone. "I guess my calls to you weren't much of an emergency, except for my own sanity. She never said anything to me about it, just canceled the phone."

"How could she do something like that? What right did she have? If you pay your bills—"

"It wasn't really my phone, Annie. I fooled myself into thinking it was. And I no longer have money. She found the credit card statement and realized I'd bought your ring." He traced the glittering stone on her finger, lifted his shoulders in a weary shrug. "I never found out until I tried to use my card off campus. She told the board members I wasn't allowed any funds because I had proven I might slack off at Yale unless I remained focused."

His fingers clenched on hers. "They're all old school. Most of them went to Yale and Harvard. They grew up on trust funds and such, and they believed her. She contacted the Dean of Students and set up a monthly stipend for me. I get enough credit for food and school supplies, as long as I make those purchases on campus. Very few actual dollars end up in my hand. At first I couldn't believe she could get away with something like this, but it's more common at the big colleges than you'd think." He dragged a hand over his face, reddening his eyes when he pushed against them. "My mother's been in control since she brought my father home from the hospital. She has his Power of Attorney. She has control of all of the companies, everything." His voice dropped to a rasp. "And she has control of me."

"Oh, Travis." Annie reached out for him and he fell into her arms. She held him close, unsure of how she could soothe him, make this better for him. How could she tell him she knew what he was going through, when she didn't? Her mama was so wonderful. His sure wasn't. Her daddy cuddled her and told her he loved her, and his daddy was unable to give Travis any support. What could she say to make him feel better?

After a minute or so, he pulled away, brushed a lock of hair from her damp cheek, and tucked it behind her ear. A trace of red still ringed his eyes, but his voice had steadied. "It's not fair of me to lay this all on you, Annie. As long as I know you understand what I'm going through and you're here for me, I'll be all right. My mother can't take that away, although if she could think of a way to do it, I bet she would. But she can't change how much I love you. She's pretty much pulled everything else from me."

"Well, she didn't take your car. At least you have a way back and forth from school."

"But I have no money for gas. I had to borrow money from Catherine, and—"

"What? What did you say?" Annie wasn't sure she'd heard correctly. She sat up slowly. "Do you mean Catherine Cabot? Why would you borrow money from her?"

"Um—" He suddenly wouldn't look at her, and instead plucked at the wrecked sheets. His cheeks held a telltale flush.

She grabbed his arm to still his movements and bring his attention back to her. "What's going on, Travis? Why would you borrow money from someone you've always told me was a pest and a nuisance, someone you don't even like?"

"Listen, Annie—"

That was as far as he got, before she jumped up from the bed and reached for her shorts. He stretched his hand toward her, and then dropped it into his lap when she moved out of reach. "It's not what you think. It's just that I see her once in a while, that's all."

She faced him with her hands on her hips. Sharp pain lanced through her as she struggled with her temper. "You see a girl your mother desperately wants you to marry someday, 'once in a while.' And you borrow money from her. That's all. So, are you two buddies, now?"

"No, of course not. Just sometimes, she comes by . . ." He trailed off and looked away.

Her hands clenched so hard that her nails scored the soft skin of her palms. "And how often would you be having her for company? I have a right to know."

Travis closed his eyes as if in defeat. "She's attending prep in New Haven. She has a year to go and then she starts at Yale. She lives in a sorority house, in town."

"And?" She steeled herself to hear the rest of it, knowing it would be very bad.

"And I . . . see her. Sometimes during the week, and on the weekends."

Oh, God. She was right. It *was* bad. Catherine Cabot, going to the same college as Travis. Seeing him any old time she wanted, with Ruth Quincy's blessing.

Annie cleared the hoarseness from her throat. "After your classes are through, she comes over. Is that what you're saying?"

He remained silent, his eyes downcast. She felt herself stiffen all over, an ache from head to foot as if someone plowed her under and kept on going. Hit and run.

What a dim bulb she'd been. How very stupid and naïve. Annie picked up a brush from her dresser, dragged it through her hair. Anything to occupy her hands so they wouldn't reach out and choke Travis.

Silence reigned in the small bedroom for perhaps a minute, until, with a furious cry, she whirled and threw the brush at his head, missing him by mere inches. "You could have told me, Travis! You could have at least fed a pay phone a handful of quarters and let me know what was going on with your mother. I would have tried to understand. Maybe I could have helped. But you had no intention of telling me anything."

"No, I would have told you. I was going to tell you, Annie." But his protest lacked conviction, and she heard it for herself.

"You only told me because you slipped up. At least be big enough to admit it." Her anger deflated, Annie bent and picked up her forgotten panties, crossed to a wicker hamper under one of the windows, and placed them inside, thinking hard all the while.

His mother was behind it. And shoving Catherine in Travis's face when he was down and vulnerable was a clever trick Ruth had pulled on Travis in the past. But he'd been different back then, and she didn't know why his attitude changed so much in just a few months. He knew better. He knew his mother, what she was capable of. That was the thing hardest to understand, why he was suddenly going along with her.

Unless—?

"Your mother has something on you. Doesn't she? For some reason she's made you accept Catherine in your life. Is that it?" She crossed the room and stood before him. "Please, just tell me the truth."

Travis seemed to search for words, hesitating before his shoulders slumped. "She doesn't have anything on me, Annie. Only the money thing, and I suppose if I wanted to badly enough, I could tell her where she could shove her money. I could quit college, get a job somewhere, and live my own life. But I don't want to quit school."

He caught her arms, his earnest gaze holding hers. "I've dreamed of going to Yale, of walking the same halls as my dad, for most of my life. I wanted to be just like my father, wanted to be the Quincy Heir, even though so much of the prep work involved my mother's pain in the ass visions of what being the Heir really meant. Golf lessons and fencing, for Christ's sake. But I put up with it because I knew what it would mean to me, once I had it all in my hands."

"Travis—"

"If I defy her, she'll cut me off. At least for now, she's paying my tuition." Self-recrimination throbbed in his voice. "It's the only funding I have available to me for college. My grades didn't make the scholarship cut. I need her money to keep going, at least right now. As much as I hate it, I need to stay on her good side."

"I need you, too. What about us? Are you going to let your mother tell you how to love, who to love, and who to marry? We're meant to be, you and I. Or have you forgotten?" She hated grasping at the last bits of hope she could find, but couldn't seem to stop herself.

He only shook his head. "I haven't forgotten our promise to each other. It's not for long, Annie. Until I can graduate and come back here to claim my own life. Once I take over for Dad, there isn't anything my mother can do. I only have to humor her, for a while. Play the game. Just for a while."

He brought her to her feet, cradled her closer, pressed a kiss to her temple, her ear, working a path to her mouth. He whispered, "She doesn't have to know. We can still see each other, and she'll never be the wiser." His lips brushed hers, using kisses to sway and persuade her.

She slapped a hand over his mouth, angry, yet resigned, as she pushed him away. "No. You're not seeing the whole picture. I'm not even sure you're able to." She rubbed at the pressure behind her eyes. "Your mother will never let you go, not as long as you do what she tells you, even if you think you're just humoring her." Turning to face him, she held a hand out to ward him off when he would have taken her in his arms again. "Just stop, Travis, and listen to me. What if she decides it's time for you to marry Catherine Cabot, and she gives you a ring and tells you to push it on Catherine's finger? Or else she'll disown you, drop her support of your schooling, ruin your chances of taking over for your daddy." She spread her hands for emphasis. "You never thought she could do half the things she's already done, and yet she has."

Stepping back until she could reach the bedroom door, Annie opened it and held it wide. Her heart broke as she looked at the only boy she'd ever loved, now a confused young man who still thought he could use half-truths to outsmart the most powerful driving force in his life. It was just sad.

"I won't be your little secret. You either love me out in the open for all to see, proudly, or you forget it." She gestured toward the dim hall beyond the doorway and choked back a sob when he stood there staring at her. "You'd better go. She might figure out where you are, and make it worse for you." Impatiently Annie jerked her thumb at the door when he failed to budge from his stance by the bed. "Go on, Travis. I mean it."

He sighed and bent to pick up the clothes he'd strewn around. She kept quiet, her eyes closed in desolation, unable to watch him dress without wanting to beg him to take everything off again and jump back into her bed.

When he finally realized he couldn't sway her, he walked through the doorway and descended the stairs. He looked back once at her as she stood in the upstairs hall. She crossed her arms and tucked her hands against her sides to keep them from reaching out. And hated herself for that lingering trace of weakness.

On the landing, he turned to her and begged, "Annie, don't do this. Please, just trust me. Give me some time to figure things out."

"Are you going to tell Catherine to go find someone else to marry? Are you going to tell your mother where she can stick all of her schemes and plans?" The words and tone were harder than she'd ever used. She saw him flinch at the sound of them.

"No. I'm—" He paused, took a breath. Swallowed. Looked away as he shook his head. "I can't."

"Then you've made your decision. And so have I. Don't call me again. Don't come back here."

"You don't mean that, Annie." Panic showed in his expression as he swung back to her.

She kept the hardness in her heart. "Oh, yes. I do."

Annie turned her back on him and walked into her room. Her body shuddered only once—when she heard the front door close behind him.

PART THREE

Turning Away

Chapter 16

August

Annie turned sideways in front of the mirror and pressed a hand on her stomach, smoothing her sleeveless shirt until it molded to her hips. Still flat. But not for long.

Pregnant. The thought of it never failed to break her out in a sweat and set her heart to pounding. A month had passed since she'd gone to the free clinic over in Weston. Her family's support eased much of her panic, and in time, she figured the shock would disappear as well. But she'd be lying to herself if she tried to pretend she wasn't scared.

It was a staggering responsibility. *Her* responsibility. And she wasn't yet seventeen.

Turning to her bed, she folded a few more tee shirts and the last of her winter sweaters, placed them in the open box on the floor, and laid underwear and socks on top. She hadn't told her mama and daddy yet, but she planned on leaving for Roanoke as soon as she could. She'd live with her Aunt Nan in the big old Victorian house that had been in her mama's family for the past eighty years.

In Roanoke, she could finish school at home. Aunt Nan said she'd help her. In Roanoke, nobody knew her and in such a big city, no one would care that she was a pregnant teenager.

In Roanoke, Ruth Quincy wouldn't find her. Annie sank down on the corner of the bed, a nightgown bunched in her hands, and took deep breaths to keep from hyperventilating. She didn't want to go, but she had no choice.

After the supper dishes were cleared, Annie took a seat next to her mama. "I think I should go live with Aunt Nan until the baby's born, maybe stay there for a while after."

"What? You can't leave. What on earth brought this on?"

Her daddy placed a hand on Mama's shoulder to soothe her, but his eyes showed his worry. "Annie, I think you'd better explain yourself."

She tried to remain matter-of-fact. "I need to get away before anyone finds out about the baby. I don't want to start senior year at Thompkin High wearing maternity clothes. You know how folks are around here, how they'd talk."

"Yes, of course I know. But running away isn't the answer." Mama gave it some thought. "I guess you don't have to go back to Thompkin High. You could home school right here. I could help you." She appealed to Daddy. "Couldn't we help her, Henry? How hard would it be to school Annie through twelfth grade?"

Before he could answer, Annie jumped in. "It's not that. I can't stay in Thompkin. Don't you see? I don't know what Travis's mama would do if she found out." She strove for inner calm. "I know something about the way the Quincy Legacy works. Travis told me a few years ago. The first-born son is the Quincy Heir."

She laid protective hands over her stomach. "If I'm carrying a boy, he'll be the next heir after Travis. Now do you understand?"

"Oh, Annie." Her mama scooted her chair close enough to hug her. "I see what you mean." She stroked Annie's hair, then eased away and touched her cheek to gain her attention.

"But you can't hide. Sooner or later you'd have to come home. And what about Travis?"

"No. You can't tell him! Promise me!" She clutched Mama's arm for emphasis.

Her daddy gazed at her with sadness in his dark eyes. "Travis will need to know, honey. Wait." He put up his hand as she started to protest. "Listen to what I have to say. This baby will be a Quincy. Travis does have a right to know he's going to be a father. Even if the two of you never end up together, nothing changes his right to be a part of the baby's life."

"No. I can't take that chance yet, Daddy. Mrs. Quincy hates me. She could threaten the baby. I'm too young to fight her if she decided to sue for custody. She's got the kind of money to buy whatever she wants. What if she wants my baby? I wouldn't stand a chance against her." Her voice threaded out to a whisper. "If I have a boy, God only knows what she would do."

She met her parents' worry with new resolve. "You have to let me handle this my way. You have to tell the boys and Susan not to say a word." She hesitated, but only for a few seconds. "I already spoke to Aunt Nan."

At her mother's exclamation of distress, Annie insisted, "Mama, I had to. She's the only one who lives far enough away. I've never mentioned her to Travis, I guess I never thought about it. I called her yesterday. "

In fact, her aunt showed more empathy than Annie initially gave her credit for. She loved Aunt Nan, but always felt a bit intimidated by her. Yet when Annie realized what was ahead for her and understood the urgent need to get away from Thompkin and Ruth Quincy, Aunt Nan became the obvious choice.

Travis's baby. She still reeled from the ramifications of it and what it would mean to her life and the lives of her family. She could never regret making love with him. But oh, they should have been more careful.

She sat up straighter and moved out of her mother's embrace. Fresh panic threatened to overwhelm her at the mere thought of what Ruth Quincy could do. And hard on the heels of that panic, the ever-present worry that Travis wouldn't—couldn't—fight for their love.

Carrying a few leftover coffee mugs to the sink gave her something to do. She could sense Mama's concerned stare boring into her back as she stood there wiping her hands on a dishtowel.

She refused to kid herself that Travis would stand for her against his mother. And though trying to gain the upper hand against Ruth would buy her some time, eventually someone at Quincy Hall would discover her secret.

Turning, she faced her parents and scraped together what self-confidence she could. "I'll leave for Roanoke in two weeks. I promise I'll call you every day. I'll write, too. Maybe I can talk Aunt Nan into getting a computer, so I'll have email. I can create a fake name and everything." Her chin wobbled, then firmed in a smile she hoped would reassure them.

When her daddy opened his arms, Annie ran to him.

Chapter 17

November

Five days after Thanksgiving, Susan sat next to Annie in the back seat of her parents' old station wagon and watched some of the pedestrians who bustled around downtown Roanoke. Occasionally, she turned to glance in concern at Annie.

It was finally sinking in. She was going to be an aunt.

Aunt Susan. It was surreal, that's what it was.

An hour ago they all viewed the ultrasound monitor, talking in hushed tones. There was no mistake. Susan hoped and prayed for a girl. So had Mama and Daddy. If Annie had a girl, the Quincys would probably leave her in peace. However, Annie carried a boy.

Damn. Susan wanted to scream aloud at the unfairness of it all, but anger was pointless now.

"It'll be all right." Annie's soft assurance brought Susan out of her dark thoughts. She turned toward her sister and formed a half smile as Annie gave her a thumbs-up sign. Susan caught hold of the thumb and twisted it playfully. They sat for a while, listening to the traffic outside and the low rise and fall of their parents' voices in the front seat.

"Aunt Nan says you're almost ready to take your final exam." Susan played with Annie's fingers as she spoke. With relief, she noticed Annie had finally taken off Travis's ring, though she'd bet the stupid thing would end up on a chain around Annie's neck. Her sister could be such a hopeless romantic.

"Yep. I can't wait. Did I mention I already have a job lined up at the college bookstore? It's minimum wage, but I can have all the hours I want. And I applied for a scholarship to Hollins." Annie rubbed a hand over her stomach. It was getting rounder, although privately Susan thought she could do with a little more weight. Annie had always been petite and slender.

"Just so long as you don't overdo it. You're not Superwoman."

Annie chuckled. "Don't I know it."

They both avoided talking about the obvious: the sex of the baby. Nobody had said much in the examining room while they watched the ultrasound. And in truth, what was there to say? Annie would stay in Roanoke indefinitely, and the family agreed to keep her secret.

"You know, there's been a few times in the past six months when I'd have loved to get right up in Travis's face and ask him what he thought he was doing, treating you the way he did." At Annie's sound of protest, Susan shrugged. "Well, that's how I feel." She glanced sideways at Annie. "He lied to you. First lie, hundredth lie, makes no difference. I used to really admire him, too."

"You had a crush on him."

"Maybe." Susan poked her in the shoulder, and smiled when Annie poked her back. She didn't want to hurt her sister's feelings. Travis had already done plenty of that.

She remembered when Annie sobbed against her shoulder as she talked about Travis, how they'd made love so frantically. It was the first time Susan realized her sister was no longer a virgin. She would have gone right up to Quincy Hall and punched him in the nose for that alone.

"Do you think he's seeing Catherine?" Susan asked idly. She didn't ask out of meanness. She just wanted to squash some of Annie's tender reminisces and keep her anger toward Travis strong. If Annie thought he stepped out regularly with Catherine, she'd start burning and stay that way.

Annie eyed her with a frown. "I know what you're doing." She rubbed her stomach again. "You don't have to, Suze. I'm not going to do anything stupid like call him, believe me."

"Don't call me—oh, I see. You're getting me back."

"Maybe." They shared a smile, before Annie slouched lower and laid her head against the seat. Susan resumed staring out the window.

More than once she'd had to slam the lid on her anger, before she said something that would hurt Annie's feelings. And yet, Annie would have to grow a thick skin, especially if she planned on coming back to Thompkin with a baby and no husband. Their old-fashioned town could never be called progressive. About the first time she walked down Main Street pushing a stroller, tongues would wag nonstop.

"Just so you know, I haven't seen Travis around town at all," she informed Annie, who sat up straighter at the mention of his name. "I bet he hasn't been home in months."

"Well, he did say his mother kept him hopping with school and all, so I wouldn't figure he'd come home very often." Annie lifted a shoulder to indicate nonchalance. Susan knew she was dying to ask questions, but wouldn't.

Sliding over in her seat, Susan curved an arm around her and hugged her. "You're stronger than you know, Annie. You'll hang tough and stay smart." She uttered a self-depreciating chuckle. "Anyhow, I was the one who flipped out when you told me about the 'Catherine Campaign.'"

Annie winced. "Don't call it that! You make it sound like a conspiracy."

"As far as I'm concerned, it is." Susan knew plenty about the entire mess, including a few things she'd found out on her own. It helped to have a friend in New Haven, a girl in her graduating class who knew Travis, and some of the people he hung out with. He'd been seen around town several times with Catherine Cabot. "I bet his mama does handsprings and slaps herself on the back for a job well done."

"No doubt she does." Annie sighed. The desolation in her voice was easy to hear. "Ruth won't give up. She won't stop trying to force things between them. I wouldn't be surprised to find out she arranged to have Catherine go to Yale. It's pointless to think on it any longer." She leaned her head against the window. "We're almost home."

Susan glanced over. Aunt Nan's rambling old house was three blocks away. She gathered up her purse and the shoes she'd kicked off as soon as she'd climbed in the car. As she slipped them on, she said, "You'll have to decide how much crap you're willing to take from any of the Quincys, once they find out about the baby. I'm figuring no crap. Am I right?" She looked expectantly at Annie, who nodded. "Then don't. Don't let any of them intimidate you. And don't think their money can buy everything, either." She gave Annie an elbow nudge for emphasis. "You'll be a great mother, and that's all that matters."

Aunt Nan met them in the driveway as they parked and climbed out of the car. "Well, home again, I see. I hope none of you brought home any germs. Nasty places, those clinics." She looked straight at Annie, who tried not to blush. "So, let's hear it. What's in that tummy of yours?"

Annie hoped her voice sounded steadier than she felt. "It's a boy, Aunt Nan."

For a few seconds Aunt Nan's eyes grew suspiciously bright, before she cleared her throat and nodded once, briskly. "Well, then. Now we know." She stepped to Annie, gave her a quick hug and planted a kiss on her cheek, before striding toward the front door. "I hope nobody minds hot turkey sandwiches. And I think we have at least two whole pies left. Either we eat them or they get tossed out." She mounted the wide-planked steps, grumbling vague insults about doctors and foul clinical smells interspersed with supper details and how wide to cut slices of apple pie.

Susan clapped a hand over her mouth to hold in the giggles, and her eyes brimmed with mirth. Annie swallowed her own giggles as they walked into the drafty old house.

"Aunt Nan, let's set a fire in the fireplace." Susan winked at Annie as she spoke.

Their aunt turned to gape at Susan. "Are you crazy, girl? And waste firewood? You think that expensive firewood grows on trees?"

Everyone erupted with laughter as they trooped through the house behind stiff-shouldered Nan. Mama threw a grin of approval over her shoulder, raised her hand, and made a victory sign with her fingers.

The next morning was dreary with rain and cold, as Annie's family piled in the station wagon and left for Thompkin. It was always hard to watch them drive away. This time the ache lessened somewhat because of the extra few days she'd been able to spend with them.

A boy. She curved both hands protectively over her stomach as she walked back into the house. A boy changed everything. She'd do anything in her power to keep her son from Ruth Quincy.

Maybe someday she and Travis could be together, when they were both older, when he got strong enough to go against his mother and forge his own way. Until then, she couldn't trust that he'd be capable of standing up for her. She wanted to be loved for who she was. She wanted strong arms around her and courage behind those arms of strength.

As for Ruth, Annie wasn't so naïve as to think the

woman would never find out about her grandson. Eventually Travis would realize there was a child. She couldn't guess what his reaction might be, and it was hard to accept. Once, she'd known his heart as well as she knew her own. It hurt to think she now fumbled in the dark, unsure, worried, and fearful.

Stifling a shaky sigh, she turned to face her aunt. Those shrewd blue eyes, so much like her mama's, crinkled at the corners in a reassuring smile. With a nudge to her shoulder, Aunt Nan urged her up the sidewalk and into the house. Pushing her toward the kitchen, she pointed to a chair and Annie obediently sat.

She watched her aunt collect milk from the fridge, a glass from the cupboard. She pulled a container of chocolate powder out of another cupboard and with efficient hands mixed up a large glass of chocolate milk.

Aunt Nan placed it in front of her. "Here. Drink every drop."

Annie stared at the foamy treat, blinked back a few sudden, burning tears, and drained the glass in three swallows. Aunt Nan tsked at her for her unladylike gulps, but there was a smile on her weathered face when she picked up the empty glass and rinsed it in the sink.

In that moment, Annie knew everything would be all right. She cupped her hands over the swell of her baby and felt the subtle, stretching movements he made. Softly, she whispered, "We'll be fine, little one. You'll see."

It was a promise and a vow.

Chapter 18

Eighteen Months Later
April

Ruth stacked the last of the invitations and set them aside. One hundred and thirteen would go out in the mail later on today, and she expected the same amount of RSVPs to be returned. Last year, when Travis became of age, he'd flatly refused a party. This year she wasn't going to let him back out of one.

Twenty-two years old. It didn't seem possible that a month from now, she'd toast her son with champagne. Where had the years gone? When Travis came home for visits and she looked at him, so tall and handsome, Ruth still felt amazement that he came from her body. She was proud of him, although she rarely told him. It wouldn't do for the boy to get a swelled head or to inflate his ego. Especially during the last few years, when she had to ride roughshod on him to keep him in line. She hadn't wanted to. Contrary to what her son thought, she did have feelings and she didn't enjoy his cold attitude toward her. Someday he'd understand, and thank her for all she'd done for him.

She thought about the upcoming party as she dropped the packet of invitations on the foyer credenza and started up the stairs toward her suite. The extensive and elegant menu promised to satisfy her most choosy guest, and the birthday cake would be both a centerpiece and a delectable confection. Fine wine, wonderful apéritifs and witty conversation blended with an atmosphere of sophistication, assured Travis's birthday party would be the talk of the county.

She made a mental note to call Janice Cabot and ask her when she and Catherine planned to arrive. Ruth so envied the closeness that Janice and her darling child shared. If only she could have the same kind of relationship with Travis. Well, he'd calm down once he returned home permanently. She'd accept nothing less.

She had one aim: to see her son take his rightful place as head of the family and the power behind the Quincy Legacy and fortune. She'd realize that aim, and when she did, Catherine would stand at his side. If everything went according to plan, not only would Catherine have the Quincy wedding set on her finger, she'd soon carry the Quincy Heir in her body, too.

Now that she had the key to Travis, and a way to assure his compliance, she was certain she'd have everything she wanted for her son.

And nothing—or no one—that she didn't.

The Cabots' invitation to Travis Quincy's birthday celebration, hand delivered to their estate later in the day, sat on a side table in the foyer. Catherine's mother found the thick vellum envelope and ran for the day room where Catherine sat reading, curled in an armchair by the sun-dappled window.

"Cathy, I have something you've been waiting for." Her mother dropped the card onto the open book in Catherine's lap.

Catherine trailed a finger over the envelope before she opened it. She read it silently, then laid it on a small side table. "I did assume I would receive one, if not directly from Travis, then of course from his mother."

Her calm nature afforded her a bland façade she used whenever something bothered her. In this case, it came from Travis's lack of enthusiasm where she was concerned.

But she wouldn't say anything, for it would get back to Ruth, who would then find a way to take Travis to task. And months of hard work on Catherine's part would be ruined. She'd grown weary of taking three steps backwards for every one forward that she gained with Travis. And she blamed her own mother almost as much as she blamed Ruth.

"Well, aren't you excited? Don't you want to talk about what you'll wear? I think a trip into Newport would be in order. You will need an especially lovely party dress for Travis." Her mother was nothing, if not predictable. Her answer to every social event centered on finding an expensive boutique and buying more clothes. Catherine's ample closet already bulged with outfits she rarely wore.

The last thing she wanted to do was to traipse around in search of yet another dress. It wouldn't matter what she wore for Travis because he wouldn't notice.

He never did.

"Mother, no. We just got home last night. I don't want to run right back out and go to Newport. Besides, I have plenty of dresses, any one of which would be suitable. Please don't worry about me—"

"But you *must* have a new dress, Cathy. You simply *cannot* wear something old. Now, let's check your calendar and see what day would be best for you." As usual, her mother steamrolled right over her in mid-sentence, already planning another shopping excursion.

When her mother strode to the mahogany secretary desk in the corner and proceeded to dig out a copy of Catherine's weekly calendar, she jumped from her comfortable armchair and snatched it away. Her mother's eyes rounded in surprise. "Catherine Elizabeth Cabot, what on earth has gotten into you?"

She tried to avoid confrontations, but Catherine suddenly had enough. If she could point a finger of blame at her mother for mucking up her chances with Travis and not suffer guilt for it, she'd have done so. For all Mother's faults, however, Catherine knew she meant well. But it was just so very frustrating.

This time, she stood her ground and chose honesty over any attempt to spare her mother's feelings. "Travis could care less what I wear. In fact, it's probably pointless for me to attend the party. He won't even know I'm there. Don't you see?"

Her mother sank onto the settee in shock. "Catherine—"

"He's never noticed me, not unless you or his mother pushed me right in front of his nose. And even then, I'd often wonder if he saw me at all." Catherine laid the calendar back on the desk as she searched for words her mother would understand and accept. "When we were children, I didn't exist for him, and now that I'm an adult, it hasn't changed very much. He's polite, so he calls me. But only after Ruth has already nagged him. He asks me to dinner because his mother would make his life miserable if he didn't."

Holding onto her composure took some effort. "Regardless of what either of you think will happen, Travis isn't for me. I used to hope—" Catherine caught her breath on a sudden, ruthlessly swallowed sob. "I really used to hope he'd *see* me, and then fall for me. But it never happened, and all of the conniving you and Ruth do together only makes it worse. You both need to stop, before I lose even his friendship."

"Catherine, darling, I don't understand." Complete bewilderment shone from her mother's eyes. "I thought you were coming along so well! Why, your father and I assumed we'd hear an announcement any day now. We thought for certain that Travis would be stopping by to ask your father formally for your hand."

"Mother, for the last time, *no*. It's not going to happen. You must know by now that Travis is in love with someone else. I think they're engaged."

At the blank look on her mother's face, Catherine knew she wasn't getting through to her. She sighed. "Mama, listen to me." Falling back on the childhood name, she knelt at her mother's feet and took her hands. "If I could have my way, I'd be the one engaged to Travis. But you can't force love, you can't schedule it, and you can't make it happen where it's not meant to. I know Ruth is your dearest friend. But if she'd just left Travis alone instead of always trying to push me on him, then maybe he would have seen me in a better light. Maybe he wouldn't have turned to someone else in the first place."

For a full minute her mother was silent, digesting Catherine's words, then she squared her shoulders. And she looked Catherine right in the eyes. "I'm surprised at you. Letting a few small difficulties get in the way of your future happiness. Allowing a challenge to go unmet. If Travis slips out of your fingers forever, then you have only yourself to blame."

Catherine protested, "Haven't you heard a word I've said?"

"Oh yes, I heard. And what I hear is a little coward, afraid to be bold and reach out for what she wants. In my heart, I believe you could have Travis tomorrow if you put your mind to it. And if you used all of the advantages you *do* have."

She pulled at Catherine until they sat side by side on the narrow settee. Her mother insisted, "You have Ruth in the palm of your hand. Maybe you don't think she has influence over her son, but she does. She favors you as a daughter-in-law. She always has. If you want Travis, you have the opportunity to get him. Use it, Cathy."

"Not like this. He wouldn't love me, Mother—"

"How do you know, darling? How do you know he wouldn't fall in love with you? For heaven's sake, you've never given him much encouragement, from what I've seen. Have you ever flirted with him, tried to get to know him other than talk of school and such? You're a lovely young woman. You certainly have as much chance, if not more than anyone else, of getting him to notice you, become fascinated by you."

"I just don't think it's an honest way to proceed. It's like I'd try to trick him."

Her mother gave a righteous huff. "And you don't think it's fair to trick a man into seeing things your way? If we women didn't use what wiles we have, none of us would ever have gotten married and had you children. Men don't think about settling down, Cathy. Men think about manly things. It's up to women to train them into considering love, commitment, family. It's up to you."

With that, her mother rose, leaned over to brush a kiss over Catherine's cheek. Her stride was its usual bustle of energy but in the open doorway, she turned and delivered one last parting shot. "If you decide you want Travis, you know what you have to do. I raised a smart, resourceful girl. Think about it."

Catherine sat there for several minutes after her mother exited the room, and wondered if, all these years, she'd simply given the impression she didn't care one way or another if she and Travis were even nodding acquaintances, much less anything more. Wondered just how much influence Ruth *did* have, over her son.

Wondered if a new dress—and possibly a complete hair and facial makeover as well as an attitude adjustment— might be the answer for her.

Oh, why not? She supposed she could fit a few more dresses into her closet. She rose, moved to the abandoned chair by the window and picked up her book, returning it to its slot on the shelf next to the desk. It looked as if she'd be too busy in the next few weeks to read much more of it.

She had a party to plan for.

Travis laid a dark blue henley shirt and a pair of comfortable jeans on the bed. Beat-up sneakers sat on the floor next to the closet. It was a far cry from the cashmere jackets and the leather tassled loafers he forced himself to wear on those occasions when he gave in to his mother's damned blackmail, and took Catherine out. At least for this evening, he'd go out for pleasure and not duty.

He'd have one last bout of fun with his frat brothers before he left for Thompkin. He'd tolerate the obligatory visit with his family and deal with the stuffy birthday party his mother planned. He should refuse to leave campus, but he knew she'd push the issue if he balked.

It suited him to let her think she had him by the short hairs, and chuckle over the phone to Janice Cabot weekly as they congratulated each other for their latest bout of scheming.

Early on, he'd struggled at Yale and let his mother's unbending attitude get to him. When it was almost too late to salvage his grade point average, he realized the only way to get through the rest of college was to get his mother off his back. The only way to accomplish *that,* was to make her think she really controlled him. And in her mind, one aspect of control meant pushing Catherine at him regularly. For his own academic sanity, Travis gave in.

He tugged on the jeans and shirt, smoothing his hair back into place, and thought about Catherine as he tied his sneakers. To be honest, she wasn't all that awful as a companion. She was easy on the eyes, intelligent, and well spoken. She knew when to be quiet and when to offer conversation. She seemed to understand and accept his silences. Another thing she'd accepted was his up-front honestly about why he saw her socially.

He still remembered their first lunch together, in a corner booth at Bali Bistro during a particularly boisterous lunchtime rush. As their stilted conversation lagged, Catherine placed her sandwich on the plate and folded her hands in her lap, her eyes steady on his face. "Why did you ask me to lunch, Travis?"

It was a blunt, yet honest, question, and he'd told her the truth. "Because if I didn't, my mother would nag me to death. I don't want to have to listen to her. How about you, Catherine?"

She flushed, but her eyes remained on his. "The same, I suppose. Nagging mother." She shrugged helplessly. "Over the years, I've tried to tell her, Travis. I've tried to get her to give it up. She doesn't listen. She never has."

He could sympathize.

That first lunch set the tone for others to come. In time, dinner dates were added, but only after a strenuous prod from his mother. Every time he protested, she'd mention the Turners, and how it would be so easy to make a few calls and "set their trashy world on its ear." Or she'd threaten to cut off his school tuition. He despised feeling weak. He'd sworn to Annie he wouldn't be manipulated, and now here he was, letting his mother dictate to him.

If his father could stand up for him, his mother wouldn't dare do this. And Travis hated feeling resentful for it, because it made him less than a good son and more of a selfish one.

Yet another reason to hold no respect and even less love, for his mother—and also to suffer guilt for the lack.

He'd just come through a hellish semester, with many of his toughest classes scheduled together, enough to frazzle his brain and exhaust his patience. Within his heart, there formed a hard kernel of resentment for the way his wants had little or no bearing any longer.

Whenever he returned to the Hall, Dad didn't know he was even there. His father sat in a chair by the window for a few hours daily, staring down at his hands. At night, he lay on his back in a bed with guardrails on each side. It broke Travis's heart each time he came home, another pressure and worry that added itself to everything else he dealt with.

Afterwards, he'd escape to campus with a sigh of relief, even though he dreaded the return plunge into his academic workload. Once eager to study at a fiendish pace and thus graduate early, he now wished for the semesters to slow way down. Because that way he could put off, a while longer, the inevitable: being pressured to slap a ring on Catherine's finger.

And, damn it, the absence of Annie in his life was a never-ending ache.

Chapter 19

Sunlight poured from the kitchen window and warmed Annie's face as she looked out over the back yard. Mama's garden showed new growth, early seedlings breaking through the soil, their tender leaves reaching toward the sun. She could relate. For it seemed the past few years, she'd been doing the same. Growing. Reaching.

She refilled her coffee cup and brought it to the table, adding a generous dollop of cream and three heaping spoons of sugar to the rich brew. The milky, sweet concoction settled on her tongue, and she hummed in appreciation as she sipped.

"Yuck." Susan voiced her opinion of Annie's chosen morning beverage and reached for her can of Coke. "How can you drink that nasty stuff at the crack of dawn?"

Annie made a face at her. "It's almost ten. I had to drag you out of bed by your toes, and you've been complaining ever since. And you've got room to talk. Who drinks warm soda pop for breakfast, anyhow?"

"Diet soda pop. I'm trying to lose five pounds."

"Why, for heaven's sake?" Annie gave her a disbelieving once over. "You're gorgeous, Susan."

"You'd say that no matter what 'cause you're my sister and you have to love me."

"Oh, brother." Annie grabbed for Susan's long ponytail and yanked it, then drained her cup and carried it to the sink. "Are you going with us or not?"

Susan pretended to consider. "Let me think. Going back to sleep or mucking around town. Which, I might remind you, we have done to death already, all our lives. Gee, I wonder which one I'll choose?"

"You always were a lazy bum." Annie dried her hands on a dishtowel. "I have to rescue Mama from Hank. Meet us for lunch, later."

"Maybe. You got your phone? I'll call you, let you know."

"I don't have any numbers loaded in."

"Well, criminy, give it to me. What's the point of having a phone if you don't use it? I'll bet you've never called anyone, have you? And you've only had it, what? Six months?" With an exasperated snort, Susan snatched the cell phone from Annie's hand and started punching buttons.

Annie mumbled, "Five and a half months. You know I hate talking into those silly things, Suze. I don't see why I have to have one."

"Don't call me *Suze*." She said it absently, as she finished programming phone numbers. "And you have to have one because they're essential for emergencies, not to mention when your sister needs to get hold of you in a hurry." She handed it back to Annie, who rudely stuck out her tongue. Identical grins split their faces, and they both chuckled.

"Don't go back to bed, okay? Come to lunch with us," Annie cajoled.

"I'll think about it." Susan opened the cupboard and grabbed another diet soda pop as Annie laughed and headed up to the narrow bedroom she'd shared with her sister, years ago.

It hadn't changed very much. She rooted in the crowded closet for a pair of jeans and a short-sleeved blouse, unsure if the clothes were hers or Susan's. She looked around as she laid the outfit on the bed and added a fresh set of underwear. The same unevenly hemmed lace curtains hung at the window that Mama had shown her and Susan how to sew.

The same old dressers they'd painted pale pink when they were kids sat, one in each corner. Mama found the antique floor mirror at a flea market for a dollar and figured out how to re-silver it so the reflection wasn't all spotty. It still stood near the door.

Annie loved this room. When she was a little girl, she'd often felt trapped in it. Now the memories that bounced off the walls and ceiling made her feel good.

"Ma-ma!" The sweet baby voice and the stomping feet, toddling down the hallway from the bathroom, also made her feel very good, as she stepped outside the door and caught the chubby body of her son in her arms. She swung him up and buried her nose in his neck, causing him to shriek in glee.

"He got away from me, slippery little dickens." Her mama came down the hallway after him, a rumpled sleeper in one hand and a damp towel in the other. She dropped the towel and made a claw out of her fingers, growling at the child, who screamed with laughter when those curled fingers caught him right in the tummy. He squirmed and wriggled, this adorable boy, caught between two women who loved him fiercely.

Henry Travis Turner, nicknamed "Hank," already knew what family meant.

With a smile, Annie gave up her son when he held out his arms for his "Gammy," and her mama hoisted him upside down for the short walk to the bedroom. She placed him on Susan's bed, and he kicked his legs happily while she wrestled him into a fresh diaper and tee shirt. As she tugged it into place and let him bounce on the mattress, she inquired, "So, what's the plan today?"

"Lunch at the Hut. Bring Susan, even if you have to drag her butt back out of bed. I don't get to spend enough time with all of you as it is, without her sleeping away most of my visit." Annie pawed through a tangle of makeup and hair ties on the vanity dresser, until she found Susan's brush. She unwound her hair from its braid and ran the bristles through the heavy strands, while she watched Hank bounce and giggle. "I'm glad we decided to stay an extra week."

Her mama ran a gentle hand over Annie's hair. "I'm glad, too. I just wish your daddy could get away from work. I know he's upset because he hasn't been home very much." She snuggled Hank when he crawled onto her lap and settled in with drowsy eyes and two fingers in his mouth. Her lips brushed his forehead in a loving kiss.

It had been a wonderful visit. Annie knew Mama was thrilled that she'd chosen to stay another week. Hank scampered all over the house now. It was hard enough being so far away. She'd badly needed her mama, too.

Mama's soft voice roused her from her thoughts. "He's so beautiful, honey. I want you to know I'm proud of you." There was a catch in her voice that Annie knew could grow into full-blown tears, which would in turn get her going. Then Hank would sense her sadness and start crying, a chain reaction she'd seen more than once.

She sat down next to her mama and wrapped her arms around both of them, Hank squished in the middle. He giggled as she declared, "It's a Hank sandwich!" The silliness did the trick, turning would-be sniffles into laughter. For a few seconds they held the position, until Hank squirmed. As she gazed at her son, Annie felt her eyes film over despite her efforts at humor.

He *was* a beautiful child, sunny tempered, loving and easygoing. Black hair, thick and silky, lay in soft curls over his head. He had Annie's deep brown eyes, but otherwise he was the image of his daddy. With a sigh, she released Hank and settled next to her mama as she finished brushing her hair.

Much of the anger she'd felt for Travis had mellowed. She hadn't spoken to him since that afternoon in late May when he'd walked away from her, not knowing what he'd left behind. Her main worry these days formed around a possible custody war. Which could be imminent if Ruth Quincy were to discover Hank's birth before Annie graduated college and could fully support him on her own. And even then, Ruth could probably hire a fleet of lawyers who'd drag it all into court, find loopholes, and buy the right to take Hank from her.

Ruth might hate the mother of her grandson, but she'd want him. Annie would do anything to protect her child, even if she had to lie and hide out. Both of which she'd done. Travis might be old enough, but he certainly wasn't mature enough to hold firm against his own mother.

But how sad that Travis missed out on the sweet boy who currently dozed against her mama's shoulder, one chubby hand clutching the front of her sweater. How very sad.

"Annie? What are you going to do, honey?"

She looked up from the neat braid she was securing with one of Susan's stretchy hair bands. "Do? What do you mean, do? About what?"

Her mama glanced down at Hank, then quirked a brow at Annie, who sighed. "You know what I mean."

"Yes, I know what you mean." She stroked her fingers over Hank's flushed cheek. "I'm not going to do anything. You know I can't. I'll stay another week before I head back to get an early start at the bookstore." She stood and gathered the clothing she'd set at the foot of the bed. "I want to see how fall semester goes before I increase my hours at work. Hank loves being with Aunt Nan, so that's one major worry off my mind." She smiled in reassurance. "It's coming together, Mama. It'll be all right."

Her mama flapped a hand in dismissal. "Oh, I know it'll be fine. You'll make it fine, and you'll do great. But sooner or later, someone's going to see Hank. Maybe not in Roanoke, although you never know. But definitely here, Annie. Someone who knows Travis or Ruth, someone who'll put one and one together and make sure the Quincys know what's what. As much as I hate to say it, the longer you stay in town—"

"Mama, I know it's a risk. But I've barely been back to Thompkin the past two years, and I needed this time at home with all of you. I've been careful. Ruth never comes to town. Her phobia seems to be as strong as ever."

"Anyone could see him and call up to Quincy Hall, honey," her mama pointed out. "You only have to look at the boy to know who his daddy is."

Blinking away sudden tears, Annie took her sleeping son and cuddled him in her arms. He sighed into her neck and snuggled as she rocked him gently. Her damp eyes glittered in painful understanding. "Yes, I know. And Ruth will never get her hands on him, Mama, no matter what I have to do. Never."

Later, as she took her bath, she thought back on the vow she'd made just an hour after Hank's birth. She ran a soapy washcloth over her face and recalled the tears she'd shed in the hospital room in Roanoke, from wanting Travis to know he had a son. Wrapped up in a soft blue blanket and sleeping like a tiny angel, Hank was a miracle she needed to share with the father of her child.

Even when her family surrounded her in unquestionable support, it still wasn't easy to pull back from making that phone call. Only her aunt said aloud what every Turner must have thought, as they all watched Hank sleep in her arms.

"He's gorgeous. And I can see he's a Quincy, down to his toes. You think it might not hurt to let his daddy know." Aunt Nan said it right to her face as Annie leaned back against the pillows and tears dampened her cheeks. Aunt Nan shook her head when Annie's drenched eyes met hers pleadingly, hoping for someone to tell her it was all right to make that call. "But you stay away from the phone, girl. Right now, while your emotions are jumping all around, is the worst time to make any kind of decisions."

As always, Aunt Nan had been right. Annie rinsed the soap away and reached for her towel, blotting her face. If some of the moisture on her cheeks came from something other than bath water, no one would know but her.

An hour later, she headed into town, Hank babbling away in his car seat. Thompkin always looked the same to her, and she had to smile as she drove toward downtown. It remained a prosperous a place that held onto its original charm while keeping abreast of modernization and growth. Annie knew the Quincy Legacy was responsible for most of what Thompkin enjoyed. The family had worked hard for their town for many generations. It was an onerous duty for Ronald Quincy, and it would be the same for Travis, when it became his turn to take over.

It was still a great place to live and to raise children. Yet, she had no intention of coming back to Thompkin permanently, not until she could be sure her son was safe from Ruth Quincy.

Chapter 20

He followed her. How could he stop himself? Travis spotted Annie as he left Nimson's Drugstore. She drove a compact blue Honda that rounded the corner of North Main, headed toward Market Street. It was pure luck he'd seen her at all, as his attention had been on slipping his wallet back in his pocket.

Travis adjusted the bill of his baseball cap to shield more of his face. He stayed back, not wanting to arouse Annie's suspicions. Hell, his Beemer was conspicuous enough. He dropped back even further, just in case.

He had no idea what he'd do when she stopped, but he was determined to at least speak to her. He didn't know if she'd listen to what he needed to say, not after a two-year silence on his part. She'd told him not to contact her again, but it was his choice not to push it. It was the only way he could think to keep his mother's hatred from tainting her further.

Two years.

Two years of denying himself even the smallest touch of her in his life, all in the name of keeping her and her family safe from his mother's threats. Without Annie, he was unbearably lonely, but at least he poured most of his concentration into his studies. He would graduate early from Yale, before his twenty-third birthday. He'd crammed three years of classes into two years, no small feat on his part. He hoped the additional year of grad study would speed by just as fast, and he'd be finished.

Then he could inform his mother—and the board of

trustees she now controlled—to go to hell. He could get down on his knees if necessary and beg Annie's forgiveness. Marry her the way they'd always planned to do. And somewhere in the midst of all those plans, he'd push the damned trustees aside and take his rightful place in the Quincy hierarchy. He'd make his dad proud of him. He'd make Annie proud, too.

He was so busy plotting all the ways to impress his loved ones, he almost lost track of Annie. He caught the taillight of her car as it turned off onto the county road that led to Boggy Creek Lane, and Bogg Pond. What the—?

She was going to Bogg Pond. Travis hadn't been back there since their breakup. It held too many bittersweet memories for him, and whenever he came home, he avoided it, and the inevitable pain of remembering happier times spent there with her.

Suddenly Travis couldn't think of a better place to confront Annie.

When she pulled off the lane and onto the rocky berm ringing the north edge of Bogg Pond, he stopped his car near the new growth of high marsh grasses. He eased out from the driver's seat and waited, desperate for his first look at the girl he'd loved for so very long.

She opened her door, stepped out, and flipped her thick braid behind her back as she raised her face to the sky and stretched her arms above her head. Her hair had grown much longer. He could tell it would fall below her waist when loosened from its braid. She'd matured, too. The pretty girl he'd known forever had become a stunning woman.

She spun in a circle, shaded her eyes with a slender hand, in much the same way she'd always done as a girl, when eyeing the calm surface of the water would net her the best pockets to fish for bullhead and pickerel. The memory made him grin.

Then his grin faded into shock when he heard the high,

babyish voice in the quiet air.

"Ma-ma! Owd! Owd, Ma-ma!"

She laughed as she turned toward the back seat, opened the door, and leaned inside. He could hear the love in her voice. Then, she lifted out a baby. Black hair curled riotously over his head. He wore a red jacket and blue jeans. Tiny white shoes completed his outfit. She swung him up into her arms, and he squealed out a happy trill of giggles, his pudgy hands clutching her around the neck.

Travis leaned weakly against the car. Annie had a little boy.

His little boy.

He couldn't wrap his mind around it. He couldn't believe what was right in front of his eyes. And fast on the heels of that disbelief, came the suddenly bitter acknowledgement that she'd kept their baby's birth a secret from him.

As Annie carried his son toward the pond and settled on the large flat rock where they used to fish, Travis pushed away from his car on unsteady legs. He wanted answers. He was damned well going to get them.

It'd been a fun, if exhausting, day. Sylvia, Annie's old boss at the Coffee Hut, served a delicious lunch and monopolized Hank all during the meal. Hank, at his most flirty, loved all the attention he'd gotten from a table full of women. He'd bounced in Sylvia's lap, gnawed on a few of her French fries, and snuggled against her shoulder, his rosy cheek trustingly pressed to her neck.

All too soon, it was time for them to leave. After she dropped Susan and Mama off at home, she decided to drive around a bit. She hadn't done much of that since she'd been back in Thompkin.

It was probably a bad idea when she followed her

impulses and drove out to Bogg Pond. Here she was, trying to get Travis out of her mind, and yet she headed toward the one place in Thompkin truly their own. She'd stayed away from it, half afraid of the memories and also worried she might run into Travis there. Although she doubted he'd really haunt Bogg Pond out of loneliness for her, she figured there was no sense in taking any chances.

She'd missed the uncomplicated goodness of the wild grasses and the grouping of flat rocks she'd stood on to fish. Memories of those casual dates with Travis, summer after summer, hung in the moist air. Maybe those memories were painful, but they were hers to cherish. They'd helped to form her, helped to strengthen her when she was at her lowest point. Whatever she now called her former relationship with the father of her son, Annie would be forever grateful a boy like Travis had once loved her very much.

The thick humidity surrounded her as she stood by the pond. It smelled the same: ripe, overly green, murky. She shielded her eyes and made her customary pass around the entire pond, grinned when she realized she looked for fish clusters the same as she'd done as a child. Some things never changed.

When Hank demanded to be let "owd," her smile broadened into complete happiness as she moved to the back of the car and unfastened her son from his seat. Some things *did* change, and wasn't that a wonderful part of life?

With Hank in her arms, she walked over to the largest flat rock and sat down, snuggling her child as he stared raptly at the rippling water. She bent her cheek to his and laughed when he reached over and wound his fingers into her braid, something he loved to do. She sighed deeply, content, happy to be home for a while longer, happy that Mark and Sissy had decided to come for a visit, too. And the thought of their coming baby, a little nephew or niece she could spoil, added to her happiness. Soon they'd know the joy of being parents—

"Annie."

Focused on her thoughts, at first she barely heard the low voice that spoke her name. She glanced around, but didn't see anyone. Hank rested his head on her shoulder and relaxed against her. She sighed again. It must have been the wind in the reeds she heard.

"Annie—"

Closer that time, and recognizable. Oh, no.

Annie whipped around, and faced Travis for the first time in two years.

Dismay, longing, and a touch of fear swamped her as she looked at him. He seemed wider in the shoulder, leaner through the cheeks, taller. His gaze locked on Hank, then flicked to her—and the expression on his face could only be described as hungry.

The urge to hide overwhelmed her, and she scrambled off the rock. She clutched her baby hard in her arms, prepared to run all the way back to Roanoke if she had to.

She'd often thought of this reunion, whatever it could be called. In her imagination, she'd stand firm and tell the only boy she ever loved he couldn't be a part of his own son's life. And he'd step aside and let her go. He'd understand why.

In reality, there was nowhere to run. There was nowhere to hide and no way to pretend his father hadn't seen Hank, was even now staring at him as if he'd like nothing better than to grab him up and take off with him. She trembled as she pressed Hank's cheek to her shoulder, and met Travis's stunned gaze with defiance in her own. She'd face whatever accusation he flung at her, and then get the hell out of Thompkin with Hank and never come back.

For endless seconds, Travis looked at his son. She knew what he'd see, the strong Quincy resemblance. She battled the trembles, but she could still feel them, deep inside.

"What's his name? How old is he?" Travis's voice held

a hoarse rasp. She edged away when his hand moved as if to reach out and touch. He hastily dropped his arm, and she saw his fingers clench, but she refused to feel guilty. Yet she ached to think she couldn't be sure of his intentions.

Her arms tightened around Hank as she answered his questions, hearing the ring of pride in her words. "His name is Henry. Henry Travis Turner. We call him Hank. And he just turned one in February."

"Turner. He doesn't have my last name?" It was as much a question as a statement. This time when he extended a hand toward his son, Annie allowed it. He touched one of the silky curls that lay against Hank's forehead.

She took a deep breath. "No. He doesn't. I won't apologize for not using your last name on the birth certificate, Travis."

"You hid him from me."

"Yes. I'm not apologizing for that, either."

"Were you ever going to tell me?"

She looked away. "I don't know. Probably not, at least not for a few years." She knew her frank admission wounded him. "You know why I wouldn't have told you."

He released a heavy sigh. "My mother. She'd have been—I don't even know. That's the entire reason. Isn't it?"

Annie nodded and adjusted Hank on her hip, cuddling him closer as he sagged in her arms. Honesty was innate to her, and now that Travis knew most of it, she wouldn't lie to him any longer. "Yes, the biggest part of it. Look, I have to sit down. He's heavy when he sleeps." She moved back to the rock, perched on the rough surface, and rested the baby against her chest. Travis crowded next to her, close enough to touch. He rubbed his finger along Hank's hand.

She wouldn't go easy on Travis. "I've stayed away from Thompkin for a long time. Right after I found out I was pregnant. I finally came back for a visit because I missed my family. I guess it was stupid of me to think you'd never find out about Hank."

It was hard to dredge up the pain from the last time she'd seen him. "When you left that day, I figured I'd never see you again. Maybe I told you to go, but you said you wouldn't stop seeing Catherine Cabot, wouldn't tell your mother where she could stuff her control of you. I ceased to be the most important person in your life. It broke my heart."

She raised a hand to cut him off when he tried to protest. "You can't deny it. You would have continued to see me, but in secret, as if I needed to be hidden away. All of the promises we made to each other didn't seem to mean a thing to you, and that hurt most of all."

"Annie—"

"I'm not through." She hitched the baby higher on her shoulder. "I understood you had to finish what you'd started. I know how important Yale was to you. I wasn't asking you to change your life, Travis, just to keep me in it, and do that out in the open, proud of what we had together. That was all I wanted. Suddenly you seemed to be ashamed of me, and it hurt, badly."

She pressed a hand against Hank's neck to support him as he dozed. "When I found out I was pregnant, I did the only thing I could do to protect my baby. I moved away, and I made a life without you. I'll tell you honestly, if I'd been carrying a girl, I'd have gotten hold of you as soon as I had the ultrasound printout in my hand. Your mama wouldn't have cared one way or another about a little girl. Would she?" Her voice remained calm and matter-of-fact, but her insides quaked as she waited for his response.

"Annie . . ."

"Answer me." She wouldn't take on another speck of guilt. She'd done what was best for Hank, and nothing else mattered. Not her feelings. Not Travis's, either.

He scrubbed a hand over his face, dropped it into his lap. Finally, he admitted, "She might not have cared about a girl. But what could make up for the year I've lost, not knowing my son? What about the two years I lost, of you? I'm trying to understand. I know you had to be scared of going through a pregnancy all alone, even though I'm sure your family helped you. But now that I'm seeing him . . ."

Travis gestured toward Hank. "I want him, Annie. I want both of you. He's my son. You have to let me be his father. And I can't bear to lose you again."

He leaned closer, but she slid sideways on the warm rock, putting a few more feet between them, refusing to allow remorse to fuel regret. What was it Susan said once, right after Hank's birth? "Sperm donation doesn't make a guy some baby's daddy." Annie remembered those words, every time she'd longed to pick up the phone and call Travis.

Now she retorted, "You're his father, but you're not his daddy. He might never have a daddy. I'm prepared to raise him by myself. I'm doing a good job of it, Travis. Don't think otherwise."

She shouldn't be telling him anything personal. She shouldn't trust him. But the need to make him understand her strive toward independence also made her less than cautious. "I've got a partial scholarship to Hollins University, and a student loan takes care of the rest. I'm standing on my own feet and starting to make my own way. In a few weeks, I'll get a head start on my sophomore year and I'm also working at the campus bookstore part-time. My manager adores Hank."

She stroked her son's downy cheek and cradled it against her palm, noting the way Travis followed the path of her hand as if wishing he were the one doing the stroking. She pushed away more remorse.

He looked up with a pained expression. "I don't know what to say, Annie. I'm proud of you, that you've done all of this on your own. But you didn't have to be alone. We could have done it together." Travis brushed his fingers over her cheek, and for a few mad moments she let him get close to her, closer than she knew was wise. Her eyes half closed from the joy of his touch after so long without it.

If only circumstances were different, Travis would be the one who held Hank right now, and she'd sit next to them both, filled with her own pride at the picture father and son made, nestled together on their favorite rock next to Bogg Pond. And she'd wear his ring.

She blinked away the fantasy and concentrated on the reality. Her subtle movement away from Travis's hand wasn't lost on him. She saw the way his jaw clenched. It seemed she couldn't help causing him pain, any more than he'd done to her in the past.

"You can't support either of us, Travis." She shook her head as he reacted to her bluntness. "No, you can't. We both know it. Still under your mother's control, aren't you? Don't bother to deny it." She waved away his protest. "I've started putting away some money now and then. I doubt you can say the same thing."

"Annie, you don't understand—"

"It doesn't matter. You don't have much claim on this child. And your mother has none. She'll never take him from me. You'd better understand that, right up front."

"She's his grandmother. I'm his father." Travis stood, his face almost even with hers as she sat on the rock and held Hank so tightly. "There are rights to consider—"

"*No.*" She was determined not to panic. "I remember the look in your mother's eyes the night of the Quincy holiday party. And at the hospital, the very next day. Hate, Travis. That's what I saw. I'll never allow my child to be exposed to hatred." She blew out a shaky breath. "As for your rights, I don't know if I could trust you not to take Hank to your mother and stand back as she tries to keep him from me."

His mouth fell open, as if stunned that she would think him capable of doing something so underhanded. "I wouldn't! You know me better than that."

Her lips quirked sadly. "I thought I did. I'm not so sure, anymore."

She soothed Hank when he awoke a bit and snuffled, a sign of fussiness. His eyes opened briefly, and he offered a drowsy smile, revealing several pearly baby teeth, before he snuggled closer to his mother and shoved two fingers into his mouth. She hummed as she rocked him and his eyes fluttered shut, asleep again.

She laid her cheek on Hank's soft hair and watched Travis through a veil of blurred tears she could no longer hold back. "He's all I have. With my family's help, I've been able to spend most of my time with him. I'm a good mother. The first thing your mama would do, if she knew about him, would be to hire a bunch of fancy lawyers and take me to court for custody." She wiped the dampness from her cheek as a few tears spilled over. "This is your heir, Travis. She doesn't want me in the family, but I'd lay odds she'd want Hank. And she'd find a way to get him."

Without another word, Annie rose and turned toward her car. Travis grasped the sleeve of her jacket to forestall her and demanded, "Where are you going? Annie, we have things we need to talk about."

She pulled away from his hold, reaching the car a second before he did. He opened the back door, and she fastened Hank in his car seat. Travis gazed at his son, but made no move to touch him again. Instead, he repeated, "We have to talk, Annie, the sooner, the better."

Weary of confrontation, all Annie wanted to do was go home to her parents. She clung to what scraps of strength she had left. "Not now, Travis. Let it rest a few days. I don't know what else there is to say, but I can't deal with it right now."

It was difficult to remain firm, yet her voice held steady. She tucked her hands in her pockets so Travis wouldn't see how her fingers shook. "I'm asking you to keep Hank to yourself. I'm asking you to tell no one, not even Martha. I'm only eighteen, Travis. You may be coming up on twenty-two, but you're still under your mother's financial thumb. I know darned well she has a lot of control over you and your life, your future. And I may not like it, but I do understand why you didn't want to get on her bad side two years ago."

Looking into his set face, she couldn't tell whether or not her words got through to him. "If your mother wanted to, she could destroy my life. I couldn't fight her, and my family is too poor to help. You're not the kind of man who could take care of us. I'm sorry if that hurts your feelings, but you know it's true."

While he remained silent, gazing at her with a stark look of misery, she slid into the front seat and rolled down the window. "I'll keep you posted on how Hank is doing. I'll think about having a talk with you, that much I can promise, but right now I have to go."

Before she could start the car, he placed his hand on her door. "Annie? I'm glad he's got your eyes."

His words made it easier to offer him a smile. "I'm glad he's got everything else, of you."

Chapter 21

As soon as Annie got back to the house, she carried Hank upstairs and settled him in his crib. He sighed once and snuggled into his blanket. He'd nap for at least another hour, and she'd need all of that hour, and probably more, to talk to her folks. Maybe they'd be able to get her past the panic she could no longer fight.

Downstairs in the kitchen, Mark's deep voice and Mama's soft tones resonated. Annie took the stairs slowly, her thoughts in turmoil. The unexpected confrontation with Travis at Bogg Pond had thrown her off-balance. If she'd known she would face him, she could have better prepared. But now she felt vulnerable, in spite of her strong words.

Coming home for this length of time was a gamble. In Roanoke, she always felt safe. She'd never worried these past two years with Aunt Nan. She hadn't run into a single person she knew, outside her family, and it wasn't as if she'd lived the life of a hermit and hidden herself away. Nobody in Roanoke ever pointed at her and exclaimed, "Look, there goes that girl who had a baby out of wedlock." It was a big place, and no one cared what anyone else did.

But Thompkin was different. You couldn't expect an entire town to keep quiet about a baby who looked like the twin of that town's leading son.

"Annie, you're finally back. What took you so long?" Her mama jumped up as soon as Annie walked into the kitchen, and poured her a tall glass of lemonade from the pitcher on the counter. Annie moved behind Mark's chair and leaned down to give him a hug and to press her cheek to his. He squeezed the hand she rested on his shoulder.

She sank into the chair across from Mama's, accepted the lemonade, and baldly announced, "Travis is in town. He saw Hank. What am I going to do?"

At Cabot Estate, Catherine sat on the rear veranda and let the glider rock her, absently pushing off with one foot. Her attention wasn't on the lovely view of the formal gardens or the tinkling waterfall that graced her mother's prized koi pond.

She'd seen the child—a boy, she felt certain—with her own eyes. And she struggled to deny who the father was.

It shouldn't have come as a complete surprise after all, that Travis would have sex with that Annie Turner. He was a healthy male, and men sowed their wild oats before they married. It was expected of them. She'd known Travis would sow a few of his. Judging by the age of the baby Annie had lifted from the back seat of that little blue car parked in front of the Coffee Hut, she would have been about sixteen when they did it, made love, had the sex.

Well, why not? They'd probably been engaged by then. If she'd been in Annie's shoes and someone like Travis kissed her, asked for more than a hug, Catherine doubted she could resist.

It was pure bad luck she'd been right across the street in her Audi, pathetically watching for Travis, as usual. She'd called up to Quincy Hall to speak with him and one of the day maids told her Travis was in town on errands for Martha. The maid provided a few places where Catherine might find him. So she'd driven into town like a lovesick idiot, hoping to see him.

Well, she hadn't found Travis, but she'd gotten an eyeful, anyway. She'd seen Annie and her baby enter the

Coffee Hut. Shaken, Catherine didn't bother to stick around. As she drove back home, her hands trembled on the steering wheel.

A baby changed everything. Travis couldn't know, or else he'd have already said something to her. He'd be so proud, he'd probably be unable to contain himself. She knew what it would mean to him.

If he hadn't yet heard about the baby, then of course Ruth was ignorant of the child's existence as well. Although, how anyone could hide in Thompkin and not be discovered by the plethora of busybodies who lived here, Catherine hadn't a clue. Unless Annie somehow found a way to have the child in secret.

That was it. It had to be. She stopped the glider abruptly, certain she had the right answer. Annie couldn't have had the baby anywhere close to Thompkin. Her family still lived here, but that didn't mean anything. They must have sent her away to have the child, and raise it, probably ashamed of her behavior.

And now she'd come back, perhaps to confront them? Make them give her a hand with the child? Maybe ask them for money? It was impossible to say. She didn't know Annie or her family. Her limited knowledge of the Turners came from what Travis had told her over the years.

If Travis loved her, then Annie had to be a decent person. But Catherine found it tough to think of her in any kind of positive light. Even though Travis and Annie had parted, it was painfully obvious to her that Annie still held his heart.

She left the glider and made her way inside. Sooner or later, Travis would find out he had a son. She sure didn't want to be the one who told him, but he'd be home for at least two more weeks. People here in Thompkin couldn't keep anything to themselves.

Maybe the next time she went to town, folks would

look at *her* in pity, although Ruth made no secret about her suitability for Travis. She could have no better champion on her side.

Except she had too much pride to resort to such means in order to get Travis for herself. She wanted him to come to her willingly, because he cared for her, desired a life with her. She had enough pride to be wanted only for herself.

Didn't she?

"I have to go back to Aunt Nan's. Right away." Annie pushed the untouched plate of food aside.

Her daddy poured another cup of coffee and sat next to her, wrapping his arm around her as a bolster and a comforter. While she leaned into him, Mark bounced a giggling Hank on his knee and remarked, "His mama might not even know, Annie. I'd bet Travis would keep his word and not tell her."

She raised her head from the security of her daddy's shoulder. "But someone else will. Anyone could have seen me. How stupid could I be? I should never have gone into town with Hank. I have to leave, tonight."

"You can't drive all night long with a baby in the back seat and trying to stay awake enough to avoid running off the road. Use your head." Susan shoved a plate of fried chicken toward her. "And for heaven's sake, eat something. You look like you're about to fall over."

"No one's going anywhere tonight," her mama declared. "I'll call Aunt Nan and tell her we'll drive you back first thing tomorrow. Your father has the day off anyhow, and I'll come with you. Susan can follow us in your car, and we'll all go home later on tomorrow afternoon." She bustled around the table and poured more lemonade, stopping next to Annie's chair long enough to rub her arm soothingly.

Annie enjoyed the loving caress, but her mind was

made up. "No. That's too much. I can't let you take a day away from Mark and Sissy. It's not fair. I can drive myself. I promise I'll eat something." She picked up a chicken wing and bit into it with forced enthusiasm. She chewed, and with her mouth half-full, assured, "I'll even take extra vitamins and get ten hours of sleep, I swear." She swallowed the wad of meat and gestured with the remaining wing. "I have to get out of here before there's trouble."

"And then what?" Susan demanded. "Once Ruth knows, do you really think she wouldn't find you and come to Roanoke to harass you? Agoraphobia or not, I guarantee the thought of getting her hands on her grandson would make her hop into the nearest limo and run right on over to land on Aunt Nan's doorstep."

When her mother clucked her tongue at Susan for her bluntness, she retorted, "Sorry, but we have to face facts. Once that woman knows, we need to be prepared. Whether you stay here or you go back to Roanoke, you have to be ready to fight."

"So what do I do? Wait for her lawyers to come to the door and hand out subpoenas?" Agitated and unable to sit still any longer, Annie jumped to her feet. Hank clapped his hands and held his arms out for her, but she was too upset to hold him.

"Yes. That's exactly what you do. You wait. *We* wait. And whether at Nan's or here, we get ourselves a lawyer of our own." Her daddy reached for her hand, pulled at her until she moved back to his side and curled into his lap. He stroked her hair as he jerked a chin toward the phone in the entryway. "Mary, call Nan right now. Let her know what's going on. I'll contact a lawyer tomorrow. And I'll take some money out from savings."

"Daddy, no!" Annie sat up and regarded him in dismay.

He gave her a squeeze. "Yes. Why do you think I've been working overtime on weekends? I've been saving the extra. We really haven't needed it, knock on wood, and I figured it would come in handy sooner or later. I guess it was sooner, huh?"

"I don't want you to use savings, Daddy. Not for this. I wouldn't feel right, letting you do this."

"You're not letting us. We're doing this because we want to. All of us," he emphasized. He caught her quivering chin with one big hand and raised her troubled eyes to his.

Annie frowned in confusion. "What do you mean, 'all of us?'"

Sissy answered in her soft, shy voice. "It was Mark's idea. We've all been saving. We started right after Hank was born. Just in case there was trouble." She blushed. "I sold things on eBay. It was fun."

"I waitressed for a while, over at Morgan's." Susan named a tavern between Thompkin and Hanover Corner. "I saved all my tips. If we didn't need the extra, then Hank would have a decent nest egg for college."

As Annie's eyes widened in surprise, Sissy hastily added, "Mark did short-order cooking at this eatery right outside the base. Danny caddied for a while at that fancy golf club in Weston and sent in his tips, too. Frankie and Bobby sent money. I'd bet we have almost five thousand dollars, maybe more. We called it the 'Hank Fund.'"

Her mama added, "Aunt Nan has money set aside, too. With her contribution, we have more than enough for a good lawyer. You're not to worry, honey. We'll let those Quincys know exactly who they're up against."

Her daddy massaged Annie's back as she burst into tears. She wiped her streaming eyes and met the determined gazes of her family, one by one. Mark winked at her. Susan dashed away her own tears and affirmed, "Hank belongs to all of us. Whatever we have to do, that's what we're going to do."

Chapter 22

In the informal parlor adjacent to her study, Ruth sipped the last of her herbal tea. She'd permitted herself a lazy day, comfortable in her casual pantsuit, her hair loose on her shoulders. Compiling a list of prospective wedding guests was a perfect task to while away an afternoon.

Tomorrow Janice and Catherine were expected for luncheon, and she anticipated getting a large chunk of the initial wedding preparations out of the way. She still had to push Travis in the correct direction and have him propose to Catherine. Ruth wasn't without feeling. She understood that a sensitive and romantic girl such as Catherine would expect Travis to ask her while down on one knee, and not informed by the prospective groom's mother that a wedding would take place in under a year.

To that end, she was determined to make it happen. The birthday party, scheduled only four days away, would be public enough to assure Travis's compliance. If she played it cleverly enough, Ruth would make the announcement herself during the party.

A sound in the outer foyer caught her attention. She hurriedly rose from the carved secretary desk. She recognized those footfalls: Travis. The boy had an irritating habit of disappearing for hours, just when she needed him to sit down and listen to her. Ruth knew he did it purposely. She also knew he'd walk right by her and not bother to come in. He'd rush through the house to see his father, but he'd never done the same for her

.

It didn't matter. She wouldn't let it. Her hide was tougher than that.

"Travis, I wish to speak with you." She stood in the parlor doorway and observed the way her son stiffened his shoulders as soon as he heard her voice. She pushed down the twinge of hurt at his attitude, and remained calm as he turned and faced her with a smooth, blank expression.

Oh, she read his thoughts so easily. The last thing in the world he'd want would be a chat with his mother. The subtle lift of his chin, the chill in his eyes, told her better than words just what her own son thought of her. She watched him take a deep breath, and she tensed, in spite of her determination to present a placid, unaffected front.

"Mother, I don't have time right now. I have plans, and I'm running late." Travis took a step toward the stairway as he spoke.

Ruth's eyes narrowed. He was lying, she could tell. Well, he wouldn't get away with it. They had much to discuss, and she wanted everything settled this evening, with no more avoidance. She crossed her arms and stared him down. "I'm sure there's nothing on your schedule more important than what we need to discuss. I'm prepared to give you fifteen minutes to freshen up. Then I expect you in my study."

"I can't. I told you, I have plans." Another step toward the stairs.

She had to concentrate to keep the anger from her tone. "And whom do you meet that would be more important than time spent with your mother?"

Oh, shit. Travis shoved both hands in the front pockets of his jeans as they clenched into fists. He despised these little power plays. Lately they'd increased, and his level of patience was just about gone. He searched for a name he knew his mother would accept, and of course only one came to mind.

"I have a date with Catherine. We haven't seen each other in a while." He was lying through his teeth. He'd forgotten when Catherine had told him she'd be back in Thompkin. He figured she'd already made it in, since she was meticulous to a fault and would want to give herself plenty of time to settle in and "prepare" for whatever the hell his mother and hers planned for them.

He wanted to tug on his own hair in frustration. It was bad enough he'd now have to spend the evening with Catherine when all he wanted to do was see his dad, then grab some time alone and think about Annie and Hank.

His mention of Catherine had his mother beaming. She walked swiftly toward him with her hands outstretched, and grasped at him when he didn't reach for her first. Giving his shoulders a squeeze, she said, "Well, how wonderful. I had no idea you were seeing Catherine tonight. Her mother never said a thing about it during our chat earlier today."

Yeah, I'd just bet she didn't. Travis pulled away from his mother slowly, so as to avoid the standard pout she usually gave him when he dodged her outward signs of affection. With a vague nod in her direction, he climbed the stairs, reluctance in his every step.

Now he'd have to call over to the Cabot Estate, request a date from Catherine, fill an evening with whatever he could, when the only thing in the world he wanted was to have Annie in his arms. Morose, he shut himself inside his suite and flopped on his bed.

The day's revelations left him depressed and aching. Worried, too, that Annie would take off again. She'd given him her word that she'd get in touch with him soon so they could talk. She'd also lied to him for two years. How could he trust her? How could he be sure she'd let him see his son again?

With an oath, Travis took out his new cell phone. He punched in Catherine's number and tried to think of something to do with her. Something very unromantic.

Catherine rushed around her bedroom, trying on and discarding outfits, while her mother sat on the edge of the bed and chattered about china patterns and the advantages of Wedgwood over Sevres.

"Mother, for heaven's sake, it's only a date. It's not as if we haven't gone out before." Catherine felt jittery with nerves, and her mother didn't help matters any. She wriggled into a deep blue sheath and gauged its overall effect in the full-length mirror.

"Not that dress, darling. Nobody wears linen until after Memorial Day. And this is much more important than just a date, Cathy. Why, it's the first time Travis called you of his own accord—" Her mother pressed her fingers over her mouth as if realizing the significance of her words.

Catherine turned to her with a thunderous frown. "What did you say? What do you mean? What have you done, Mother?" The three sentences shot out like bullets.

"I haven't done a thing. I don't know what you mean." Her mother got to her feet and backed away. "I have a few things to do. Enjoy your evening." She made a dash for the door, but Catherine was faster. Dress still unzipped and barefoot, she barred the way and confronted her mother, whose sudden flush reddened her cheeks.

"Tell me right now, or I swear I'll never see Travis again under any circumstances. I mean it, Mother." Catherine crossed her arms and waited.

With a sigh, her mother trudged back to the bed and sat down. Flinging her hands out in entreaty, she blustered, "Now, Cathy, it was for your own good. I could see how much you love Travis. Haven't I always tried to give you everything you want?"

Frustrated, Catherine groaned. "You can't go around giving love where there isn't any! You can't invent something that isn't there. And you can't force someone to feel what is impossible for him to feel. Just because Travis chose to call me without his mother's knowledge and permission doesn't mean he's ready to fall on his knees, flip a ring out of his pocket, and shove it on my finger!"

While her mother sat in shock, Catherine yanked off the linen dress and wrapped herself in the chenille robe at the foot of her bed. She tied the sash, then reached for her phone and started punching in numbers.

"Who are you calling?"

She met her mother's suspicious gaze with a deceptively bland expression. "I'm canceling the date. I don't believe I want to see Travis tonight."

With a gasp, her mother slapped the phone out of Catherine's hand. "Are you out of your mind? You have him calling you, Cathy, willingly. His mother had nothing to do with it this time. I feel badly at my own duplicity, but think about it. I had nothing to do with it, either. Travis wants to see you. Here's your chance, and you think to toss it away out of some silly anger against two mothers who only want your happiness? I don't understand you."

Catherine whirled away from the reproach she saw on her mother's face. She'd perfected the expression over the years, using it whenever she wanted Catherine to bend to her will. She loved her mother dearly, but the woman was a relentless steamroller. And without doubt, she could get to the heart of the matter in a hurry.

Yes, she wanted to marry Travis. She was probably desperate enough to take him knowing he did not, could not, love her in return, at least not as long as his heart still belonged to Annie Turner.

But could she marry him without telling him he was a father, if indeed he didn't yet know Annie had given birth to his child? Could she cash in on his mother's single-minded determination to have Catherine herself as a daughter-in-law?

She just didn't know. And this continuous pushing made it more stressful for her.

"Are you listening to me?" Her mother grasped her arm and shook her. Catherine blinked and pulled her arm away. Picking up the discarded linen dress, she wriggled into it, and then presented her back, silently demanding to be zipped up.

"No, you should really wear that dark green cashmere I bought you—"

Catherine sent one narrowed glare over her shoulder. Her mother pressed her lips together and said no more.

Dressed at last, Catherine slipped on her shoes while her mother drifted around the bedroom, looking as if she badly wanted to speak. Another firm glare from Catherine kept her silent. She picked up the clutch purse that matched her dress and caught her mother's eyes. "I don't know what time I'll be home. But I want you to stay off the phone with Ruth, do you understand? I am teetering on the edge of my patience, and I promise you, Travis is right there with me, on the edge of his. You have *got* to let us work things out— whatever there is to work out—between us. For God's sake, no more meddling."

Ignoring the self-righteous huff behind her, she marched down the stairs and out the front door. She let loose a huge sigh of relief at finally being alone. Butterflies threatened to revolt inside her stomach, her usual reaction when she anticipated seeing Travis.

This time, she needed to decide whether or not to say anything to him about what she knew.

And whether or not to speak of it to Ruth.

Travis drove through Thompkin, noting the clusters of people downtown on a weeknight. The last thing he wanted to do was escort Catherine around when he knew how many busybodies milled about. People would have them engaged and picking out china patterns, for Christ's sake. He made a quick turn, took a side street, and caught Market Avenue, out of town.

Next to him, Catherine sat quietly, hands clasped together, staring out the side window. Aside from a soft greeting, she hadn't spoken. Travis stole a quick glance at her calm face.

He cleared his throat, and she turned toward him. She parted her lips to speak, hesitated, and then offered, "Travis, you don't have to take me anywhere. I know your mother has been putting pressure on you, and I figured you only asked me out to get away from her, um, interference. Really, I don't mind."

"Catherine, no. I called because I wanted to. Although I will admit, getting away from my mother is a side benefit. I sure can't lie about that." He grinned when one side of her mouth turned up in a brief smile. "I thought we'd drive to Weston, maybe stop at Maison for dinner. I'm not exactly dressed for it." He indicated his casual shirt and black denim jeans. "But they'll probably let us in."

"I'd rather have a pizza. I'm not in the mood for fancy. When I'm home, I never get to eat pizza because Mother thinks it's a peasant's meal."

"Yeah, that sounds familiar. But Martha makes a mean pizza and she'll bake one once in a while just to piss my mother off." He downshifted and caught the expressway outside of town, heading toward Weston.

"Your mother is a wonderful woman, Travis." There was no censure in her voice.

"No. She isn't. She's cold and manipulative and bitter and unbending. She's given me nothing but grief since I was twelve years old, and the only buffer I ever had against her, my dad, is now—unaware." He swallowed painfully. "Gone."

"Travis, no."

"Yes. And my mother has just taken over. You know what it's like. You have a mother who rolls right over your wants and choices, don't you? I've seen Janice Cabot in action. At least your mother genuinely loves you and wants you to be happy."

"Your mother wants the same thing for you." The short, pithy expletive he spit out halted anything else she might have said, and she settled back in her seat with a distressed expression on her face. He cursed himself for making her feel uncomfortable.

She drew in a ragged breath. Damn it, he'd hurt her feelings. They needed to clear the air, somehow needed to settle what was between them.

And what so obviously wasn't.

There was a sign up ahead indicating a rest area in three miles. Before he could suggest they stop there for a while, she pointed to it. "Can you pull into that next rest stop? I would like to talk to you about something."

"Sure."

Five minutes later, they were parked in the deserted rest area. He left the car running and turned toward her, waiting for her to speak.

A huge lump of what seemed like desert sand embedded itself in her throat as she looked at him. He was so beautiful. There was no other word for it. She could remember as a child feeling as if she'd been knocked sideways with a lightening bolt every time their parents brought them together for a play date. She'd only been eight years old, but even that young, she'd wanted to be near Travis Quincy. At least she was smart enough now to understand he'd be unhappy and resentful if their mothers succeeded in forcing them into a relationship he didn't want.

Her scattered thoughts were interrupted by his firm, "Catherine, you wanted to stop and talk. You can say anything to me. You should know that by now."

She felt herself flush, tried to keep her focus and not slide into a deep puddle right in her seat because she had his undivided attention. Twisting her fingers together, she searched for a vague opening to what she knew needed airing, and instead found herself blurting, "I saw Annie Turner in town yesterday, carrying a baby. I think it's your baby."

Immediately she clapped her hands over her mouth in horror. Oh, Lord.

But he just nodded. "I know. I saw Annie yesterday, too. And yes. He's mine."

In spite of her best efforts, a tear slipped down her cheek. Then another. She cleared her throat. "Are you glad about it, Travis? It's so hard to think of you as a father. Are you and Annie going to—will you—"

"Are we getting married? I asked Annie to marry me two years ago. She still has my engagement ring. Yes, I want to marry her. I would have married her the night I gave her the ring, if it had been at all possible." The certainty in his voice couldn't be doubted.

"What about your mother? Does she know about the baby?"

"No, she doesn't. And I have to ask you to keep quiet about this, Catherine. Please don't tell anyone, especially your parents. I don't know what my mother might do when she finds out. For all I know, she'd sue for custody and have Annie declared an unfit mother."

Shocked, Catherine exclaimed, "She wouldn't do that! Would she?"

"She might. I would put nothing past her, given the way she feels about Annie." He leaned his head back against the seat, a sign of weariness. She longed to reach out to him, offer some kind of reassurance, comfort. He wouldn't welcome it from her, though. She clasped her hands together to keep from doing just that. More tears pricked her eyes and slid down her face.

He turned in his seat, and she quickly wiped at her cheeks. She didn't want him to see her crying and feel sorry for her. Pity from Travis would be too awful to take. He'd never encourage her when there was no hope of a future between them. These last few minutes of revelation between them brought home to her like nothing else, how hopeless her dreams truly were.

Chapter 23

Annoyed at the intrusive knock on her study door, Ruth called, "Come in."

Bette stepped into the room. "Mrs. Quincy, Mr. Marley is here to see you."

Ruth looked up from the pile of notes and folders on her desk and frowned at the young day maid. "Did he call ahead for an appointment?" When Bette shook her head, Ruth sighed impatiently. "All right. Send him in."

Blast it, she just found the perfect wedding invitation. She'd been about to call Janice and tell her all about it. Now it would have to wait. Dan Marley, her most trusted employee, didn't make a habit of dropping by for some frivolous reason.

A minute later Dan entered her study, and Ruth waved him to a seat. "Come in, Dan." She regarded him quizzically. "Is everything all right with Dorothy?" Dan's wife suffered from a congenital heart condition, and Ruth knew the poor woman had her good and bad days.

"She's doing quite well, Ruth. In fact, she went to brunch on Sunday with some of the Garden Guild ladies. They asked about you." He offered a somewhat harried smile that she returned, even as she wondered why he seemed shaken. It was so unlike him.

Social pleasantries over, he moved toward the door and locked it, before he took the chair closest to her desk. Her eyebrows shot up in surprise at his actions, but she waited for him to speak.

He didn't waste any time. "I'm sorry for not calling

first, Ruth. I know you're busy. But I have something urgent to share with you. When Dorothy was in town on Sunday, she saw Annie Turner over on Main Street carrying a black-haired child, about a year or so old. Do you know anything about this?"

Ruth gasped and her hands gripped the edge of the desk. She half-rose from her seat, then sank back into the rich leather as shock rendered her lightheaded.

He shook his head and muttered, "Apparently you didn't." He hurried to the small sideboard and fetched a glass, poured a measure of brandy in it, and brought it to her. "Here. Drink it." He waited until she'd taken a few sips and set the glass down with fingers that trembled.

Her tongue felt thick. "A child. Boy or girl?"

"A boy, Dorothy was fairly certain. She said the child was wearing a jacket and pants."

Ruth drained the rest of her brandy and motioned for Dan to pour her another. While he complied, she strove for outward calm, unwilling to reveal further turmoil in front of Dan. But it was difficult not to react to such a bombshell.

A child with black hair. She turned as he handed her the drink. "Was she sure? Heaven knows that Turner girl could have easily become pregnant by any number of young men."

"I don't know, Ruth. She just said the girl was holding a baby with the same hair color as Travis. They went into the Coffee Hut, which she thought was strange because the Hut is closed on Sunday. That's all. She was curious as to whether or not the child could possibly be Travis's, but you know Dorothy isn't a gossip. She merely told me so I could in turn inform you."

He remained quiet as Ruth tried to deal with her shock and distress. She could feel a damned migraine coming on as well, which didn't help matters any.

Finally, she raised her head and pinned him with a determined stare. "Say nothing more about this, not even to your wife."

"Should I—"

"*No*. Nothing, you'll do nothing. I'll check into it myself." She rose from her seat with admirable calm—considering her insides felt as if they were being ripped out of her—and saw Dan out with a dismissive assurance and vague thanks for his diligence. Although he looked a bit bewildered at her haste, he departed without protest.

Alone, she locked the door and took perhaps three steps before her knees gave out. She collapsed onto the leather settee across from her desk. All her satisfaction from poring over wedding invitations drained right out of her as she processed what Dan had told her.

Intolerable. Impossible. *Unthinkable*.

That her son would actually *bed* a Turner, and get her pregnant. That she in turn *dared* to actually give birth to it! Abomination. Ruth couldn't even bear to think of it.

Then, she gave herself a firm shake. She *had* to think of it. She had to consider this baby was a result of Travis's sexual escapade with the Turner girl.

What on earth he'd ever seen in that skinny, homely child, when he could have on his arm a lovely young woman like Catherine . . . Ruth had never understood his single-minded infatuation with those horrid Turners.

She moaned aloud. Would she never be free of the name? Twenty-five years, and she still sometimes awoke in tears from nightmares, feeling Franklin Turner's hands on her.

As long as there was a Turner in her town, she'd never be safe. Even after Travis married Catherine and settled into his rightful place here at Quincy Hall, Ruth wouldn't be free of that family's taint. Not as long as such trash lived here.

Not as long as Annie Turner held any level of fascination for her son.

She buried her face in her hands, gave in to the weakness

of tears. And now there was a baby to consider. God, why her? Why was she cursed with such a contrary, rebellious, and careless son?

Young men often forgot to practice safe sex in the heat of their passion, she knew this. And although utterly mortifying, a pregnancy could have been handled discreetly with a quick abortion. They'd all have continued with their lives, no one the wiser.

Her head snapped up as she suddenly realized something vital: *Travis didn't know.* He couldn't know, otherwise he'd have come to her, would have found a way to rub that kind of knowledge right in her face. He'd have used it, wouldn't he, to forge a wedge between his silly desires and her plans for his future. Travis wouldn't have been able to resist thwarting her.

Think. It might be a girl. A girl would pose little threat to the Quincy name.

A boy, however—what a disaster. The child would legally be the next Quincy Heir. It could be denied, of course, but Ruth wasn't stupid. DNA tests could prove it easily enough, and she'd be forced to acknowledge the child as Travis's son and heir. The board of trustees, fond of Travis, thought he could do no wrong. They might tut-tut his impulsive behavior, but they'd welcome the child. And regardless of her feelings on the matter, she would be forced to recognize the child's mother as having a place within the Quincy Legacy.

No. She could not, would not, accept such an infiltration by Annie Turner into their lives.

Ruth jerked to her feet. Her temples now throbbed and she rubbed furiously to alleviate the pain. No Turners, that was the first rule. The child would have to be claimed as a Quincy, as soon as possible. Which meant Travis, as the father, needed full custody.

As soon as she thought about it, Ruth discounted it with

a frustrated wave of her hand. No court would give a young college boy sole custody of a baby. It was ridiculous to even think of it.

But—

She steepled her fingers under her chin, considering. A court would give custody to that child's paternal grandmother, once said court saw proof of its mother's unsuitability and the emotional immaturity of its father. A court would award custody to the matriarch of one of the most influential and powerful families in the state of Virginia.

Ruth straightened her spine and smoothed back her upswept hair. It was time to flex some of that power, and she knew just whom to call.

Chapter 24

Travis drove by Annie's house three times. He'd resisted the temptation for so long, knowing if he gave in, then he'd stop and knock on the door. He'd beg anyone answering that door to tell him where Annie had gone. So he'd stayed away from this side of town for almost two years.

He knuckled his gritty eyes. Thoughts of Annie and Hank made for several sleepless nights. Worried about his mother's inevitable reaction to Hank's existence, he drove himself nuts over what she would do to Annie and her family if she decided to take legal action. He knew how her mind worked: if she wanted Hank, she'd figure out a way to get him, no matter who she trod on or hurt in the process.

Sometime before sunrise, Travis found a small and ugly knot inside himself, a person he didn't want to recognize, wondering if his mother could help him gain his son. She had power and the financial influence necessary to win in court. If Annie tried to run with Hank, his mother would find them. As the day lightened outside, he broke out in an actual sweat when he replayed his thoughts. He sat up in bed and dropped his head into his hands.

What the hell was the *matter* with him? Had he learned nothing from watching the way his mother operated, the way she took over and manipulated? Did he honestly think she'd let him obtain custody of his child, without controlling everything herself? He had to be out of his mind.

Feeling an overwhelming need to be away from Quincy Hall, he'd sprang from his bed and hurriedly dressed. If he stayed there any longer, he'd go insane.

Now, hours later, Travis parked across the street and killed the engine, staring at the weathered old house. For all its air of outer neglect, the yard was raked and nicely green, and there was no clutter on the old porch. Flowers bloomed along the front and sides, a mixture of lingering tulips and budding columbine, clumps of primroses. Lilac bushes, Mary's pride and joy, dotted the borders of the lawn area.

He'd spent so many wonderful hours in that house. All the meals he'd eaten there, devouring Mary's delicious cooking. Surrounded by Annie and her brothers, with Susan trading insults and jokes, as she'd do with any other member of her family. Henry would wink at him as they bickered over the last spoonful of peach cobbler. Mary would slide a piece of corn pone from her plate to his with the insistence she was too full to eat it.

And Annie would hold his hand, laugh with him, her brown eyes glowing with happiness at how easily her family accepted him. They gave him what he'd been starved for. Not necessarily home-cooked meals, but love. He'd enjoyed those meals, but he'd needed the love, and they'd been more than generous to him. They made him an honorary Turner, and he'd pushed them all away, just as he'd pushed Annie away through his own cowardice.

And now she might lose Hank. With a groan of despair, Travis leaned his head on the steering wheel.

"Travis?" The voice and the knock on his partially open window startled him. He sat up and blinked at Henry Turner, who stood next to the car with a concerned look in his eyes. "What's wrong, son?"

Travis stifled a sigh as he opened his door and stepped out. He hadn't a clue what excuse to offer as to why he'd been in effect staking out the house.

Dressed in old, loose-fitting clothes, Henry was as dear and familiar to him as his own father. And when he curved an arm around Travis in a hug, he felt as if he were fourteen years old again.

Suddenly Travis was holding on with two hands fisted in Henry's shirt, soaking it with hot tears.

"Travis, whatever it is, it'll be all right. Come on in. Have a cup of coffee and a piece of Mary's apple pie, and then you tell me what's wrong, okay?" Henry urged him across the street while Travis blotted his damp face on his sleeve.

Once they stepped onto the porch, Travis hesitated. "Annie might not want to see me."

Henry took his hand and pulled him inside the cool interior of the small foyer. "She's not here right now. Come sit at the table. You look pretty rough."

He pushed Travis toward the kitchen and settled him at the table. He reached into a cupboard for a plate and a mug, poured a cup of coffee and set it in front of him, then found a knife and unwrapped the pie. Two generous slices were already missing and Henry cut another wide slab and laid it on a plate for Travis. He added a fork and a paper napkin. "Here, eat."

The pie, packed with apples and brown sugar syrup, had a light, flaky crust. The fragrance of tangy fruit and sweet spice called to him like a siren song. Travis recalled many times when he'd eaten his share of one of Mary's pies. Slowly, he picked up the fork and cut into the pie, lifted a chunk of it to his mouth and almost broke down again when the familiar taste exploded on his tongue.

Travis ate four large bites before he set down his fork and gulped half his coffee. He had to tell Annie's father what he suspected would happen as soon as his mother found out about Hank. He had to warn them to expect serious trouble up ahead. And he had to decide fast what his role in the upcoming battle would be.

He parted his lips to speak, but before he could say a word, there was a commotion at the door. Susan darted into the kitchen, her blue eyes ablaze with fury. She skidded to a halt in front of Travis and swung her fists up in a defensive pose. Her voice lashed out, cold and rough.

"What the hell are *you* doing here, Quincy? Haven't you caused enough trouble for Annie?"

"*Susan!*" Henry's voice snapped, uncharacteristically firm, and Susan lowered her hands and pressed her lips together. She continued to glare at Travis, who paled and got to his feet, preparing to flee. Henry gripped his shoulder in reassurance. Susan huffed out a last warning growl as Henry pointed at her with the index finger of his free hand. It was enough to make her subside. He pointed to the empty chair next to him, and she flopped down on the seat.

"I should go." Travis tried to ease out from under Henry's hand and found out just how strong the older man was.

"No, I think you should stay, Travis. You drove over here for a reason. Judging by the state of your emotions when I came up to your car, I'd say you need to talk. Now's as good a time as any."

"But, Daddy—"

Henry sent Susan a quelling glance. "Quiet. If you don't want to hear, you can always go up to your room."

"I'm not a three-year-old any longer! You can't send me to my room."

"Oh, can't I?" His voice deepened, low and silky. Even Susan could surely hear the command behind it. She slumped in the chair and offered no further disruption.

"Now, then. Travis, why don't you tell us what's going on? Whatever it is, son, it can be dealt with. You know that, don't you?" Henry urged Travis back into his seat and sat beside him, his eyes steady and warm.

Travis couldn't hold that loving gaze. "I know about Hank. I know he's my son. And if I know, then it won't be long before my mother finds out, too. I think she'll take

Annie to court for custody, and if she does, she has the kind of legal counsel to assure she'll win." He kept his eyes averted, afraid of what he'd see in the face of the man he'd considered his second father.

Then Henry knocked him sideways when he calmly replied, "Annie told us. She's worried about the same thing, that your mother will find out and do everything she can to declare Annie an unfit mother in hopes of taking Hank. It's not going to happen." Henry clasped his shoulder and gave it a comforting rub. "We just got back from our attorney's office, and—"

"Daddy, don't *tell* him that. He's the enemy!"

"Susan, hush right now, or leave the room. I mean it." Henry turned back to Travis. "As I was saying, we have legal counsel too, and she's assured us we have nothing to worry about. Your mother can't take Hank."

"Yes, she can. I promise you, she can. She knows things, she'll make terrible trouble—" Travis couldn't sit still any longer. He spun away from Henry, and his agitated steps brought him right into Annie's path. He stopped short at the sight of her. She stood in the doorway of the kitchen with Hank in her arms, her eyes wide with worry.

"What does she know, Travis? What could she possibly know that would make a judge agree to let her take my child from me?"

"I'd like the answer to that, too." Mark came up behind Annie and stood next to her with one arm around her shoulders and his free hand curved over his nephew's back. Hank snuggled his cheek into Annie's neck as he yawned. He spotted his grandfather and with a sleepy chirp, held his chubby arms out to Henry, who rose and silently took him. Henry sat back down with Hank on his lap as Travis looked on with longing.

"Travis, I think you'd better start talking." Mark's voice jerked his attention from Hank, and he met Mark's stern look with something akin to panic. Mary stepped into the kitchen and took up a position next to Henry, running a gentle hand over Hank's tousled hair. She gave him an affectionate smile.

Annie's chin lifted as she faced him. "I don't know what you could say to make me think your mother has any sort of case for taking my son, Travis. Our lawyer says she doesn't."

He wanted, needed to touch her. "Annie, my mother will think she can get Hank just because she's Ruth Quincy. She knows high-powered people all over the state. A lot of them have been family friends for years, and they'll go for anything she tells them." Travis dared to reach out for one of her hands, relieved when she allowed it to rest in his.

He gripped her fingers and turned his attention to the room in general. "I came to see Annie and Hank. When I got here, I sat out in the car and all I could think of was how much you all gave to me when I was a kid, how much you all cared about me. You made me a part of your family, and I've missed it like crazy."

"If you miss it so much, then why did you push it aside?" Annie pulled her hand away and wrapped her arms around her waist. "Why did you let your mother dictate to you like that? You said she'd never tell you what to do once you became of age. Well, from what I've seen, she's doing just that, isn't she?"

"But there's a reason, Annie. There's a reason I let my mother have her way—"

"Oh, yes." Her voice held sharp sarcasm. "Your schooling. I'm sure that was most important, having the Quincy money backing your Yale education. For your information, Travis, you can get scholarships to any school if your grades are good. Including Yale. You could have worked hard to improve your grades and then gone there on your own."

"It wasn't just college tuition that she held over my

head. I wouldn't have done what I did only because my mother threatened to take away Yale."

"Then what else, Travis? You can tell us." Mary moved to his side and took his shoulders in her hands. He could feel his body start to shake. Under her steady regard, Travis buckled. A part of him admitted one of the very reasons he'd driven down Spring Street in the first place today was to get it all off his chest once and for all. He was so afraid of losing Annie and Hank forever. Someone needed to stop his mother and warn the Turners of what was coming, though they were smart enough to take action themselves.

But it might not be enough, not unless they had all the information he could give them. And that was going to be the hardest thing for them to hear.

When Mary urged him back to his chair, Travis slumped there. Henry patted his knee. Annie leaned against the counter closest to where Hank dozed in her father's lap, keeping a watchful eye on the baby.

Travis took a deep breath and scanned the faces surrounding him. Susan and Mark. Mary, on one side of him, Henry on the other, holding his son. Annie stood with her arms crossed and a worried frown on her face. He saw how two years had changed her, how motherhood and responsibility had molded her into a beautiful young woman. Yet for all her newfound maturity, she was still so innocent.

God, they all were, these gentle people. He'd never known a family more innocent of the uglier side of life. And he was about to disillusion them in the worst way. At that moment, Travis felt so damned old.

His voice came out in a low croak. He cleared it, and tried again. "Two years ago I had a horrible fight with my mother, the morning after our annual Christmas party." At Annie's sudden intake of breath, he flicked her an apologetic glance and nodded slightly. "Yeah, that one. She'd said some rotten things about you, Annie—and your family. I couldn't take it any longer, and I demanded to know why she felt this way about all of you, why she had always hated you so much. I told her I'd leave and never come back, if she didn't tell me why. I must have gotten across to her how serious I was because she finally told me."

He blew out a shuddery breath. "She said a lot about her past, things she'd always kept hidden from me. How she grew up dirt-poor in West Virginia, the oldest daughter of an alcoholic mother and an abusive stepfather. How, when she was only fifteen years old, her parents sold her in a poker game. Her stepfather had played and lost, and the man he lost to would have killed him if he hadn't offered my mother as payment for his debt."

"Oh, Travis. Oh, my Lord. Poor little girl. What a terrible way to live." Mary's eyes filled with sympathetic tears. She took one of his hands in comfort and winced when his fingers latched onto hers in a bruising, needy grip.

Everyone in the kitchen gaped at him in horror, no doubt trying to imagine people so heartless and inhuman as to sell their own child to pay off a gambling debt. Travis dreaded what he needed to say next, for he knew it would hit them worse than anything else ever could.

"The man who took my mother, who won her in that game . . . was Franklin Turner. Your father." Travis held Henry's gaze as he spoke, and watched fresh horror spill into his eyes.

"My father? I don't—how could—" Shock robbed Henry of his breath as he stammered.

Surprisingly, Susan came forward to reassure Travis first. Rising from her seat, she moved to his side and knelt in front of him, took hold of his free hand. "Finish it, Travis. There's obviously a great deal more. Say it, and then we can deal with it."

He nodded, grateful, and he clutched her hand as well as Mary's. Searching for enough inner courage to get the rest of it out, his eyes locked with Annie's compassionate gaze. He found all he needed, there.

He turned back to Henry. "Franklin Turner took my mother as his winnings that night, and he . . . he raped her several times." He heard gasps around the table and gritted his teeth, determined to purge it all out. "He would have kept her locked up somewhere and done it to her again and again. But she got away from him and she ran for miles, until she found the driveway to Quincy Hall. My father and grandmother took her in." Hot tears rolled down his cheeks, but he couldn't let go long enough to dash them away. "They took care of her, and a year after it happened, Dad married her." His voice reduced to a whispery croak. "She never reported it to the police, never spoke of it again until the day she told me. The same day my father had his second stroke."

His face white and drawn, Henry stood and handed Hank to Mark, who balanced him on his hip and let him play with the ID tags he wore around his neck.

Mary wiped at her wet cheeks and eyed Henry with helpless concern. Travis could imagine what went through her mind: how could anyone related to her wonderful husband have been so plain evil?

"My God, I can't process this," Henry rasped. "My father was a bastard and treated my mother abominably. He drank almost every day of his life that I can remember, gambled away all of our savings, sold off Mama's few pieces of good heirloom jewelry. He sold my valuable rare stamp collection for whiskey and gambling at the track. But *this*—" He looked sick to his stomach.

"There's more." Travis broke into Henry's pained reverie with reluctance. What he had to say next was the very worst. Henry seemed to almost brace himself, and the room got deathly quiet as Travis admitted, "My mother told me she'd found a hammer on the floor of the car's backseat. She got the hammer in her hand, and when the car swung around a curve, she hit him in the head. The blow knocked him out, and the car crashed into an embankment. That's how she got away. My father said Franklin Turner was found dead in his car the next morning. An autopsy revealed he'd had a heart attack, too. They were never able to find out if he'd died from that, or from the hammer."

Henry sank slowly onto his chair again and groped for his wife's hand, then wrapped an arm around her hips when she hastened to his side. She stroked her palm against his nape soothingly. Henry's breath caught in a choke before he could speak coherently. "Travis, your mother . . . I can't even begin to tell you how sorry, that my—my—that he would have committed such a terrible crime against her—"

"It's not your fault," Travis protested. "I told my mother that the sins of the father—or mother, in my own maternal grandmother's case—don't always leave a smear on their children. I told her, but she wouldn't listen. All she wants to think of is how I fell in with the relatives of a monster."

Travis stood up to face everyone, and his heart sank at the shock and anger he saw on each face. How could any of them accept this story based on nothing more than his word? Hell, he sure wouldn't have accepted it, if he were in their place.

"Look," he appealed, "My mother is dead wrong about so many things. She never made an effort to get to know Annie. She plotted to get me away from all of you. Every single time I've tried to live my own life these past two years, she's threatened to reveal this information to ruin your family. Now she'll use it as ammunition against you once she finds out about Hank, and not suffer a speck of guilt over it. She'll try to discredit you. To prove Annie couldn't possibly be a decent mother."

He had to push it out of his mind, that his mother might have any kind of right to Hank. Never, not with the kind of hatred she felt.

Tears coursed down Travis's face as he met the devastation his story left behind. "I wanted you to know. Because if there's a way for her to use this to her advantage, and if she can find an attorney and a judge she can put in her pocket, she'll do it."

He edged toward the door, knowing as a family, they needed time to process this. "I'm going to go. I'm sorry," he whispered to Henry, who still looked shaken and crushed. "So sorry. Whatever you need, testimony, anything, you've got it. I just want you to know I'm on your side. My mother has no right to do this to you. No right to treat Annie this way." With that, he moved to the back door and let himself out, before he broke down any further. He didn't dare look at Annie or Hank, otherwise he'd beg to stay. The door swung shut behind him.

Annie hurried to catch up with Travis as he strode down the sidewalk. He turned to face her, his body slumped, his hands shoved into his pockets.

She came to a stop three feet from him. Her eyes searched his and her heart clenched at the anguish she could see in their drenched blue depths. "Travis—"

"It's all right. I won't bother you again, Annie. Just let me know if you need me for anything, okay? If my mother's attorneys contact you, I'll be there for you and your family." He took several steps backward. She could see the way he trembled.

"Travis, listen to me—"

He kept his head down, shoulders hunched inward as if to ward off pain. "I don't have much money right now, but I promise as soon as I can get something set up for Hank, I'll be sending you regular support for him, and I'll—"

"*Stop!*" she shouted, and watched him flinch. His air of

utter defeat cracked her aching heart. She stepped forward and pulled him into her embrace. His arms snapped around her body reflexively and he shook even harder.

She buried her face against his shoulder. "I don't want your money. Hank doesn't need your money. But he does need his daddy. You can't put a price on family, Travis. Don't even try." She raised her face to his and tenderly brushed at the fresh tears on his cheeks, knowing hers were just as wet. "If you mean it, if you want to be part of this family, if you're ready to tell your mother what she can do with her control, that's all I need to know."

He released a shuddery breath and rested his forehead against hers. Intoxicated by the feel of his arms around her after two years of starvation, Annie clung to him. Maybe it was wrong to put herself through it, or take a chance he wouldn't hold steady this time. Maybe she courted another broken heart. But she'd never stopped needing him.

"It could get ugly, Annie." He rumbled the warning against her temple.

Her lips curved into a relieved smile. "I can handle ugly. Just as long as you're beside me, I can handle just about anything."

Travis slipped his hands up her arms and cupped her face, and she could have drowned in the love she saw there. He whispered, "Do you still have my ring?"

She nodded. "I still have it."

"Will you wear it again, Annie? Will you let me put it back in your finger?"

Her head tilted to one side as she considered his request. She wore the ring on a chain around her neck, hidden beneath her clothes. She'd placed it there a few days after their breakup. Except for when she'd been in the hospital giving birth to Hank, it never left her side.

"You first have to tell me what the ring means to you, once it's back on my finger."

In her ear he affirmed, "It means I marry you as soon as we can find a preacher. You're almost nineteen. I'm over twenty-one. I've never stopped loving you, not for an instant." He brushed his mouth over her lobe, and she shivered. He raised her chin with a finger until her eyes met his. "I need you, Annie. You and Hank."

Her smile bloomed.

"Yes."

First, Susan noticed the huge smile on Annie's face when she and Travis returned to the kitchen. Then she saw the sparkle of Travis's topaz and diamond ring, back on her sister's finger. Even the most insensitive clod in the world could have felt the love between them.

Maybe it was a match made in heaven, after all. But Susan knew they had a hell of a lot of challenges to face and tribulations to overcome, including Ruth Quincy.

Silently she stepped to Mark and took Hank from his arms. As soon as their brother realized what was going on, he'd probably be too angry to want to cuddle his nephew. Mark used to like Travis. But a lot had happened, and Mark protected the women in their family. Plus, he sported a mean temper.

"Mama? Daddy? We're getting married." Soft words from Annie, but the tone stayed firm. Her hand clasped Travis's as they faced the family, determination on both their faces. Susan leaned against the counter and grinned. Seemed she was getting herself a brother-in-law, after all. She brushed her fingers over Hank's hair and felt him cuddle closer. He yawned against her neck, needing a proper nap. But no way would she leave the kitchen long enough to take him upstairs. Judging by the dark frown on Mark's face, she might miss some entertainment.

Next to Annie, Travis seemed to radiate youthful confidence as well, but even from several feet away, Susan spied a film of nervous sweat on his upper lip. He feared they'd all reject him for leaving Annie the way he did. For things that were his fault and all the things which weren't. For telling them what kind of monster Franklin Turner had been.

Susan watched as Mama got to her feet and shushed Mark for whatever he muttered under his breath. She spoke in an undertone to him, and he ground his teeth together. Susan pursed her lips at him in a mock-kiss and almost laughed aloud at the nasty glare he shot her.

Annie and Travis both clung to Mama when she slipped an arm around each of them. Daddy took her place as soon as she let them go, and he hugged them as well. Annie wiped her tears away and took Hank from Susan's arms, then carried him over to Travis.

They faced each other. Two identical heads of silky black hair, two sets of eyes, one bright blue and one deep brown. Hank tilted his head to the side, and when Susan glanced at Travis, she saw the same tilt to his head. It brought a sting of emotion to her eyes.

Annie must have seen the similarity as well because she gulped back a laugh/sob, and said to Hank, "Can you say 'Daddy,' Hank? This is your daddy. Can you give your daddy a hug?"

Without hesitation, Hank held out his arms to Travis, who awkwardly balanced him on one hip. He flung a look of new-father panic around the room, before his eyes fastened on Hank. The baby stared at him, fascinated.

"Hi, Hank." Travis visibly shook with emotion.

Hank fluttered long, inky lashes at his father and smiled, showing off several baby teeth. He patted Travis's cheek with one dimpled hand and exclaimed, "Da!"

Travis brought Hank close to bury his face in his son's neck. "Yeah. That's who I am." His voice broke. "I'm your Da."

PART FOUR

Reunion

Chapter 25

Every muscle in her body tightened, Ruth perched on the settee in her study. Fury rushed through her.

The old fool! How *dare* he patronize her? How dare he treat her with such triviality?

She'd expected Judge Timothy Harbawker's cooperation, his agreement to instigate the paperwork necessary to serve the Turners with a custody challenge. She'd expected him to assure she'd win.

Instead, Timothy patted her hand as if she were a five-year-old imbecile, mouthed a few ridiculous platitudes, and hurried up the stairs, eager to spend his time with Ronald, her vegetative spouse.

She'd have to obtain her grandson on her own. Which meant she'd have to leave Quincy Hall.

Her stomach instantly clutched and she broke into a sweat. She hadn't been past those doors since she'd brought Ronald home from the hospital, two years ago.

Ruth moved to the sideboard, feeling the need for a restorative. Ordinarily she abstained from alcohol before seven o'clock in the evening, of the opinion that daytime indulgence was a sign of weakness. But perhaps a small drink would banish her insistent headache. She poured a healthy splash of brandy into a glass and downed it in three gulps. The potent liquor surged through her body.

Steadier, she returned to her desk to plot her next move. It did seem pointless to engage Timothy Harbawker, unless she could prove the Turner brat to be a poor mother and report those findings to him. She would need to have the girl watched and followed, her personal habits documented. As distasteful as it might be, she'd have to hire an investigator.

Dan Marley could find one for her. Of what use were dedicated employees, if they couldn't take on the more unpleasant tasks? She'd call Dan this evening and give him explicit instructions.

She would speak to Travis and let him know she was going to intercede on his behalf, although he certainly didn't deserve her courtesy. Yesterday he came home briefly to check on his father, and ran back out the front door before she could accost him. At the time, she thought little of it. But this morning, she called Janice to ask how their children's outing had gone, only to discover Catherine hadn't seen him since that night. Ruth puzzled over where on earth he'd spent the day and most of the evening. She'd gone to bed at eleven, her usual bedtime, uneasy because Travis was still out. And this morning, he'd been up and gone before she came downstairs.

She reached for the telephone to call Dan, but laid the receiver back in its cradle as a disturbing thought came to her.

What if Travis had been—God forbid—over at the Turner house? What if he knew about his son? *Even worse, what if he'd run off with the wretched girl?*

He wouldn't.

But of course he would. She had to face reality. Even with sweet Catherine patiently awaiting his marriage proposal, Travis possessed enough contrariness to run out and marry Annie Turner, just to spite his own mother.

Trembles overtook her at the mere thought of Travis doing something so recklessly disastrous. She groped for the nearest chair. Her headache, beginning to abate, came back twice as strong.

She had to speak to him. He might be at the Turner's house this very minute. She had no idea where the family lived. They probably didn't even have a telephone.

Two minutes later, she flipped through the phone directory on a search for Henry Turner's name. When she found it, she reached for a pen, clenched her fingers tightly, then snatched it up and dug for a notepad. She scribbled down the address and tossed the pen aside, wondering how on earth she'd find the inner fortitude to actually step outside the doors of Quincy Hall and into her car. Which she'd never learned how to drive. Well, no matter, she'd find someone to drive her.

Her fingers shook. She cursed her damned weakness. She had to do this. She had to get over her phobias. She had to take care of family business as befitted a Quincy. No one else could do it but her.

Travis held Annie in one arm and nuzzled her temple, catching the fine, silky hairs that grew there. Utterly content for the first time in two years, he closed his eyes and relaxed on the old sofa. He was really here, with her. He was whole again, at last.

They'd left a single lamp glowing in a far corner of the living room. Henry thoughtfully hustled his family out the door right after supper with a promise of banana splits at the Creamery. Susan allowed herself to be herded with a mock grumble and a wink to her sister, who blushed and tried to look nonchalant about being left alone with Travis. He just grinned.

Mark hadn't wanted to leave Sissy and refused to go with them. Then he'd refused to leave the living room. Mary persuaded him to keep Sissy company upstairs and with visible reluctance, he'd conceded. He'd glared at Travis, and Annie stuck her tongue out at him as he tromped upstairs.

Once the rest of the family left, Hank awoke from his

nap and made his usual babyish demands. One diaper change and a milk and fruit snack later, he entertained himself by bouncing on Travis's knees. Every so often he fell back in a fit of giggles, when Travis gave his belly a tickle. Happy to be the center of attention, he crawled all over his parents, from one lap to the other, babbling away at both of them.

Surely this must be heaven. After the loneliness of many months, after all his mother's unrelenting pressure, it was so good to have Annie back in his arms. And there were no words for how wonderful Hank was. Travis couldn't get over his luck.

Still, he worried. His gut feeling told him his mother knew about Hank. He and Annie needed to get some plans made, fast.

"Annie?" He turned her until she gazed up at him, a happy smile on her face. That smile faded somewhat when he said, "We have to figure out what to do, sweetheart." He sat Hank between them on the sofa, and the baby grabbed at their hands to clap them together. Travis let him play with their fingers and enjoyed his antics, but with a serious tone he added, "I don't mean to pressure you, but the sooner we get married, the better."

"We can go to Roanoke first. Then we wouldn't have to be in a hurry. It's a big city, and—"

"Annie, we can't hide somewhere. You think my mother wouldn't come after us? If not her, then some attorney with a subpoena. She'll get legal counsel as soon as she hears about Hank. I'd bet money she's been told and has already pulled in some favors."

"Favors?"

"Mother has a lot of influential friends all over the state. My dad would help anyone and expect nothing in return, but Mother's not like that," he explained.

"It doesn't matter what she does. We're not minors any longer, Travis," she reminded him.

"No. We're not. But we're both still in school. I have an allowance and that's about it. I live in a small apartment in New Haven funded by the Quincy Legacy. Dad bought my car, probably with Legacy funds. I'm not even sure whose name is on the title. I never thought to look." He exhaled an embittered breath. "I've skated along, trying to outwit my mother where my private life is concerned. Only to realize I never *had* a private life."

"Look, I own my car. My job doesn't pay a lot, but I have money in the bank. I have a room at my aunt's house in Roanoke. Aunt Nan takes care of Hank for me when I'm in class or at work. We could live there, Travis. There's nothing wrong with it, and I can't see any judge saying a life like that would be bad for Hank." Annie gripped his hands. "You could go to school there, too. Maybe it's not Yale but you could still get a degree."

"I need to go to Yale, Annie. I need to graduate from there. It's a Quincy tradition. If I'm to take over for my father, then I have to have Yale." His words were gentle, but adamant.

"Do you really think your mother will let you step in for your daddy, once you marry me?" She let him go and made a cutting motion with her hand. "She'll disown you. She'll take all of it away from you. You're fooling yourself if you think any differently." He shook his head in denial before Annie finished speaking.

She got to her feet and went to the window, leaning against the glass and staring out at the quiet street. "We could have a good life in Roanoke. There are lots of jobs available for someone with a solid education. It wouldn't take long at all, and we could have our own place, maybe a house with a yard for Hank to play in. I could plant a garden, like Mama—"

Her voice faltered when his reflection joined hers. He'd come to stand behind her. In the glass he could see his own lack of enthusiasm at her suggestion of a life like that.

He urged her to turn and face him, cupped her slender neck, looked down at her and saw dreams in those soft brown eyes. Dreams he couldn't bear to ruin. Yet he had to be honest with her.

"Annie." He tried to choose his words with care. "I'm the Quincy Heir. Someday, Hank will be the next Heir. I need to take over for my father, which means living at Quincy Hall. I need the board of trustees' approval."

He held her in place when she tried to step back. "No, listen to me. This can work out. All we have to do is get married. There isn't anything she can do, once we're married. We'll live at the Hall, she can't stop us."

"Oh, Travis. Now who's dreaming?" She pulled away and moved to the center of the room, where Hank had unraveled a skein of her mother's yarn. She scooped up the baby and ignored his squawks of protest as his mischievous game was thwarted. "Come on, my boy, we're getting you ready for bed." She started up the stairs, and Travis trailed after her.

Mindful of the presence of Mark and Sissy down the hall, he closed the bedroom door and watched as Annie wrestled Hank out of his pants and shirt. She changed his diaper and Hank chortled, wriggling in ecstasy at being naked for about thirty seconds before she slapped on a fresh one. For the first time, Travis realized she used cloth diapers instead of disposables. More than likely she couldn't afford anything but cloth, since disposable diapers probably cost a lot of money to use every day. He'd never given it much thought, accustomed to a life of wealth and ease. He'd never given any thought to a lot of things he'd taken for granted, his entire life.

But once they were married and living at the Hall, Annie wouldn't have to use cloth diapers ever again. He watched her tug a pair of rubber pants up over the diaper, then slip Hank into his knit sleeper and let him bounce on the bed. She avoided Travis's eyes.

They had to settle this before it drove a wedge between them. He waited until she laid Hank in his crib. His son rolled onto his side and pulled his teddy bear to him, spooned the stuffed toy, and babbled to it. Annie motioned Travis toward the door, and they tiptoed out, leaving one of the bedside lamps on.

"He'll talk to his Pooh until he falls asleep. It's a nightly ritual." She left the door partially open, and they moved silently down the stairs, back to the living room.

Once settled on the sofa again with Annie cuddled in his arms, Travis was eager to resume the discussion. "As soon as we apply for the license, we'll go see Judge Harbawker. He has offices in Clarion. Our family has known him for years, and I'm sure he'll be glad to marry us."

"Travis, I told you I want to get married in our church. I don't want to stand in some judge's office and have a hasty wedding." She turned to face him, gesturing with both hands in supplication. "This is our wedding. We only get to do it once. It's important to me, being in our church, when we exchange our vows."

"We don't have time for that. We need to get it done fast. Tomorrow would be best. If I thought we could get the license and schedule the Judge's chambers—"

"*No.* Haven't you heard anything I've said? Marrying in a hurry to thwart your mother isn't going to do a bit of good. You think she'll let you come home with Hank and me tied to your shirttails. You think she'll welcome us and let us live there. She *won't.* Getting married and then trying to bring us to the Hall to live won't do anything except make her even madder at you. And give her more of a reason to keep you right under her thumb."

"She will have to accept the marriage."

"No, she won't. Maybe if your daddy were strong

enough to stand for us, maybe it wouldn't be so bad. And even then, she wouldn't accept us. All she has to do is see one thing she thinks we're doing wrong with Hank, and she'd have what she figures is reason enough to sue for custody. It would only be worse, living there with her."

"Annie—"

The doorbell cut off whatever Travis was going to say. With a sigh, he watched Annie rise and walk to the front door.

"I can't imagine who it could be." She looked through the peephole, a relatively new addition to the front door. Aunt Nan had insisted the simple addition was a good safety measure, even in Thompkin.

In this case, Aunt Nan was right, for when Annie squinted and glanced through the tiny security device, she spun to Travis, a look of complete panic on her face.

She whispered urgently, "Travis! Your mother is out there!"

Ruth shivered and her entire body ached from clenching her muscles so tightly. Not from a chill, but because bone-deep panic gripped her. She'd dug her fingers into the edges of the back seat for the entire trip from Quincy Hall to the Turners' slovenly side of town. Bette, who drove sedately, hadn't seemed to notice Ruth's breathing difficulties.

All the way down the long driveway and out onto the road, Ruth told herself she could do this. It was worth the terror of being away from her sanctuary, outside of her safety zone, to save Travis from making a terrible mistake and to rescue her grandson from a life of squalor. For the opportunity to put Annie Turner and the rest of her family in their place, she'd have endured far worse.

She curled her lip in revulsion as she gave the house

the once-over. This hovel, with its peeling paint and cracked walkway, was where Travis chose to be. Even now, his car sat right out in front. She wanted to scream aloud.

"Mrs. Quincy?" Bette turned to look at her, and Ruth made an effort to compose herself. This battle was better won with cold logic instead of hot emotion. She smoothed her hair back and nodded, then opened the door. It took every ounce of inner fortitude she possessed to step out of the car.

"Please wait for me, Bette. I won't be long." Ruth slammed the door and walked up the sidewalk, her posture stiffly erect, her purse tucked under one elbow.

She had a few seconds to take steadying breaths after she rang the doorbell and waited until the door finally opened and Annie Turner stood before her. Ruth's eyes swept over her, from her tangled hair to her bare feet. The girl looked like a homeless person. Ruth had seen street beggars who were better-dressed. Spots of what appeared to be food stained her loose tee shirt. Her jeans had a rip on one knee.

Ruth allowed her disgust to show, standing poker-straight. "I wish to speak to my son. Now."

To the girl's credit, she showed no outward sign of distress as Ruth swept in. Annie closed the door and motioned to the living room. "Travis is in there. Would you like to sit down?"

In answer, Ruth gave her a look of loathing.

She moved toward a faded old sofa that couldn't have been appealing even when new, her resentful eyes taking due note of the way her son reclined against sagging cushions. He looked so much at home, it was all Ruth could do not to reach out and throttle him. Instead, she waited until Annie joined him, pressed to his side. Ruth tightened her jaw to keep from grinding her teeth together.

Travis nodded toward her. "Mother. What got you up and out of the house?" Without breaking eye contact with her, he stroked a hand over the girl's tangled hair.

Of course he only did it to irritate her. Still, Ruth followed the caress with a cold stare. Her spine stiffened even more. "I wish to speak with you, Travis. Privately."

He didn't move. "Anything you need to say can be said in front of Annie, Mother."

Ruth drew an affronted breath through her nose in an attempt to control her temper. "Very well. It has come to my attention that you have fathered a child by this girl. Of course, tests will have to be accomplished to assure paternity, and I will arrange for the procedure to be done immediately."

When Annie bristled, Ruth spared her a second of frigid attention. "Miss Turner, you cannot stop me from petitioning a court for paternity testing. Protest all you like." She turned back to Travis and took note of the fury in his eyes. "Once paternity is established, I expect the child to be brought to Quincy Hall to live."

She addressed Annie with sparse courtesy. "I guarantee you, Miss Turner, my grandchild will be generously provided for and given every advantage. He will be raised in the Quincy tradition as was his father and his grandfather, and will someday become the next Quincy Heir."

Annie surged to her feet. "You *can't* take my son, Mrs. Quincy. You know it and I know it. If you think you can prove I'm an unfit mother, you're sadly mistaken—"

Ruth interrupted brusquely, "Oh, but I can. Make no mistake about it. I can easily prove your unsuitability in a court of law, and your family's inability to assist you."

"I'm eighteen and legally able to raise my own child!"

"That doesn't matter one bit. You haven't enough power to fight me, Miss Turner." She stepped closer, smiling grimly when the girl retreated, fear plain to see on her face. "You thought you could involve yourself with my son in the hopes he'd marry you, bring you to Quincy Hall, beget children by you. Well, you accomplished part of it. But, marriage? Think again. Travis will never marry a person like you."

"That's where you're wrong, Mother." Travis stood and wrapped a supporting arm around the girl, who visibly trembled. "Annie and I are getting married. I'm of age and no longer need your consent." His chin lifted in defiance, and there was conviction in his eyes.

There was also the insecurity of youth, and Ruth saw it for herself. Briefly she faltered as she recognized his courage.

She wanted the world for him. But she knew what was best for her son. And this ragged, skinny white-trash girl wasn't it.

Ruth squashed every drop of emotionalism within her heart and issued an ultimatum. "You will *not* marry this girl, Travis. You will leave this house with me, now, and assist me in compiling what information is necessary to begin custody proceedings. You will contact Catherine, immediately. You have a wonderful young woman waiting for you, one who has received attention from you and expects you to honor her with your proposal of marriage." She took his arm and, despite his struggles, maneuvered him toward the door.

"No, I won't marry anyone but Annie! Catherine already knows it, Mother. You're wasting your time." Travis dug in his heels and wrenched his arm from her grip in a blatant attempt to ignore her authority. "Once Annie and I are married, we'll be moving to New Haven to get ready for fall semester."

Ruth permitted herself one short, sarcastic laugh. "Fall semester? Is that what you think?" She narrowed her eyes at her son. "I think not." Her voice lowered. "If you disobey me, you will never step foot back on Yale property, Travis. This I promise you. Persist in this madness of yours, and I will disown you without one speck of guilt. No education, no prospects. No Legacy. Nothing. And I'll still obtain custody of my grandson. You will never see the boy, once he's under my guardianship."

Both Travis and Annie blanched as they processed

Ruth's threat. Satisfied, she added, "See if your little girlfriend can replace all you will lose, should you rebel against your destiny. And you can also forget about coming back to Quincy Hall to visit your father."

Ruth moved forward as she spoke, until she was mere inches from Travis. Her breath fanned his ashen cheeks as she issued her final blow. "You'll lose everything."

"Whose car is that?" Susan nodded at the stately silver Mercedes parked out in front of the house. "Maybe one of our neighbors won the lottery?" She grinned at Henry as he glanced in the rear-view mirror. He mugged a face at her before he pulled into the driveway and killed the engine. Then he gave the expensive sedan another perusal, and sobered.

"Oh, Lord, this isn't good." He exchanged a worried look with Mary as he climbed out of the driver's seat and hurried toward the back door with her fast on his heels.

Ruth Quincy. Who else in town owned a car like that?

They heard raised voices coming from the living room. Henry headed for the narrow hallway as Mark tore down the stairs, his face dark with anger and concern. He muttered, "I never even heard the damn doorbell." Henry nodded as they both strode into the living room with Susan and Mary close behind.

Travis stood trembling before his mother, and Ruth Quincy's face had never looked so harsh, so cold. Next to Travis, Annie pressed both hands to her mouth.

"Mrs. Quincy, what are you doing here, intimidating my daughter?" Henry moved to Annie and slipped an arm around her shoulders, drew her close to his side. She turned her face into his chest.

Without taking her eyes from Travis, Ruth addressed

Henry. "I apologize on behalf of my son for disrupting your household. As I have already explained to your daughter, I plan to arrange for paternity tests, to assure the child in question was indeed fathered by my son. After that, we will finalize the transfer of custody from your daughter, to me."

A harsh growl behind her drew Ruth's attention. She glanced over her shoulder. And paled at the sight of Mark, who stood near Mary and scrutinized her with revulsion.

Swaying, she reached for something to hold onto. She brushed Travis's arm and gripped his elbow.

"Mother, what the hell is wrong with you?" Travis took her arms in a hard grip, holding her upright when it seemed her legs would give out beneath her.

Ruth raised a shaky hand and gestured. Travis turned and frowned as he looked where she pointed. "That's Mark, Annie's big brother. I doubt he'd stand aside and let you take his nephew."

Mark came farther into the room and rasped, "No one is taking Hank anywhere, ma'am. I can guarantee that." At the sound of his voice, Ruth's knees buckled. Travis wrapped an arm around her, bewilderment plain to see on his face.

It suddenly dawned on Henry. Of all the Turner children, Mark was the only one who bore a marked resemblance to his grandfather, Franklin: similar coloring, the same husky build and the same eyes. Even the same heavy brows and distinctively shaped nose. That striking similarity seemed to scare Ruth half to death. Henry wasn't by nature mean, but right now he was glad to use anything at hand to rid the house of Ruth Quincy.

Including his own offspring. He gestured to Mark, who nodded and narrowed his dark brown eyes at the cowering woman. "Leave please, ma'am. Now." Turning, Mark addressed Travis, who still held onto his mother. "Take her home, Travis. And understand this: she'll never get her hands on Hank. You got that?"

"Mark, none of this is Travis's fault." Annie confronted her brother and caught his arm.

Mark shook her off. "I don't care whose fault it is, or isn't. I only care about you, Annie. Our family." He jerked his chin toward the stairs. "My nephew."

As if on cue, Hank started to fuss. Annie rushed toward the hall, but at the bottom of the stairway, she stopped and looked over at Travis. "You have a choice, Travis. Your mother got here by herself, and she can leave just as easily." Ruth sucked in an audible breath, but Annie ignored her. She held Travis's gaze. "You want to marry me, be a father to Hank? Then stay here, and send your mother home."

"Annie—" Travis stepped away from his mother, and she instantly grabbed hold of him. He tried to pull his arm away, but she held fast.

"Mother, let *go*."

"You will come home with me *now*, Travis."

"Travis, I'm warning you. Get your mother out of here," Mark ground out furiously.

"*Stop it!*" Sissy's loud protest shut everyone up, and they all turned to look at her, poised on the stairs. While everyone had been arguing, she'd come down, with Hank held in her arms. Flushed from sleep and teary, he popped two fingers into his mouth and nestled his head on her shoulder.

Sissy frowned at them and chastised, "You woke him up. All of you, stop shouting. Annie, take him, I need to sit down." Annie hurried to retrieve Hank, and Mark swung Sissy off the stairs and into the living room. He settled her in the armchair, and she sank onto the cushions, rubbing at her distended belly.

"Are you all right? Did you have a contraction?" He hovered over Sissy.

She offered a faint smile. "I'm okay. Just indigestion. But you know I can't stand to hear a baby crying." Sissy flicked an apologetic glance at Annie. "I didn't mean to yell at you."

"No, you're right. It's wrong of us to fight this way. And I'm glad you checked on Hank. I've never been able to let him cry, either. He's such a good little boy." Annie pressed her lips to her son's temple, and smiled when he let out a huge, contented sigh against her shoulder.

Henry watched the astonishment steal over Ruth's face when she saw for herself how much Hank resembled his father. Maybe it was a mistake for Sissy to bring him downstairs while there was shouting going on, but Hank so seldom cried. Besides, it was time to settle this once and for all.

Still, when Ruth took a few hesitant steps toward Annie, she stepped close to her brother. Mark crossed his arms over his chest, and Ruth wisely kept her distance. But her eyes never left Hank's face.

Hank looked all around the room, wide-eyed, caught sight of Travis and pulled his fingers out of his mouth, waving them wildly. "Da!"

He managed to grin. "Hi, buddy." Hank wriggled, wanting his daddy, and Travis sent a pleading look towards Annie. She hesitated, nodded, and Travis held out his arms for Hank. He settled the boy on one hip, placed his free arm around Annie's waist, and linked the three of them together. It was a visual unit even Ruth couldn't possibly miss.

For endless seconds, nobody moved or spoke. Then, Ruth strode toward the foyer with her head held high, giving Mark a wide berth as she did so. The rest of the family moved back to let her pass.

As she opened the door, Ruth tossed Henry a final, cold glare. "My attorneys will be in touch."

Chapter 26

Warm air stirred the lace curtains at the window. Annie held down a squirmy Hank while she finished pinning his diaper and slid the rubber pants in place. Travis, lounging on the edge of the bed, handed her the pullover shirt and jeans she'd laid out for him to wear. She looked up with a smile of thanks. "That was fast. You're already done with the dishes?"

"I didn't do them. Your mother kicked me out of the kitchen." He made silly faces at Hank while Annie finished dressing him. As soon as she let him go, Hank crawled to Travis and climbed all over him. They fell back in the bed, Hank giggling madly as he gained his feet and stood on Travis's chest.

"Look what a big boy you are. You're taller than me!" He winced as Hank did a rapid tap dance on his ribs. "Wow, he's heavy." He poked a finger into his son's tummy and laughed as Hank shrieked and collapsed next to him.

For the last four days, he'd stayed with the Turners. He didn't want to go back to Quincy Hall any more than Annie and her family wanted him to leave. Even Mark, whose improved attitude meant a lot, had urged him to stay.

Earlier in the morning, the family surprised him by throwing him a breakfast birthday party. With so much going on, Travis had forgotten about his birthday. He'd received cards, small gifts, and everyone feasted on cobbler thick with fresh peaches and accompanied by home-cranked ice cream. It was wonderful, the best birthday he'd ever had.

Now, cuddling his son close, Travis tried to imagine

Hank at Quincy Hall, surrounded by regimented luxury instead of a place where he was free to be a rowdy little boy. Relegated to an extravagantly decorated nursery instead of this simple, warm and happy room. Wearing designer baby gear instead of the comfy cotton knit shirt and denim pants he currently had on.

Being cared for by an impersonal nanny, or worse, his mother . . . instead of Annie and the rest of her loving family.

"What are you thinking? You've got a strange look on your face." Annie nudged his shoulder, and he shook his head to clear it.

"Just trying to visualize Hank living at Quincy Hall. And remaining the well-rounded baby he is right now." He dropped a kiss on his boy's forehead as Hank snuggled against his shoulder, two fingers in his mouth.

"And?"

He caught her hand and pulled her close, caressed her cheek. Leaned in and brushed his mouth to hers. "And I just can't see it."

She nodded. "Now you know how I feel. Where do we go from here?"

"Well, a fast marriage at City Hall is still an option, but I agree with you. It won't stop my mother. It's obvious she'll try ruining life as I know it, unless I fall in with her plans. Since that's not going to happen, I guess you're stuck with me." With Hank curled into his side, he slipped his free arm around Annie and completed the circle, holding them both close. "My mother will do what she wants, and we can't change it. So maybe we should plan that wedding, the way you've dreamed. And then go to Roanoke."

After a speechless few seconds, she pressed her cheek to his in the sweet gesture he'd always adored. "My aunt Nan will love you."

Travis squeezed her tightly. He wanted to be alone with her, though he knew it was selfish of him. He should get down on his knees and thank God he'd been given a second chance. But oh, he needed her. He wanted to make love to her. It had been so long. He struggled to put his desires aside for a while longer, and instead basked in the wonder of holding his family.

Susan suddenly burst through the open doorway of the bedroom, interrupting their quiet moment. Worry flared in her eyes.

"Annie, you'd better get downstairs. There's some creepy guy in a suit on the front porch, asking for you. He's got a big manila envelope in his hand. Mama thinks it might be a subpoena. It's got your name on it."

Ruth leaned back in her chair and watched Jenny and Bette dismantle the contents of the dining room table. Watched them remove the remnants of smoked salmon and grilled crab cakes dripping with tangy horseradish sauce, which her party guests raved over. She had served artfully arranged crudités, select cheeses from around the world, crackers and assorted snacks.

A dizzying variety of sweet and savory graced her expansive buffet. Everything a tasteful birthday celebration needed to be a smashing success, all displayed around the three-tiered masterpiece of a birthday cake. The design crew from Newport, who'd decorated the downstairs rooms and the more informal patio area, outdid themselves. Her party guests exclaimed in rapture over the food, the cake, and the atmosphere.

She did it all for her son. Ruth spent a small fortune to make this birthday memorable for him. She hired a jazz ensemble instead of the small, classically trained orchestra she'd first leaned toward. Personally, she thought jazz music sounded like discordant noise, but Catherine assured her the party guests would love it.

And they had. She heard many compliments as the young people enthusiastically indulged in dancing. Dear Catherine had been right. She would make the most splendid daughter-in-law. Ruth allowed herself a brief, sentimental smile.

Then her smile faded as she rose to her feet and walked stiffly from the dining room. She couldn't sit still any longer. Not when there was so much anger and fury whipping through her body, it was a wonder her hair didn't stand straight on end.

She'd made Travis's birthday party a true event. Except it wasn't much of a birthday party.

Because the birthday boy hadn't bothered to attend.

At first, she didn't believe it. She fully expected Travis to walk through the door in plenty of time for his own party. She'd welcomed the early arrival of Janice and Catherine, such a great help with the final preparations. Catherine looked sweetly young in a sundress of palest blue, with a heart-shaped bodice and thin straps crisscrossing over her shoulders, the full skirt falling to just above her knees. She'd swept her long blond hair to one side and had applied a tasteful amount of eye makeup. The Cabot pearls glowed around her slender neck and the matching pearl bracelet played up the delicacy of her wrist.

Ruth could hardly wait to see Travis slip the diamond and pearl Quincy betrothal ring onto Catherine's finger. It would look perfect against the lovely bracelet she wore.

She'd planned for this union. Yearned for it. She'd contacted the jazz ensemble in advance of the party and asked for as much romantic music as possible to be included in their repertoire. She'd ordered extra champagne for toasting the newly engaged couple.

As the hour of the party loomed closer, however, her anxiety became hot anger. She knew where her rebellious son was: on the dirty side of town, with those accursed Turners.

He didn't come home, didn't call. Nothing. To be fair, she'd provoked him with her parting shot three days ago when she'd swept out of that tacky, run-down house. And she kept her promise, had contacted her attorneys as soon as she arrived back at Quincy Hall. Ruth began immediate subpoena proceedings and her attorneys promised to serve within the week, directly to Annie Turner.

But foolishly she expected Travis to return home, to understand and accept his duties as the future Quincy Heir and to put aside his childishness. She never thought he would continue to act so contrarily. It was the ultimate betrayal.

When one guest after another inquired after Travis, her quickly contrived excuse—about him having to run back to New Haven concerning Yale-related business—had been easily accepted.

One fib after another emerged. No, it was sudden. Yes, it was important, but he hoped to make it back in time for the party. But in case he didn't, Travis asked her to offer his apologies to his guests and for them to carry on. Have a wonderful time in his name. Saving face was vital, and she'd accomplished it. No one guessed how she'd seethed in fury beneath the social mask she wore.

"Mrs. Quincy?" Catherine's soft voice intruded on her dark thoughts, and Ruth hastily composed her features before turning and smiling at her standing beside the dining room table. Poor child, Travis humiliated her this evening. It would never happen again, she promised herself.

She drew on her innate poise and approached Catherine, placing an arm about her shoulders. With effort, Ruth kept her anger in check. "I am so sorry, my dear child. I don't always understand my son. I apologize for his insensitivity and his lack of decency in not attending his own party."

"It's all right, Mrs. Quincy. Really, it is. I just wanted to ask you if there was anything else Mother and I could do for you before we leave. I'm driving back to New Haven in a few days and I have more packing to do—"

"But Catherine," Ruth felt a resurgence of her earlier panic. "My dear, you must stay here in Thompkin. I feel certain once Travis understands the gravity of the injustice he has done to you, he'll be quite remorseful and present his proposal."

Catherine moved away, dislodging Ruth's arm. She stepped back toward the wide archway of the front foyer. Her smile held, calm and steady as ever, but her lovely eyes showed pain. Ruth held out her hands, wanting to comfort the darling girl, but Catherine's next statement stopped her cold.

"No. Travis won't offer for me, Mrs. Quincy. And even if he did, for any reason at all, I wouldn't accept him. I don't want to marry your son."

Ruth didn't think she'd heard right, and she regarded Catherine in shock. Not marry Travis? Not become her cherished daughter-in-law, the mother of her grandchildren? She sputtered, "What sort of nonsense is this?"

"It's not nonsense, ma'am." Catherine remained polite, but firm, as she clasped her hands at her waist, ever the perfect young lady. "I will always consider Travis my very good friend. I will always care about him. But there will be no marriage. Please, let it go."

"Let *what* go? Cathy, what insanity are you spouting now?" Janice bustled into the dining room, her heels clicking with each step. Ruth sighed in relief. Her dearest friend would help her. Janice would convince her daughter to have patience. Fortitude.

Taking Catherine's shoulders in a strong grip, Janice spun her around. "Why would you say such a thing, Cathy? You're not going back to New Haven. Why, it's weeks until you need to leave. Explain yourself, immediately. After all Ruth has done for you, I don't understand your mindset."

"No, neither of you do, and it looks as if you never will!" Catherine wrenched away from her mother and faced them both. Tears formed in her eyes and spilled down her cheeks. In a splintered voice, she pleaded, "Why can't you see the truth, for once? I am not meant for Travis. I never was. You have pushed us together and interfered, until I'm the last person on earth he'd ever want to be in the same room with."

She dashed tears from her cheeks. "Travis is engaged to Annie Turner. They have a child together. Yes, they do," she affirmed, as her mother exclaimed in distress. "If he marries anyone, it will be the mother of his child. Now, I'm telling you to let it go. Or else the relationship I have with both of you will be severely damaged." Without another word, she whirled and sped to the wide double doors, one of which was partially open. It swung shut behind her.

Janice turned, shock still apparent on her face, and queried shakily, "Ruth?"

Chapter 27

"Are you sure you don't mind me going? I can put it off." Travis stood in the kitchen doorway and watched as Annie fed Hank his cereal and bananas. In a feisty mood, his son alternately took his meal like a sweet angel, and then grabbed cereal off his rubber-coated spoon and flung it about. Consequently, bits of oatmeal clung to her tee shirt, her hair, and even her nose, which she wiped with a sigh.

She put the dish and spoon down and turned to offer him a reassuring, if harried, smile. "Go ahead. He'll settle down and take his nap soon. If you don't take care of this now, it'll be too easy to procrastinate, and you can't afford to delay it."

Travis nodded and slung the backpack over his shoulder. He would spend the day in New Haven and clear out as much as he could from the apartment he'd once lived in. If he had time and Yale's business office was open, he'd request copies of all his transcripts. Sooner or later he'd have to transfer to another college. He refused to feel bitter.

He could load a lot into the trunk of his Beemer. Might as well take advantage of having it, since he expected his mother to pull the keys out from under him any day now.

He stepped into the kitchen and, avoiding his son's sticky, outthrust hands, pressed a kiss to Hank's forehead. When he turned to kiss Annie, what started out as warm and innocent turned deep and sensuous in a hurry, and he scooped her into his arms. They kissed endlessly, while Hank babbled to himself and played with the oatmeal on his fingers.

Breathless, leaning his forehead against hers, Travis

groaned, "You know I love staying here, but it's sure hard finding time to be alone with you. I wish you'd come with me." He whispered seductively, "We could use the bed in the apartment." She shivered against his lips as they trailed over her neck.

They'd only gotten one opportunity to be together since he moved in, their lovemaking hurried and a bit shy and hesitant. Two years had passed since the last time they'd made love, the result being Hank's birth. But the rest of the family was absent one afternoon, by design or coincidence, they'd never be sure. So they'd tiptoed into Travis's room, after Hank went down for his nap. They'd left the doors open in case he awoke, and they took advantage of what time they could snatch.

Travis's hands trembled as he undressed Annie, and her fingers hadn't been much steadier. For the first time in his life, he'd worn a condom. He'd worried about the right size, the right texture, and how resilient the latex rings truly were. He'd rolled it on without tearing it, and he must have gotten the correct size because it stayed in place. Then all of his worry faded away once he pressed Annie beneath his overheated body in the lumpy old bed. Those two years of abstinence melted away as if they were nothing.

Now, the need for her always present, he tried to persuade her. "Annie? Why don't you pack a few things for Hank? We could make a day of it, just the three of us."

She uttered a regretful moan of her own. "I can't. Not with everything going on around here." Sissy awoke early that morning with cramps, which became contractions as soon as her water broke while she sat at the kitchen table. Since she was almost three weeks early, Mark fell apart. Mary calmed him down, gathered everyone up, including an overnight bag for Sissy, and got them to the hospital. Susan went along for moral support and Henry even spent ten minutes at the hospital, before he had to rush off to work.

"It's anyone's guess how long Sissy will be in labor," she added. "Probably all day and evening at the very least. Mama said she wasn't dilated very much, and that was just an hour ago. Hank's being a little monkey-devil, too. It's best if we stay home."

Annie stood on the porch and watched Travis drive off, smiling to think how his silver convertible seemed to suit him, with its understated class. Her husband-to-be could dress as casually as the next person, but he was first and foremost pure class. He'd been born into it.

She still recalled how, when they were kids, he could fish all day in a white shirt and never get a speck of worm grime or fish slime on him. And how her clothes and face would be smeared with nasty pond stuff within ten minutes of baiting her pole.

Her grin widened at the memory, then faded as the sounds of one very rambunctious little boy sent her through the front door and hurrying into the kitchen. It sounded as if Hank had gotten hold of his dish and spoon and was having a great time banging them together, if the noisy din she heard was anything to go by.

She came to a halt inside the kitchen door, coughing back her own helpless laughter at the sight that met her eyes. Hank pounded and giggled, his leftover oatmeal flung on the table, finger-painted on his tee shirt and ground into his hair. Surely there hadn't been that much cereal left on his tray. Then she remembered. Travis distracted her just enough that she'd set the bowl on the tray, instead of out of reach on the table.

She sighed as she rolled up her sleeves and grasped the highchair tray. The release mechanism refused to budge. All the kids had used the old highchair, and the tray glides required a lot of effort. Most of the time it was easier to just pull Hank straight out of the seat without taking off the tray, but he was growing fast, and his sturdy body now made it difficult to get him out of the seat without removing the tray.

So she tugged at it while Hank, delighted with having his mama and her long hair so close and within reach, grabbed her braid with oatmeal-sticky hands, and yanked, hard.

"*Ouch.* Hank, stop that." She tried to pull away, but his grip on her hair was too strong. He pulled again, bringing tears to her eyes. She let go of the tray and reached for his hands, just as the rusted mechanism gave way and the tray swung to the side. Highchairs this old also didn't have seat buckles, and Hank slid right out of it, his fingers still twined in her hair. She grabbed his arms in a tight grip and pulled him up—but not before he whacked his forehead hard on the dangling metal tray. He burst into loud tears.

"Shh, shh, it's okay, poor sweetheart. It's okay." She cuddled him close and stood on shaky legs. Still hungry, Hank needed a morning nap, but a sore head would only put him in a worse mood. She kissed the rapidly forming bump on his damp forehead and knew she couldn't lay him down, not just yet. A tiny cut right in the center of the bump oozed a bit of blood, and she felt like crying herself when she saw the way his fragile skin tore from hitting his head so hard. Hank had such delicate skin, but he'd never once gotten any kind of serious owie. It had to hurt like the very dickens, but he'd heal rapidly. Babies were so resilient.

Still, she had to keep him awake, which would make him even more miserable. She'd calm him down, and then they'd both take a warm bath.

Annie paced around the sunlight-dappled kitchen with Hank sobbing in her arms, and sang to him softly, the soothing tones barely audible above his babyish distress.

Louise Morgan sat in the car and looked at the dilapidated house. She hated coming to this side of town. She'd grown up only four streets away, in an old three-bedroom shack made of inferior wood siding with a leaking tarpaper roof. Five children in the same sad dump, locked in day after day and year after year with their drunken mother and indifferent father. She suppressed a shudder at the unwelcome memory.

Living in small, smelly rooms and going to bed hungry every night taught her that some people should never be parents. The day the county welfare office sent two social workers to arrest her parents for neglect was the best day of her life.

Clarence and Sarah Morgan had taken her in, given her their name, and a new life on their dairy farm outside Thompkin. Louise owed them everything she now had. And whenever she came to the shoddy side of any town within the county seat, she thought of them. Thanked God for them. Because if things had been different for her, she'd still be in that stinking, rotten old house, or perhaps one just like it. In her adoptive parents' name, she was relentless in her determination to save these neglected and abused children.

Like the one suspected of being the victim of abuse, in the house she now watched. Such neglect and abuse would have to be proven in a court of law. But a reliable source told her the young, unwed mother who lived there hadn't a clue how to care for her baby. Louise heard of neglect, the careless lifestyle the mother led, and the child's maternal grandparents not much better as suitable guardians. Usually, she required concrete proof of this level of neglect and abuse. But the source of her information was as reliable as they came: the child's paternal grandmother, who also happened to be a scion of the community.

She knew nothing of the family who currently had possession of the child in question, but Ruth Quincy was a generous and kind patron of Thompkin. Louise owed it to her to go in and see for herself if abuse was present.

And if she found a frightened, bruised child in that house, there would be hell to pay.

She stepped from the car, smoothed down the skirt of her dark green suit. Slipping the strap of her purse over her shoulder, she walked up to the porch.

Then she froze in place at the sounds coming from within, the sobs of a child and an older, but still youthful voice, urging the child to be quiet. The baby only sobbed louder, and Louise could feel her insides clench in sympathy and outrage. She knew just how that little boy felt. How many times had she sobbed and cried either from hunger or from the stinging slaps her mother could dole out with sly and quicksilver accuracy no matter how drunk she might be?

She straightened her shoulders and rang the rusted bell several times. As the child shrieked louder, the door opened to reveal a narrow, dim foyer. The girl who stood there didn't look old enough to be in high school, much less the mother of a child. Shadows bloomed beneath her red-rimmed eyes, and matted hair hung to her waist. She wore baggy clothes smeared with food. And perched on her hip, a baby in a soiled cloth diaper and a stained tee shirt rubbed at his wet eyes and sniffled pitifully. Had this girl thrown food at her own baby? It was in the tangled black curls on his head and on his bare legs and arms.

His arms. Louise looked at the baby-pure skin, pale and fragile, and noted with mounting fury the bruises on each arm. Finger shaped bruises. And she spotted the bump, already dark and puffy, on his forehead. There was a small cut in the center of it that seeped blood. A fist, wearing a ring, would make a knot and cause a cut such as that.

The girl had a ring on her finger. An expensive ring, from the looks of it. With a stone large enough to do the kind of damage she saw on the poor child's head.

Louise's fury grew.

Holding onto her composure as best as she could, she faced the thin young woman. "I'm from the county Child Welfare office. I'm here to talk to you about your relationship with your son." She watched with some satisfaction as the girl's already pale cheeks blanched even further. Louise waited until shock overtook the girl's narrow face. "Our office has received reports of an abusive relationship involving this minor child." She nodded in the direction of the fretful baby, and the girl actually swayed where she stood as if her body could no longer support her legs.

Louise suppressed a savage smile. *This one's for you, Mom and Dad.* The thought stayed firmly in her head as she pushed her way past the trembling girl.

As he exited off the expressway, Travis whistled to himself. He'd severed a pathological tie, and it was a better feeling than he thought it would be. Packing up his belongings had been therapeutic. He'd been able to go into his place and think of it as a temporary stop in the road for him. Even the loss of Yale hadn't caused too much of a hurtful ping for him.

He'd boxed some of the more trendy and costly articles of clothing his mother purchased and then pushed on him. He'd take it to the closest Salvation Army. Someone who shopped there might want cashmere jackets and sweaters, silk shirts. But he knew those things didn't fit his way of life anymore. Maybe they never had.

Now he was almost home. Another five miles and he'd be in Thompkin. Soon he'd walk through the door on Spring Street. Maybe Sissy's baby would have been born by now and Annie would be at the hospital. Travis thought about just going straight over there, but decided against it. If Sissy delivered and Annie was gone, then someone would be home with Hank. Travis just wanted to be home, too.

In all the years he'd known them, the Turner house represented home like no other place. He'd walk in the door and smell fresh flowers cut from the backyard garden, the lemon oil Mary used to wipe down the banister and the woodwork. There would always be something delicious cooking on the stove and the fragrance would mix with the other, familiar smells and wrap around him like a security blanket.

Thirteen, sixteen, nineteen; at any age it was always the same. He'd return from the Academy, and the welcome he got was warm and caring and good. Soon he'd legally belong to them. He couldn't wait. Even the subpoena his mother conjured up, meant to intimidate and threaten, couldn't break his good mood. They'd deal with her in court, and they'd do it as a family.

He turned onto Spring Street and looked toward the house. Only Annie's car was there. Sissy was probably still in labor. He winced in sympathy at the thought of it. He pulled into the driveway, grabbed his duffel bag, and strode up the steps to the door. The cramped foyer was dim, so he snapped on a light. And paused in surprise at the sight of Annie, sitting on the stairway, slumped over with her head in her hands.

Travis dropped his bag and rushed to her side. He touched her bent head worriedly. "What is it? Sissy? Is she all right? Has she had the baby yet?"

Annie raised a face ravaged with tears, cheeks splotchy, her eyes swollen and red. She uttered a wordless cry and reached for him. He sat on the step and pulled her into his arms. "Annie? Come on. Talk to me." He stroked her tangled hair.

Her entire body trembled against him. "He's gone. I tried to c-call you. You had your ph-phone off."

"I turn it off when I'm driving. I must have forgotten to

turn it back—wait, who's gone? What's going on?" He eased her away until he could see her face.

She whispered raggedly, "Hank. A woman from the welfare office came and t-took him. About an hour ago. She said I was a b-bad mother, she'd heard I a-abused Hank. She wouldn't let me explain anything. She yanked him right out of my arms! He was screaming for me, Travis. Screaming." Fresh tears poured from her bruised eyes.

Travis fell back against the staircase, dumbfounded. Hank, taken? Right out of their home? How in hell could something like this happen? Why would it happen?

"Annie, sweetheart, calm down and tell me everything."

She drew in a shuddering breath. "Hank bumped his head on the highchair tray, and he was crying when she came to the door. She thought I'd h-hit him. My baby, how could anyone think I'd hit my baby? She said I s-shook him and hit him. Asked me if I were on drugs. Drugs, Travis! Then she drove away, and I could hear Hank crying all the way down the street!"

"Why didn't you call your mother or Susan?"

She rubbed at her wet face with a hand still dotted with oatmeal. "I tried to call you. I didn't think about anyone else. Then I guess I just sat here and cried myself sick. I don't know what to do. I don't know who'd say such awful things about me."

It didn't take much thinking for Travis to come up with a surefire answer as to who would have done this: his mother. Who the hell else commanded such power and pull around here? Her final words to them all, just a few days ago, hinted at her attorneys contacting them. Other than the hastily delivered subpoena, they'd heard nothing further from her.

He'd bet anything if the family attorneys knew about what she'd done, they'd have tried to talk her out of it. No, she must have pulled strings directly with county Child Services. Travis was certain she had some high-ranking pals there, too.

This was a nightmare.

He slipped an arm around Annie's shoulders and gently urged her to her feet. He led her into the living room and sat her on the sofa. Taking a handkerchief from the back pocket of his jeans, he wiped her eyes, then held it under her nose. She dutifully blew into the soft linen, and rested her head wearily against his shoulder. Travis rubbed his cheek on her silky hair, trying to soothe her.

His mother wouldn't get away with this.

Two years of controlling the Quincy Legacy had made her just powerful and arrogant enough to think she could do whatever she pleased, to feel confident enough to demand support from the movers and shakers around the county. God only knew what level of authority she'd appealed to. For all he knew, she'd gone straight to the governor, who incidentally was his honorary godfather.

He urged Annie to recline on the sofa. "I'll be right back." In the foyer, he dug the phone book from the small telephone table near the kitchen door. He found the number for the hospital and called them first. As soon as he explained things to Mary, he'd call Aunt Nan in Roanoke.

The phone clicked in his ear twice before Mary's soft voice came on. "Hello? Annie, is that you?"

Annie came into the foyer and huddled into his side as he managed, "It's Travis. Mar—" He swallowed, painfully. "Mom, we've got trouble."

Chapter 28

Ruth dressed the boy in a one-piece nautical style romper that once belonged to Travis, and it actually fit decently. He jerked in her grasp and screamed the entire time she fought to get him into the designer outfit. Finally dressed, she left him in the Jenny Lind crib Travis had used as a baby. His incessant sobs grated on her nerves. She'd probably have to move the nursery to a guestroom in the other wing, otherwise, listening to him might keep her up at night.

She watched him warily as he gained his feet and clutched the crib rails. Tears streamed down his face and dampened the collar of his romper. Damn it. That ensemble was an expensive "Happy Baby Togs" original, and the boy would no doubt ruin it with his blubbering.

Yet, he was of her blood. He could be her second chance at motherhood, for she was certain once Travis and Catherine were wed and expecting their own, Travis would forget his desire to raise this child himself. Ruth could not imagine Catherine taking on the care of another woman's baby. Who could blame her? The boy's birth was a mistake. He would be illegitimate until legally adopted, and Ruth planned to attain the adoption herself. It was up to her to rear him as befitted a proper Quincy, to eradicate any Turner influence that might have already formed in his malleable little mind.

She might wish with all her heart a child conceived by Travis and Catherine would have the honor of being the next heir, but Ruth knew the legalities of the Quincy Legacy. She despised this child's mother, but she would adhere to the Legacy. The Turners would be devastated about losing the boy, a nice side bonus for her. She decided a 'thank-you' card sent to Lawrence Bailey would be apropos, since his office had moved with such swiftness in bringing the boy to his rightful home. Besides, Lawrence had always been a dear friend of Ronald's.

She'd puzzled over what to do about the child's name. She wanted no reminder of the family whose presence in Thompkin had plagued her for so many years. After much consideration, Ruth decided to call him "Duncan Adams Quincy," after the first Quincy, and borrow Ronald's middle name of "Adams." She let the full name roll off her tongue, pleased at how dignified it sounded. She'd have the papers drawn up at once.

A gasp at the open doorway drew her attention from the crib and its noisy occupant, and Ruth spun around.

"Oh, my Lord, what have you *done*, Ruth?"

Martha ignored Ruth and her hostile glares. Instead, her attention centered on the exhausted child who nestled against her shoulder. He hiccupped a teary sob once or twice, which thankfully didn't awaken him. How utterly stressful the past several hours must have been for him.

From the kitchen, Martha heard the wails and she'd run upstairs in a sudden panic. Ruth wouldn't have done it, she'd repeated over and over. Ruth wouldn't have stolen Annie's child.

But she'd done exactly that. Martha had halted inside the guestroom and gazed at the boy, a mirror image of his daddy, except for those big brown eyes. Annie's eyes. As soon as the child saw her, he held out his chubby little arms. The poor mite hadn't stopped crying until Martha picked him up and crooned to him.

"Leave my grandson alone," Ruth had seethed at her. She'd advanced toward the crib, but the fury in Martha's eyes must have gotten through to her, because she didn't move any too close.

Her voice a tender chime of comfort, Martha had carried him downstairs, and Ruth trailed after her.

Now, determined to get to the bottom of this latest mess, Martha faced off with Ruth in the main foyer. Her eyes, soft with instant love as they looked down on the boy's sweet face, hardened and narrowed when she raised them.

"You are out of your damned mind, Ruth." The low, furious words didn't stir the sleeping baby she held.

"I did what I had to do. I did the right thing for my grandson." Ruth haughtily lifted her chin.

Martha only shook her head and rocked back and forth, humming softly as she stroked a hand across the child's back. He snuffled and cuddled closer, two fingers in his mouth. Her arms tightened and she brushed a kiss across his damp forehead, then frowned at the lump that protruded and the tiny cut, already crusted over and beginning to heal.

Ruth pointed to the wound. "Annie Turner did that. She hit my grandson."

"Oh, bullshit," Martha retorted, eyeing Ruth with disgust. "Children fall down and whack their heads all the time. There is no way on God's green earth that Annie hit this child."

"Well, what about those marks on his arms? And he was filthy when the social worker visited. Covered in heaven knows what kind of foulness. Bruises, screaming in pain. I'm sure photos were taken to document this hideous abuse."

Martha's fingers smoothed lightly over the bruises visible beneath the fancy short-sleeved romper the boy wore. Ruth probably did it herself when she tried to dress him. What the idiot woman knew about dealing with babies could be printed on the head of a pin with room to spare.

"You *are* insane, Ruth. It's not only all in your mind, but it's also a passel of lies." Martha hitched the baby closer to her body, uneasy when she noted how Ruth watched the child as if she'd like to grab him and run away with him. Predatory possessiveness was there in her eyes, in her stance.

It hadn't come as a surprise when Martha heard about Travis's son. She'd known something urgent had to be behind Annie's departure from Thompkin, and given Ruth's attitude toward Annie over the years, her fear of Ruth's reaction to the news made sense. The situation Martha now found herself in, holding this exhausted child in the foyer of Quincy Hall instead of where he rightfully belonged, proved how far Ruth would go in her vengeance against an innocent like Annie.

Anger churned in her as she turned to Ruth. "You tore the boy from his mother—no, that's not quite right, is it? You hired someone to go to Annie's home and frighten her, intimidate her, and then steal her own son from her. Do you have *any* idea what you put him through, today? Any idea what you've done to Annie? To Travis, when he finds out about this? Do you even care?"

Ruth shifted closer, her eyes focused on the baby. "Give him to me." She held out her arms and frowned when Martha backed up and shook her head. "I said, give him to me! He's my grandson. Soon he'll be my adopted son. I wish to hold him."

Martha spat, "You don't deserve to hold him, Ruth, not after what you've done. Kidnapping, missy. Has an ugly ring to it, wouldn't you say? Well, that's what you've done. And if you think the Turner family will allow you to get away with it, think again. I wouldn't be surprised to see the police on the doorstep before very long." With that, Martha turned and strode toward the kitchen with the sleeping child locked in her arms.

"You are dismissed, Martha! You are fired. Do you

hear me? *FIRED!*" Ruth screamed the words at her, but Martha merely flung a furious look over her shoulder and disappeared around the corner. She took the back stairs at a run and didn't slow down until she was behind the locked door of her suite. She sank into the closest chair, her heart pounding, and looked down at Travis's son, still fast asleep in her arms.

She pressed her lips to his silky curls. "Don't you worry, sugarpie. Martha's got you now."

Mary wiped the tears from Annie's face. Susan stomped around the room in a circle and tossed out a few inventive ways to kill off Ruth Quincy. Travis, slumped in a chair across the room with his head in his hands while Henry patted his back, made no attempt to defend his mother against Susan's rages. If his mother stood before him right now, he'd have strangled her himself. He doubted a court system in the state would condemn him for it.

Mark entered the waiting room and attempted a smile. "Well, they're sleeping. Sissy's worn out, but she's doing fine." He stepped over to where his mother sat with Annie, and pressed a kiss to both their cheeks. "She wanted to see you, Annie. Toby's still in the room with her and the nurse said he can stay there all night. Why don't you go in and spend some time getting to know your new nephew? Take your mind off your troubles, okay?"

Annie raised tear-swollen eyes to her brother and nodded, reaching up to hug him as he drew her to her feet. She laid her forehead against his shoulder. "I'm so sorry, Mark. So sorry this happened during what should be the happiest day for all of us. I'm thrilled to have a nephew to spoil." For a few seconds brother and sister stood clasped together, before she stepped back. The door of the private waiting room swung shut behind her.

"Where's Nan?" Mary's voice faltered, and she cleared her throat as she looked up at her son. Mark took the seat Annie vacated and Mary caught one of his hands, holding it between both of her palms.

He gripped her fingers. "She went in search of coffee, after ordering me to send in Annie. Told me it would do her good to stop crying and come sit with Sissy for a while." He smiled. "Aunt Nan might be starchy, but she's as mush-hearted as they come. She told me she'd already called the lawyer, and the woman promised to investigate and get right back to us." He sighed. "You should probably all go home. I'm staying here with Sissy."

Susan stopped pacing, and scowled at each of her family members in turn. "What's that lawyer going to do about this? I'd bet all the money in my savings account that no-good social worker didn't have a warrant, or whatever they need to take children from their homes. It happened too fast." She spun toward Travis. "Don't you think it happened too fast, for it to be a legal procedure?"

He nodded as he scrubbed his palms over his cheeks. "Yes, I think so." He dropped his hands into his lap, feeling helpless, as usual, where his mother was concerned. "It's easy enough for my mother to make a few calls and get almost anything she wants." He gathered some facts from memory. "To achieve this legally, she would have to contact County Child Welfare and report suspected abuse or neglect. Someone would then come to the house to investigate. Not to just grab Hank," he stressed, at the resurgent fury in Susan's expression. "Just to investigate. If it seemed Hank was in any immediate danger, steps would have been taken to remove him into protective custody."

Wearily he shrugged and leaned his elbows on his knees. "He had bruises on his arms and a cut on his forehead. That was probably enough for Child Welfare to justify taking him away." At Susan's low growl and Mark's soft exclamation of anger, Travis hastened to add, "But to have Hank brought immediately to Quincy Hall? Mother can't have gone through proper channels. No way."

"What were you thinking, Morgan? No, don't answer that. Obviously you weren't thinking at all." Lawrence Bailey dropped his considerable bulk into his office chair. Louise Morgan opened her mouth to protest, but he silenced her with a single blunt-edged finger pointed at her. She wisely closed her mouth, but her eyes remained hostile.

He was indifferent to her attitude. "You let Ruth Quincy have the child."

"I—"

"Shut up." His booming voice roughened. "You walked into that girl's house, interrogated her, took her child, and ignored legal procedure when you gave him to his grandmother. With no documentation, no paperwork of any kind." He didn't hide his exasperation from her. "You have no proof the child was abused, because you neglected to bring him to Child Services first and then record whatever evidence you claim to have seen. As a result of your bungling, we have utter squat at this time, no photo evidence, not to mention a ruling by a judge for the child's temporary guardianship. All we have is your rash and impulsive actions, which I'm sure resulted in the Turner family's ability to lawyer up in a hurry. And can't say that I blame them."

She tried to defend herself. "Sir, I know what I saw—"

"I told you to shut up. And it doesn't *matter* what you saw. Without going through proper channels, without photo documentation, you could have seen the kid wrapped in manure stained bed sheets and hanging on a hook as wall art, and it wouldn't have mattered. That's what procedure is for. Jesus save me from the idiots of the world," Lawrence griped as he tugged on his thinning hair and made what sparse amount he possessed stand on end.

"I'm *not* an idiot. I did what I thought was best. The boy was sobbing hysterically. He had on a soaking wet diaper. That speaks of neglect. He had a knot on his head where that simpleton girl had hit him, and—"

"What does a wet diaper have to do with it, for pity's sake?" Lawrence couldn't contain his ire. "I've got a news flash for you, Morgan: babies piss their diapers until they're soaked, and boy babies can soak their britches on a single piss. And did you actually *see* how that knot on his head got there?"

He wanted to grab onto his assistant and shake some sense into her. His pale blue eyes, framed by thick, dark eyebrows, narrowed as they took in her visible defiance. Stating the obvious, he growled, "Babies cry when they're wet, or when they fall down and hit their heads. That's all we can assume happened. And you of course know what happens when you *assume*, don't you?"

Louise hissed, "Yes. *Sir.*"

Lawrence heaved himself to his feet and gave his troublemaker of an assistant a few final orders. "Go home, Louise. I want a report of this on my desk, first thing in the morning. Next time you receive a call from an anxious grandmother, you might want to make sure you have all your legal ducks in a row, before you go tearing off to save the child from the clutches of its loving family. You got that? Oh, and one more thing." He tossed it out to her before she could reach his door and make her escape. "Next time don't bring your personal junk to your job. As of right now, consider yourself on suspension."

Chapter 29

Annie collapsed on the living room sofa and expelled a breath of utter relief. If she'd had to remain at the county offices for even five more minutes, she'd have screamed her head off.

What a nightmare. She rubbed at eyes still gritty and swollen from all the tears she'd shed. But Hank was safe now, and that was the most important thing.

She looked up with a tired smile when Travis sat next to her. He pulled on a strand of hair near her temple. "I found breakfast." With a flourish, he held out a small piece of dried oatmeal.

"Oh, good grief. I walked around with food in my hair—why didn't you say anything?" Annie protested, horrified.

"I don't think any of us cared that you had food in your hair, sweetheart." He leaned close and kissed her. Their lips clung as his arm slipped around her and he pressed her close. Annie sank into his embrace and let his warmth soothe her.

From the doorway, someone cleared their throat, and Annie pulled away with a flush to her cheeks. Aunt Nan stood there with two steaming mugs in her hands.

"Here. Hot cocoa." She brought them over to the coffee table and set them down. "You could both do with some extra calories." She perched on the edge of the sofa near Travis and ruffled his hair. "And you could use a trim, my boy. When was the last time you went to a barber?"

"It's kind of slipped my mind lately, Aunt Nan," he replied. Annie could see the pleasure on her aunt's face when Travis called her "Aunt."

"Hmph. Let Susan cut it. She's got a way with shears." Aunt Nan laughed aloud when he paled. Annie loosed a rusty-sounding snicker. Actually, the thought of Susan wielding anything with sharp blades *was* pretty scary.

"Um—"

"Don't tease him, Nan. He's had a rough night." Her mama chastised Aunt Nan as she entered the living room. Travis gave her a grateful smile. Annie's eyes lingered on the lines weariness had left on Mama's face. Well, they were all weary. It had been an awful few days.

Hank was out of her arms for almost forty-eight hours before she and Travis got him back. For a lot of that time, he'd been in Ruth's hands. Just the thought of Ruth anywhere near her precious baby still sent shivers of fear up her spine. Luckily, Martha had kept Hank with her, the two of them locked in her bedroom.

She felt a smile quiver at one corner of her mouth, and her mama raised her eyebrows in query. "What? Thinking of a joke? We could all use a laugh right about now."

Annie let some mirth bubble over. "I'm just trying to picture Martha with Hank in her arms behind a locked door, and Ruth, hopping mad on the other side." As everyone released tired chuckles, she sobered. "I guess it's not that funny, when you think of it. What if she'd gotten inside? Would they have had a tug-of-war with our baby?" she appealed to Travis worriedly.

"No, I doubt it. Even my mother isn't that clueless around babies. And she's always been intimidated by Martha." He tried to reassure her.

After giving her a final squeeze, Travis got to his feet and faced everyone. Mama, Aunt Nan, Mark, who stepped through the door quietly with Susan on his heels. Travis met their eyes with a look of apology in his own, and Annie ached with empathy for what she knew he must feel. When her daddy walked in the room carrying Hank, dressed in his own pajamas and drowsy from his nap, she watched tears slip down Travis's cheeks.

"I—I'm sorry. For what my mother put you through, I'm so sorry. She had no right. You must think she's the most awful person in the world, and I couldn't blame you at all for thinking that way."

"Now, stop that." Mark was the first to step forward. He clapped Travis on the back, pulling him in for a brotherly hug. Travis clung as Mark admonished, "How could you know what your mama had planned? None of us really thought she would." He held Travis's shoulders, made him listen. "Trav, what your mama did . . . I don't think she can help herself. She's got problems. I hope she gets help someday. In the meantime, I think we'd all best remember that her reasons for doing what she did are based on strong feeling. Maybe it's the wrong feeling." He gave Travis a brief shake. "But she's still your mama. I'm willing to cut her some slack. Not much," he winked, "but a little."

"Mark's right." Annie got to her feet and wrapped an arm around Travis, caught her brother with her free hand, and squeezed his fingers in thanks. "And there's blame, but it isn't on you, Travis. You're not in control of what your mother does."

No, he wasn't in control of his mother's actions, Travis knew. It didn't lessen the bitterness or the hurt. He sat with Annie on the sofa and snuggled her in one arm and Hank in the other, while the rise and fall of conversation around him soothed over his jangled nerves. He wouldn't forget this day, not for a long time.

It was far from over. They still had to face the damned subpoena, and a court date had already been set. But this latest escapade would undoubtedly cost his mother some credibility points.

A few hours passed peacefully. One by one, the Turner family said their goodnights and trooped upstairs to bed, leaving Travis and his precious family clustered together on the sofa. Aunt Nan, the last to head up, kissed their cheeks before she left the room.

Sleepy-eyed, Hank babbled to the old stuffed dog in his arms. Travis recognized it as one he'd played with when he wasn't much older than his son. Martha must have saved it all these years and given it to Hank when she had him upstairs with her at Quincy Hall.

He still couldn't quite believe his mother had, in effect, kidnapped her own grandson. Though she kept him overnight, County Child Services ordered her to release Hank into their custody first thing the next morning, and two uniformed police had come to Quincy Hall and taken him. Travis found out Martha had refused to unlock the bedroom door, even after she heard their voices on the other side. Picturing it made him laugh aloud.

"What now?" Annie sent him a puzzled look.

He nestled her closer. "Oh, thinking about Martha, demanding to see some ID from those cops. She wouldn't open the door until they slid their badges under so she could examine them."

Annie released a coughing laugh. "Oh, Lord. I can see her doing it, too." She rested her head on his shoulder. "We should head up. We're both wiped out, and we have to go see that lawyer, Ms. Findley, tomorrow." She moved away, stretched, and grabbed hold of the sofa arm to hoist herself up.

"Yeah, my energy levels spiked downward many hours ago." Travis struggled to his feet with his son's heavy weight on his shoulder, one hand still gripping the stuffed dog. "Let's get the big guy to bed." He carried Hank toward the foyer. Behind him, Annie snapped off lights.

"I think we should bring Hank with us tomorrow," she commented as they climbed the stairs. "I don't want him out of our sight."

"You won't get an argument from me."

In the dark bedroom, Annie stroked Hank's hair as he curled on his side and hugged the stuffed dog to his face. Seconds later she heard a tiny snort, Hank's own baby version of a snore. She muffled a chuckle, afraid she'd awaken Susan.

When she turned to whisper goodnight to Travis, her jaw dropped at the sight of him, unbuttoning his shirt. "What are you—Susan's in here!"

He snapped on the low-wattage lamp between the beds, and she squeaked in alarm as she spun toward Susan. Only to stare, confused, at the empty bed.

"Where's Susan?"

"She suggested we swap rooms for the next few nights. She thought we'd feel better if we're both in here with Hank." Travis sat down on Annie's bed and pulled off his sneakers and socks, calmly undressing in front of her with her folks just down the hallway from them.

She sputtered, "My parents, Travis!"

He shrugged and sent her a slow smile as he stood and unfastened his jeans. "Your mama heard what Susan said to me. She just patted me on the head, the way she usually does."

He slipped out of his jeans, and her mouth went dry at the look of him, the tanned, smooth skin and lean muscles. He took a step toward her, his eyes darkened with emotion. "We're getting married soon. Your mama knows how much we love each other. If she's okay with me sleeping in the same room with you and Hank, then I'm sure okay with it."

He reached her side and ran a hand over her braided hair, loosening it. Strong fingers slid against her scalp and massaged away her tension, while his other hand brought her closer as he worked at the tangles. She leaned into his body, loving the feel of his bare skin beneath her cheek. He stroked his thumb along the curve of her mouth until it reached her chin, then tipped her head back and took her lips in a deep kiss.

How easy and familiar, to fall back on the old, faded bedspread with him. How exciting, as well as a touch forbidden, the idea they'd make love with family members three doors down from them. Even if they were married, she was certain she'd have been self-conscious.

Then her hesitancy melted away, at the force of need Travis's kisses aroused in her. She met each one of them with hunger, moaning when he tugged at her clothes.

The soft creak of the bedsprings beneath them, as they shifted on the mattress, didn't disturb the child who slept in the crib tucked into one corner of the room. In the dim light, their gazes locked as he rose above her.

"Annie." He breathed her name into the warm, shadowed room. Her arms reached for him, welcomed him. When he pressed against her and their bodies meshed together, they both sighed.

Chapter 30

Catherine hadn't been sleeping well at all.

It was her own fault. Listeners at keyholes usually heard things they'd rather not know about, and she had done a very stupid thing: she'd listened at the keyhole over at Quincy Hall. The evening of Travis's birthday, she should have just kept walking right out of the house. But she hadn't. Instead, after the bombshell she'd dropped concerning Travis's and Annie's baby, she'd made her exit but crept back toward the wide doors and hid behind them like the worst sort of eavesdropper. Why, she still wasn't sure. Perhaps she'd needed to hear her mother finally acknowledge defeat, and then somehow persuade Ruth to give up, too.

Instead, her mother chose to conspire with Ruth. Some of the words were muted, but Catherine heard more than enough. She pressed a hand to her mouth, aghast, as Ruth plotted out what amounted to kidnapping her own grandson. A court would no doubt call it something else. They'd probably say it was a concerned and loving grandmother worried about the welfare and well-being of a small child.

But Catherine knew better. And so did her mother, damn it.

Just the other day Catherine had found bridal magazines—and heaven save her, upholstery swatches—in the library. It *had* to stop. Now, before her mother actually mailed out the engagement announcements stacked next to the swatches. Catherine was afraid to ask how long ago they'd been purchased.

She planned to drive out in about two hours, headed

to New Haven. She nodded decisively as she snapped the suitcase shut and hefted it to the floor to sit beside the rest of the matched set. She'd had enough of Thompkin, enough of parental machinations. She longed for her uncomplicated, comfortable apartment.

But first she had to make it out to her car with her suitcases. And do it without the additional guilt, remorse, and disappointment her mother could so expertly heap on her.

She succeeded in getting all of her luggage out to the car, which was parked at the side of the house. As she went upstairs a final time for her purse and a small tote bag, her mother appeared at the bottom of the stairs and peered up at her.

"Cathy?" Just her name, but Catherine could hear the plea, as well as the demand, in her mother's voice.

With a sigh she turned, smoothing down the skirt of her navy summer-weight suit. "Yes, Mother. I was coming to the parlor to say goodbye." She paused, astonished at the sudden sheen of emotion in her mother's eyes and the way she wrung her slender hands together.

"But, Cathy, why leave now, just when everything is coming together—"

"You know why I'm leaving now," she reminded her mother as she descended the stairs. "I told you, and Ruth, too. I really don't want to be here right now."

One tear spilled over her mother's lower lid and tracked slowly down her cheek. "You are so close, my dear, so close to attaining everything you've always wanted. Why would you throw it all away when you only have to reach out for it?"

Though her mother's tears made her feel horrendous guilt, as they usually did, Catherine held firm. "It's not what I want. It's what *you* want. What Ruth wants. Please don't insult my intelligence any further. If I'm very lucky, I won't have lost Travis's friendship during this entire debacle."

"Travis won't marry that girl, Cathy. Why, he's coming home very soon. Ruth said—"

"For heaven's sake, stop listening to what Ruth says. She knows nothing about her son, his goals and dreams, his needs. She never did." Catherine fought her temper. She wanted to yank her hair out by the roots and stomp on it.

With a fortifying breath, she reached for her mother's hand. "You have *got* to let me live my own life. For too long, I've gone along with this insane plot to capture Travis, thinking I was in love with him and he was the one for me. But he's not, understand that. I deserve a man who'll look at me the way Travis looks at Annie, Mother. I deserve no less than that.

"Please." Catherine held her mother's sad gaze. "Let me do what I think is best for me. Stop buying into Ruth's madness."

She leaned in and kissed her mother's damp cheek, then released her hand and walked to the door. Turning, Catherine offered a strained smile. "I'll call you in a few days. Maybe you can come up to New Haven and help me get ready for the semester. Stay a while. We could eat out at fast food diners and go shopping."

"You know I abhor fast food." There was a steadier note in her mother's voice, though tears still streamed from her eyes. "I'll miss you, Cathy. I love you so much."

"I love you too, Mother. I'll call you when I get to New Haven." Catherine pulled the heavy door open and stepped out into the warm sunshine, breathed deeply, tasting her freedom, as well as the sweet scent of the primroses that grew in tangled profusion along the side porch.

After one more important stop, she'd be out of Thompkin. There was a lilt in her step, all the way to the car.

Annie paused in the open doorway of Mark's old room with a purposely cheery smile on her face as she watched Sissy nursing Toby. That kind of bond between mother and child was so important. Remembering how incredible it had felt to nurse Hank, Annie was thrilled for Sissy to have a chance to experience it for herself.

Sissy looked up from admiring her son as Annie stepped through the door. Her cheeks flushed pink, but she made no move to cover herself, which in itself spoke volumes about the way her role as wife and now motherhood had matured her. Sissy was so painfully shy, it had amazed the family when Mark snared a first date with her. And look at her now; well balanced, secure, and content. It was wonderful.

"I just wanted to see this sweet boy, before we take off for Weston. We'll be gone most of the day, and Mark mentioned last night that y'all might leave today?" There was a question in Annie's voice as she sat down on the bed next to Sissy and caressed Toby's downy cheek.

"I talked him out of it," Sissy replied. "Your folks want to spoil Toby some more, and I'm not ready to leave everyone. We've got another three weeks, if we want to take them. I think we should stay right here. What if there's more trouble?" Her voice dropped to a whisper. "Travis's mama might try pulling something else. It's best we stay awhile." She supported the baby's head and tiny shoulders when his mouth slipped from her nipple, his milky lips already going slack with sleep.

"Well, you sure won't get any argument from me." Annie held out her arms and Sissy handed Toby over. She rested against the pillows and fastened the front of her nightgown as Annie worked a noisy little burp from the dozing infant. She propped him on her shoulder and nuzzled him, loving the tender feel of him in her arms. "Oh, he's so very adorable. He makes me want to have another of my own."

"You're not—" Sissy gestured with one hand and blushed.

"Oh, no!" Annie hastened to reassure her. "We've only been, um—" Now it was her turn to pinken. Sissy nodded in understanding as Annie confessed, "We've had only a few opportunities to be together. And we've been careful. I know it's just a few weeks until the wedding, but we can't afford another baby, at least not for a few years. I'm going to get a prescription for pills, I think. It's the best thing to do."

"Well, there, you see? We need to stay, for the wedding. In all the excitement of these past few days, I forgot. I'm so sorry." Sissy was sweetly contrite, and Annie waved it away as she rocked her nephew in her arms.

"Gee, I wonder why you'd forget a thing like that? It's not as if you had other pressing things to think about." With reluctance, Annie handed the baby back to Sissy and stood, moving toward the door. One final glance over her shoulder and she just had to tease the new mother. "Enjoy it now, Sissy. Before you know it, he'll be biting when he nurses."

Sissy went milk-pale and gaped at her, then stared down in dawning horror at the innocent angel she held. Then back at Annie as she stammered, "They bite? Nobody told me they bite!" There was a note of panic in her voice that had Annie laughing all the way down the stairs.

In the kitchen, her mother cleaned Hank's breakfast off his face. He bounced in his high chair as soon as he saw Annie in the doorway.

"Hank, hold still. You'll fall right out and land on your head again." Her mother scolded him as she scrubbed at his chin.

"Owd, owd, owd! Gammy! Owd!" Hank shrieked and clapped his pudgy hands, then stretched them out to Annie as she walked over to him. "Bye-bye, Ma-Ma? Bye-bye?" His eyes widened with excitement as he spied the sweater she held.

"Yes, you messy little monkey. Bye-bye. Now, sit still and let Gammy finish washing your face." Annie frowned in mock-ferociousness, and Hank quieted in his seat and grinned angelically as her mother cleaned him up.

She bent and kissed his pink cheek, then laughed when he turned his head and gave her a smacking kiss on her mouth. "What a flirt you are. Be a good boy for your mama and daddy, you hear?" She ruffled his hair and deftly lifted him out of the chair.

Annie dressed him in his bright blue sweater, then patted his denim-covered rump and instructed, "Go find Daddy." Hank tottered off in the direction of the living room, calling for "Da" with every bounce he took on his hi-top sneakers.

"Well, he's full of pee and vinegar this morning. You sure you want to take him with you?" Her mother swiped the wet cloth over the highchair, cleaning off a few smears of cereal.

"I'll feel better having him with us, Mama. He'll probably fall asleep in the car." Annie picked up the diaper bag that sat by the front door and commented, "By the way, I talked to Sissy. They decided to stay another few weeks."

"That's just fine. I hoped, but I didn't like to ask, you know. I haven't had near enough time with Toby."

"No, neither have I. And things might start to get ugly with Ruth Quincy." Annie hated to formulate in words what her thoughts didn't want to admit to.

"Now, there'll be none of that. It's going to work out. There's nothing she can throw at us that we can't work through, honey. Aunt Nan decided to stay a while longer too, at least as long as Mark and Sissy. She's got some crazy idea that I might overdo it, doting on a newborn baby day and night." Her mother slipped her arms around Annie and cradled her, diaper bag and all. Annie rested her head on her mother's shoulder and gave in to the luxury of being treated like a little girl.

How many times had her mama been there for her, with open arms and loving reassurances? All of her life. She was so very lucky. Surely her luck would continue to hold through anything.

For a minute they snuggled together with Hank's blue plaid diaper bag hanging off Annie's arm, and they drew what both needed from each other. Annie raised her head and smiled into her mother's eyes, about to speak, when the doorbell suddenly pealed.

"Who could that be?" Annie set the diaper bag down and walked to the door. Just before she grasped the knob, she turned to her mother. "You think it could be that county child welfare office again?"

"Well, there's only one way to find out."

Annie nodded and peeked through the tiny peephole. "Oh, Lord." She pulled the inside door open and stood behind the screen, staring at the young woman who stood there in a dark blue suit. It had been over two years, but Annie knew who she was.

"Hello, Annie. I—" Catherine Cabot faltered, then straightened her shoulders determinedly. "May I come in?"

A few minutes later, Catherine sat on the living room sofa, her feet pressed together, toe to heel. Her hands, with their short, neat nails, lay folded in her lap. In her pretty navy suit, she seemed calm and capable, but Annie could see the uncertainty in her eyes.

On the floor, Hank played with his dump truck and plastic cars, occasionally pounding them together and then giggling with glee. Next to him, Travis sat cross-legged and kept one eye on their son and the other eye warily on Catherine, probably wondering the same as Annie wondered what on earth had brought her to Spring Street.

She should be furious that Catherine would just show up on the doorstep and ask to speak to her, then sit there silently and look all around at the room and the furnishings as if she'd never seen anything like it before. Annie doubted Catherine's ability to understand or be able to relate to a life so foreign to her own.

As if to confound her, Catherine raised her eyes from watching Hank play with his toys. "He's a lovely boy. You're very lucky, Annie. I'm sure you know that." She glanced around the room again and added, "Your home is so warm. It feels happy. It seems like a good place to raise a child."

"Thank you." Annie was stunned, to say the least. For years she'd envied this girl, jealous of the preference Travis's mother showed toward her. But now, she looked at her rival's face and saw only wistful envy. No vindictiveness, just longing and regret in Catherine's pale gray eyes.

Suddenly, the threat she used to pose seemed ridiculous. Annie's lips curved into a smile, which widened even more when Catherine hesitantly returned it.

"Catherine, what's going on? Why are you here?" Travis asked bluntly.

"I wanted you to know—" She paused and wet her lips. "Travis, I overheard your mother telling mine that she was going to send someone from the county here, about your little boy." She glanced down just as Hank raised his head and looked straight at her, then sent her a flirtatious smile. Her eyes lit up and she breathed, "Oh, Travis. He looks so much like you."

"He does, doesn't he?" Travis beamed. Meeting Annie's compassionate gaze, he rose from the floor and sat next to Catherine on the sofa. "We know about Mother's plans. She already sent a social worker, and the woman wasted her time coming here."

"Thank goodness she failed. But I don't see your mother quitting so easily. Do you?" Catherine asked.

"No, she won't. We're driving into Weston to meet with our attorney. Ten minutes later and you wouldn't have caught us," Annie explained.

"Then I'm glad I was on time. I wanted to meet Hank, Annie." Catherine turned back to her. "And I wanted to tell you myself there has never been anything but friendship between Travis and me. It was all in our mothers' heads, and there were times when just giving in was easier than fighting either of them." She took a breath and rushed on, "If there's anything you need from me, if I can tell your attorney anything that will help you, please let me know."

"Do you mean it? You'd help us? Why would you do that?" Annie hadn't meant to blurt it out quite that impolitely, but Catherine's friendliness bewildered her. When she glanced at Travis, she saw the same confusion on his face.

Catherine spread her hands in appeal. "Because our mothers have gone too far, and I'm tired of having my life controlled. I think I finally got through to my mother today, but I know I hurt her in the process." She stifled a sigh. "I'm going back to New Haven and get a head start on the semester. But if I can be of help to you, I'm happy to do what I can."

"Would you be willing to—no, that's too much to ask. Forget it." Travis got to his feet and reached down for Hank, swinging him up into his arms, while Annie collected the scattered toys and deposited them in Hank's toy box.

"What? Truly, if I can do anything, anything at all. . ." Catherine said earnestly.

Annie started to speak, glanced at Travis first, and caught his nod of agreement. "Would you come to Weston with us today? We meet with our attorney at ten. Any ammunition we can get is better than none at all." She aimed a tentative smile at Catherine. "I think what you have to say, maybe your observations, would be a big help."

"I can follow you in my car. It won't delay me much at all." Catherine extended her hand to Annie.

Annie took the narrow hand between both of her palms in silent thanks. She met Catherine's eyes. "We'll be leaving the attorney's office about noon, unless there's a delay. Hank will be hungry by then, and it's not smart for you to drive all the way to New Haven on an empty stomach. What do you think about joining us at the downtown diner for some greasy, but very good, food?"

"I think I'd like greasy food. I've never had onion rings before. Will they have onion rings?" Catherine asked hopefully.

"The biggest onion rings you ever saw," Travis replied. "Hank loves them, don't you, buddy?"

"Onwee! Owd, owd, owd!" Hank bounced in Travis's arms, ready to visit the diner and demolish a plateful of onion rings with the seven baby teeth he possessed.

Travis escorted them to the front door and called up the stairs. "We're heading out. Wish us luck."

"Good luck!" Two feminine voices floated down the stairs to them. A third, more gruff voice coming from the direction of the kitchen ordered Travis to make sure everyone in the car wore their seat belts and warned him to keep within the speed limit. Annie smothered a laugh at Aunt Nan's often caustic commands.

As Catherine walked to her car, she turned and smiled at Annie. "I was just thinking how comfortable you look in your blue jeans. I wish I had a pair."

"And I was thinking how classic and lovely you look in that pretty suit," Annie chuckled. "Maybe we should go shopping together one of these days. I can help you find some nice jeans. Maybe a sweatshirt. And you could give me some advice on dresses and such." She winked at Catherine.

Catherine winked back. "I'd like that."

Chapter 31

"I should change into the black dress." The green print blouse and matching skirt Annie wore looked too girlish for someone who was trying to convince a judge that she was mature enough to take care of a young child. She turned to Susan. "What do you think?"

"No. You look like the Grim Reaper's girlfriend in that thing. It drains all the color out of your skin and straightens what curves you have. Leave yourself alone." Susan fastened small enameled hoops in her ears and fluffed her hair expertly, until it fell down her back in a golden cloud. "Anyway, Mama called us downstairs five minutes ago."

"What about my hair?" Annie trailed a hand along the thick length. "Should I put it up on top of my head? Maybe if you cut some of it off—"

"Are you crazy? I'm not touching it. Your hair is fabulous, so you're going to leave it alone, too. You're gorgeous, I'm gorgeous and between the two of us we'll dazzle the judge silly." Susan swung back to the mirror and applied yet another layer of mascara.

Feeling more and more nervous, Annie faced her sister. "Susan, it's not a joke. This is important. I have to do everything right. I only get one shot at this. We don't know what Ruth might say in court. For all I know, she's got a bunch of people agreeing to perjure themselves on the stand against me. Ms. Findley says the judge is fair and will listen objectively, but, well, I don't seem to have a lot of confidence right about now."

"And you can't help being worried. We all are, Twerp."

Susan rose from the small vanity stool and grasped Annie's arm, tugged her toward the nearest bed and sat down next to her on the edge of the mattress. She massaged Annie's shoulder and her voice took on a bracing note. "You've got all of the family there, and believe me, Aunt Nan's ready to do battle. Did you see that glint in her eyes, last night at dinner?"

Susan nudged at Annie with her elbow until she nodded in agreement. "And the folks at Daddy's company? A bunch of them, including Daddy's manager, promised to be there. Martha will be there. And didn't you say Catherine Cabot's even coming in from New Haven? That's a lot of support, don't you think? It'll be all right."

"Yes. I know. I'm just," Annie waved her hand in dismissal, "I'm just being paranoid. I'm being a baby. If I go in there with that attitude, then I deserve to get myself stomped on." She squared her shoulders, stood and brushed a hand down the straight lines of her skirt to bolster herself. "Okay, positive mindset. Self-confidence. I think, no, I *know* we're going to win." Pushing away the doubt and the worry, she set her head at a cocky angle. "Plus, I look damned good. Let's go kick ass."

Susan choked out a laugh as she bounced off the bed and pulled Annie after her. "Potty-mouth. Okay, chin up. Bosom out. Oh, sorry." She spared a sideways glance toward Annie as they hurried down the stairs. "You don't have enough bosom for that. Well, fake it." She snickered at the look Annie sent her.

"I'll get you for that, Suze."

"*Don't* call me *Suze*."

The silly, back and forth bickering was just what Annie needed, she realized, as they rounded the corner and stepped into the living room where the rest of the family gathered. And bless Susan for knowing it.

Five minutes later, Sissy waved them off. She and Mark

volunteered to be the designated babysitters. Annie agonized over leaving Hank, but she didn't want him anywhere near Ruth. She wouldn't say that to Travis, though. He might have few illusions left where his mother was concerned, but Annie didn't want to make him feel any worse. Their latest session with Muriel Findley, their attorney, had been difficult enough for him.

His strong voice cracked with emotion several times as he told Muriel what his mother endured at Annie's grandfather's hands. But before that, all of them—Travis, Annie, and Catherine, too—described Ruth's absolute determination to force a marriage between Travis and Catherine. How far she was willing to go in order to take Hank away from Annie and raise him as her own son. They'd told Muriel everything.

Their attorney sat, nonplussed, while she processed Travis's words. Then she commented dryly, "No offense, Travis, but your mother is a piece of work."

Annie clapped a hand over her mouth to hold in a startled giggle, while Catherine turned her own giggle into a cough as Travis chuckled. Muriel's small bit of levity helped to lighten the overall mood considerably.

Muriel asked questions about Annie's daddy, too, and it was hard for Annie to view her own father objectively. But she'd been as honest as she knew how to be.

"Nobody could ever ask for a better father. You bring in any of us kids and ask that question and you'll get the same answer, over and over again. Whatever ugliness was inside Franklin Turner, it never spread any further. And there's a lot of people, in Thompkin as well as here in Weston, who'd be happy to lay their hand on a Bible and swear to it." Her response seemed to be exactly what Muriel had hoped for. In turn, she calmed Annie and Travis down a lot.

But now all those calm butterflies were stirring themselves up again.

In the back seat of Susan's car, Annie gripped Travis's hand when he twined his fingers through hers. "It'll be all right, Annie. I promise you." He kissed her cheek and held her close.

She nodded. Yes, it would. It had to be.

Travis figured his mother would voluntarily drag out her version of the Turner family history, if it would sway the judge in her favor. She considered Judge Perdue to be in her pocket. He vaguely remembered the man from past Christmas parties at Quincy Hall. He also knew Benson Perdue had been a frat brother of his father's, graduating two years ahead of Dad. It didn't surprise Travis to see Perdue's name on the bench today, but he hoped it was just a coincidence.

The courtroom was about half filled. Looking through the open door at the people already seated, he whispered to Annie, "Martha's here."

She nodded distractedly. "I'm so nervous, Travis."

"Oh, sweetheart, don't be. It's going to work out, I know it." He curled an arm around her waist and drew her back against him. Annie leaned into his chest, a hand on his arm to hold it in place around her. In that position they stood, until Muriel Findley, somber yet elegant in a dark gray suit, walked over to them and urged them to sit down. Travis released Annie and they followed Muriel to their seats.

"Relax. No tears, Annie. Look at me." Muriel's quiet, firm voice was close to Annie's ear and she turned her head, gulped in a breath. Muriel looked from Annie to Travis with warmth and assurance. "I want you to see all the people who came to support both of you. It's a good sign, trust me."

Muriel slipped one arm around Annie's shoulder and the other around Travis's waist, briefly linking them all together.

"You are both great parents. You have a support system that far exceeds the norm. You have bright futures ahead of you, and nobody can take that away or prove anything to the contrary. Remember that, okay?"

"We're starting in five minutes, Mrs. Quincy." Randolph Louden, one of Ruth's attorneys, shuffled the papers in front of him. "I'm asking you one final time. Is there anything you've left out? Anything more we can use in this case? As I cautioned you before, we haven't much to go on, here." His low voice grated in Ruth's ear and she glared at him. He merely raised his eyebrows and waited.

Incompetent idiot. Ruth turned to look at the other, older attorney, Walter Sheffield, who sat on her left. Both men, employed by the legal offices of the Quincy Legacy, were reputed to be the best. She'd given them a concise description of the hovel-like interior of the Turner home. She'd detailed the unsavory quality of the neighborhood itself. They had a copy of the report Child Services filed after poor Duncan had been rescued from that wretched place. The condition of his person, the bruises and the abuse he'd suffered was documented. What on earth more could they possibly need?

"Mrs. Quincy?" Louden brought her regard back to him.

She kept her expression bland, certain everyone in the courtroom was watching her. "I have explained, Mr. Louden, you have in your possession enough to assure a successful custody victory. The filed report from Child Services is more than adequate—"

"And both Mr. Sheffield and I have explained to *you* that your case is thin and needs more evidence. We both cautioned you against a push for this court date. We want to see you get the boy, Mrs. Quincy. But frankly, we haven't enough at this time to guarantee the judge's favor. We think we should reschedule."

"No. I refuse to wait any longer. Each day my grandson spends in that horrid family's presence damages him. We have enough evidence. I also have character witnesses. We will go forward." Ruth gave both of them a narrowed, biting stare. "I expect your litigation to be skillful and successful. Your employment depends on it, gentlemen. Please don't forget that."

Satisfied at the way both men seemed taken aback at her blunt threat, she relaxed in her seat and glanced around the courtroom. When she saw not only Janice Cabot but Catherine as well, seated a few rows behind, she hid a victorious smile. Her dear friend and her darling future daughter-in-law, here to offer support should she need it. How fortunate she was.

Of course, their testimony would not be required. After all, she was a Quincy. Her word alone was stellar in this state. Her motives, pure as they were, would never be brought into question.

Ruth nodded to herself in satisfaction. She'd win.

Annie tried to stay calm, which wasn't easy. Judge Perdue, large and gruff, resembled a hefty bird-of-prey, sitting behind the massive bench in his black robes. His face held no expression. Of course, impartiality was part of his job. He had thick hair as dark as Travis's and the blackest eyes she'd ever seen in her life. Annie took several quick, steadying breaths, then held the last one, until the panic fluttering inside her passed somewhat. She curled against Travis and he tightened his arm.

"All right?" His mouth brushed her ear.

"I'm okay. I just can't seem to control my jitters."

"I'm nervous too, sweetheart. It'll be over soon, and we'll walk out of here and go back home to Hank. Never doubt it." Travis pressed his lips to her temple and kept them there for a few seconds.

Muriel caught Annie's eyes. "I noticed Mrs. Quincy's attorneys conferring rather urgently with her several times already. I'd venture to say it was to drop this whole mess. It's what I would have done. Unless she or her boys over there have some last-minute surprises up their sleeves, I predict the judge will most likely toss her case out."

"I'm too nervous to think that positively," Annie confessed, as she gripped Travis's hand.

The pound of the gavel made them both jump. "Here we go," Travis muttered, sitting up straighter in his seat.

Annie listened as Ruth reiterated the Child Welfare Services report, using her frostiest and most precise tone. Her attorneys waited until she'd finished, then one spoke up. "Mrs. Quincy, do you think perhaps the child's emotional outburst might have been caused by being forcibly taken from his home by a stranger, and then held in an unfamiliar place until he was brought to you?"

Fury showed on Ruth's face, probably because her own attorneys would ask such a question. But she seemed to hold on to her calm. "Certainly not. The boy should have had no reason to be hysterical. He was being rescued, after all. His incessant crying was a direct result of the pain of the bruises. His head injury compounded the residual discomfort of wet diapers."

Muriel stood to address her. "Mrs. Quincy, do you understand that Lawrence Bailey, the head of Child Welfare for this county, ordered the return of the child to his biological mother based on lack of evidence of any kind of abuse?"

"Yes, and it has proven to me the utter incompetence of some county offices. I intend to look into the matter myself, as a representative of the Quincy Legacy." There was a self-righteous sniff in Ruth's voice as she answered, a tone Annie had heard in one or another form, for as long as she'd known the woman.

A few minutes later, Travis's mother made a grave tactical error. When Muriel mentioned Hank by name, Ruth interrupted emphatically, "His name is *Duncan Adams Quincy*. Kindly refer to my grandson correctly."

The murmur that rippled through the courtroom was loud enough for the judge to tap his gavel and demand order. Perdue asked all three attorneys to approach the bench. It was impossible to hear what was said, but Annie had a healthy imagination. Ruth had made a big mistake.

When Muriel returned to her questioning, she gently but firmly stated, "Mrs. Quincy, your grandson's legal name is Henry Travis Turner. Why do you refer to him otherwise?"

"It's an inferior, common name. My grandson requires an impressive title. Therefore, his name *will* be Duncan Adams Quincy, after I have adopted him."

"And why do you want to adopt your grandson, Mrs. Quincy? Aside from your allegations of neglect and abuse which my client supposedly perpetrated on her own child?"

"He is the next Quincy Heir. Under my tutelage and guidance the boy will realize his full potential as befits the family legacy. If left to the devices of his mother and her family, I have no doubt he will grow to be as common and inferior as they all are." Ruth's voice rang with superior disdain. Everyone in the courtroom had to have heard it. Annie winced.

Before Annie rose from her seat and approached the witness bench, she clenched Travis's fingers, hard. When she took the stand, she raised her hand and without a single ripple of nervousness swore to tell the truth. But Travis knew how frightened she felt. He also knew she'd come across as exactly the kind of person she was: intelligent, loving, an endearing combination of youth and capability.

Muriel easily guided Annie through the events of the day Hank was taken, and in such a way that Annie responded with maturity and calm composure. By the time his mother's attorneys got hold of her, Annie was ready for them.

They gave it a fair shot. They must have realized their client wasn't playing with a straight deck. But they worked for Ruth Quincy. Travis didn't doubt she'd already threatened their jobs if she didn't win today. Being faced with the loss of a prestigious and well-paying job would make anyone toe the line, even if—as he suspected—her attorneys didn't believe much of what his mother had told them.

They asked Annie about the knot on Hank's forehead, and she explained how he slid out of his highchair and when she tried to catch him, the tray caught him in the head.

One of the attorneys queried, "Why use such a substandard piece of children's furniture for your son, if he could be in danger of sliding out of his seat?"

Annie lifted her chin. "I've been saving money for a new highchair."

They asked about the bruises on his arms, and she replied that in her panic to get a grip on him before he hit the floor, she grasped his arms tightly. Hank's tender baby skin bruised easily.

They wanted to know if she was in the habit of leaving her child in soaked diapers and tee shirts crusted with food. With admirable restraint, Annie said, "Bath time could wait. It was more important to calm my son down."

The attorney smoothly changed tactics. "You cannot

deny your inability to care for your son by yourself, at your age. When you start college—"

"I have already started college, sir." Annie interrupted the man without apology. "I'm going to be a sophomore. I also have a job at the university bookstore. I have a full scholarship this semester provided I maintain a three-point-five grade average. Which I intend to do. And Hank has a daddy, too."

"We are not establishing the dependability of the child's father at this time, Miss Turner."

"All right, if you want to leave him out of it, fine. I can do it myself, if I have to. I can take care of my son, work part-time, attend college and still maintain three-point-five or better."

"You cannot predict—" the attorney began.

"Oh yes, sir. I can. I graduated in-home high school study at college level, with a four-point-zero average, two days after Hank was born. To get this full scholarship, to be able to pay for most of my schooling and not have to burden my family with the cost, I can do another four-point-zero, and I can do it on my head if I have to." Annie was on a roll. It was all Travis could do not to laugh aloud in profound relief.

She paused as if to calm herself, and looked the attorney dead in the eye. "I can do it without sacrificing my son's well-being. I can do it without having to depend on strangers. Would you like to know *how* I'm sure I can do it?"

He started to say something, hesitated and then shrugged. "Certainly, Miss Turner."

"Because my family's behind me. They want me to succeed. I don't have to beg them for help because they'd offer it anyhow." Annie paused again and tilted her head curiously. "You must not know much about big families, sir."

"Well, I—"

"Big families take care of each other. Big families have

a lot of love to pass around. When I was a kid, my mama and daddy weren't always right there to stick a band-aid on my finger if I hurt it, or to read me a bedtime story. But my older brothers were, and before I knew it I'd be tucked up in bed and falling asleep and it didn't matter if it was Mama or someone else who took care of me. I once had the measles and couldn't do my chores, so my sister and my brothers did them for me. There wasn't much money but there was always lots of love, and that was more than enough. Family is family. We help each other out. That's the way it should be."

And that, Travis thought, was that. Annie summed it up in her soft, sweet voice, without anger, and with strong conviction. He was so proud of her.

Finally, the Quincy legal team let her go. Annie started to step down, but instead turned toward his mother's attorneys. "I'm sorry I interrupted you so many times, sir. It's true I had something to say. But I was raised better, and I was taught to always respect my elders and not interrupt them while they're talking."

With that, and amidst chuckling that rippled through the courtroom, Annie returned to her seat. Travis guessed the younger attorney was none too pleased at being referred to as someone's "elder," judging by the pinkish tips of his ears. Travis stifled his own chuckle.

Then it was his turn. He took the oath and seated himself, locked away his nerves, knowing he needed his wits about him. He felt positive the case had already swung in his and Annie's favor, but it was unwise to assume anything. He'd learned that particular lesson the hard way.

"Travis, your son's welfare and safety must mean a great deal to you." The attorney—Sheffield, if Travis wasn't mistaken—began his examination with what passed for avuncular concern.

Without a blink of hesitancy Travis answered, "Yes of

course. And Annie always—"

"And yet, you allow your son to be cared for by a young woman who doesn't appear to understand the first thing about proper childcare. Bruises on his arms and neglected diaper changes seem to be the scope of her nurturing, wouldn't you say?"

"Objection. Your Honor, this is ridiculous. The circumstance behind the child's alleged condition that day has already been established." Muriel jumped in quickly.

Judge Perdue leveled a frown toward Sheffield. "Sustained. Mr. Sheffield, watch yourself."

"I'll rephrase. Travis, how long have you known your son, Henry Travis Turner?"

"Approximately two months."

"And in that time have you been satisfied with his upbringing and care under his biological mother, Annie Turner?"

"Yes, very satisfied. Annie is a wonderful mother, and—"

"And hasn't it worried you that your own mother would make allegations of neglect and abuse against the mother of your son? Wouldn't you need to find out just how factual these allegations might be?"

"I don't *need* to find out anything. I know Annie. I know her family, and I can see for myself how much they love and care for Hank. His nickname is Hank," Travis added wearily, right before Sheffield could open his mouth and say anything. "I was introduced to him as 'Hank.'"

"Yes, exactly. "Introduced." To your own son. Doesn't it bother you that your son's biological mother hid his existence from you, including her pregnancy? By your own admission you have only known your son for two months. Doesn't it upset you that Annie Turner and her family kept you from your own son?"

"Not anymore. Because I understand the reasoning

behind their decision to—"

"And now that you have had a chance to know your son, wouldn't you do anything to keep that child? Wouldn't you be willing to overlook some aspects of his upbringing, for the chance of a continued relationship with your son?"

"Your Honor, I have to object—" Muriel interjected.

"Your Honor, I am trying to establish a reason why the witness would allow his son to live under slovenly conditions and less than desirable guardianship—"

"*Enough*!" Judge Perdue slammed his gavel down hard, held in one broad hand. His black brows furrowed and his eyes flared with impatience. He leveled a thick finger at Sheffield. "Sit down, Mr. Sheffield. You too, Ms. Findley." Both attorneys resumed their seats. "Now, then. I have presided over many a custody case, and I guarantee you, there are two sides to every single story. Often there are even three or more. I have heard Mrs. Quincy's side of the story. I have heard Annie Turner's side, too. Now I would like to hear Travis Quincy's, and without further interruption. Is that clear, Mr. Sheffield?"

"Your Honor, I merely attempt to establish—"

"*Is that clear,* Mr. Sheffield?" Judge Perdue stressed.

Sheffield wisely subsided. "Yes, Your Honor."

The judge nodded toward Muriel. "Ms. Findley? Is that clear for you as well?"

"Yes, Your Honor."

"All right. Since we're all clear, the witness will answer the original question, which I believe queried whether or not he was upset from attempts by the Turner family to keep his son's identity from him." Judge Perdue looked over at Travis. "Answer the question, please."

Travis didn't hesitate at all. "At first, I was angry. I missed out not only on the first year of my son's life, but also the preparatory excitement that goes along with planning for a baby. I would have been scared knowing I was to become a father so soon, but thrilled to share in all of that with Annie and her family." Travis smiled directly at Annie, and saw the way her eyes glittered with emotion. "But I understood why Hank's birth was hidden from me for as long as it was."

Travis paused, looking not to either attorney but to Judge Perdue for permission to continue. The judge nodded encouragingly, and Travis realized that 'go-ahead' nod may have helped them turn an important corner.

"My mother, Ruth Quincy, has disapproved of my relationship with Annie since we were children. She treated the Turner family badly, spoke against them in slanderous terms, and threatened them verbally. She used my affection for the family as well as my love for Annie as a way to manipulate me, and threatened to cause trouble for the Turners if I didn't sever my relationship with Annie. That's why I broke things off with her. Consequently I was kept in the dark about the pregnancy and Hank's birth, and I don't blame Annie or her family one bit, given the way I acted."

With his words, Travis might have felt a twinge of guilt at the way he aligned himself against his mother, but only a twinge. Because there was fury on his mother's face. Fury, and something else. Something ugly.

Judge Perdue asked, "And what did she threaten the Turner family with, young man? What sort of trouble could she have caused?"

From the plaintiff's table, Travis saw the look of puzzlement and then worry that Louden shot in his mother's direction. He and Sheffield crowded in, and both whispered urgently to her. With a swipe of two hands, his mother cut them off. Her spine steel-rod stiff, she glared at Travis.

A frisson of panic made him falter. God, he didn't want to push his mother's past into the open like this. But then he looked at Henry and saw the smile of reassurance, the nod of acquiescence. In Annie's eyes he saw only love and pride.

As Travis parted his lips to speak, Muriel got to her feet

and sent a pleading glance toward Sheffield. He resignedly stood to address the bench. "Your Honor, we respectfully request a short recess, to confer privately with you and with our clients."

One thick black eyebrow shot up. "Ms. Findley, is this acceptable to you?"

At the judge's gruff query, Muriel spoke up, "Yes, Your Honor. With your permission."

"All right, then. Twenty minutes."

Chapter 32

"Everybody take a seat. If there's not enough to go around, too bad. You'll have to stand." In his chambers, Benson Perdue settled his large frame behind his desk.

"Let's get this over with. Mr. Sheffield and Mr. Louden, Ms. Findley, I assume you all know what this impromptu conference is about?" When the Quincy attorneys merely looked confused, Perdue sighed, and turned to Muriel. "All right, Ms. Findley. You're up."

With a quick glance at Travis, Muriel began, "Your Honor, you wanted to know what Mrs. Quincy could have used as a threat against the Turner family—"

"I know what I requested, Counselor. Now, why doesn't somebody just give me the answer?" Perdue barked.

"Your Honor, may I speak?" Travis asked.

The judge gestured with his hand. "By all means."

Travis cleared his throat. "My mother hates the Turners, Your Honor, because years ago when she was just fifteen, Henry Turner's father, Franklin Turner, sexually abused her repeatedly—"

"*Travis, you will be silent.*" His mother half-rose from her seat and hissed at him.

"Mrs. Quincy, you never mentioned this," Sheffield sputtered at her, trying to catch hold of her arm. She pushed him away.

"Mother, it needs to be told. It's festered inside you for far too long," Travis pleaded.

"It has *nothing* to do with how horrible that girl is as a mother to my grandson," she spat.

"It has *everything* to do with your opinion of me and my family, Mrs. Quincy," Annie protested.

"*Shut up*! Good God Almighty, can't I get a straight answer when I ask for one?" Perdue looked ready to pitch all of them out the door. "Everyone sit down, and stay there. You," he pointed to Sheffield, "can shut up as well. And you," his finger swung toward Annie, "young lady, I don't want to hear a peep out of you, either. Now, sit." He waited until his commands were obeyed, then gestured to Travis. "As I said before, let's hear it. You have ten minutes, so make it count."

It took roughly seven minutes. Travis kept to the facts and reiterated those with as much straightforward economy as he could. At one point, his mother covered her face with both hands and didn't pull away when Sheffield placed a bracing arm around her. And by the end of it, Annie as well as Muriel blinked away tears.

"Anything else to add?" Perdue asked. Throughout the telling of it, his expression hadn't altered one iota. It was impossible for Travis to gauge what the judge might be thinking.

"No, Your Honor. That's about it." Travis started when he felt Annie's hand squeeze his. He hadn't realized he'd clung to her shoulder for dear life.

"All right. I'm going to extend the recess by ten additional minutes, while I give this latest information my attention and thought. I will make my ruling presently. You're all excused, and will repair to the courtroom."

Judge Perdue cast his black eyes around the room. "But, before you all leave, let me just say this." He settled on Travis's mother first. "Mrs. Quincy, it was extremely unfortunate that you had to endure such a crime, and at such a young age. There is no ready excuse nor condoning what was done to you. However, if you had reported it at the time, I believe valuable counseling could have been arranged for you to help you past the pain of your ordeal. That you chose to conceal it for all these years, tells me you need closure badly. My advice to you is to get yourself into counseling, the sooner the better."

Travis was certain Perdue's gruffness hid his very genuine concern over the wife of his good friend. But his mother sat ramrod straight in her chair and refused to acknowledge the judge's words. Only her eyes seemed alive, and they were a blistering blue.

With a sigh, Perdue regarded Annie. "Miss Turner, this episode of your family history must be difficult for you to accept. Maybe you're afraid there might be repercussions, should this information about your grandfather become public knowledge. But in a court of law, the sins of the father stay with the father and are not visited upon his children. Your own father need not worry about his good reputation. The law doesn't bend that way."

"Thank you, Your Honor." It was a husky whisper. "And thank you, in my daddy's name."

Judge Perdue stood, and the attorneys jumped to their feet. He addressed them all. "Counsel will take this information as background evidence inasmuch as it applies to the plaintiff's mindset, because that's exactly what it is. I trust the three of you will use some common sense while you're at it. Dismissed." He waved everyone toward the door. "Ah, Mr. Quincy? A moment, please." Perdue motioned to Travis, who obediently remained behind while everyone else shuffled out.

"Take a seat, Travis, I won't be long-winded." The judge gestured to the chair nearest his desk and Travis sat down, trying not to feel too much panic.

"Relax, son. I just wanted to thank you for this additional information. I have often felt—well, it doesn't matter. Your story does go a ways toward helping me to understand somewhat better. Now," Perdue took a pad and pen, and scribbled a few lines, "I am writing down the name and number of an excellent therapist who focuses on the victims of sexual crimes and deviant behavior. She's sympathetic and knowledgeable and holds several three-month counseling sessions a year. I think the sooner you get your mother into one of these sessions, the better." He ripped off the note and handed it to Travis, who folded it into his pocket.

"I'll try, Judge Perdue. I really will. But if you know anything about my mother, you also know how stubborn she is."

Perdue chuffed out a brief chuckle. "Oh, yes. That I *do* know. Nevertheless, see what you can accomplish with her."

Benson Perdue adjusted his robes and slipped on a pair of thick-rimmed reading glasses. He sorted through the papers in his hands one more time, before he raised his head and fixed that intensity on the two groups in front of him. Travis gripped Annie's hand.

"In my experience," Perdue began, "custody cases are amongst the toughest of domestic disputes. Someone wins, someone loses. If we are lucky, the children involved are always on the winning side, and we as public servants have done the right thing, made the best choice for that young life.

"I made a choice today, one I feel is in the best interest of the child, Henry Travis Turner. After weighing evidence, such as it is, and hearing from everyone concerned, I have made my decision based on what has been proven. I see no evidence that Annie Turner, or her fiancé, Travis Quincy, are anything other than good parents, therefore they shall retain full custody of their minor child, Henry Travis Turner."

He paused for a second as Annie turned to Travis and flung her arms around his neck, then rapped his gavel sharply to dispel the congratulatory rumble already forming. "Order, please, I'm not finished. Annie and Travis," Perdue eyed them over the rim of his reading glasses, "I trust you won't mind a visit from County Child Welfare once in a while, say, quarterly, for a period of one year. Said visit not to exceed one hour, for the purpose of verifying the child care progress of Henry Travis Turner. Unannounced visits," he clarified.

"No, Your Honor. I mean, yes, Your Honor. I mean, visits are fine," Annie stammered out.

"Good. Child Welfare will be happy to hear of it," Perdue retorted dryly, and unbent enough to bestow a smile on them.

He glanced over at Travis's mother, who stood as if turned to stone between the hapless attorneys assigned to her. "Mrs. Quincy, your son and future daughter-in-law will be randomly visited within the next twelve months, to assure they are taking proper care of your grandson, Henry Travis Turner. I trust this will appease your worry concerning your grandson's well-being. I am sure you'd like to set some kind of visitation schedule in motion, and I am certain Travis and Annie will find it within their hearts and in the child's best interests to allow his grandmother access now and then. Court is adjourned."

With a slam of his gavel, Perdue brought everyone to their feet. He stepped down from his bench and strode out the door. Behind him in the courtroom, the Turner family hugged Annie, and slapped Travis on the back before taking turns hugging him, too.

While Mary Turner kissed his cheek, Travis couldn't help but look over at his mother, as she stood and tugged on pale leather gloves as creamy and delicate as her own skin. She smoothed them carefully, tucked her purse under her arm, and swept from the courtroom without so much as a glance his way. Travis refused to feel guilty for the judge's decision. But he couldn't deny the piercing hurt, deep inside. He couldn't help but feel he'd just become an orphan.

"Let's get out of here, huh?" Henry slung his arm over Travis's shoulder. "I know two little boys who are very anxious to see the family. And I'd bet you anything there's a few pies in the refrigerator, compliments of Aunt Nan." He winked at his sister-in-law, and a rosy flush stole over her cheeks.

"Pie? Why on earth would I make you a pie, Henry Turner? You think all those ingredients grow on trees?" She huffed her way toward the courtroom's double doors.

Chapter 33

The gown hung in Mary's closet. She rounded the corner toward her bedroom and smiled when she saw the door wide open and Annie mooning over it for about the fourth time that day.

Mary and Annie had both scolded Nan, but Mary knew her sister would do as she pleased, and it had pleased her to buy Annie a wedding gown. A few days ago Nan drove to Thompkin and laid it in Annie's arms. While Annie cried on her shoulder in reaction to the lovely dress, Nan had cuddled her close and whispered gruffly, "Every bride deserves the gown of her dreams."

"But the cost, Aunt Nan—" Annie tried to protest.

"Oh, faddle. Haven't you ever heard of clearance sales, my girl?" Mary looked on, amused, as Nan gave Annie's ear a quick tweak. "I went to Bridal Palace, over in that newfangled mall. They were practically giving their gowns away. And as soon as I saw this one, I knew it was meant for you."

Nan plucked a hankie out of her pocket and wiped Annie's tears. "You can still have your daisy bouquet, if you must be thrifty. If we can find decent springtime daisies by now. They don't grow on trees, you know." That now-standard line was just what Annie needed to turn the sob in her throat to a watery snicker. She hugged Nan again, fiercely, then caught Mary around the neck and squeezed her, too.

Mary could have sewn a simple gown in just a few days with minimal expense. The last thing she knew her baby girl wanted was to burden anyone with wedding costs they couldn't afford. Annie would marry the man she loved and nothing else was more important.

But the dress *was* perfect. Simple in design, the heart-shaped neckline slipped off Annie's shoulders at just the right spot. Small, dainty cap sleeves showcased her slender arms and the fitted bodice curved into a dropped waist, which erupted into a flutter of scalloped chiffon panels. The back panels lengthened to form a subtle train. There wasn't any beading. No seed pearls. Instead, its very simplicity made it special.

When Mary came up behind Annie, she already had the protective bag unzipped and was sighing yet again over the chiffon panels. "Caught you! How many times have you looked at it today?" Mary snagged her at the waist.

Annie leaned her head back on Mary's shoulder. "Once or twice." That understatement earned her a pinch, and Annie giggled. "Okay, four or five times. I can't stop myself. It's so beautiful, Mama." She turned to face Mary. "Aunt Nan said it was on clearance, but this time of year, why would a bridal shop have a sale like that?"

Thoughtfully, Mary tucked a wayward strand of hair behind her daughter's ear. Annie was nobody's fool. She'd told Nan as much when her sister called from the mall in Roanoke and announced she'd found the perfect dress for Annie.

"You know how set Annie is against you spending your money, Nan." Mary spoke softly so Annie, upstairs with Hank, wouldn't overhear her.

"It's not my money, it's Annie's," Nan retorted in satisfaction. "All that "rent" she tried to pay me went into a savings account for her. There was enough to buy the gown. Why, I only had to toss in a few dollars of my own."

"Nan—"

"Well, maybe more than a few. So what? That child

deserves a wedding gown. Heaven knows I have money in my bank account that sits there and grows dusty. Now, I'll bring it up at the end of the week. You're not to tell Annie, you hear? She was proud of herself, giving me room and board money. I'd sooner cut off a hand than upset her or make her feel badly that I didn't keep it in the bank."

Mary promised not to say a thing, not even to Henry, about how Annie really came to have her dress. And now, seeing the way Annie sighed over it, her hands reverent when she touched it, Mary was glad Nan had gone with her instincts. Annie would look like a dream, wearing it. Her sister was the sweetest person in the world, and her gruff exterior hid a heart of pure gold.

To diffuse her own emotional state, Mary took one of Annie's hands and examined it. "There better not be anything on your fingers that can smear this dress, young lady, as much as you've been pawing at it." In spite of her teasing words, a catch roughened her voice.

"I'm going to be so happy, Mama. Please don't cry." Annie pulled her close.

Mary stroked her girl's soft brown hair. "I know you will, Munchkin. It's all I ever wanted for you." She eased away and kissed Annie's cheeks. "Your happiness. It's all your daddy ever wanted, too. And he'll be the proudest daddy in the world when he walks you down the aisle, with you on his arm wearing your pretty gown."

"I'm worried about Mrs. Quincy," Bette said to Phoebe Sherman.

Phoebe looked up from her lunch preparation and frowned at the blunt statement. Curious, she asked, "What's she been doing that would cause you worry?"

"For one thing, she's holed up in that study of hers all

hours of the day and night." Bette jerked her chin toward the foyer and the locked study door. "She paces and mutters to herself. She canceled her Wednesday bridge club and her Monday Guild luncheon. Said she doesn't want any of those women in the house ever again."

Bette's concern showed on her ruddy face. "She's not eating properly. All she ever seems to want is tea and those thin little lemon cookies that you can practically see through. And I tried asking her if I could swap Friday with Jenny, because Dougie and I—well, we have our blood tests for the marriage license that day. But she told me," Bette dropped her voice to a scandalized whisper, "she told me to "fuck off." Can you imagine, Mrs. Quincy saying a word like that? I've never, ever heard her swear, not even the mildest cuss word."

Phoebe rinsed her hands in the sink and wiped them off, as she processed Bette's concerns. Ruth *had* changed since losing that custody case two weeks ago. Never overly pleasant to the staff, she'd become downright hateful and surly to everyone from Phoebe herself to Charles, her gardener, whom Ruth had always seemed to hold in such high esteem. She even rebuffed her friend, Janice Cabot, who'd called three times to speak to Ruth. Janice had finally given up, probably certain Ruth would never forgive her for what had appeared to be lack of support during the custody hearing.

If only Martha were still at the Hall. Phoebe missed her calmness and common sense at times like these. She sighed once, then put it aside. She added a few finishing touches to Mr. Ronald's lunch, which was more important right now than anxiety over Martha's dismissal or Ruth's bizarre behavior.

Mr. Ronald was her biggest worry. His appetite had plummeted in the past year, and Phoebe often thought she prepared his meals for nothing, as he rarely ate them. She managed to get one or two prescribed protein drinks down him each day, and considered it a small victory. But his body seemed to be shutting down. It hurt her heart to think of how short his time on this earth might be.

"Phoebe? What should we do?"

Bette's fretful voice brought Phoebe back from her unwelcome thoughts, and she hastily folded a napkin and laid it on Ronald's tray. "I don't know. But right now I can't be thinking about it. I have to try and get as much of this lunch into Mr. Ronald as I can. Let me give Martha a call later on today, and maybe I'll call Dan Marley, too. He deals with Legacy business, doesn't he?" At Bette's nod, Phoebe hefted the tray and carried it out of the kitchen. As she headed toward the elevator, she glanced over her shoulder. "When I speak to Mr. Marley, I'm going to ask him to reinstate Martha. She needs to be here."

In her suite of rooms, Ruth stood at the window glaring at the beautiful grounds, faithfully groomed daily by Charles and two other day helpers. She didn't know their names nor did she give a shit if she ever learned them. All of the roses were in full bloom. She didn't give a shit about them, either.

What was the point of having flowers, or a carpet of perfect lawn that stretched over the rolling hills? The formal gardens, the luxurious pool area, the tennis court? The three-hole golf course? What was the point of tastefully decorated rooms, precious heirlooms and priceless works of art?

What was the goddamned point of having Quincy Hall, without an heir? Ruth pressed on her aching temples and cursed the onset of yet another headache. She'd been having them every day for over a week. It was the fault of all the people in her life who tromped on her and caused her untold pain. Her own son had betrayed her in the most heinous way.

Her grandson was beyond her reach. Her moronic attorneys resigned before she could have the satisfaction of firing them. And her husband—her once-handsome, once-strong husband—was a fucking rutabaga.

"Fuck." Ruth whispered the word. "Fuck it." A bit louder. It felt satisfying, she decided. A taboo word, never spoken in this hallowed house by anyone. Ladies didn't curse, ever. Ladies never used this most foul of all curse words.

"*FUCK YOU ALL!*" Ruth screamed it at the top of her lungs.

She'd tried her best to follow Mama Quincy's genteel principles, for all the good it had done her. Her son still left her for the trashy granddaughter of a monster. Her husband still suffered two strokes and was now useless to her. Yes, being a lady certainly afforded her a wonderful life, hadn't it?

Ruth pressed harder on her temples, finally giving in to the need for medication. She staggered to her private bath and fumbled in the medicine cabinet for aspirin, uncapped the bottle and shook five of them into her palm. She nearly broke her etched crystal water glass in her rush to fill it with enough tap water to swallow the pills. Finally she got them down, and carefully replaced the glass in its matching crystal holder. It wouldn't do for her to break either and have glass shards everywhere. Besides, the lovely glass and holder once belonged to Mama Quincy, and Ruth treasured it.

Mama Quincy—how Ruth longed for her guidance, her thoughtful advice and caring warmth. Mama would have known how to best handle the Turners, offering valuable advice to deflect all of the suffering they had visited upon the Quincys. Mama would have lent added strength in the goddamned courtroom, too. She would have won the boy, if Mama had been there.

Ruth wandered through her elegant rooms, unable to

take pleasure in them as she usually did. There had to be a way to get the child. Benson Perdue, the fool, spouted legal jargon in his idiotic ruling, going on about visitations and such. As if she'd be satisfied with just a visit now and then. She barely felt the way her nails cut into her palms when she curled them into tight fists.

She didn't want a stingy schedule of damned visits. She wanted her grandson, in this house. She wanted him under her singular control and she wanted to raise him as truly befitted a Quincy.

With Duncan, there'd be no mistakes, no errors in judgment. His time outside of the Academy would be regimented and geared toward preparing him for the life he had been born to assume.

She wouldn't allow him to dodge his lessons, or to run off in the summer to some horrid, smelly pond, grubbing about in brackish water for nasty, slimy fish.

No more association with the utter dregs of Thompkin, either.

Duncan would be hers to mold and shape. He'd wear designer clothes chosen by her, sleep in a lovely room painted blue, to match his eyes . . .

She frowned briefly, trying to remember. Blue. Not brown. Her darling boy's eyes could never be brown.

If she could only see him. Ruth stopped in the middle of her sitting room and imagined how he'd run toward her with his arms open wide and a smile on his face for his Nana. She'd find another judge, a better judge, one who would understand the boy belonged with the only person who could open doors and pave his way with wealth and stature, prestige and opportunity. Why, under her guidance and authority, young Duncan might one day aspire to the Presidency.

With the right force behind him, it could happen. But if left in that dismal hovel on the foul side of Thompkin—well, it would *never* happen, would it?

She had to save him. He was the Quincy future.

"You mean, you didn't want to go along on the great shoe-shopping expedition? I'm shocked." Mary ruffled Travis's hair as she stepped into the kitchen. He sat at the table with Hank in his lap, and for once Hank wasn't trying to play with his breakfast, instead taking his scrambled eggs and applesauce with cherubic placidness.

Travis shuddered. "Shopping is painful enough. Going along with two excitable women on the hunt for the perfect shoes? No, thanks. Besides, I have to head over to the library. There's registration I can only do online, and I need to use the computer lab." He scooped up more fruit and made airplane noises as he sent the rubber-coated spoon toward Hank's mouth. The baby giggled and opened wide, clapping his hands. He sucked and then bit at the spoon.

Mary winced. "I'm sure glad Annie stopped nursing that boy. He's been biting on his spoons for months. Better them than his poor mama."

"She told Sissy babies bite. I hear Sissy turned white as a sheet. Annie's got a mean streak. I can't imagine who in the family she gets it from." Travis sent Mary a sidelong glance as he fed Hank the last spoonful, and she laughed as she held her arms out for her grandson.

"Well, I'm almost certain I said the same thing to Annie. And I'm almost certain she turned just as white. We mothers have such rare moments of rottenness, you know. Most of the time we have to be perfect." She patted Hank on the back as he burped loudly, then looked proud of himself. "Good one, honey-pot! Let's get you settled in your sandbox, okay? It's a shame to waste time indoors on such a sunny day." Hank planted a smacking, sticky kiss on her cheek and burbled happily at the mention of his beloved sandbox.

"Can I pick up anything while I'm out? It shouldn't take very long provided I can get right online and don't have to wait for a cubicle." Travis hefted his backpack over his shoulder and reached in his pocket for his keys.

"Well, it wouldn't hurt to get some more milk. Maybe a couple of gallons. Sissy's drinking it like crazy and I swear Henry could slurp down a quart at every meal."

Mary started to go for her purse, and Travis waved her off. "No way. I have money. I could also pick up some pizzas for dinner, you know. Save you from having to cook. Pepperoni and black olive," he enticed.

"Oh, you shouldn't! It's not like I don't have time to make something—although Lambelli's *does* have the loveliest crust, far better than anything I can make." Thinking about her favorite pizza, Mary dithered, undecided, hating to see Travis spend his money. Finally she exclaimed, "Go ahead! Before I change my mind." She caught hold of his arm and stood on tiptoe to kiss his cheek. "You're a sweetheart for thinking of it, my dear." She walked with him to the door. "Now, you take your time. Hank and I are going to have a nice play date outside, then he'll have his bath and a nap. I reckon the girls will traipse all over Weston and maybe end up in Collette, before they find those shoes Annie needs for her dress. And I have no idea when Mark and Sissy might make it back in, what with visiting her mama. So, take all the time you need, all right?"

"I will, thanks."

A few minutes later, standing at the door and admonishing Hank to wave to his Da, Mary sighed with contentment. She had a wonderful afternoon ahead of her, playing with her favorite boy. With the wedding coming up so quickly, she knew these precious days would soon be gone, as her children found their places out in the world. It was happening too fast, but she was happy for all of them.

Mark's transfer to Andrews Air Force Base would bring him and Sissy closer, and she'd see her sweet Toby more often. The twins would start tech school outside of Charlottesville. They'd worked hard these past few years and saved their money. Student loans would take care of whatever they lacked. Bobby's decision to enlist in the Air Force and follow in his big brother's footsteps had pleased everyone, and Susan would work and live in Weston. All of her chicks, settled and thriving, and all but Bobby remaining comfortably close to their parents. Truly, what more could she and Henry ask for?

Nan would keep a protective eye on Annie and Travis in Roanoke, and it was only a matter of time before they came back to Thompkin. Travis's application for a student loan would get him through Radford, his new choice of university. With his current Yale credits, if he buckled down and took extra classes, he'd be able to graduate from Radford in a semester and a half. Mary knew he was more than capable of handling such a load, and this time Annie would help him.

"Boc! Boc, Gammy!" Hank bounced in her arms, impatient to get out the back door and into his sandbox, and Mary snapped out of her daydreaming and closed the front door.

She kissed his forehead, over the fading bruise, relieved at the way the broken skin had healed. "Boc, huh? Well, let's go play in the boc! And afterwards, lunch and a bath, and a nap. In that order." Mary set Hank on his feet and he toddled to the kitchen, shrieking excitedly the entire way. Mary followed, envying his endless energy supply as she opened the back door for him and helped him down the steps.

Chapter 34

Ruth placed a steadying hand against her racing heart. The harrowing trip from Quincy Hall left her trembling badly. She'd never driven a car in her life, and at first it was all she could do simply to open the door and climb into the driver's seat. Her old insecurities reared up once again, suffocating her.

She'd watched Ronald enough times that she felt confident in her ability to at least start the car. She knew there was an accelerator pedal and a brake. Her hand shook when she inserted the key and it took her four tries to slot the damned thing into the ignition.

She'd gotten the car started, but then had to think hard about what came next. A foot on the gas. Hands on the wheel. Shifting into gear. She'd mistakenly pushed the gear stick into "drive" instead of "reverse," nearly crashing into a side wall of the expansive garage.

Three more attempts, and Ruth finally figured out how to shift properly. By then she was damp with sweat and panting in near-hysteria. If her panic didn't ease, she'd never make it any further.

Creeping along, far under the speed limit, she drove through intersections and along lesser streets. Hoping no one would notice her erratic steering, she reached the downtrodden side of town in one piece. But she'd entered a wrong street somewhere and ended up on the other side of the railroad tracks, facing the rear side of Spring Street instead of where she needed to be.

Ruth climbed out of the car and stood on trembling

legs, fighting to rebalance her equilibrium. It wasn't until she heard the childish giggles that she realized she was almost directly across from the Turner's crumbling back porch. She saw her grandson in Mary Turner's arms.

Bitter hate burned through her body like acid. If she had a gun in her hands, there wasn't a doubt in her mind. She would have lifted it, aimed at the woman's head, and pulled the trigger. To hell with the consequences.

She watched Mary Turner place the boy in what appeared to be a box filled with dirty sand, littered with old dishes. In heaven's name, how could the woman allow a child to sit in such filth? Ruth's face twisted in disgust. Little Duncan looked happy enough as he banged on a pot with his hands and giggled over the horrid din he created. And why shouldn't he look happy? He didn't know any better. What kind of example were these people setting for her grandson? Grubbing about in dirt. Pounding on inferior kitchen equipment. His diaper was probably wet again. She couldn't bear to think of what might be crawling out of that nasty dirt and under his clothes. It was disgraceful. Unacceptable.

Every second she wasted over here was a second her poor grandson had to endure being separated from her. But she needed to compose herself a bit longer before she attempted to drive again. She closed her hand over the small prescription bottle in the pocket of her slacks. One pill, they were so very tiny, weren't they? One pill would settle her nerves.

She drew the bottle out and thumbed off the cap. Without taking her eyes from Mary Turner, she shook a pill into her palm, brought it to her lips and swallowed it, dry. Immediately she felt more in control, though she knew the pill couldn't possibly have taken effect that quickly. No, it was her own self-assurance coming into play, her own confidence.

She was ready now. Ready to take control. Ready to rescue the Quincy Heir.

Mary brushed at the sand in Hank's hair, trying to get to it before it dripped down into his eyes. As usual, the imp didn't seem to feel any discomfort from having sand stuffed into all of his little nooks and crannies. He shook his head, sending sand flying, chortling and clapping his hands.

"Stop that, you monkey!" She gave up, laughing too hard herself to scold him with any real effect. She sat on the edge of the sandbox and watched as he dumped yet another bucket of sand across his legs and squealed in glee. He fisted his fingers in the sand and held it out, then pulled his arm back to fling the damp clump right at her head.

"Don't you dare. Hank, you put that down!" Mary held out both hands to stop him, but she was weak from laughter and Hank was too mischievous to listen, anyhow. The sand went flying, missed her hair and landed on the collar of her shirt, where it broke apart and slid down under the material, right into the loose cup of her bra.

"Yuck!" She tried to peel the shirt away and shake out the sand still clinging to her collar, but she only succeeded in getting more of it down her shirt. She regarded her grandson with glinting eyes as he slid sideways in the box, giggling like a fiend.

Messy or not, she loved her boy, but she shook a finger at him, scolding, "You're such a little dickens! I think it's past time for your lunch. *And* a bath, what do you think of that, hmmm? A nice bath to clear out all the gunk. I think Gammy needs one, too." She got to her feet and held out her hands, and Hank grasped hold and pulled himself up, babbling in excitement. He loved his bath as much as he loved rolling in sand.

He stood still for her as she brushed the worst of it from his hair and his clothes. The rest would rinse down the drain as soon as she got him in the tub. He smiled at her, seven teeth gleaming pearly white, angelic as all-get-out despite the sand smudges on his face.

"Something else, that's what you are, my boy," she declared, as she took him by one hand and turned to walk to the porch. And her eyes rounded in shock when she saw the woman step out of the shadows from one of the largest lilac trees growing along the side of the house.

Dressed in black from head to toe and sweating in the hot sun, her hair tangled and hanging down her back, Ruth Quincy stood between Mary and the back porch. Her eyes were wild, her hands were curled into claws. Her mouth, bracketed by harsh grooves, pressed into a thin line as she stared at Mary and then down at Hank, who shrank against Mary's legs as if he'd suddenly remembered who this lady was.

Oh, this wasn't good.

"Mrs. Quincy. You aren't supposed to come over without calling first." She tried to remain calm and speak rationally. Backing up a step, she lifted Hank. He wrapped his arms around her neck and clung to her. Ruth emitted a warning hiss, but Mary stood her ground.

"I want my grandson. Let go of him and give him to me. *Now.*" Ruth advanced on her, reaching out her hands, and Mary skittered back two more steps.

Hank started whimpering in fright at the guttural voice, and Mary held him tighter. "You'd better go, Mrs. Quincy. I'm calling the police, unless you leave right now. You aren't taking Hank anywhere—"

"*STOP CALLING HIM BY THAT REVOLTING NAME!*" Ruth screamed, her face contorted with fury. Hank burst into sobs, burrowing into Mary's neck.

She had no idea what Ruth might be capable of. The

woman seemed horribly unstable. In despair, Mary's eyes darted around the yard. They were boxed in. Behind them sat the sandbox and a strip of yard that narrowed down to the uneven banks of Crum Creek. A rickety fence kept anyone from slipping into the creek, but she knew that fence would fall down in a second if someone got thrown against it. And right now, Ruth sure looked strong enough to toss her around.

Chicken wire fenced in Mary's garden on the left side of the yard, and Ruth partially blocked the other side. No matter which way she turned, with a child in her arms Mary couldn't move any too fast. Ruth would quickly be on them—both of them.

She stammered, "Ruth, you don't want to h-hurt your grandson, do you? You can see how s-scared he is."

"If I have to break him in half to get him away from you, I will. I know lots of doctors, world-renowned doctors. They can put him back together again. Let him go. Let Duncan come to me, and I won't hurt either of you." Her voice dropping to a low growl, Ruth reached into the front pocket of her slacks and produced what looked like a steak knife. Mary trembled violently when she saw the sharp, serrated blade.

In the hand of someone rapidly losing her hold on her sanity, a steak knife could do plenty of damage. Mary knew for Hank's safety, she had to obey.

Almost paralyzed with dread, she let Hank slide to the ground, but he wouldn't release her neck, and his sobs intensified. Fighting to keep her voice from shaking, Mary murmured to him, "Honey-pot, you let go, all right? You just sit right here on the grass and be a good boy for Gammy, can you do that for me?"

"*Nooooooo!*" It was a piteous wail, and Hank wouldn't budge. He tried to climb up her legs to reach the safety of her arms. Tears poured down her face. She couldn't refuse her sweet boy. She knelt on the grass and gathered him into her arms.

"I told you to let my grandson *go!*" Ruth darted forward. "You don't listen very well, do you? Nobody ever *listens* to me!" She brandished the knife and Mary jerked away when the blade slashed erratically in front of her eyes. She slithered back, crab-walking with Hank clinging to her, and tried to place several feet between her and Ruth.

Above the pounding of her heart she could hear her own voice sobbing out prayers, pleas, anything she could offer up to God. Hank was hysterical now, shuddering so hard in her arms that she could hear his tiny baby teeth clattering together. Or maybe that was her own teeth. Mary wasn't sure. She only knew she had to get away from this crazed woman, before whatever small thread tethering Ruth's sanity fully snapped.

"I-I'm listening, Mrs. Quincy. I am. Talk to me. Our grandson is so s-scared. Won't you please p-put down the knife?"

Ruth slapped her free hand to her temple as the boy's screaming cut through her aching head. The aspirin must have worn off. Well, she'd had enough of this, at any rate.

Unwilling to participate in a stand-off any longer, she raised the knife. She intended only to scare Mary into letting the child go. But she slipped on the grass just as Mary curled herself around the boy's body, and the knife glanced off her shoulder. It didn't look to be a deep wound but it caused the idiot woman to scream and loosen her grip on Duncan. Ruth was able to get hold of his leg. She tugged, hard, and the boy finally slipped free. Panting, Ruth dragged him, still holding onto one leg. Dimly she registered a popping sound, and fresh howls of pain erupted from the child, further hammering into her aching skull.

"*Shut up! Shut up! Shut up!*" She grabbed the boy under his armpits and hauled him up, then tucked him against her side like a football and stumbled from the yard, glancing back to assure Mary hadn't gotten to her feet. No, she was still down, but trying to rise to her knees. Blood coated her arm. Ruth dismissed her and concentrated on getting to the car, parked half on and half off the median.

"Ho there! What are you doing with that boy? Mary, are you all—oh, God! *Mary*!" A middle-aged woman came out of the house next door, another hovel as bad as the Turner dump, and ran toward the back yard where Mary knelt. Dimly Ruth heard the woman yell, "Arthur! Call nine-one-one! Call the police!"

"Fuck them all," Ruth huffed under her breath, as she shoved her grandson in the back seat, ignoring his cries.

She leapt into the front seat and slammed her foot down on the accelerator. The car shot forward, the powerful engine of the Mercedes gaining control over her shaking hands clinging to the steering wheel and her foot that pressed too hard on the pedal.

She drove on the wrong side of the pot-holed street. Ruth couldn't think past the stabbing pain in her head, now a full-blown migraine. That damned pill she'd taken for her nerves finally caught up to her, though, and her motor skills were sluggish. The intersection loomed before her, she swerved wildly, and in the back seat the boy shrieked, adding to her emotional overload.

She tried to ease up on the accelerator. Up, which way was up? Instead of letting off the gas, Ruth mashed her foot down, harder, and the car shot forward into the intersection, narrowly missing a car that slammed on the brakes to the right of her.

But the car on her left wasn't so lucky and neither was she—and the front of her car hit the other in its side, head-on. Dimly she registered the sound of crunching metal and shattering glass, a child's high-pitched scream and her own cry of terror as her body snapped forward and then slumped back against the seat.

Chapter 35

Travis ran through the small urgent care clinic toward the emergency room, his mind frozen, still locked on the shaky panic in Beatrice Fulton's voice when she'd called him on his cell phone.

"Travis, your mother—your son—oh, hurry! Get over to the clinic, *now*!"

He'd been ass deep in online registration forms not only for Radford, but also the student loan he'd be required to take out for his final two semesters. It was a wonder he even responded to his cell phone since he had set it on vibrate. But today it had been resting in his shirt pocket, thank God.

His mother. Hank. In a car accident. How bad, he had no idea. But Beatrice, the Turner's neighbor, witnessed it herself. Before he'd shoved the phone in his pocket and taken off at a dead run, he heard Beatrice say Mary was also wounded.

Mary, wounded? How the hell could this have happened? He'd been gone less than two hours! Thankfully Susan had been behind the wheel when Travis called Annie. Otherwise she would surely have driven right off the road when she heard his panicked voice. They'd reach the clinic within the hour. Henry was on his way home from Weston. Susan had called him.

What had his mother been doing, that she was in a car with Hank? None of it made any sense. For Christ's sake, his mother couldn't even drive a damned car!

He rounded the corner into the compact emergency room and strode up to the first nurse he saw. "Hank Turner and Ruth Quincy, where are they?"

She looked him over. "You're family?"

"Yes, damn it! I'm the boy's father, and Ruth Quincy is my mother."

She nodded and pointed toward an open doorway. "In there." Travis ran through the door, his knees buckling when he saw Hank in a hospital crib, asleep. A nurse and a police officer stood by the crib, and they turned when Travis approached.

"I'm his father, Travis Quincy. What happened?" Travis reached for his son's hand, shock almost immobilizing him as he took in the sight of the bruises and cuts on Hank's pale cheeks. His left arm was in a child-sized sling, his right leg encased in an inflatable cast. An ace bandage compressed his ribcage. Hooked up to an IV drip, the sight of his boy in this condition brought Travis to tears, and he sank onto the nearest chair, holding onto Hank's tiny fingers for dear life.

The police officer spoke up. "The child's grandmother was in a vehicular accident. Your son was unrestrained in the back seat. She ran through the intersection at Spring Street and Maple Hollow, and hit a car head-on. It was a miracle the child didn't suffer worse injuries." He took out a notebook and flipped it open. "My partner and I were first on scene, and we took your mother into custody after we brought her here to be treated for facial lacerations and a concussion. She also broke her wrist."

"My mother doesn't know how to drive. She's never had a license. What was she doing on that side of town? What was she doing with my son? I don't understand any of this." He pressed a hand to his head. It pounded as though he'd been knocked seven ways to sideways himself.

"Travis? Oh, I'm so glad you're here!" Beatrice rushed into the room and hugged him, patting his back. "Hank's going to be fine. So is Mary—"

"What happened to Mary? Where is she?" He looked

around as if she'd magically appear.

Beatrice removed her eyeglasses and wiped her damp eyes. "Honey, your mama came to the house and caused a horrible scene. I heard some of the ruckus, but by the time I ran outside, most of it had already happened. Your mama wanted Hank. She had a knife. Mary tried to protect Hank, and Ruth cut Mary's shoulder. Then she got hold of Hank and drove off. But she ran right through the stop sign and there was another car coming up Maple Hollow. I don't know, maybe she tried to stop. It was all very fast and confusing." Beatrice sighed and squeezed his arm comfortingly as he tried to take it all in. "She wasn't right in the head, Travis. It was like she snapped or something. And I would bet she put her foot down thinking she had it on the brake, but actually she hit the gas."

"I can't even believe this." He took a ragged breath. "I want to know how seriously injured my son is." Travis made the demand in the general vicinity of the nurse, who hurried away to find a doctor. Beatrice knelt at Travis's side when he dropped his face into his hands. His shoulders shook with sobs.

"Now, don't you take on so, Travis. Children are resilient, they truly are. Things that would knock an adult flat on their butt, well, children just breeze right through it. Hank's going to be fine."

Travis raised his head and looked at her. Beatrice and Arthur Fulton had lived on Spring Street for a lot of years, and when he and Annie were kids she often had a smile and a wave for him when he came to the Turners' house. She was a sweet lady, and trying her best to calm him down, but he didn't want to be placated. He could feel himself rapidly filling with anger. With fury.

"What was my mother doing at the house, Mrs. Fulton? What did you hear?" He grabbed hold of her hand.

"Honey, your mama's not—" Beatrice started to say.

She must have seen the ferocity in Travis's eyes, because she sighed and amended, "Your mama seems to have some troubles, and I think she might need to see someone, you know, professionally."

"Christ. Why did she have a knife? How badly is Mary hurt?" Travis gripped her fingers so hard, Beatrice winced. He mumbled an apology and released her. "Where's Mary right now?"

"Well, I expect she's getting her shoulder looked after, honey. It wasn't bad, kind of shallow, I suppose you'd say. It looked a lot worse than it is, I promise you."

Just then Annie came tearing around the corner, her face streaked with tears. He scrambled to his feet and caught her as she flung herself at him, one hand immediately reaching for Hank.

"Shh, he's all right, Annie. He's going to be all right." Travis went from helpless boy to strong protector as he held Annie. Her breath snagged on a sob.

Beatrice whispered, "I'll go find your mama, Annie," and she tiptoed out, passing a weary-looking doctor in a rumpled white lab coat.

He looked at them hovering over Hank. "I'm Doctor Bledsoe. And you're no doubt this young man's folks, right?" They nodded as Bledsoe hastened to assure them, "He's going to be fine. The worst of it was a dislocated knee. Sometimes they can be tricky. His arm is broken but it was a clean break. Should knit back together well. He has a cracked rib and some colorful bruises. But all in all, your son was lucky. It could have been a lot worse."

"Lucky. You call *this* lucky? I want to talk to my mother. She's the cause of this. Where is she?" Travis started forward blindly, beside himself with fury, and Annie wrapped her arms around him, putting herself in his path. His eyes glittered down at her. "Let me go, Annie. She's my mother, and she could have killed our son. I have to talk to her."

"Travis, just wait—" Annie wouldn't let go.

"I want to talk to her!"

"Not like this, you won't." Bledsoe retorted. "She's my patient too, regardless of what she's done. Right now she's under police escort. She's not going anywhere. They're trying to get the story out of her, son, and you need to let them do their job."

He checked Hank's chart, adjusted the IV drip. "Now, your boy is going to be sore for a few days. I'd like to keep him overnight at the very least, as he's going to be sleeping a lot and I want to check on him often to make sure he's not in too much pain. I can prescribe a gentle painkiller that'll make him sleepy, and really that's the best thing for him, anyhow. Young bones have a lot of flexibility to them, you know. If everything looks good, you can take him home tomorrow afternoon."

"We want to stay. Can we stay?" As Annie slowly released him, Travis cupped his hand protectively over Hank's bandaged chest.

"I'll have one of those reclining chairs brought in. No sense moving the boy into a regular room, anyhow. They're on the cramped side. Better to keep him down here." Bledsoe replied.

He moved toward the open doorway but turned and cautioned, "No hysterics, Mr. Quincy. Not on my shift or anyone else's, you hear? There'll be time enough for confrontation, later."

As the doctor's steps echoed down the hallway, Travis slumped into the chair closest to the hospital crib. "God. I don't know what—I can't think, Annie! Why would my mother do this?"

"I don't know." She bent to him, curled her arms around him, resting her cheek against his hair. "I just don't know. But we're going to find out." She brushed a kiss across his forehead. "Stay with him, okay? I've got to find my mama."

"I'm here, honey." Mary appeared in the doorway, dressed in her usual blue jeans, a short hospital gown covering her to the waist. She looked exhausted but steady. Susan stood behind her, a supporting arm about her waist.

"Mama." Annie rushed to her side, her hands fluttering as if unsure where to place them without hurting her further. Mary got hold of all ten fingers and pulled Annie into a careful embrace. Annie promptly burst into tears.

"I'm all right! I am." She lifted Annie's face to hers and gave her a reassuring smile, which Annie couldn't return. Mary glanced over her shoulder at the crib where Hank lay. "Poor little boy. He's had a rough day, hasn't he? But he's tough. He'll be fine, too."

With Annie in her arms, Mary glanced over at Travis. Softly she spoke his name and his body jerked. "Travis, are you all right?"

He shook his head, mutely.

Mary sighed. "Travis, won't you talk to me?"

His shoulders hunched as he wrapped his arms around his waist. He couldn't meet her eyes, he just couldn't. She might have bled to death, right in her own back yard. And it would have been his fault. If he'd gone with his mother that first time, when she'd come to the house and demanded he leave with her, if he'd listened to his instincts that told him his mother was losing touch with reality—

"Travis?" Mary's voice was as loving as ever. He shuddered with the need to be held and comforted by someone he'd always known was there for him. But he didn't deserve to be comforted by her.

"I don't know what to say to you." Guilt-stricken, he could hardly get the words out.

Mary stepped away from Annie and moved to his side. One hand slipped around his neck, stroking gently, until with a harsh sob Travis turned to her and buried his face against her. She placed her other hand on his back.

She bent to him. "Travis, it was a shallow cut. Just a few stitches. And none of this was your fault, you hear me? Not one second of it. I told you once before not to take on the things in life you have no control over, and I'm telling you again." She held him close as he cried hot tears. "Your mama has problems and she's the only one who can deal with them. She's got to be willing to accept help to get over them. Some things can't be fixed, honey. Not by you or anyone else."

"She hurt you. She hurt Hank. She could have killed—"

"But she didn't. And now, she'll get the help she needs, won't she? Maybe it had to go this far, Travis. God works His miracles in ways we can't begin to understand. All we can do is have faith." Mary kissed his cheek and reached for Annie, pulling her close, until the three of them were connected as a family unit. Annie grabbed for Susan, drawing her into the huddle. For almost a minute, no one moved.

Finally, Susan kissed Travis's other cheek, then her habitual need to add some kind of levity kicked in. "Listen to her, Travis. Or she'll never let go of us. We might freeze in position like this."

He uttered a rough chuckle. It wasn't much, but it was better than tears. He let go of Mary, gave Susan's waist a grateful squeeze, and stood up, retaining hold of Annie's hand. A glance at Hank assured him their boy was still sleeping peacefully, and Susan plopped herself down in the chair next to his crib and laid her hand on his tummy.

She nodded at them both. "I'd like to sit with him for a while."

Travis moved closer to Mary. "Annie and I need to see my mother. Do you know where she is?"

Mary watched him steadily for a few seconds, as if gauging his emotional stability. Without a word, she led them out of the room and down the short hallway. She pointed toward a closed door. A uniformed policeman stood in front of it. "In there. I don't know if they'll let you see her, Travis."

It was too cold in the room. Thermal blankets covered Ruth, yet she shivered violently.

Voices prodded at her, asking her things her ears were too muffled to comprehend. After a while, she refused to raise her head and look in the direction of those voices. It was all jumbled-up sounds, anyway.

She'd done a Very Bad Thing. When you did a Very Bad Thing, you got punished. And punishment always hurt. She huddled under the blankets, cradling her wrist. It hurt, too. Maybe that was part of her punishment. But she somehow knew the hurt was nothing compared to what awaited her.

She wasn't allowed to play with things like knives. She wasn't allowed to be in a car, pretending to drive it. Doing all those forbidden things made her a Very Bad Person. Very Bad Persons went to Hell when they died. Very Bad Persons never had anyone to love them and take care of them.

Ruth pulled the blanket over her head, shutting out the voices that were now poking at her. Everything ached, from her head to her feet. Punishment, she knew. Her fault, and now she'd go to Hell and nobody would care.

They told her she'd hurt Mary. She didn't know who Mary was, and she didn't remember hurting her. They told her she'd hurt Hank. Ruth didn't know any Hank, either. All she knew was that she'd been in a car when she wasn't supposed to, and there had been a knife, and she was a Very Bad Person and had to be punished. Maybe they'd use the knife to cut the badness out of her.

She moaned, low in her throat. It didn't sound human, even to herself.

"I'm Detective Sorenson." The forty-ish woman standing just inside the room wore a dark gray pantsuit and sensible heels, her light brown hair wound into a neat bun at the nape of her neck. Travis shook her hand while his eyes focused beyond her to the huddled form in the hospital bed. He knew his mother was there, under the mound of blankets. He could feel himself tighten all over as the anguished fury started to build.

Obviously Detective Sorenson sensed it too, for she placed her palm on his tensed forearm, a light touch that nevertheless cautioned him to tread with care. "Mr. Quincy, your mother isn't talking. We've asked her several times what happened, but she hasn't spoken a word. Now, there were witnesses to her actions, so it's not like we have to get a confession out of her right away. The doctor on duty here has told us he'll release her into our custody, probably in another hour or so."

"What's going to happen to her?" Annie asked.

"She'll have to be booked. Assault with a dangerous weapon. It wasn't a large knife but its serrated edge can do plenty of damage. Child endangerment. I could add attempted child abduction in the mix, but she is the boy's grandmother, so I'm not sure about that one," Detective Sorenson replied. "She'll have to stand trial."

"Is she," Travis cleared his dry throat but his words were still raspy. "Is she mentally competent to stand trial?" He couldn't take his eyes from the mound of blankets on the bed or ignore the keening, broken sounds emanating from under them. She sounded like an animal in terrible pain.

"Well, that'll be for a psychiatric team to decide. If she's not competent, then she'll likely be institutionalized. Could be lengthy or short term. It'll depend on how her mental capacity stabilizes. She'll need to understand what she did before she can be brought to trial. At this point we can't get a thing out of her, much less try to gauge how she might want to plead."

"What if—what if I refuse to press charges? What if Mary Turner refuses to press charges?" As he spoke, Travis locked eyes with Annie, and saw in hers compassion as well as frustration. His mother assaulted her mother with a knife. His mother endangered the life of their child.

And his mother hunched beneath a small mountain of blankets in a hospital bed, rocking back and forth and moaning like something not quite human. How the hell could he condemn her to prison? How could he live with himself, if he did that? And what kind of beginning was this to the life he wanted so badly with Annie and Hank?

"What are you saying, Mr. Quincy?" Detective Sorenson asked quietly.

Travis turned eyes swimming in emotion toward her. "I want her to have the best help possible. I don't think she'd survive prison, if it came to that. Please," he entreated, "Detective, help me. Tell me what I need to do, to assure my mother is placed somewhere that will get her what she needs. Tell me how to take care of her."

"Miss Turner? Do you agree? What about your mother? Would she agree to something like this?" Detective Sorenson wanted to know.

Annie nodded slowly, and her arms went around Travis. He leaned on her, a slip of a girl who looked as if a substantial wind could blow her away. But there was steel in that tender spine of hers. Nobody knew that better than he did. She was stronger than any of them.

She hesitated, only a second or two, as she prepared to speak in Mary's behalf. "My mother's a Christian woman, raised to show empathy and kindness toward those who would slap her down. She'd bring a crust of bread to a ravenous dog and hand-feed it."

Travis could almost read her mind when she glanced up at him. Years filled with nothing but troubles and discord, caused by his mother. How could she get past all of that and refuse to press charges? It was one thing to speak for her mother and another to apply Mary's teachings to a situation none of them could have seen coming.

But her arms tightened around him, and she must have found the empathy she needed as his grip remained warm and steady against her waist.

She took a deep breath and let it out, slowly. "Ruth Quincy needs help, Detective. She's my son's grandmother, and she's been through so much in her life, things that have formed her and skewed her judgment. My mother won't press charges, I'm certain. And neither will I."

EPILOGUE

Hank peeked around the corner, tiptoed down the carpeted hallway and stopped in front of a wide door. He looked over his shoulder. "Hurry up, Mama."

Annie grinned at his impatience. "No one's going to leave without you, silly goose." She caught up with him and tousled his black curls with her free hand. "Remember, you don't stay very long. Okay?"

"Okay. Are you going to give her the flowers?" He pointed to the crystal vase she held.

"Yes, I'm going to give her the flowers, Mister Nosy." He giggled at the nickname and knocked on the door, hopping up and down eagerly. Annie stifled a laugh. Hank had been bouncing on his feet since the first day he'd taken a step.

Edward, the day nurse, answered the door with his usual placid smile. "Good morning, young Quincy! She's been waiting for you." He extended the smile to Annie.

"How is she today?" she inquired, as she stepped inside.

"She's doing very well, ma'am."

Annie stood by the door as Hank ran into the room and threw his arms around the tall, thin woman whose hair was the same exact color as his. "Good morning, Nana. Did you sleep well?"

"I slept very well, my dear one." She snuggled him close when he climbed carefully into her lap. He leaned on her shoulder.

She ran her hand over the robe she wore. "What do you think of my new robe?"

"It's pretty. It's like your eyes." He patted the soft fabric.

"Your mother gave it to me." The sincere pleasure in her voice made Annie smile even as she felt the sting of tears.

Today would be a good day. She briefly closed her eyes on the small, daily prayer of thanks, and watched her son work his charm on Ruth Quincy.

There was a tray on the Hepplewhite credenza, next to the comfortable armchair. It held all of Ruth's morning favorites, from her signature rosehip tea, to the lemon cookies she loved to snack on in place of a heavier breakfast. Her correspondence from the day before sat neatly stacked and ready for her.

Cupping his chin, Ruth gave Hank a few nose-kisses, making him giggle. "Have you eaten yet? You are up so early."

"I'm going with Da this morning. He wants me to see the op-opnation." Hank struggled over the word.

"Operation. You're going to go into the office with your father? How lovely for you." She pressed her cheek against his hair. "You will undoubtedly live up to your potential as the Quincy Heir, my sweet Dun—ah, Henry." The stumble made Annie wince, but she knew Ruth *was* trying.

"Nana, why am I a hair?" Hank wanted to know. Annie bit her lips to hold in a chuckle. Next to her, Edward's shoulders shook in silent laughter.

"Hair?"

"Yes. You said I was a Quincy hair. I got lots of hair on my head, right?" Hank looked up at her endearingly, and Annie could see Ruth almost melt with love.

"Ask your father, sweet boy. Or your mother." As she spoke, Ruth looked right at Annie, and smiled.

"Okay!" Hank wriggled to get down and Ruth released him, after coaxing one last kiss from him. He smacked his mouth on both her cheeks, then skipped out of the room.

"Don't run down the stairs, young man," Annie called after him, shaking her head when she heard his feet clomping despite her warning. She waited until Ruth beckoned to her, before advancing any further into the room.

Until the last six or so months, days that started out with a smile on Ruth's face were few and far between. At first, Annie often found herself searching for excuses to avoid visiting her mother-in-law. It was difficult to look at Ruth and not recall that awful day when Annie had held Hank's hand in the emergency room, sobbing when she'd seen the bruises covering his body and the cuts standing out in stark relief against his pale skin. His poor arm—his leg, his ribs. Her little boy, hurt like that.

She and Travis had to work at reducing that all-consuming anger. By the time their wedding day arrived, Ruth was safely locked behind the elegant yet very secure gates of the Shane Ark Institute, receiving the help she needed. It took time, but with the ability to relax and feel secure once more, came the capability of learning how to be a family. They gave it their all, as they approached everything together.

Equally hard to deal with were the letters Ruth was allowed to send Travis, as part of her rehabilitation. They were filled with remorse, with pleas for forgiveness. At first Ruth asked that forgiveness only of Travis, somehow forgetting what she'd done to Annie and her family. Eventually she understood she needed Annie's absolution as well. So in that respect the letters were therapeutic for Ruth. Over time, Annie and Travis found something therapeutic as well, in the reading of them.

The final step, of bringing Ruth home and making a place for her in their lives, had been more difficult for Travis than it was for Annie. He struggled with residual anger and hurt over what his mother had done. But Annie dug deeply within herself to understand much of Ruth's behavior. It became easier for her to finally accept than it was for Travis. And after all, it had been their choice not to press charges.

Travis visited his mother almost every day and there was still awkwardness between them, but she seemed willing to let him set the pace. She wisely didn't ask for more. She'd come a long way from the blanket-wrapped form in the bed at Thompkin Urgent Care, who'd rocked back and forth, moaning like a wounded animal.

Now Annie stepped over to Ruth's side, comfortable in her faded jeans and bright yellow sweater. She placed the vase she carried on a nearby credenza. "Good morning, Ruth. I brought you an early birthday present."

"They're lovely! Who sent them?" Ruth eyed the roses with delight.

"Dan Marley sent them over. He'll be by later on today, to see you." Flipping her long braid over one shoulder, Annie stood next to the bureau, her hands folded at her waist, and patiently waited to see what her mother-in-law might need, though the battle for that patience had been hard-won.

There had never been any question of allowing Ruth to be incarcerated. Especially when two separate psychiatric evaluations diagnosed her as mentally incompetent to stand trial. Hospitalization was best, the doctors advised.

A week after their evaluation, Ronald suffered a massive heart attack and passed away in his sleep. The entire Quincy household was in an uproar. Travis and Annie, trying to sort out their own lives amidst having to bury Travis's father, had far more than they could handle. Admitting Ruth to Shane Ark was the best solution, allowing them to work through the grieving process and deal sanely with a quiet, private wedding.

After Ronald's funeral, Phoebe Sherman decided to re-negotiate her previous position at Weston Medical, and left Quincy Hall. Martha had already returned, to everyone's relief, and her calm, fortifying presence was a godsend. Even

Annie's family pitched in, with Mama taking Hank two days a week and Susan helping Annie move into the Hall and get settled.

Eventually it calmed down, and both Travis and Annie concentrated on their schooling. They'd juggled their classes with frequent trips home as well as to the Shane Ark Institute. Close enough that traveling there on the weekends was doable, being an hour out of Roanoke, they'd often combined the Institute visits with a quick overnight stay at Aunt Nan's.

Two months after graduation, Travis began working with Dan Marley. Last month, Dan retired, and now Travis fully held the reins of the Quincy Legacy. Despite his youth, he handled it well.

Travis and Annie converted most of the west wing of the Hall into a lovely, spacious apartment, where Ruth happily lived. Her nurses took excellent care of her and she saw Hank every day. She refused to leave her rooms, claiming she felt safe and secure there. Not once, since coming back to the Hall, had Ruth been in any other part of the house.

As for Annie's relationship with her mother-in-law, it had its ups and downs, but so far this proved to be an up day.

Annie checked her watch. "Ruth, I will need to run off for a while, all right? I want to say goodbye to Travis and Hank before they leave for the office." She offered a bright smile and was gratified to see it returned. "I'll come back later, how does that sound?"

Ruth nodded as Edward, her daytime nurse, came to help her from her chair. She had medication to take and she'd sleep for a few hours, a daily occurrence in her routine. Annie sent another prayer heavenward, as she did every single day, that Ruth's morning nap would be restful and free of disturbing dreams.

"In you go, Mrs. Quincy." Edward led Ruth to the bedroom. Annie followed and waited until Ruth dutifully removed her robe and slid between the covers, sitting up long enough to take the small paper cup of pills he handed to her. She sipped her water and nibbled on a lemon wafer, with Annie assuring her the rest of the cookies would be waiting for her when she awoke.

Annie sat on the edge of the bed holding one of Ruth's hands, while her mother-in-law's blue eyes grew heavy and her body sank into the mound of pillows at her back.

"Annie?" Ruth's voice slurred. Her eyes were already closed.

"Yes, Ruth. I'm here."

"You're a good girl, Annie. How I wish—"

"Shh, I know. Everything's all right. Everything's good. You're safe here. And later on today, your rambunctious grandson will come by and tell you all about his exciting day. How does that sound?" Annie stroked the thin, blue-veined hand she held.

Ruth pursed her lips in a cross between a smile and a yawn. "Lovely. I'm so sleepy." Her head slipped to the side against the pillows, and she mumbled, "I don't want to dream—"

"Then you won't. Just sleep." Annie waited until Ruth's chest rose and fell steadily, indicating deep sleep. With her free hand, she touched gentle fingers to her mother-in-law's soft cheek. "Just sleep, Ruth."

"You're a sweetheart, Annie Quincy." The low voice from the doorway sent a shiver of awareness down her spine, as always. She laid Ruth's hand on the embroidered coverlet and rose from the bed, reaching Travis's side and placing a cautionary finger to her lips as she stepped from the bedroom, pushing him ahead of her out of the apartment and into the hallway.

"Where's Hank?"

"Downstairs. Martha's getting him ready to go." Travis kept his voice low. "We'll leave in about ten minutes."

Behind them, Edward closed the door. He'd retreat to the comfortable recliner next to Ruth's bed, sometimes reading and sometimes working a puzzle, until Ruth awoke.

"Ten minutes, huh? Well, in that case . . ." She pounced, her slight body pushing her husband's much-larger and very willing frame against the wall.

She pulled his head down until she could reach his lips. The kiss he gave her just about spun the top of her head off. He groaned when she bit his bottom lip. Finally coming up for air, they kept their arms locked around each other. She giggled against his shoulder. Her feet were several inches in the air, and Travis tortured both of them by letting her slide down his hardened body until her sneakers touched the polished parquet floor.

"You're lethal, do you know that? For such a little squirt," he breathlessly teased her.

Annie smirked at him. "Yes, I know. Lucky for you."

He gave her braid a tug. "Brat." He leaned against the wall, elegant in his three-piece suit, the tie hanging crookedly. "So, how was she this morning?"

She straightened his tie for him and then left her hands on his lapels. "Fine. Really. She said I was a good girl."

"Well, you *are* a good girl." He cuddled her close and spoke against her hair. "What would I do without your fairness, Annie? Your caring. Any other woman would hate my mother. Any other woman would condemn her for what she did." He looked down at her. "But then, you're not any other woman." He kissed her lingeringly.

As their lips parted, she quipped, "You're right. Lately, I'm just another good girl." She was still uncomfortable with praise, when she was just doing what she considered the right thing.

"You don't mind, do you? Any other woman—"

"Travis, seriously, I don't mind. She's better. She hasn't had a nightmare in weeks, according to the night nurse. And she's doing well with Hank." Annie nestled into his arms. "Besides, I have everything in the world I want. It's pointless to hold onto anger and resentment, isn't it? So much of your mother's trouble was never her fault."

Easing back, she slipped her hands around to Travis's face, cradling his lean cheeks. His eyes glowed deep blue in the dimmer light of the hallway, his expression tender and loving. And all for her, that was the miracle. Always, all for her.

A tiny pulse beat at the corner of her mouth, proof of her burgeoning emotions, as she whispered, "I promised you, years ago, that I'd love you, want only you, no matter what. I knew it wouldn't always be easy, and it hasn't been. But it doesn't matter how impossible it all seemed, because we were meant, Travis. And nothing else could ever get in the way of that."

"Nothing," he echoed in a husky rasp. He slipped a hand over her hip and around to the slight thickening of her waist, caressing her there, an unspoken question in his touch.

She gave him a resigned look. "You know I didn't tell her. Not yet. When the time is right, when she's having a really good day, we'll tell her together. How do you think she'll feel about another grandchild?"

"I think she'll be happy. And if for any reason she's not, we'll deal with it, Annie. The way we've dealt with everything." He twined the fingers of both hands through hers, and held them up to his lips, kissing her knuckles. His ardent gaze swept over her and his body pressed against hers, warm and reassuring. "Together, okay? Always, together. I promise."

There was a huge lump in her throat, a hundred frogs preventing her from normal speech, but somehow Annie managed a husky, "I promise, too."

CPSIA information can be obtained at www.ICGtesting.com
Printed in the USA
LVOW01s0953140714

394196LV00001B/6/P

9 781619 351004